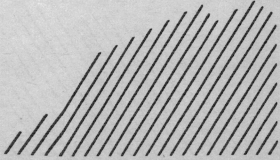

A SPECIAL SOMETHING

"Choose something special for your birthday," wealthy Tony Parish urged his sister Leslie. After all, reaching the big three-oh *was* a landmark. Jokingly, Leslie pointed to the sexy hunk sprawled in the men's cologne ad. "I'd like a week in the Caribbean—with him!" No one was more shocked than Leslie when she arrived in St. Barts. Guess who was sprawled on *her* bed... waiting to be unwrapped.

THE FOREVER INSTINCT

Marriage was supposed to last forever. It hadn't worked out that way for gorgeous Jordanna Kirkland. So she was wary when she encountered rugged Patrick Clayes again. Patrick and her ex had been fierce rivals—both on and off the football field. When Patrick finally made a sexual play for her, Jordanna couldn't trust him or herself. Her instincts had been wrong once before....

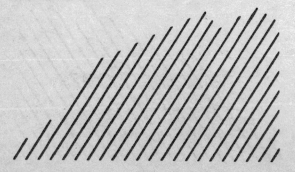

Barbara Delinsky

A SPECIAL SOMETHING

THE FOREVER INSTINCT

Harlequin Books

TORONTO • NEW YORK • LONDON
AMSTERDAM • PARIS • SYDNEY • HAMBURG
STOCKHOLM • ATHENS • TOKYO • MILAN

HARLEQUIN BOOKS

First Harlequin Books edition published October 1991

BARBARA DELINSKY REISSUE
© 1991 HARLEQUIN ENTERPRISES LIMITED

A SPECIAL SOMETHING © 1984 Barbara Delinsky
First published as a Harlequin Temptation

THE FOREVER INSTINCT © 1985 Barbara Delinsky
First published as a Harlequin Temptation

ISBN: 0-373-83240-0

Printed in U.S.A.

CONTENTS

About the Author

Barbara Delinsky was born and raised in suburban Boston. She worked as a researcher, photographer and reporter before turning to writing full-time in 1980. With more than fifty novels to her credit, she is truly one of the shining stars of contemporary romance fiction!

In 1984, Barbara was one of the four launch authors for an exciting, new, sensuous series—Harlequin Temptation. She's been writing for the line ever since, recently completing her twenty-fourth outstanding Temptation. The recipient of numerous awards and honors in her field, Barbara lives near Boston with her husband and three sons.

Dear Reader,

As you open this book, I will be putting the finishing touches to my fifty-seventh labor of love. Labor of love? By all means! Writing is a wonderful challenge, with deeply personal rewards for a scene well written, a relationship well developed, a plot well resolved. I have a fertile imagination, which means that my supply of story lines is never ending. Wherever I go in life, whatever I see or hear or experience can inspire a story.

The two stories that Harlequin has chosen to reprint, two of my favorites, are cases in point. *A Special Something* was inspired by a magazine ad that I saw in a beauty shop while my children were having haircuts. The ad was for cologne and was sensually appealing, a wonderful model for my own hero and his story. Inspiration for *The Forever Instinct* came from newspaper articles spotlighting the rival quarterbacks of teams in the Super Bowl that year. It was an easy jump from athletic competition to love-life competition.

I am delighted that Harlequin is offering you these two special stories. Please enjoy reading them as much as I enjoyed writing them!

All my best,

Barbara Delinsky

A SPECIAL SOMETHING

Barbara Delinsky

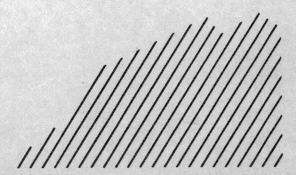

"What are you afraid of, Leslie?"

Oliver's eyes roved her face. She turned stubbornly toward the sea. But he gave a gentle tug and pulled her down onto the sand, into his arms. "Now," he murmured, "look at me and tell me what's on your mind."

"You!" Leslie cried. "You! You shouldn't be here, Oliver Ames. You're all wrong for me. I need..." Her voice trailed off as the damp warmth of his skin enveloped her.
"I need..."

"I know what you need," Oliver whispered. "You need a man's loving." He pressed his lips to her throat as she gave a convulsive swallow, then moved his body over hers. "You need me...."

1

HELLO?

How's America's answer to Michelangelo?

Feeling more like a frustrated David.

After last night?

After this morning. I was hoping to wake up with you in my arms. What time did you leave?

Just after dawn. You were sleeping so soundly I didn't have the heart to disturb you.

Some lover. Leaves me all alone to fight the Monday-morning blues wearing nothing but a bedsheet and the very last of my Homme Premier cologne.

Mmm. Sounds enticing.

That's the point. When will you be back?

Tomorrow night. What would you like from New Orleans?

Just you. Dressed in soft pink. With a silky white negligee in your bag. And . . . darling?

Yes?

Bring a bottle of Homme Premier, will you? No David should be without it.

Rogue!

FASCINATED, Leslie Parish stared at the advertisement for a long time. He was magnificent, this one whose lover had deserted him at dawn. A sculptor, his tools lay scattered atop the distant workbench at the base of a half-finished piece of art. A man, his studio apartment was a blend of muted browns and charcoals and sunlit whites. A lover, his bed was large and strewn with a sensual array of sheets barely covering one leg, and that part David hadn't tried to hide. Again and again Leslie's gaze returned to the taunting strip of flesh at his hip. Sucking in a wistful breath, she let her eyes creep back up, over the broad and sinewed expanse of his lightly haired chest to his face.

Dark wavy hair, mussed by sleep, fell across his brow. His jaw bore the faintest shadow of a beard. His nose was straight; his lips firm, slightly parted. But what intrigued her most was the expression that the camera's soft lens had captured as he'd stared into his dreams with the phone cradled against his ear. A moment of vulnerability, an exquisite blend of lonely and loving that reached out to every woman on earth who had ever glimpsed a masterpiece and craved to touch it....

"That's a crock!" The angry voice of Anthony Parish suddenly filled the room, startling her from her reverie, bringing her head sharply up. Her brother's hand gripped the phone, and his good-looking features were harsh in contrast to those of the face beneath her fingertips. "I don't care *how* long it takes to substantiate those facts! I'm paying top dollar and I want results!" He cast a glance at Leslie, then shook his head. "No, no. Not that way. Listen, you work on it. I'll be in touch later."

Replacing the receiver, he pushed himself from his chair and rounded the desk to take the seat beside her. Despite the flecks of gray that whispered through his hair, he was tall and lean, carrying his forty years well. "Sorry about that, Les," he murmured, "but someone's got to keep on top of them."

"I thought you had assistants to handle things like that."

Steepling his fingers, he leaned forward with a sigh. "The buck stops here. If I want this publishing house to make it in a struggling economy, it's *my* responsibility. Quality is the name of the game. At least for me it is. I want every story we print to be right." He shot a glance at the magazine that lay open on Leslie's lap. "*Man's Mode* has done well precisely because it's a notch above." He sighed again. "But that's not your worry—" he sent her a teasing smile "—unless you'd like to change your mind and join us."

Leslie held up a slender hand. "No, thanks. I rather like being the black sheep of the family. I mean, you've got the publishing end and Diane's got sporting goods and Brenda's tied up in computers, while dad sits up there as chairman of the board. No," she smiled, "I'll stick to my kids."

Teasing yielded to a moment's admiration. "You love your work, don't you?"

"Um hmm."

"I'm glad. Les. Hey!" The rotating file in Tony's mind must have given a sudden flip. "You've got a birthday coming up."

"Um hmm."

"A big one."

She'd been trying to forget. "Um hmm."

"What do you want?"

She crinkled up her nose. "Nothing. Really."

"Come on. It's not every day that a woman turns thirty."

"Thank God."

"Leslie," her brother chided, "you're not feeling your age, are you? Hell, self-made woman and all, you're doing better than ever."

On the surface she was. Inside, though, there was a growing sense of restlessness. "I suppose," she said thoughtfully.

"So what's your pleasure?" He sat back in his chair and eyed her speculatively. "A watch? Better still—" his brown eyes lit up "—how about a fur jacket? Something soft and chic?"

"Really, Tony. I don't want anything...."

He arched a brow. "I won't take no for an answer. You may be a successful professional, but you're still my little sister. In my book, that gives me the right to dote. So," he breathed, as though the matter was settled, "what'll it be? For your thirtieth—a special something...."

Leslie thought for a moment. Her gaze dropped to the advertisement that still lay open on her lap. Her forefinger traced the swath of skin whose lightly bronzed color ran unbroken from head to foot. She chewed on her bottom lip, then smiled. "What I'd *really* like," she announced boldly, "is the use of the house on St. Barts for a week...and *him*."

THREE WEEKS LATER she arrived on St. Barthélémy. Having woken up at four-thirty that morning to pack and catch the first plane out of JFK, she was tired. Wearing the wools that a frigid predawn February morning in New York had demanded, she was sweaty. Greeting the beauty of the Caribbean through hot, heavy eyes, she was miserable. To top it all, the taxi she'd taken from the airport had had a flat tire several hundred yards from the villa, and desperate to lay her head on a fresh, cool pillow, she'd taken her things and left the driver to deal with his jack and spare.

Toting a duffel bag over one arm and a bag of books and her purse over the other, she struggled along the narrow road, which wound uphill. Though she clung to its shoulder, where the succession of palm parasols might protect her from the strong midday Caribbean sun, she felt beads of sweat gather along her hairline, moisten her neck, trickle in a tiny stream down the valley between her breasts. For the moment the beauty of the island was lost on her. She simply wanted to lie down.

She sneezed once and sniffled as the road curved, then moaned aloud when the familiar structure with its red-tiled roof and white stucco walls emerged from its tropical camouflage. That was all the incentive she needed to quicken her step. Her legs felt like rubber, but she didn't care. Another two minutes and she'd be there, sprawled in her favorite room—in *everybody*'s favorite room—with the overhead fan gently cooling the air, the palm fronds dancing on the skylight overhead, the sea strutting its lush azure stuff beyond the open sliding doors, from the sparkling white sands of the beachfront to the far horizon.

Fairly running the last few steps, she shifted from one elbow to the other the heavy wool sweater she'd already stripped off and dug into her purse for the key. When it eluded her, she tugged the purse around and peered bleary-eyed into the scrambled abyss of its interior. She rummaged again, whispered a soft oath and peered a second time, finally shaking the bag to hear the telltale rattle that helped her zero in on the spot. Another minute's ferreting produced the key.

With a twist of her hand, the front door opened. As cool air enveloped her, she smiled her relief. "Thank you, Martine," she rasped softly, vowing to repeat it louder later in the week when she came face to face with the woman who must have been in earlier that morning in anticipation of her arrival. And a twist of fate it was that Martine was a morning person. Leslie's original plans had been to arrive that evening; only a last-minute cancellation on the early-bird flight had brought her in at noontime.

Closing the door behind her, she stooped to let her bags fall from her damp and tired shoulders. Her purse and sweater slid to the floor nearby. Mopping her clammy forehead on her sleeve, she stepped out of her leather pumps and, with her fingers at the button of her plum-and-plaid skirt, started down the stairs.

After ten years of family vacations here, she'd come to take the villa for granted. Only a visitor would be entranced by its unique design. Nestled into the cliffs rising above the sands on the western end of the small island, it sprawled across three spacious levels. The top level, even with the road, held the front foyer, one wall of which was glassed and looked out toward the ocean, the other two walls of which opened to lateral bedrooms. The bottom level, to the right as the house followed the natural cropping of the cliff, held the airy kitchen and living room and opened on to a flagstoned terrace, itself graduated on two planes, the lowest of which was a hop, skip and jump from the beach.

It was the middle level of the house to which Leslie headed unswervingly. Connected to top and bottom by an open staircase, it was the one most coveted by whichever family member had the good fortune to arrive first, or, all too often and to Leslie's misfortune, needed the space. This level held an airy den and the exquisite master-bedroom suite, of which Leslie had every intention of taking sole possession for the week.

Bent on undressing and showering, she had her skirt unzipped and halfway down her hips by the time she reached the foot of the stairs. Quickly hopping free of the heavy wool, she tossed it over the back of a chair in the den, then reached down to pull her lavender turtleneck jersey from the elastic confines of her matching wool tights. Feeling more like a wilting violet than a stylish New Yorker, she padded toward the bedroom.

The door was open. Tugging the turtleneck over her head, she stumbled across the threshold, and was in the process of peeling the clinging fabric from her sweaty arms when she cried out in alarm and came to an abrupt halt. Clamping her teeth into her soft lower lip, she stared at the bed.

It was supposed to be empty. It was supposed to be freshly made and waiting just for her. It was supposed to be all hers for the week.

Instead, the covers were pulled back, and the rumpled sheets were draped—just barely—over a large body that was very definitely male and just as definitely sound asleep.

Sagging against the doorjamb with her turtleneck crushed against the pale mauve lace of her bra, she was seized by a wave of fury. Tony had promised! He'd said he would clear it with the others so that she might have the villa to herself for the week! Was this a friend of his? Or Diane's . . . or Brenda's? It just wasn't fair! The one time she'd wanted it . . . wanted it. . . .

Suddenly her anger faded as a memory seemed to mesh with the tableau before her. Decorated in white and rattan, with pillows and cushions of an imported Italian weave, the room glowed beneath the noontime sun, which stole through the palms above the skylight to lend a dreamlike quality to the air. The ceiling fan whirred softly overhead, augmenting the gentlest of breezes that danced off the ocean and whispered in through the open glass sliding doors. But it was to the bed that Leslie's eyes were riveted. To the bed . . . and the figure so carelessly spread atop it.

There was something familiar about him. Feeling a sneeze coming on, she pressed her hand to her nose in hopes of suppressing it as, entranced, she studied the limp torso and sprawled limbs. The length of lightly bronzed leg that extended from the sheet spoke of superior height. The firmness of his thigh and corresponding leanness of his stomach attested to commendable fitness. The solidly muscular structure of his shoulder hinted at bodily pride. He was, in a word, stunning.

He lay on his back with his head fallen to the side. One hand, fingers splayed, rested on his stomach. She couldn't help but note how comfortable it looked, cushioned by the soft ribbon of hair that narrowed from the more ambitious covering of his chest. His other hand was thrown out to the side in a gesture she might have seen as pure invitation had the man not been so very obviously asleep.

Hugging her jersey to her throat, Leslie dared creep closer. Eyes wide in disbelief, she stared. She'd seen that face before. Even in repose it held a certain expression of vulnerability that immediately conjured up images of another bed, another setting. There was the hair, dark and mussed by sleep . . . the nose, straight, almost aristocratic . . . the sensually enticing shadow of a beard. As her eye tripped down his body once more, her heart began to pound with understanding. Oh, yes, she'd seen that face before. *And* that body. This time there was no workbench in the background, no sculptor's tools, no half-finished piece of art. This time his sheet covered the strip of flesh at his hip that had so taunted her before. This time the bed was in no photographer's studio but in her family's own villa.

Without realizing what she was doing, she sniffed the air in search of the unique scent of Homme Premier. But her nose was so stuffed she only succeeded in sending herself in a paroxysm of coughing, from which she emerged in horror to watch the man on the bed begin to move.

First his chest expanded with a deep, indrawn breath. His lips thinned, his brow furrowed. He turned his dark head on the pillow, stretching the outflung arm up over his head. Leslie swallowed hard when the sheet slipped precariously low on his abdomen.

Her gaze returned to his face in time to see one eye open—and stare at her blankly. When it was joined by the other, she saw that they were a warm shade of brown. The man blinked, dusting thick mahogany fringes against the high line of his cheek, then frowned, then blinked again and stared at her. Finally, as though abruptly recalling something, he bolted upright.

"My God!" he exclaimed, thrusting his fingers through the thick swath of hair that waved gently over his brow. "I'm sorry! I was going to be up and showered and dressed long before you arrived!" Frowning again, he looked toward the skylight, then reached for his watch from the stand beside the bed and stared at it in confusion. "Twelve-forty? But you weren't supposed to be in until seven tonight."

"I got an early flight," Leslie droned in a near monotone, then shook her blond head in distress. "I...don't...believe it."

"What don't you believe?"

"You."

His expression was immediately endearing, as though his only purpose in life was to please her, and having failed that, he was crushed. "I've done something wrong already?"

"You're here. I don't . . . believe it."

All vestige of drowsiness gone, the man looked down at his body innocently, before breaking into a gentle smile. "I am here."

"An understatement," she muttered, then watched him hoist himself up against the headboard. He seemed to dominate not only the bed but the entire room. In turn, Leslie's eyes held dismay. "He really did it."

Her reference was clear. "Your brother? Of course he did it. It sounds like he adores you. Most likely he'd have given you *anything* you'd asked."

"But . . . a man? *You?*" Her dismay was fast turning to mortification. "I was supposed to be here alone," she said in a very small voice. Above and beyond all the special things she had planned for herself, she suddenly realized that this man was not only gorgeous, but he was a male model who was *paid* to be pleasing to women. In this case he'd been paid by her brother, *her own brother*, to spend the week with her! Her cheeks felt hotter than ever.

Beneath the sheet, he bent one knee out to the side. Leslie eyed its vivid outline with something akin to anguish, breathing only a marginal sigh when he safely adjusted the sheet over his hips.

"Alone is no fun," he countered softly. His eyes dropped from her face to her chest, taking in the straps of her bra, the disarray of her jersey, which was clutched more fiercely than ever to her breasts, the slender expanse of purple wool running from her waist to her toes. She assumed she must look like a lavender elf; in truth, she felt more like the court jester.

Following his gaze and for the first time realizing her state of dress, Leslie took a step backward. "Alone can be lots of fun," she argued, recalling the plans she had to read, to sunbathe in the buff, to amble around the island to her heart's content with no thought of any other living soul, for a change. It simply wasn't fair, she mused, then slanted him an accusing glance. "You're in *my* bed, you know." She felt on the defense both physically and emotionally.

But her brief spurt of belligerence was feeble and reflected her growing torment. Not only was she appalled that her brother had taken seriously what she'd said purely tongue-in-cheek, but she felt sicker by the minute.

"I thought this was the master suite," came the deep rejoinder.

"It is. And this time round, *I'm* the master." So she'd been telling herself for the past few weeks; it had been part of the lure of spending her vacation at the villa in solitude.

The man on the bed arched a brow and skimmed her defensive pose. "You don't look terribly masterful right now.

As a matter of fact—" his dark brows knit and he sat forward "—you don't look terribly well. Are you feeling all right?"

In no mood to be witty or subtle, Leslie simply shook her head. "I was up before dawn to get to JFK and had to wait forever sweltering on St. Martin to catch the island hopper here. I'm hot and sweaty and just want to get out of these things and into a cool shower. Besides that, I've got a splitting headache and one hell of a cold." She took a stuffy breath. "In short, I feel awful!"

When the man quickly pushed himself up from the bed, she shut her eyes. All too well she remembered the sliver of smooth flesh by his hip. She didn't think she could take that just now.

"You mean your normal voice isn't as nasal?" came the note of amusement not far from her ear. Simultaneously an arm circled her shoulder and propelled her forward.

Feeling perfectly stupid, she opened her eyes, careful to keep them straight ahead as the bathroom door neared. "No, it's not," she managed, struggling with the *n*'s.

"That's too bad," the man replied softly, teasingly. "It's sexy. Deep and . . . sultry. That's it. Sultry."

"Sultry, as in hot and humid. And sweaty." Sexy was the last thing she felt.

At the bathroom door he slipped a hand to her forehead. "And feverish. Wait here."

Sagging against the jamb, she closed her eyes. Then, hit by a wave of dizziness, she gave up even the idea of a cooling shower. Suddenly nothing mattered more than lying flat. Turning, she stumbled back to the bed. The thought that the man whose body had warmed its sheets moments before might have a god-awful social disease was totally irrelevant to the situation. Her legs simply wouldn't hold her any longer.

With a soft moan she curled on her side, then, forgetting her company, rolled onto her back, clutching her jersey to her stomach with one hand and throwing the other arm across her eyes. When, moments later, the same arm that had led her toward the bathroom lifted her to a half-seated position, she groaned.

"Let me rest," she whispered, but her protector had other ideas.

"First, aspirin," he said gently. "Are you taking anything else?" She shook her head and docilely swallowed the tablets, washing them down with the water he'd brought. "There." He took the glass from her and eased her back onto the bed. Then he reached for the waistband of her tights and began to shimmy them over her hips.

"What are you doing?" she cried in alarm and squirmed away. When she tried to sit up, though, a firm hand pressed her flat. For the effort she'd made, her only reward was the sight of the pale blue briefs that ringed his hips. With strong, knowing hands he proceeded to peel the tights to her toes and off.

"Better?"

By twenty degrees at least. "Oh, yes."

"Want a shower now?"

She shook her head and rolled to her side again, pulling one of the pillows against her for comfort. "Not yet. I think I'll just lie like this for a while."

"Then I'll shower. Where are your bags?"

Her eyes were closed, his voice distant. If the man wished to rob her, she couldn't stop him. Her total concentration was on finding relief from the aches and pains that seemed to have suddenly invaded her body. "Upstairs. . . ."

If she was aware of the pad of footsteps on the stairs going up, then down, she made no sign. Nor did she turn her head when the faint hum of an electric razor filled the air, or when the spray of the shower rang out, or when the rustle of clothes in a suitcase ended with the glide of smooth cotton over hair-roughened flesh. It was only when the aspirin began to take effect, when she felt just warm, rather than hot, when the pounding in her head had subsided to a dull throb, that she opened her eyes again.

Seated in a chair by the bed, wearing nothing but a pair of pleated khaki shorts, was the man she'd been given for her birthday. A rush of mortification hit her anew. For, sitting there, his hair and skin damp and fresh, his chest broad and manly, his shoulders strong and inviting, he looked more magnificent than he had in his ad. By contrast she felt as though she'd been dredged up from hell.

"I don't believe it!" she moaned, then felt all the more gauche when the faintest of smiles curved his lips.

Propping his elbows on the arms of the chair, he threaded his fingers together. "I think you've said that already."

"I don't care! This is incredible!"

"What is?"

"This . . ." She waved toward him, then herself, then extended her fingers to take in the situation as a whole. "I can't believe Tony would do this to me!"

"As I was told, you specifically requested it."

Her chest rose and fell as she labored to breathe. "It was a *joke!* I was being facetious! Tony must have known that." When the man opposite her slowly shook his head, she went quickly on. "And besides, the man I pointed to was a fictitious character."

"He had a face and a body. You had to know he was real."

"He was a paid model! I never expected Tony to go out and track him down, then hire him to entertain me for the week!" The thought instantly revived her embarrassment. Pink-cheeked, she turned her face away and shut her eyes. "God," she moaned beneath her breath, "I feel so lousy.

Maybe I'd be laughing if I felt all right. But I can barely breathe, let alone think straight."

The mattress yielded to another form. Though she tensed up, she didn't have the strength to move, even when a cool hand began to stroke damp strands of blond hair from her brow. Quite against her will, she found the gesture a comfort.

"How long have you felt this way?" the deep voice probed with such concern that she couldn't help but answer.

"Since last night."

"Sore throat?"

She shook her head, then opened her eyes and peered up into his, which were studying her carefully. "You can't stay here, you know."

"Oh?" The twinkle in his eye spoke of his amusement.

"No."

"And why not?"

"Because *I'm* here."

The man made a ceremony of looking around the bed. "We seem to be doing just fine here together." Anticipating her, he had a hand at her shoulder before she could begin to raise it from the bed. "Besides, I'm your gift. You can't just discard me along with the wrapping."

"What wrapping?" she quipped. "Seems to me you weren't wearing much of anything."

"I was wearing something."

"Not much."

"So you *did* notice. I was beginning to think I'd lost my touch."

Leslie sighed and closed her eyes. "You haven't lost your touch," she granted. It was moving in slow circles against her temples. "Great for headaches...."

"And...?"

Her eyes flew open. "That's all," she said quickly. "I meant what I said before. You can't. . . ." Her voice trailed off as a sneeze approached. "Damn," she whispered, covering her mouth and sneezing. She sat up in time to sneeze a second time, then took the tissue he offered and blew her nose. "Do I ever feel lousy. . . ."

The same hand that had smoothed her hair from her brow now tucked random strands behind her ear. "Why don't you take that shower? In the meantime, I'll fix you a cold drink."

"You can't stay. . . ."

"Have you had any lunch?"

"Lunch? I haven't had any *breakfast*. Feed a cold, starve a fever . . . I've got both. What do I do?" She raised her eyes to those above her. They were reassuring and confident.

"Don't worry, sweetheart. I know what to do. Here, you stay put." He pushed himself from the bed and reached for her bag. "What do you want to put on?" Unzipping the stylish duffel, he began rummaging inside. "Is there a nightgown in here?"

Leslie recalled the ad that had started this farce. Her voice held more than a trace of sarcasm. "Nightgown as in silky white negligee?" She shook her head. "Sorry."

For a minute the man eyed her strangely. Then, as understanding dawned, he cast her a punishing glance, and turned his attention back to her bag.

Perhaps it was her reference to the ad that did it. Perhaps it was simply the aspirin clearing her head. But in the moment's pause it occurred to Leslie that she was lying on a rumpled bed in nothing but scant wisps of mauve lace, watching a total stranger fish through her clothes.

"Here, let me do that," she said crossly as she pushed herself up. Within seconds she'd managed to extract the oversize T-shirt she'd come to think of as her Caribbean negligee. A very pale aqua from too many washings, it was likewise soft and comfortable. Easily reaching her thighs, it would be suitably unappealing. "If it's sexy you're looking for," she muttered, "you've come to the wrong place."

Mustering her pride, she snatched her bag of toiletries from the duffel and headed for the bathroom, totally unaware of how truly sexy she looked. The man watching her, however, was not. He stood holding the picture of her in his mind's eye long after the bathroom door had closed.

On the other side of the door, Leslie pressed her palms to her hot cheeks, then slid her fingers up to push her hair away from her face. A mess. She was a mess. The entire situation was a mess. How had she ever managed it . . . careful, conservative Leslie?

Angrily plopping the bag of toiletries atop the vanity, she dug inside for makeup remover. Makeup? Hah! What a wasted effort that had been. She'd looked deathly regardless. But New York was New York, and one didn't show one's face in public unless it was suitably protected from the elements. Lips thinning with sarcasm, she squeezed a gob of cold cream onto her fingers and began to scrub at her cheeks. Protected from the elements? More likely camouflaged. Hidden. Shielded from the world by a manufactured sheen. How phony it all was!

With a vengeance she tissued off the cold cream, then bent low to rinse her face with water. There she lingered, savoring the sensation of coolness on her cheeks and eyes. At last she straightened and pressed a towel more gently to her skin.

She should have known . . . should have known never to even joke with Tony about the state of her love life. He'd been after her for years to marry, have an affair, get involved, live it up. Wasn't that what he'd been doing since his own divorce six years before? Not that she criticized him. He'd married young and had been faithful to the letter to Laura. In the end she had been the one to run off with someone else, leaving him to cope with three growing children. He was a hardworking, devoted father who needed time off once in a while; Leslie certainly couldn't fault him for his own choice of outlet.

On the other hand, she reasoned, as she turned on the shower and stepped beneath its tepid spray, he should have known not to foist something as . . . as preposterous as this pretty boy on her! Hadn't she spent the past ten years trying to show the world how different she was? She'd had her fill of high society back in high school. And in college, well, Joe Durand had soured her on men, period. But then, Tony knew nothing about Joe. She hadn't spoken of him to anyone. The self-reproach with which she lived was bad enough, but to air her folly for the sake of others' enjoyment . . . *that* she didn't need.

Adjusting the water to a warmer temperature, she shampooed her hair, then soaped herself. It was several minutes later when she stepped from beneath the soothing spray. After toweling herself as vigorously as her tired arms would allow, she drew on the T-shirt and a fresh pair of panties and blew her hair nearly dry. Then, standing opposite the misted mirror, she studied herself. Even the mist couldn't soften the image.

"Pale, Leslie. Too pale," she announced, then sneezed and reached for a piece of Kleenex. By the time she faced herself again, the mist had begun to clear, and what she saw gave her a jolt. Oh, the features were fine—soft amethyst eyes that were large and, if anything, set a bit too far apart; a nose that was certainly small enough to balance the delicacy of her mouth and chin; hair that was an enviable shade of blond, cut into long bangs across the brow, trimmed crisply an inch above the shoulder, cropped stylishly at the sideburns and falling into place as Diego had promised. No, the features were fine, taken one by one. Put together, however, they formed the image of a lost and lonely waif.

Reaching up, she brushed her bangs from her eyes. What was she going to do? Granted, it was unfortunate that the one week she'd chosen to spend in the sun should be hampered by a mean winter cold. That, though, she could live with. And the sun, the warm weather, would be potent medicine.

But this man, this model...this very handsome model...was something else. Never in a million years would she have sought such a man on her own. Indeed, pausing to think of the man's occupation, of the many women he must have serviced over the years, she was appalled. And embarrassed. She wasn't that type at all! She wouldn't know what to *do* with such a man....

Shaking her head half in regret, she left the sanctuary of the bathroom to find the bedroom immaculate. The man's suitcase that had lain on the low glass table was gone, as were odds and ends atop the nightstand. The bed had been freshly made, its covers turned back invitingly. Padding barefoot to the walk-in closet, she peered inside, then turned. There was no sign of him.

While urging herself to simply climb into bed and be grateful she'd been left alone, Leslie headed downstairs toward the kitchen. He'd said he'd make her a cool drink. Well, she was thirsty.

Indeed he was in the kitchen, though his attention was not on making a cool drink. Rather, he stood before the open window, his back to her, his arms crossed over his chest, one bare foot propped on the low rung of a nearby stool. He wore the same shorts he'd put on earlier, and all in all, he presented a perfect image of reflective masculinity.

For a lingering moment she studied him. Though his hair was thick and on the long side, it was well trimmed. From the sturdy nape to the soles of his feet, he looked clean. He also looked older than she'd imagined him to be, despite the prime condition of his body. From where she stood she caught shadings of silver following the gentle curve of each ear. Rather than detracting from his appearance, these silver streaks lent him an air of dignity that puzzled her all the more.

In short, there was nothing unsavory-looking about him. She wasn't sure what she'd expected from a gigolo. Certainly not . . . this.

With practically no warning she sneezed, ending her moment of invisibility. The man by the window turned quickly, his features instantly released from whatever thoughts had held them taut.

"There you are," he said, taking the few steps necessary to end their separation. "Feeling better?"

She had been, she thought. Now, though, looking up that great distance into a face that seemed so gentle, so knowing, she felt suddenly small and utterly insignificant.

"A little," she murmured, adding "self-conscious" to the list. What had made her think that a T-shirt would protect her from the eyes of a professional lover? When those eyes began to wander across her chest and down, she slithered from their touch and took refuge on the stool by the window.

"Why aren't you in bed?" he asked softly.

"I felt like seeing what you were up to," she answered defensively, then turned her face to catch the ocean's gentle breath. "Where's that cool drink you promised?" Even to her own ears her tone held a touch of arrogance. It bothered her. She didn't much care for hired help . . . certainly not of this sort!

After a pause came a murmured, "Coming right up." Only when Leslie heard the refrigerator door open did she dare look back to find her attendant on his haunches sorting through the packed shelves. "It looks like someone was far more prepared for your arrival than I was," he said, pushing aside a bushy head of lettuce to get at a carton of eggs. "I wouldn't have believed they had all this fresh produce down here."

"Some of it is home grown, but most of it's imported. And it was Martine who did the marketing. She's a marvel. She comes in to clean once or twice while we're here and keeps an eye on things when we're not. All it takes is one call from the States and the house is open, cool and stocked to the hilt."

"You don't ever rent it out."

"No. Friends use it sometimes. But more often it's just us." She tried desperately to be tactful. "We were very lucky to get this land. It's on a prime part of the island. Most of the space is owned by small inns. In fact, there's one quaint one just around the bend. You could probably get a room there...."

Ignoring her suggestion, he added a quart of milk and a package of neatly wrapped cheese to the growing assortment in his arms. "Nice cheese. Any lemon? Ah, there." When, arms laden, he stood at last, his knees cracked in protest. He flexed them gingerly as he deposited his armload on the counter.

Leslie focused in on the knees. "How old are you?"

"Thirty-nine."

"That old?" Even with creaking knees and the twin streaks of gray behind his ears, she would have given him no more than thirty-five. "Aren't you a little...beyond this type of thing?"

"Beyond cooking?"

"Beyond modeling. And...." She waved her arm in a gesture to indicate his dubious role as her supposed birthday present. "I always thought you had to be younger...."

"To bring pleasure?"

"To do it ... like this...." The heat on her cheeks soared when he turned teasing eyes her way.

"Are you trying to say something, Leslie?"

"Yes," she declared in frustration, growing clammy all over. "You can't stay here for a week! You've got to leave; it's as simple as that!"

Reaching for a skillet, he put it on the stove, added a dollop of butter and lit the gas. "While you're under the weather? No way. As it is, I've got to redeem myself for not being up and ready when you arrived."

She held up a hand. "No apologies. I'm sure someone in your...field...is used to sleeping late." It had been twelve-forty, for heaven's sake! She couldn't remember the last time she'd slept that late herself. On second thought, she could. It had been the summer before, when she'd been hooked on *Noble House*. Not that she'd loved it that much, but she made a practice of never leaving a book midway through, and there had been another book she'd been dying to start. "Late nights and all...."

"And all."

"So—" she sent him an accusatory glance "—you've found your way around the island? Gustavia has its lively spots. When did you say you arrived?"

"Yesterday. And I haven't been anywhere but the airport and here. Actually, I was up late reading. I was in the middle of a book I didn't really care for and I wanted to start another, but I have this practice of never leaving a book midway through, and it wasn't until five this morning that I finally finished it."

Leslie swallowed hard, sneezed again and put her palm to her head. Things weren't going as she'd planned. Not by a long shot.

"What are you doing?" she cried when she felt her feet leave the floor.

"Getting you back to bed. Don't worry. These weary old bones won't drop you."

"That's not the point."

"Then what is?" He took the stairs two at a time, carrying her as though she weighed no more than a small child.

The point? What *was* it, anyway? Her head was suddenly muddled again so badly that Leslie neither knew nor cared. When she felt the coolness of the sheets she breathed a sigh of relief and, curling onto her side, closed her eyes.

SHE MUST HAVE dozed off. By the time she awoke, the face of the sun had shifted from the skylight overhead to the sliding doors, lower and farther west. Blinking away her grogginess, she followed its rays to the tall figure propped casually in the chair by her bed.

Deep in thought, he didn't see her at first. His legs were sprawled before him, his elbows bent on the cushioned arms of the chair, his hands fisted inside each other and pressed to his lips. She wondered what thoughts held him in his distant world, then shuddered when she realized how very far that world was from her own. The faint movement was enough to bring him back.

The slowest of smiles gentled his lips. "Hi, there."

"Hello."

Reaching to the stand beside him, he lifted two more pills and an ice-filled glass. Without a word, she swallowed the aspirin, washed it down with several gulps of what proved to be fresh lemonade, then drained the glass. When she leaned back, it was to rest against the pillows that he'd newly puffed.

"Not bad . . . the lemonade, that is." In truth, what she'd been thinking was how nice it was to have someone taking care of her for a change. A small luxury . . . a birthday gift. Her expression grew exquisitely soft. "When I was a child I loved Steiff pets—you know, those little stuffed animals—" she reached up and caught the upper part of her ear "—with the tiny tag right about here? They used to come with names attached to their ribbons." She moved her hand to the hollow of her throat, then, almost timidly, raised her eyes to his. "Do you have a name?"

For a heart-stopping moment, he held her gaze. She felt drawn to him, much as earlier she'd been drawn to the kitchen when she'd known she should have stayed in bed. He had power. It had touched her from the pages of *Man's Mode*. It had touched her when he'd stood at the kitchen window with his back to her. It had touched her moments before when his eyes had been distant. A kind of dreamlike quality. A depth. A puzzlement.

Slowly, with the corners of his eyes crinkling in a most effective way, he smiled. "Oliver Ames, at your service."

Oliver Ames. Her heart skipped a beat.

2

"OLIVER AMES." She said it aloud, testing it on her tongue. It flowed without any effort at all. Just right for a model— or a playboy. "Is that your . . . professional name?"

His mouth twitched at one corner. "Yes."

"And your real name," she asked more softly. "What's that? Or . . . is it off limits?" There were rules governing this sort of thing; unfortunately, she wasn't well versed in them.

Oliver smiled openly, his lips mirroring the dance of humor in his eyes. Sitting forward now, he was fully attentive. . . . *As rightly he should be,* Leslie mused. Wasn't he paid to be attentive? He was also paid to be attractive: bare chested, bare legged, large and vibrantly male—she found him disconcertingly so.

"No," he allowed lightly, "it's not off limits. As long as you don't spread it around."

"And who would I spread it to?" she snapped in response to the unsettling twist of her thoughts. "In case you haven't noticed, I'm not too . . . comfortable with this situation. Not much of a chance of my running back to Manhattan shouting the name of the guy my brother *bought* for me." She grimaced. "No woman wants to think she can't find someone on her own."

For an instant, when his dark brows knit, she feared that she'd offended him. Yet when he spoke, his voice held only curiosity.

"Can't you?"

"I'm not looking."

"And if you were? Surely there are men in New York who'd give their right arms for a Parish."

Leslie's lips grew taut, her expression grim. "If a man needed a Parish badly enough to sacrifice his right arm, I'd say he's sold himself short. And yes, there are many men like that around. Funny how money can screw up priorities." Closing her eyes, she slid lower on the pillows.

The creak of the rattan chair gave warning that Oliver Ames had moved. It wasn't until the bed dipped by her side, though, that she felt alarm. Eyes flying open, she found him settled near her hip, his arms propped on either side of her, hemming her in.

"You sound bitter," he observed. His voice was deep and kind and not at all taunting, as it might have been, given the fact that it was a Parish who had dreamed up the very scheme that had brought him to St. Barts. "You've been hurt?"

She shrugged, unwilling to elaborate. For she couldn't think of the past when the man before her dominated the present. What was it about him, she asked herself, as she stared into eyes the texture of warm chocolate, that made her want to forget that he was what he was? What was it that made her want to reach up and brush the hair from his brow, trace the firm line of his lips, scale the gentle swell of his shoulder? What was it that stirred senses on which she'd long since given up? What was it that affected her so, that even now, as she lay in bed with a stuffy head and clenched fists, entranced her to the point of distraction?

"Your name," she whispered, then moistened her lips with her tongue. "Your real name. What is it?" Her expectant gaze fell to his lips and she waited, admiring the strong shape of them, until at last they moved to form the words.

"Oliver Ames," he mouthed, then gave a boyish grin.

"You're making fun of me," she contended soberly. "It was an innocent question."

"And an innocent answer. My name *is* Oliver Ames. Personal. Professional. Oliver Ames." He tipped his head to the side. "Perhaps you're the one doing the mocking. Is there something wrong with Oliver Ames?"

"Oh, no!" she breathed. "It's fine. It's more than fine. I like it. It's just that...well...it flows so easily I thought you'd made it up." She was babbling and she knew it. He seemed so close, his voice so deep and smooth that she felt rattled.

"My parents made it up. You can thank them one day."

Embarrassed, Leslie wrinkled her nose. "Oh, I couldn't do that...." Her voice trailed off. A lover for hire...and his parents? Great! Then she grew curious. "Do your parents...do they know what you do for a living?"

"Sure."

"And...they don't mind?"

"Why would they mind?"

She shrugged and fumbled. It didn't help that Oliver had moved his hands closer, that his thumbs had slyly found their way into her sleeves to ever so faintly caress the soft skin of her upper arms. "Oh, you know.... Modeling, and...this...." She waved one arm half in hopes of dislodging his hand. The gesture only seemed to solidify his grasp. And Oliver Ames was more amused than ever.

"Actually," he offered wide-eyed, "they're quite proud of me."

"Oh."

"Uh huh." He grinned. "A parent's love is all-abiding, wouldn't you say?"

She couldn't say much. A breathy, "I guess so," was all his closeness would permit. Her gaze fell briefly to his chest, but the sight of the light furring of hair there was all the more unsettling, so she forced her attention back to his eyes. Her insides burned; much as she wanted to blame the sensation on the aspirin she'd taken, she couldn't.

"You'll catch my cold if you sit this close," she warned as she tried to sink more deeply into the bed.

"I don't mind," came the silky reply.

"But . . . then where would you be?" she persisted, unable to free herself from his sensual spell, struggling against its hold by voicing frantic wisps of thought. "I mean, who wants a red-nosed model with glassy eyes? Who wants a lover with a stuffed nose and the sneezes? As it is there are already too many communicable diseases rampant in your trade—"

"Ah, so that's what frightens you—catching something from *me?*"

"I'm not frightened."

"Then why are you trembling?"

"Because . . . I'm sick."

To her chagrin he moved one hand to her forehead. "You feel cooler. You're not even as pale. No, there must be something else that's given you the shakes."

"I don't have the shakes!" she declared loudly, then clamped her mouth shut when even her voice belied her claim. It was sheer chemistry. She knew it, and it mortified her. Granted, he was a pro. But to be so totally susceptible to him appalled her. "And if I do, it's your fault. You're the one who's making me nervous. Damn it, you should be some kind of arrogant, unsavory creep, with little bugs crawling around here and there."

"I'm not," he stated, his voice calm. "And there aren't any bugs."

"I know," she replied miserably. It was obvious that the man was both clean and healthy. She didn't have to ask; she just knew. Besides, she trusted Tony. Though his sense of humor was sadly misguided, he did love her. And he was protective. Hadn't she kept her experience with Joe Durand from him partly out of fear of what he might do to Joe? No, Tony would never have invited anyone objectionable to spend the week alone in a villa with his little sister. Tony would have checked everything out. Strange. A male model checking out? A paid escort? In *Tony's* book?

"Well . . . ?" Oliver asked softly, his face no more than a hand's width from hers.

"Well what?" she managed to whisper.

"The verdict. I can see those little wheels going round and round in your head. Will you let me kiss you . . . or am I going to have to be forceful about it?"

"Forceful? Truly?" she asked softly.

His forearms came to rest flush on the sheet, bringing his abdomen into contact with hers. Leslie caught her breath, aware of his warmth and of the precious nothings she wore beneath her shirt. Meanwhile, hidden high up her sleeves, his fingers cupped her shoulders and gently massaged their tautness. Her response, an instinctive coil of heat that sizzled its way to her toes and back, made moot the point. He would never use force. He wouldn't have to. He was good, she mused in dismay. Too good.

"Don't . . ." she heard herself say, then looked as puzzled as he.

"Don't what? Don't touch you? Don't kiss you? Don't take care of you?"

She wanted . . . she didn't. "Just don't. . . ."

"But I have to," he whispered.

Her voice was no louder, though tinged with regret. "Because you were hired?" The word stuck in her throat like a large piece of overcooked liver. She swallowed hard to dislodge it, managing to produce only a tiny moan. He'd been hired to love her . . . and it hurt.

When he slid his fingers to the back of her neck and pressed feathery circles in her skin, she closed her eyes and turned her face away. "What is it?" he murmured. She simply shook her head and squeezed her eyes tighter. "Come on, Les," he coaxed. "Tell me." His thumb slid across her cheek to stroke the taut line of her jaw.

"This is . . . humiliating. . . ."

"Why?"

"Because Tony. . . arranged for you," she said, feeling ugly and sick and sexless.

"And if I said that had no bearing on this moment . . . ?"

"I'd wonder whether it, too, wasn't part of the act." Very cautiously, she opened her eyes to find Oliver studying her intently. Then, easing up, he clicked his tongue against the roof of his mouth.

"So distrustful . . . and at such a young age."

"I feel about twelve. And, yes, I'm distrustful. I. . .I guess I just want more out of life than the buying and selling of favors."

He thought for a minute. "What if you thought of this as a fix-up? Haven't you ever had a blind date?"

"Oh, yes." Her lips twisted. "Charming invention, the blind date."

"It has been known to work."

"Not in my book."

"And why not?"

"Because a blind date is never really blind. I mean, the person who agrees to a blind date usually does so at the convincing of a salesman in the guise of a matchmaker." When Oliver frowned she grew insistent. "Really." She stared at the ceiling and spoke in a mocking tone. "He's in his late thirties, is tall, dark and handsome, is a stockbroker, drives a Porsche and has a horse farm in upstate New York."

Oliver nodded. "Sounds interesting."

"Sounds vile! Who gives a damn if he's tall, dark and handsome, and has enough money to put DuPont to shame? I certainly don't! And I dislike the thought that I've in turn been marketed, based on similarly meaningless data."

"Ah . . . the Parish curse."

"Among other things," she mused, then took a breath and, emboldened by indignation, faced her tormentor. "So, Oliver Ames, if you want to kiss me, do so knowing that I earn my own living as a preschool teacher, that I drive a four-year-old VW Rabbit, that I hate parties, love picnics and abide by intrusions into my privacy only with great reluctance." Energy waning, she lowered her voice. "Also know that I'm very conservative. I don't sleep around."

He pressed his lips together, stifling a grin. "Then I don't have to fear catching something from you?"

"Yes. A cold."

"Which I'll risk. . . ."

Certain her diatribe would have discouraged him, Leslie was taken by surprise. She tried to tell herself who he was, *what* he was, but the fact of his presence muddled her brain. He was so near, so vibrant. When his head lowered, she closed her eyes. Her breath came faster; she heard its rasping. Surely that would put him off . . . but no. His lips touched her left eye first, whispering a kiss on its lid once, then a second time before inching away. The bridge of her nose received similar treatment, then her right eye and its adjoining temple.

What astonished her most was the reassurance she felt from his touch. It was light and gentle, imbuing her with an unexpected sense of contentment. From her temple it fell to her cheekbone, dotting that sculpted line with a string of feather kisses before moving on to savor the delicate curve of her ear. The warmth of his breath made her tingle. Unknowingly she tipped her head to the side to ease his access.

"Nice?" he whispered against the high point of her jaw.

"Mmm."

"Relaxing?"

"Very."

"I'm glad," he murmured against her skin as he nibbled his way along her jaw, giving special attention to the delicacy of her chin before raising his head.

In a daze of pleasure, Leslie opened her eyes to find Oliver's, warm and alive, trained on her lips. His touch was a tangible thing, in the name of seduction doing something destructive to relaxation.

"I shouldn't let you . . ." she whispered meekly.

"But you can't help yourself . . . any more than I can," he answered, moments before he lowered his head and touched his lips to hers.

She stiffened at first, struck by the utter intimacy of the act. Only a kiss . . . yet it probed her entire being. Though his lips were gentle, they slid over hers with expertise—lightly at first, sampling, tasting, then with greater conviction as he sought her essence.

"Relax, Les," he whispered. "It's all right." His hands emerged from her sleeves to caress her shoulders from without.

"No . . . don't. . . ." It felt too good. She didn't trust herself."

Again he raised his head, and she met his gaze. His eyes were more smoky this time; she badly wanted to believe that she'd excited him.

"Kiss me," he said in a shaky breath, his eyes on her lips, then sliding upward. "Kiss me, and then decide." When she shook her head, he took a different tack, dropping his gaze to his hands, which glided up her shoulder to her neck, then inched downward from the hollow of her throat, downward over her chest, downward to separate over the straining fullness of her breasts.

Unable to push him away, unable to invite his advances, Leslie bit her lip to keep from crying out. Her eyes begged that he free her from the prison of his spell, yet her breasts swelled toward his touch in primal betrayal. His fingers circled her, working systematically inward, coming at last to the turgid peaks that spoke so eloquently of her arousal.

In self-defense she grasped his wrists and put a halt to the torture by pressing his hands hard against her. "Oliver, please don't."

"Will you kiss me?"

"I don't want to."

"You might like it."

"That's what worries me!"

Silence hung in the air, made heavy by the honesty of her argument. Frowning, Oliver studied her as though she was a creature like no other he'd ever known. In turn, she pleaded silently. She was sick . . . and aroused. It was a disturbing duo.

"You have the eyes of a fawn," he said at last. "Has anyone ever told you that?"

The spell was broken. With a shy smile of relief, she shook her head. "No."

"Well, you do." He sat straighter. "The eyes of a fawn. I could never hurt a fawn. So free and alive, so soft and vulnerable."

"You must be a poet. Funny, I thought you were supposed to be a sculptor."

"All illusion," he breathed magnanimously as he pushed himself off the bed. Only then did Leslie see what she wanted to. Very subtly and from the corner of her eye she saw sign of his arousal. Illusion? Not that. It was a heady thought on which to roll over and go to sleep.

SHE SLEPT through the late afternoon and early evening, awakening only to eat the light omelet Oliver had fixed, to take the aspirin he supplied, to drink the juice he'd chilled. She felt lazy and pampered and stuffy enough neither to object to the attention nor to raise the issue of his leaving the villa again. There would be time aplenty to discuss the latter when she felt better. For the time being, having a caretaker was rather nice.

Not used to sleeping at such length, she awakened periodically throughout the night. Each time, Oliver was in his chair by her bed, either sitting quietly, reading, or, at last, dozing. Though she might have enjoyed the luxury of watching him sleep, her slightest movement roused him every time.

"How do you feel?" he asked softly, leaning forward to touch the back of his hand to her brow.

"Okay."

"Any better?"

"I think so."

"Want a drink?"

"I just had one."

"That was two hours ago. Another would do you good," he argued, bounding from his chair to return to the kitchen for juice. In his absence, Leslie marveled not only at the image of his moonlit torso edged in silver, but at the easy intimacy of their soft-spoken conversation. To her astonishment there was something warm and reassuring about it.

Then he was back, standing guard while she drained the entire glass.

"I'll float away pretty soon."

"I'm your anchor. You won't get far. Now, be a good girl and go back to sleep."

"Hmmph. 'Be a good girl.' Lucky for you I'm the docile type. What would you have done if you'd had a wildcat on your hands?"

"I guess I'd have had to tie her hand and foot to the bed. Are you going to go to sleep?"

"In a minute. What time is it?"

"Two-twenty."

"Aren't *you* going to bed?"

"Is that an invitation?"

"Uh uh. Just a touch of concern. After all, if you let yourself get run down, you'll catch this cold but good!"

"Hey . . . which one of us is the doctor here?"

"Funny, I didn't think we had one."

"Oh, we have one, and it's me! Now go to sleep."

"I'm not tired."

"Not tired? You've got to be tired. You're sick."

"But I've been sleeping for hours." She started up from the bed. "What I really feel like doing is taking a walk on the beach."

Just as quickly, her shoulders were pressed flat. "No way, sweetheart. The bathroom is about your limit tonight."

"Come on. It's no fun walking around the bathroom. No sand, no shells, no waves—"

"Right! That gives you great incentive to get well."

"Really, Dr. Ames. I'm *not* tired."

He paused then. Even in the dark she felt the brand of his gaze. When, puzzled, she raised her head, she saw him push himself from his chair and approach the tape deck.

"Then we'll have some music. What'll it be?"

Sighing her resignation, she laid her head back. "You choose." Then, recalling his occupation and suddenly fearing that his choice might be something loud and swinging, she wavered. "On second thought—"

"Too late. My choice it is."

Moments later the soft and gentle strains of Debussy wafted into the air. Leslie lasted for all of five minutes before she fell back to sleep.

WHEN SHE AWOKE it was dawn. Pale purples and blues lit the sky, filling the room with their opalescent hues. She was alone. Alone and unguarded. Quickly shaking off the last traces of sleep, she put her feet on the floor and stood up. Cold or no cold, she'd had her fill of bed. This was her vacation. Oliver Ames could do something quite pithy with his orders, *she* was going to the beach.

Walking stealthily, half expecting her keeper to pop up from around the corner and usher her back to bed, she left the bedroom. Finding the den empty she headed for the stairs, tiptoeing down their bleached wood planks and pausing on the lowest rung. Still no sign of him. The kitchen was empty. The tile felt cool beneath her bare feet as she sped toward the glass sliding doors. When she flipped back the lock, its echo made her wince. Looking cautiously behind her, she waited. Still nothing. Dallying no longer, she quietly slid the door open and stepped out onto the terrace.

A long, deep breath told her that her cold was better. For the first time since she'd arrived, she smelled the special aroma of the island. Fresh in the morning's first light, it was a blend of sand and salt and lush tropical verdancy, a bouquet evoking lavish thoughts of laziness and leisure.

With a smile, she crossed beneath the palms of the terrace, trotted down the few stairs to the lower level, paused once again to savor the setting, then took the last set of steps at a clip. Ahh, to be finally on the beach!

Her smile spread into a full-scale beam. There was nothing like it! She wiggled her toes in the superfine sand, squished forward several steps, wiggled her toes some more, then sat down. It was beautiful as always, the beach, the sea. Her lungs drank it in, her eyes devoured it. Every one of her senses opened greedily.

Sitting cross-legged with the cushion of sand conforming to the lines of her bottom, her thighs, her calves, she thrust her fingers into the fine white stuff, heedless of the grains catching beneath her nails, simply eager to feel it all close up. Her eyes tripped forward over the softest of sand to that damp area where the surf had recently played. Here and there small shells winked, half buried in the tawny beach. And beyond was the restful ribbon of the tide, swishing this way and that with each incoming wave, rhythmic and gentle and positively addictive.

She was glad she'd come. She needed this—this sense of the warm, the familiar, the relaxing. She'd always been able to think here, to walk off on her own or sit on the beach and put things into perspective. She needed that now. She'd been troubled of late. Where was she going? What did she want in life? Oh, yes, the preschool thrived, and indeed she loved her work. But something was lacking . . . something with which she had to come to terms.

On impulse she swiveled around on the sand until she faced the villa. Arms now straight behind, supporting her, she studied the sprawling house set into the rocks. Where was he? Surely he hadn't given up so easily and left in the predawn hours to find a more hospitable welcome in town. No, chances were he had simply made use of one of the bedrooms on the upper floor.

Her gaze rose to that level, slipping from one to the other of the large glass panes that marked each of the bedrooms in turn. Was he sleeping? Sprawled out in bed as he'd been when she'd first arrived? Wearing nothing but the bedsheet . . . and his Homme Premier cologne? Today she'd be able to smell it. Would it be musky? Tart? Woodsy? Spicy?

What was she going to do about him? Her plans hadn't included a live-in companion, particularly one as tall and good-looking as Oliver Ames. The mere mention of his name set small butterflies aflutter in her stomach. She'd wanted to spend her time here in total relaxation, letting it all hang out, so to speak. Yet, sexy as sin, Oliver Ames intimidated her. What was she going to do about him?

Whirling around in frustration, she hugged her knees to her chest. Moments later she scrambled to her feet and began to walk slowly, pensively, along the water line. The soles of her feet slapped the wet sand; distractedly she eyed the pattern of granules dislodged from beneath her toes. Bending, she lifted a tiny mollusk shell, studied its spiral design, tossed it lightly back into the surf. Then she turned to face the ocean head-on, wishing she could find something, *anything* offensive about Oliver Ames. To her chagrin, there was only one thing—his occupation. A paid smile. A manufactured daydream. Prepackaged virility. And, oh yes, bedroom eyes. No doubt he was good at his job.

Perturbed, she returned to the powdery sand of the beach, stretched out with her hands layered beneath her head and closed her eyes. The sky was brightening steadily; the sun wasn't far behind. A tan. That was one of the things she wanted this week. A soft, even tan. All over.

Oliver Ames would have to leave! He'd just have to! How could she possibly lie nude in the sun with him around? Smiling, she recalled the first time she'd gone topless on a beach. It had been the year before they'd had the villa built, when she and her father and Tony and Laura and Brenda and John had flown down here to scout around. She'd been eighteen at the time, confident of her youth, if not her future. In no time she'd discovered that on the beaches of St. Barts one was more conspicuous with a bikini top than without. In no time she'd discovered the delightful intimacy of the sun's warm touch on her breasts. And the rest, oh, she'd discovered that several years later, on the only other occasion she'd chanced to be alone at the villa. She'd felt free and uninhibited and sensual then. It had been wonderful....

Opening her eyes, she squinted toward the rooftop of the house. Another hour and the sun would scale it. Would he be sleeping still? Closing her eyes again, she pictured *him* bathing nude in the sun. Long limbs connected by sinewed bonds, tautly drawn skin, swells here, indentations there, a mat of hair extending in varied patterns from chest to ankle....

Sharply sucking in her breath, she sat upright. Eyes wide, she dug her teeth into her knee, welcoming the pain. Then, when the slightest movement caught her eye, she lifted her gaze to the villa.

He was there, standing at the window of her room, hands on his hips, his dark head moving slowly from side to side. She stared for a minute, then hugged her knees tighter and lowered her head again. She could almost hear it. *What are you doing out of bed? And on the beach before sunup? If it's pneumonia you're looking for, you're on the right track!*

Hearing the patter of his feet on the planking connecting the terrace levels, she stood quickly, propped her hands on her hips and adopted her most belligerent stance. "I don't care what you say, Oliver Ames," she called to the fast-approaching figure, "but I'm here! And I'm fine! And I have every intention of making the best of my vacation!" She paused only for a breath as Oliver's long legs carried him toward her. "Now—" she held up a hand "—I do appreciate what you did for me last night, but I'm fine. Really fine. So you don't need to feel any further responsibility—"

The breath was knocked out of her when Oliver took her firmly in his arms. His eyes glowed, his body pulsed. "Damn it, but you look sexy," he growled, then took her lips in a kiss so masterfully gentle it shattered all pretense of fight. "Good morning," he whispered against her mouth seconds later. "Sleep well?"

Leslie stared at him in shock. "Good morning?" she echoed blankly, then watched him eye the sky in amusement.

"It is morning, I believe. And a beautiful one at that." His arms remained around her waist, holding her lower body snug against his.

"But . . . what are *you* doing up at this hour? I was sure you'd be out 'til noon. I mean, you didn't get to bed until after two-thirty."

"Actually it was closer to three-thirty. But I like getting up early. Morning's the best time."

Was it the velvet softness of his voice or the glimmer in his eye that lent deeper meaning to his words? She didn't know. She didn't want to find out. Coward that she was, she put light pressure on his arms. When he released her instantly, she was only momentarily relieved. When without another word he took off at a trot toward the water, she felt disappointed. When he splashed in to thigh level, then dived forward in a graceful arc and began to swim away from shore, she felt abandoned.

Lips on the verge of a pout, she sank down on the sand and watched the dark head turn rhythmically with each stroke. He was a good swimmer. *But why not*, she asked herself. Men of his ilk were bound to have access to villas such as these, or estates with pools. Indeed, part of his appeal would be the slickness of his limbs as they propelled him smoothly through the waves. Even now he was probably wondering whether she was watching. Perversely, she twisted sideways on the sand and studied the nearby palm. Tall and sturdy, graceful in a majestic kind of way, powerful, dignified, protective.... With a soft moan, she turned back to the sea.

Moments later Oliver emerged from the waves, his body wet and gleaming in the early morning light. Pulse racing, Leslie watched him approach.

"That was nice," he said breathlessly, rubbing a hand across his chest. Then, ducking behind her, he dragged a pad cushion from one of the lounge chairs tucked beneath the rocks and, returning to her side, spread the cushion flat. Within moments he lay on his back, his eyes closed, his hands folded on his stomach.

Unable to help herself, Leslie stared. Fit, indeed. His body was beautiful. Not perfect, mind you—there was a mole on his left shoulder, a tiny scar beneath his ribs. The gift of a jealous husband, perhaps? Or a scorned mistress?

Another scar caught her eye, this one slashing ever so slightly above the band of the slim-fitting trunks he wore. A low blow from a dissatisfied client?

"Appendectomy," came the timely explanation.

When Leslie's gaze shot upward, it caught Oliver's knowing smile. "I was wondering," she said hotly, "whether it was a battle scar."

He tucked in his chin to study his body. "This one is," he said, touching a finger to the small mark beneath the ribs. Then he moved the finger lower, following into his trunks and out again the faint ridge of the more daring scar. "This one's still pretty pink. I would have thought it should have faded more by now."

"When was it done?"

"Last winter." He put his head back down, closed his eyes again and gave a soft chuckle. "I'm not the best of patients. It was as much of a trial for the hospital as it was for me."

Somehow she couldn't believe it. Turning her head to the side, she eyed him askance. "You mean to say that the nurses didn't appreciate your presence?"

"Not by a long shot. I suppose I wasn't very cooperative, but after two days of being pushed and pulled, rolled and prodded, undressed and bathed and powdered, I'd had it!" He inhaled a deep breath through his nose. "I guess I'm just not meant to be pampered."

A shame, she mused, since he seemed the perfect subject. Lucky nurses, to have free access to that body....

She cleared her throat. "So you prefer to do the pampering, do you? I suppose . . . if the reward's great enough . . ." She took a breath, then shut her mouth and slowly exhaled through her nose.

Oliver opened one eye. "What were you going to say?"

"Nothing."

"Do you gulp air often?" he teased gently.

"Only when it's preferable to putting my foot in my mouth."

"Come on. You can say anything to me." When she simply turned her head and studied the waves, he reached out to slide his fingers around her wrist. "Come on, Leslie . . . anything."

"Actually," she began timidly, "I was just wondering why you do it."

"Why I do what?"

"Model. Rent yourself out. I would think you'd want something a little more . . . more lasting."

"You don't approve of my . . . avocation?"

Avocation. On the nose. Part-time hobby or source of amusement. "Perhaps I don't understand it. I guess I'm more attuned to occupations. You know, full-time career types of things."

"As in preschool teaching?"

"Uh huh."

"But what about fun?" he asked, suddenly up on an elbow looking at her. "You must have outside interests. There must be things you do on a lark."

"Is that what this is to you . . . a lark?"

For the first time there was a hint of impatience in his voice. "It's far more than that, Leslie, and you know it."

Of course. Tony had hired him. "Listen," she began, looking evasively at her toes, "this whole situation is extremely awkward. I appreciate Tony's thought in sending you down here, but now that we've had our laughs you can go on back to New York."

"I can't do that."

"Why not?"

"Because we haven't had our laughs. You stumbled in here sick as a dog yesterday. All I've had a chance to do is force liquid down your throat. Tony wouldn't be pleased."

"Tony doesn't have to know. You can go quietly back to New York, and I can tell Tony what a wonderful time we had. He'll never be any the wiser."

"And what about me? I've been looking forward to ten full days in the sun."

"Then I'll make a call and get you a room down the road."

"I don't want a room down the road."

"Don't you see," she exclaimed, growing more frustrated by the minute, "you can't stay here!"

For a minute he was quiet. His eyes roved her face, returning time and again to her eyes. "What are you afraid of, Leslie?" he asked at last. "There's got to be something hanging you up."

"There's nothing," she said quietly, all the while thinking how soft and coaxing his voice was.

"Look at me and tell me that."

She kept her eyes glued to the horizon. "There's nothing."

"Look at me," he whispered, his fingers tightening almost imperceptibly around her wrist. When still she didn't comply, he gave a gentle tug. Catching her off balance, he pulled her down onto the sand. Before she could begin to recover, he'd pinned her down. "Now," he murmured, his eyes an ardent brown, "look at me and tell me what's on your mind."

"You!" she cried. "You! You shouldn't be here, Oliver Ames! You're all wrong for me! I need...I need..." Her voice trailed off, caught in her throat as the damp warmth of his body seeped through to her. "I need..." she whispered, mesmerized by the low glimmer of his gaze.

"I know what you need," Oliver whispered in turn, lowering his lips to her neck. "You need a man's loving." He pressed his mouth to her throat as she gave a convulsive swallow, then ran his tongue along an imaginary line to her chin. When he lifted his head to meet her gaze once more, he moved his body over hers. "You need me...."

3

HE WAS RIGHT in a way, she was later to muse. She *did* need a man's loving. But not just in the physical sense Oliver offered. She needed something deeper. A relationship—that was what was missing from her life. That was what she'd read in the ad. That was what she'd wanted when she had fingered Oliver's picture in response to Tony's magnanimous offer. She wanted love. A man, family, a home. And Oliver Ames, whose body was his prime negotiable commodity, was not the one to give it! Oh, yes, she found him attractive. Her body responded to him in precisely the way he intended. But there was far more to love than desire alone. Blinded by passion, she had made a fool of herself once. Never again.

"You need me," Oliver repeated in a husky whisper.

Leslie shook her head, her eyes awash with apprehension. "No. That's not true," she gasped, fighting his pull with every bit of determination she could muster.

Threading his fingers through hers, Oliver anchored her hands to the sand on either side of her head. "It is," he insisted. "Don't you see it? Don't you *feel* it?"

What she felt was the boldness of his body, hard and warm and aggressive, imprinting its maleness onto her. What she felt was the answering tremor of her limbs, the gathering of a heat deep within, the stoking of unbidden fires.

"I feel it," she cried softly, "but I can't, Oliver, I can't give in to it. Don't you see?" Her fingers clutched tightly at his, her eyes held a hint of desperation. "I can't view it the way you do. You may be able to jump from relationship to relationship, but I can't. I suppose I'm an anachronism in this day and age. But that's the way I am." Her voice lowered to a mere quaver. "I'm sorry."

With a harsh chuckle, Oliver rolled off her and sat up to stare at the sea. "Don't be sorry. It's really very... lovely."

Leslie watched the muscles of his back flex with a tenseness echoed by his jaw. Without a doubt, she'd made her point. What must he think of her now? Drawing in an unsteady breath, she sat up, then rolled to her knees. On a whim, wishing only to soften her dictate, she reached out to touch him, then thought twice and let her hand waver in the air before dropping it to her side. She'd wanted him to leave; now she'd simply given him further incentive.

Pushing herself from the sand, she headed for the stairs.

"Leslie?"

She paused, head down, her bare foot on the lowest rung. *Move, Leslie, move. Show him your grit. Show him you really don't care.* But she couldn't. Because she did care. Dubious life-style or no, she couldn't help but feel something for Oliver Ames.

"Leslie?" His voice was directly behind her now. She turned and looked up, then felt her insides flip-flop. His expression—so vulnerable, so very like that he'd worn in the ad.... But it couldn't be an act; there was something far too deep and needy.... "Listen, Les, I've got a proposition."

"Proposition?" *Oh, God, what now? He's imposing and appealing and powerful. A woman can only withstand so much....*

At her look of fear, his gaze gentled all the more. "Nothing compromising," he soothed, his lips curving into the ghost of a smile. "Just practical." When she stood her ground, he went on. "This is your vacation. The week was to be something special for you." He lifted a hand to her shoulder, wavered, dropped it. She couldn't help but recall her own similarly thwarted gesture moments before. "What say we call a truce? You go your way, I'll go mine. You take the master suite, I'll take the bedroom I used last night. I'd like to explore the island, so I'll stay out of your hair. You can do anything you'd intended to do all by yourself...unless you change your mind. If that happens—" his gaze dropped to her lips "—I'll be here."

Leslie studied him, trying to equate what he was with what he proposed. "You're apt to be very bored," she warned.

He laughed gently. "I doubt that." He cast a glance behind him. "With all this—and a good book, and a kitchen at my disposal—how could I be bored?"

She wondered what the kitchen had to do with anything. There wasn't a spare ounce of fat on the man, so he couldn't be that much of a glutton. "I can't promise you anything...."

"I'm not asking for promises."

"But...why? Why would you rather spend a quiet and uneventful week here than go to one of the resorts? I mean, I'm sure there'd be lots of women..."

At Oliver's punishing glance, she shut her mouth. "I don't want lots of women. Or action. You may not believe it, but quiet and uneventful *do* sound perfect to me." He thrust long fingers through his hair, only to have the damp swath fall right back over his forehead. Leslie was grateful that something else dared defy him, and grew bolder.

"You're right. I don't believe it," she quipped lightly. "I'm sure your life is an endless whirlwind of pleasure back in New York."

He grew more serious. "Pleasure? Not always. Sometimes the whirlwind seems more like a tempest. Which is one of the reasons I jumped at the opportunity to come down here. I need the break, Leslie. I'm tired." Indeed, she heard it in his voice at that moment. "Maybe you're right. Maybe I am getting too old for this kind of—" a glint of humor returned to his eye "—rootless existence. Maybe a week of...abstinence will do me good. Build my character, so to speak. Reform me. Set me on the straight and narrow."

"Fat chance," she muttered, but her resistance was token. True, she'd hoped to have the villa all to herself. True, his presence would keep her on her guard. But there was something quite...appealing about him. If she had to share the villa, she could have done far worse.

"What do you say?" he prodded in earnest.

"What *can* I say? After your talk of character building, I'd feel like a heel to refuse." Her eyes narrowed. "You were counting on that, weren't you?" He simply shrugged and broke away to start up the steps. "Where are you going?" she called.

On the terrace and fast receding, he yelled back, "I'm disappearing. As promised." Sure enough, within seconds he'd been swallowed up by the house.

Smiling, Leslie followed as far as the lower terrace, where she sank into one of the deck chairs to track the progress of a fishing boat as it returned to Gustavia with its early-morning catch.

An hour later her nose twitched, rousing her from her peaceful contemplation of the beauty of the sea. At first she thought she was about to sneeze, then realized that the awareness was of something quite different. Lifting her head, she sniffed the air, then she stood up and moved hesitantly toward the steps. Curious, she climbed them. Stomach growling, she crossed the upper tier of the terrace. Only when she pushed back the screen and stepped onto the inner tile did she have her first glimmer of under-standing of Oliver's attraction to the kitchen.

"What have you *made?*" she asked, mouth watering, eyes wide and hungrily homing in on the kitchen counter.

Oliver sat at the table, deeply immersed in a book. Be-fore him was a plate containing the swirling remnants of some maple syrup. "Belgian waffles," he said without looking up. "There are two left. Help yourself."

Sure enough, on a plate covered by foil were two plump, warm waffles. In nearby dishes were strawberries, confec-tionery sugar, maple syrup and whipped cream. She felt as though she'd been treated to a breakfast buffet brought in from one of the local resorts. Had it not been for the waffle iron, well scrubbed and dripping dry beside the sink, she might have suspected he'd done just that.

His empty plate settled into the sink. "When you're done," he murmured near her ear, "just leave everything. I'll be in later to clean up." She looked up in time to see him turn. The next thing she knew, she was alone.

She hesitated for only a minute before reaching for a clean plate and helping herself to the feast he'd prepared. It was delicious. But then, she'd been starved. What had she had yesterday—one light omelet and twenty glasses of juice? Surely she was on the mend, what with this newfound ap-petite.

Without a second thought, she cleaned everything when she'd finished, then climbed the stairs to ferret a bathing suit from her bag. Though there was no sign of Oliver, she wasn't taking any chances. Her suit was one piece—albeit cut out in back with a bevy of crisscrossing straps—and appropriately demure. Satisfied that her appearance would preclude invitation, she armed herself with a bottle of sun-tan lotion and a towel and headed for the beach.

The day was utterly restful. She sunned for a while, returned to the kitchen for a cold drink and her book, then spent several hours back on the beach in a lounge chair, reading beneath the shade of the waving palm, even dozing to the gentle swish of the waves. In response to the sun, the warmth and the rest, her cold continued to improve. She felt stronger by the hour and more encouraged. For true to his word, Oliver had gone his own way. Or so she assumed, since she saw neither hide nor hair of him. She felt relaxed and free, almost as though she had the villa to herself.

She didn't see him again that day. When she finally left the beach at afternoon's end, she found a large brown bag and a note on the kitchen table.

"Dinner," it read, "if you're in the mood. I've taken the bike and gone exploring. Hear the sunset is spectacular from Castelets. If I'm not back by dawn, I bequeath you my bag of books. Particularly enjoyed...."

Tuning out, she lifted her eyes in dismay. The motorbike. Of course, she wouldn't be able to hear it from the beach. But...to Castelets? Steep and jagged, the approaching drive had turned back many a cabbie in its day! So, she scowled and crushed the note in her fist, in the case of his demise, she'd inherit his books? How thoughtful. No doubt his choice of reading matter would fascinate her.

Then she caught herself. Hadn't she had similar thoughts regarding his choice of music? She'd been pleasantly surprised on that one. What if.... Bidden by curiosity, she straightened the crumpled note in her hand and finished reading. "Particularly enjoyed the new Ludlum. Why not try it?"

Indeed she'd had every intention of doing just that when she'd bought the book and put it in her own bag to bring to St. Barts. He liked adventure, did he? But then he probably lived it, while she was content to read it on occasion. With a wry headshake, she opened the bag on the table and removed, one by one, the small cartons. Langouste creole, potato puffs, fresh pastry—from La Rotisserie, no doubt. Impressed by his apparent familiarity with the offerings of the island, she wondered for an instant whether he'd been on St. Barts before. Perhaps on another job? With another woman?

Fortunately at the moment hunger was a far greater force than jealousy. Setting aside all thought of Oliver and his lively if dubious past, she ate. Then read. Then slept, awakening only once, well before midnight, to hear movements on the upper level before smiling softly and closing her eyes again.

WITH THE SUN rising brightly, Sunday promised to be as pleasant a day as Saturday had been. Once more Leslie spent the morning on the beach. This day, however, even before she'd been able to drag herself from the sand to get a drink and a bite for lunch, she was brought to attention by the sound of footsteps on the planks leading down from the terrace. Looking up from where she lay on her stomach, she saw Oliver approaching, a large basket in one hand, a blanket in the other.

"Hi," he said, placing the basket on the sand and spreading out the blanket. "How're you doing?"

"Not bad," she answered cautiously. She half wondered if she should excuse herself and give him his turn on the beach, then was too intrigued watching him unpack the basket to budge. "What have you got?"

"A picnic." He cast her a fleeting eye. "Hungry?"

"A little."

"Good." Within a matter of minutes, the blanket was spread with plates bearing a thick wedge of cheese, an assortment of fresh fruit, a loaf of French bread and a carafe of white wine. When he extracted two glasses, filled them and handed one to her, she accepted it graciously.

"Thanks."

"*De nada.*"

"*Rien,*" she corrected softly.

"Excuse me?"

"*Rien.* The island's French." Reaching out, she touched the bread with one finger. "Still warm? Don't tell me you baked it yourself."

"I won't," he said jauntily, producing a knife and moving to attack the loaf. "Actually—" he made a neat cut and handed her a slice, then made a similar incision in the cheese "—it was baked in a charming little bakery."

Sitting up, she grinned. "I know." Many times had she visited that very one. "But how did you? Have you been here before?"

"To St. Barts?" He popped a grape into his mouth, started to toss her one, then, seeing that her hands were full, leaned forward to press it between her lips. "Nope. But I read...and ask. Even guidebooks can be quite informative." Stretching his legs out and crossing them at the ankles, he leaned back on his elbow and took a sip of his wine.

He was wearing bathing trunks, black ones this time with a white stripe down each hip. If anything, his bare skin had an even richer tone than it had had the day before—richer and warmer and all the more tempting to touch. Stuffing a hunk of bread into her mouth, Leslie chewed forcefully. Only when she'd swallowed did she give a despairing, "Hmmph! Guidebooks. You're right. They give away every secret worth keeping. As a matter of fact, when we first started coming here, St. Barts itself was a secret. For Americans, at least. Now, Gustavia's that much more crowded. Things have changed."

"It's still quite beautiful." His gaze slipped down the nearby stretch of beach. "And very private here."

Tearing her eyes from the dashing silver wings behind his ears, she followed his gaze. "Mmm. We're lucky."

He offered her a slice of cheese before helping himself to one. "You don't like crowds?" he asked, taking a bite as he waited for her reply.

"I don't mind them. I mean, I guess they're unavoidable at home. If one wants the pluses of a big city, one has to be willing to put up with the minuses."

"You live right in the city?"

She shook her head. "On the island."

"Is that where you teach?"

"Um hmm."

He paused to put a piece of cheese on his bread, ate it, then washed it down with his wine. Then he sat back and turned his avid gaze on her. "How did you get started?"

"Teaching?"

"Mmm."

"I started in the city, as a matter of fact. It seemed like a good enough place to begin. I knew I wanted to work at the preschool level and, with the growing number of women working, there were preschool centers cropping up all over the place. After a year, though, I realized that . . . well . . . I wanted to be a little farther out."

"Away from your family?"

He was right on the button. "Uh huh."

"You don't like your family?"

"I love my family," she countered quickly. "It's just that . . . I needed some distance. And there were other challenges. . . ."

"Such as . . . ?"

She faced him squarely, filled with conviction. "Such as meeting the as-yet-untapped need in the suburbs. There had already been a slew of day-care centers established there, also to meet the need of the working woman. But those centers did just that: they met the women's needs rather than those of the kids themselves. What was required was something a step above day care, a very controlled environment in which children could learn rather than simply pass the time." She paused to sip her wine. Oliver quickly lifted the carafe and added more to her glass.

"So you found something there?"

"I made something there. Another woman and I set up a small center in a room we rented in a church, put together what we thought to be a stimulating curriculum, found a super gal to teach with us, and it worked. We incorporated a year later, opened second and third branches in neighboring towns the following year. Last fall we opened our fourth. Two more are in the planning stages."

He cocked a brow. "Not bad . . . for a teacher."

"Hmmph. Sometimes I wonder about that. There are times when the managerial end supersedes everything." Then she smiled. "But I do love it. Both teaching and managing."

"You love kids?"

"Mmm." She tore off the corner of a piece of bread and ate it. "They're such honest little creatures. Something's on their minds and they say it. Something bothers them and they cry. No pretense at all. It's delightful."

"Doesn't say much for us big creatures, does it?"

"Nope." She reached for another grape, tipped her face up to the sun and closed her eyes as she savored the grape's sweet juice. "This is great. Thanks. I do love a picnic."

"So you said."

She blushed, recalling her stormy outburst. "So I did."

"That's pretty."

She opened her eyes to find Oliver's gaze warming her. "What is?"

"Your color."

"It's the wine. Or the sun." Far be it from her to admit that his presence might have an effect.

"You look good. You sound good. Your cold really is better."

"Yes, doctor," she mocked, then held her breath, mockery fast forgotten beneath the power of his lambent gaze. His heat reached into her, stirring her blood, quickening her pulse. She wondered whether any woman could be immune to this silent command of his, a command as vocal in his eyes as in the long, sinuous strain of his body. She bit her lip and looked away, but he was one step ahead, bounding to his feet and heading for the surf.

"I need a dip," he muttered on the run, leaving Leslie to admire his athletic grace as he hit the water and dived.

"You'll get a cramp," she murmured to the breeze alone, for he was well out of earshot, intent on stroking swiftly from shore. She glanced back at the food spread on the blanket, then up at the house. Old habits died hard, but he was trying. And he was sweet. Dinner last night, a picnic today. He really *had* left her alone most of the time. Once more it occurred to her to simply disappear and leave him in peace; he'd obviously had something quite different in mind for his vacation than the innocent cohabitation she'd agreed to. But he'd suggested it, and he could leave at any time, she reasoned, though she found the thought vaguely disturbing.

With a sigh of confusion, she settled back on her towel, closed her eyes and gave herself up to the soft caress of the sun. It was far less complicated than any man, she mused. Less complicated...less satisfying. Even now, with her body alive in heretofore forgotten crannies, she pondered the risks of each. While the sun could cause skin cancer, a man could break her heart. Yet here she lay, complacent as a basking lizard, taking her chances on the goodness of the sun. Could she take her chances with Oliver?

What she needed, she mused, was Oliver-block—something to optimize the pleasure and minimize the risk of overexposure to such a potently virile man. Did such a thing exist? She laughed aloud. It was the wine. Straight to her head. The wine....

Moments later Oliver emerged from the sea. Eyes still closed, Leslie listened as he panted toward the blanket, caught up the towel he'd brought inside the basket, rubbed it across his chest and face, then settled down on the sand by her side. For a brief instant she felt her skin tingle and knew he was looking at her.

"All right?" he asked softly.

"All right," she answered, then relaxed when he closed his eyes.

They lay together in a companionable silence, rising every so often to munch on the goodies he'd brought, to dip in the water and cool off, to turn in the sun or move into the shade and read. It was Leslie who excused herself first, gathering her things and returning to the house, phoning to have a rental car delivered, then showering. Donning a strappy yellow sundress and sandals, she drove into town to eat at a small port-side café.

The sunset was beautiful, tripping over the harbor with its pert gathering of assorted small boats. Time and again, though, her eye was drawn to the couples surrounding her at other tables on the open-air terrace. Healthy and tanned, they sat close together, hands entwined, heads bent toward one another with an air of intimacy she envied. She wondered where they'd come from, whether they were married, whether the happiness they appeared to have captured was simply a product of the romantic setting or whether the setting had enhanced something that had been good from the start.

Leaving without dessert, she returned to the villa, only to find it empty. For a time she wandered from room to room making a pretense of admiring the fresh tropical decor before she settled at last in the den with the book she'd abandoned earlier. This was what she'd wanted, she reminded herself pointedly. Peace and solitude.

Three times she read the same page before finally absorbing its words.

By MONDAY MORNING her cold was nothing more than a memory. She rose in time to spot the dark-haired figure swimming in the early-morning sun, and, not daring to join him, retreated to the kitchen to fix a breakfast of bacon and eggs and muffins. There was more than enough for two. Quickly eating her share, she left the rest on the stove and returned to her room. Then, on a whim, she packed up a towel, a wide-brimmed straw hat, her lotion and a book, and went into town to buy a newspaper, which she read over a cup of coffee before heading for the public beach.

Spreading her towel on the sand, she shimmied out of her terry cover-up, then, with a glance around to assure herself that the mode hadn't changed, gracefully removed her bikini top and lay down in the sun.

It felt wonderful, as she'd known it would. Strange that she could do this so easily on a public beach, while she'd persisted in wearing her one-piece suit in the privacy of the villa. But the villa wasn't totally private this time round, was it?

Squinting in the sun, she wrestled her lotion from the bag and squirted a generous dollop onto her stomach. It spread easily beneath her hands. She worked it up past her ribs, around and over her breasts to her shoulders, finally smoothing the remainder down her arms before lying back. Better. Warm. Relaxing.

Why *couldn't* she do this at the villa? Was there truly safety in numbers? Peeking through the shadow of her lashes, she scanned the growing crowd. The bodies were beautiful, few of them covered by more than slim bands of material at their hips. Men and women. Lean and fit. Well, she was lean and fit, too. What objection could she have to Oliver's seeing her like this?

Oliver was lean and fit. She recalled how he'd looked this morning with the sun glancing off his limbs as he swam. She recalled how he'd looked yesterday, lying beside her on the sand. His shoulders were sturdy and tanned, his hips narrow, his legs well formed. She liked the soft matting of hair that roughened those legs, the broader patch on his chest, the tapering line down his stomach. His body was every bit as beautiful as that of any man on the beach today. And his hands—those hands that had so deftly poured the wine, sliced cheese, popped a single grape into her mouth—had those fingers touched her lips? She remembered how easily they'd circled her wrist to tug her back down to the sand. What might they have been like spreading lotion on her body...?

To her dismay, she felt her breasts grow taut. Peering down in embarrassment, she flipped angrily over onto her stomach and silently tore into herself for the foolishness of her thoughts. Was she that starved for the touch of a man? True, it had been a long time since she'd been reckless enough to trust one to the point of making love. But she'd never known the kind of frustration that would make her body respond out of sheer imagination. Opening one eye, she skimmed the bodies nearby, pausing at that of one attractive man, then another. Nothing. *Damn him!*

Defiantly she rolled over once more and concentrated on her life back home. The preschool centers were thriving. Six by next fall...quite an accomplishment. What now? Should she continue to teach? Go back to school for a business degree? Focus on the managerial skills she'd inadvertently picked up? There were many options, not the least of which was to take Tony up on his offer of signing on with the corporation. Even in spite of the distance she purposely placed between it and herself, she was neither deaf nor blind. Had she not caught talk at family gatherings of the corporation's spreading interests, she had certainly read of them in the newspapers. There were new divisions forming all the time, any one of which she could take over if she showed the slightest inclination.

But she didn't. And she wouldn't. There was something about high power and the almighty buck that stuck in her craw. Misplaced values. Misguided loyalties. Marriages of convenience rather than love.

Look at Tony. He'd married Laura because she'd promised to be the kind of wife every chief executive needed. Only problem was that every *other* chief executive needed her, or wanted her...or simply took her, so it seemed.

Sensing the dry, parched feel to her legs, Leslie sat up and smoothed lotion on them liberally, then lay down again. And Brenda—she was working on number two. Number one had been her high-school sweetheart and had unfortunately developed a penchant for gambling away every cent she earned. Poor Brenda. John had been a disappointment. Perhaps Larry would be better for her.

And then there was Diane. Slim, petite Diane, who'd wanted nothing more than to be a gymnastics star until she'd discovered that all the money in the world couldn't buy her the gold. Unable to settle for silver or bronze, she'd quit gymnastics and, by way of consolation, had been awarded the sporting-goods division of the corporation.

From the start she'd been in over her head. Even Tony had seen that. When she'd quite opportunely fallen in love with Brad Weitz, himself a senior vice-president of his family's development firm, things looked good. What with Brad's business acumen and that of the circle of lesser executives he helped Diane gather, she was able to focus her attentions on the content of the Parish line, rather than its high-level management.

Unfortunately, while the business flourished, her marriage floundered. Brad wandered, always returning to soothe Diane's injured pride, yet inevitably straying again before long. More than once Diane had eyed Leslie in envy at the latter's unencumbered state.

If only she knew, Leslie reflected wryly as she turned onto her stomach and tuned in to the sounds of the gentle Caribbean air. They were soft sounds—the murmur of easy conversation from parties nearby, the light laughter of those near the water's edge, the occasional cry of a bird flying overhead. How delightful it was to be here, she mused, to leave that other world where it was. Soon enough she'd be back to face it again. Soon enough she'd have to decide where she wanted to go with her life. But for now she wanted to relax and enjoy. That was all...that was all...that was all....

Lulled by the sun, she lay in a semisomnolent state, breathing slowly and evenly, savoring anonymity and the total absence of responsibility. When she felt hot, she stood and unselfconsciously walked into the water, swam about in the pale aqua surf, then returned to her towel. Stretching out on her back, she closed her eyes. It was divine. Thoroughly divine. She felt herself a part of the crowd, at ease and more in the spirit of the island than she had since she'd arrived.

Bathers came and went as the sun crept to its apex. Lathering her body frequently, Leslie knew she was beginning to blend in with the bronzed bodies all around. With a sigh she closed her eyes and returned to her worship. Once, maybe twice a year she could do this. Any more and not only would she get bored, but her body would wrinkle like a prune. Once... maybe twice a year... it was nice....

With a self-indulgent smile on her face, she turned her head slightly to one side and peered at the world through the shade of thick, tawny lashes. Then her smile froze in place and her complacency vanished. A man lay close by, sprawled stomach down on a towel, with his head turned away. Dark brown hair with a distinct C of gray behind his ear.... *Him!* When had he come? How could he have found her? His back glistened with suntan lotion; his breathing was even. It appeared he'd been there for some time, while she'd lain half nude, oblivious to all but the sun....

For the second time that day she twisted onto her stomach in embarrassment. The first time she'd simply imagined him and her body had reacted. Now he was here, beside her. What was she going to do? Head turned away, eyes open wide, heart pounding, she examined her alternatives. She could nonchalantly slip on her top and as nonchalantly lie back down. But he'd know, and she'd feel more the coward for it. She could simply dress and leave, but then she'd be deprived of her time on the beach. She could lie where she was until he tired of the beach and left. But he wouldn't do that without a word to her, would he? Not after having so conveniently selected her body from all those others on the beach beside which to stretch his sexy six-foot-plus frame! Besides, was she supposed to lie on her stomach for the rest of the day?

There was one other alternative and, damn it, she was going to take it. She'd come to the beach on her own and had been perfectly happy and comfortable. Oliver or no Oliver, she was going to stay. In the sun. And on her back, if she so pleased.

On a rebellious impulse, she flipped back as she'd been when first she'd spotted Oliver beside her. When her head fell his way, she gasped in genuine surprise. He was looking straight at her.

"Oliver!" she whispered, her breath in scarce supply. "You startled me!" It was the truth. Somehow she'd been count-ing on time to adjust to the fact of his presence.

As though relieved that she'd only been startled, he smiled gently. "I'm sorry. I didn't mean to do that." His eyes held hers without straying.

"How long have you been here?"

"Not long. Maybe fifteen, twenty minutes."

"Oh."

"Nice beach."

"Mmm."

"Tired of yours?"

She turned down the corners of her mouth and shook her head, felt her breasts shimmy and lost her courage. As gracefully as she could—and as casually—she rolled to her stomach again. Though the move brought her all the closer to Oliver, she felt somehow let off the hook. "It's nice here once in a while," she murmured, then managed to feign a relaxed sigh. Facing him, she closed her eyes. His next words brought them open in a hurry.

"I didn't think you'd do this, Les."

She knew precisely what he meant. "Why not?"

"You seem more . . . inhibited."

"I usually am," she confessed in the same half whisper in which the rest of the conversation was being carried on.

There was something intimate about their talk; Leslie found she liked the feeling.

Arching his back, he folded his arms beneath his chin. "What makes things different here?"

Had there been the faintest hint of mockery in his tone, she might have been put on the defensive instantly. But his voice remained gentle and curious, his eyes simply warm and pleased.

"I don't know. Maybe the other people. They're strangers."

"And safe?"

"I guess."

"Impersonal."

"Um hmm."

"Like . . . a gynecologist?"

"Come on, Oliver. What is this?"

"Just trying to understand why you'd bare yourself for them . . . but not for me."

"Oliver!" He had almost sounded hurt. When she opened her eyes in alarm, she indeed read that same gut-wrenching vulnerability written across his chiseled face. In response, she took her lip between her teeth. As quickly, he reached out a hand.

"Don't do that," he murmured, rubbing the tip of his forefinger against her lip until she'd released it herself. His finger lingered a moment longer in caress of her softly parted mouth. Then he put his hand on her back. The subtle incursion brought him inches closer. "God, your skin is hot. You'll be burned to a crisp."

"I'm okay." She felt strangely restful and raised no objection when he began to move his hand in a gentle kneading caress. For several seconds they just lay and stared at each other. "Oliver?"

"Mmm?"

"What's it like to model?"

His hand paused for only an instant before resuming its soothing motion. "It's . . . fun."

"You said that once before. But . . . I've always heard talk of the trying pace—you know, hours doing the same thing over and over again. Is it like that?"

"I don't know," he said simply. "I've never had to do the same thing over and over again."

"You're that good?" She smiled in accompaniment to her teasing tone and was rewarded by his total absence of arrogance.

"No. It just . . . works."

Her thoughts joined his on the set of the Homme Premier ad. "Is it ever . . . awkward?"

"What do you mean?"

"When you . . . I mean . . . you are nude, aren't you?"

He dared a tiny grin. "Yes."

"Does it bother you?"

"I like nudity."

"So, if this were a nude beach, you would . . . ?" Her brief glance toward his trunks said it all.

"No," he murmured without hesitation.

"Why not?"

"Because it would be embarrassing."

"Embarrassing? But you've got a beautiful body!"

Again that tiny grin. "How do you know? You haven't seen it all."

Again her downward glance. "There's not much left covered."

He arched a brow. "Some men might take offense at that."

"Come on," she chided. "You knew what I meant. Would you really be embarrassed to *un*cover it?"

"On this beach . . . beside you . . . yes."

"Because of *me?*" So she wasn't the only neurotic one?

"Yes." He inched closer. His lips were a breath from hers. "I don't think I could lie quite as impassively as—" he cocked his head "—most of these other men seem to be doing. It was bad enough when I first got here and saw your car in the lot. I've been to this beach before; I knew what the style was." His hand slowed its motion, coming to a rest just beneath her armpit. Leslie felt her breasts tingle at the nearness, but she couldn't move. His eyes held hers with binding warmth. "There are lots of pretty women here, Les, but I was totally unaffected . . . until I saw you."

"Sounds like the lyric to a song," she teased by way of self-defense, lifting her eyes and singing. "'Til I saw you . . .'" Then, recalling how boldly she'd been lying on her back with her breasts bare, exposed to the sun, she blushed.

"I'm serious," he said, brushing the back of his fingers against the swell of her breast. Suddenly she was, too.

"I know," she whispered. Had his earnestness been faked, something would have given it away—the glimmer of an eye, the twitch of a mouth, the rush to offer other lofty words. Oliver's expression, however, was solemn, every feature in harmony with the intensity of his gaze. He said nothing more, simply looked at Leslie as though imprisoned by the very charm that gave credence to his claim. Only his hand moved, sliding very gently along the side of her breast, up and back, doing ragged things to her pulse, damaging things to her composure. She felt his touch through every inch of her being. Her gaze dropped to his lips.

"You're very soft," he mouthed. He slid his thumb forward until it skimmed her aureole.

Leslie caught her breath, then, swept up in the sensual magic of the moment, released it and whispered his name. It was as though her entire life had been in a state of limbo . . . and only now took direction once more.

4

HER LIPS WERE PARTED. Stealing forward, he accepted their invitation, grazing her in soft, slow mouthfuls until she closed her eyes and yielded to his quiet fire. Her insides burned, and still he teased, growing evasive between lingering kisses, forcing her mouth to be more aggressive in its search for satisfaction.

"Oliver!" she whispered, angling her body just high enough to slip his hand beneath and press it to her breast. "I can't stand this!" she gasped, watching the slow opening of his eyes.

"*You* can't stand it?" he growled hoarsely. "They're apt to arrest us in a minute." He wiggled a finger against her throbbing nipple and took pleasure in the moan she suppressed. Her fingers tightened over his, yet she didn't pull his hand away. She couldn't. His touch felt far too good, as though that of a long-lost lover who'd just come home. Feeling suddenly light-headed, she gave a mischievous grin.

"Do you think they would?" She cast a surreptitious glance around. "I mean, there have to be other people fooling around here." Then she frowned. "Why don't I ever see it?"

"Because you're not a voyeur," he returned simply. "If you were looking, you'd find it."

"You did?" she asked, eyes alight, curious. "Come on, Oliver," she whispered conspiratorially. She tugged his hand upward and cushioned it against her cheek so that his arm fully crossed her nakedness. Their bodies were snug, side by side. She felt wonderfully alive. "Tell me."

"I will not. It might give you ideas."

"Ideas? What ideas?"

When he grinned, the groove at the corner of his mouth deepened. She hadn't noticed it before; it had a lazy sensuality to it. "Now if I told you that, you'd know what I've seen. I think I'd better go back to sleep." Turning his head away, he raised his hips and resettled them in a bid to ease his discomfort. Leslie appreciated the gesture, appreciated even more his attempt at self-control, appreciated most of all that strong, hairy arm that tickled her where it counted.

"Sleep?" she challenged. "Is that what you were doing?"

He turned back until their heads were intimately close. "No. I suppose not. I was lying here thinking. . . ." His tone was up; he seemed ready to go on. Then, expelling a soft breath, he simply repeated the word with a proper period at its end. "Thinking."

"Are you pleased with St. Barts?" she asked, nestling more comfortably against the arm he seemed in no hurry to remove.

"Yes." An affirmation it was, yet it dangled in the air.

"You don't sound convinced."

"Oh, it's fine."

"But?"

"Just about everyone's coupled up. It makes me feel lonely."

She sent him a look of doubt. "Does it mean that much to you to be with a date?"

"For the sake of a date? No way. For the sake of pleasant talk and easy companionship, yes. That's what I see here— on the beach, in shops and cafés. Warmth. I envy it."

"I know the feeling," she murmured half to herself as she recalled similar feelings she'd harbored the night before. She lifted her head for an instant to look forward. "Who do you think they are, Oliver? Friends? Lovers? Husbands and wives?"

His gaze followed hers, lighting on a couple lying on the sand several yards away. "Some of each, I suppose." He tossed his chin at the pair. "They're married."

"Oh?"

"Sure. See his wedding band?"

"Where's hers?"

"Oh. Hmm, that shoots that theory."

"Oliver?"

He settled his head down again, returning his mouth to within a whisper of hers. "Um hmm?"

"Were you ever married?"

"No."

"Why not?"

"Never wanted to."

"Not even for the sake of that warmth?"

"The woman, not the marriage, brings the warmth."

"True. But what about kids?" Strange. By stereotype, she'd assume he'd have no interest in children. Somehow, though, she could easily picture him with a brood. "Wouldn't you marry for the sake of having them?"

"A bad marriage for the sake of kids can be disastrous."

"You could have a good marriage."

"I could...I suppose. It's been hard finding good women—" he smirked "—what with my job and all."

She nodded. "Your job and all."

"How about you?"

"*My* job's no problem."

"Then why aren't you married? You seem like a warm, affectionate sort." He moved one finger ever so slightly against her cheek. "And you love kids. Wouldn't you like your own?"

"To quote you, 'A bad marriage for the sake of kids can be disastrous.'"

"To quote you back, 'You could have a good marriage.'"

She grew more serious. "If only. It seems that wherever I look I see divorces piling up. Divorces, or couples in the throes of counseling or those who are simply miserable. Maybe you don't see it, or maybe you take it for granted in your line of work, but I see it every day and it bothers me. Not only has my family struck out, but many of the kids at the centers are products of broken homes. And many of them are suffering terribly."

Oliver studied the look of anguish on her face. "But now you're getting onto the issue of kids again. What about the marriages to start with? Why is it that they're not working?"

She thought for a minute, then shrugged. "I don't know. Too much ambition. Too little honesty. Too much independence. Too little trust. Maybe it's the times, and what we're going through is an emotional evolution of sorts. Maybe love has to take on different meanings to make it feasible in this day and age. Take that couple over there. For all we know, his wife may be off with someone, too. But if she's in love and they're in love, and all four are happy, far be it from us to criticize them, particularly if we've got nothing better."

As Oliver pondered her words, his brow furrowed. "You condone infidelity?"

"No, not really." She was frowning, too. "Maybe what I'm saying is that love is the most important factor, that it makes allowance for other slips. Only problem is that where love is involved, those other slips can cause terrible, terrible pain. . . ."

"You sound very sure."

"I am."

"You've had personal experience with that kind of pain?"

Realizing she'd strayed far from the beaten path and in a direction she loathed, she shrugged. "It's not important." She sighed and forced a lighter smile. "Besides, it all may be an illusion, anyway. These people may not be in love, they might simply be swept up in the atmosphere of this place. There's something about a tropical island in the middle of winter...."

"Something daring, like lying on a beach half nude?"

In that instant, the more serious discussion was shelved. Leslie grinned. "Something like that."

"Why don't you turn over?" he teased.

She fought fire with fire, enjoying the banter. "Why don't *you?*"

"Because I keep thinking of *your* doing it and I get . . . hot and bothered."

"Hot and bothered. Interesting."

"Tell you what. I'll go down the beach a way and pretend you're not here. If you do the same, we'll be all right."

"I don't know." She wavered, reluctant to lose his company. "Maybe we could do it here...."

His eyes gaped. "Do what?"

"Lie cool and comfortable...." She felt so very close to him that it seemed absurd, this modesty of hers. Avoiding his gaze, she released his arm and turned over with slow and studied nonchalance. "There," she sighed, eyes closed, body aware of far more than the sun. "Your turn."

He offered a pithy oath beneath his breath, then coughed away the frog in his throat. "I think I'll take that walk."

"Don't go," she whispered, turning her head and opening her eyes. "I mean, it's really all right. There's no reason you can't stay here. It's all a matter . . . of the mind."

His eyes pierced hers, then seared a path to her breasts. "Is that all it is?" he asked, his voice thick. "A matter of the mind?"

Leslie felt his gaze as long, sinewed fingers caressing her fullness, belying her claim. Her breathing was already disturbed when he pushed himself up on his forearms and put his mouth to her ear.

"You've got beautiful breasts, Leslie."

"So do three-quarters of the women on this beach."

"I'm not looking at their breasts, I'm looking at yours."

She felt the truth of his words. Her breasts were ready to explode. "Well, you shouldn't be."

He ignored her. "Need some lotion? I'm great at spreading lotion up over—"

"Oliver!" she exclaimed in strangled protest. "You could try, at least—"

"I'm trying. I'm trying."

"Sure. To get me aroused." She gave him a withering stare. "Now try to get me *unaroused*."

"What fun would that be?"

"Oliver," she warned, growing frustrated in, oh, so many ways, "you promised you wouldn't push."

Before her beseeching expression, he grew serious. "I did, didn't I?" She nodded, her face inches below his. "Then," he began slowly, a look of regret in his mocha gaze, "I guess I'd better take that walk after all." He kissed the tip of her nose and was on his feet before Leslie could respond. But it was just as well. Bracing herself on her elbows, she watched him jog toward the water, submerge completely in the waves, swim off his own arousal, then emerge and walk thoughtfully down the beach.

She would have loved to have gone with him. It would have been nice, walking side by side with the lace of the surf curling at their feet. It would have been nice to have talked more. She enjoyed talking with him. He was easygoing, quick to smile and curious. She would have assumed the beautiful model-type to be self-centered, yet he wasn't. He seemed far more interested in hearing her thoughts than in impressing her with his own. Come to think of it, he'd spoken little of himself in the discussions they'd had.

With a sigh, she dropped back to the towel. In this, too, it was probably just as well. Given the source of his income, the less she knew about his life-style the better. Hmmph, she mused, he had all the lines. Beautiful breasts . . . attracted to no body but hers—baloney! He was a pro, and hanky-panky or no, he was still on the job. The only problem was that she wanted to believe him. She wanted to believe that he found her breasts beautiful, that he was more attracted to her than to any other woman on the beach. She wanted to believe . . . how she wanted to believe. . . .

Abruptly sitting up, she put on her bikini top, tugged on her terry cover-up and gathered her things together. She'd had enough of the beach for now. A long, slow drive around the island would clear her brain. That was what she needed—a long, slow drive.

It filled the bill. By the time she returned to the villa she had her mind in working order once more. She was Leslie Parish, loner, spending the week at her family's villa. Oliver Ames just happened, by a quirk of fate attributable to her brother Tony and worthy of no further mention, to be staying at the villa as well. That was all. Each went his own way, did his own thing. Period. She had it all straightened out...which made it doubly hard for her to understand her continuing restlessness.

After her return, she fell asleep on her bed. At some point during that time, Oliver quietly returned to the villa. When she awoke, she found his sprawled form spilling over one of the terrace chairs. He was reading a book.

Wearing the one-piece terry sunsuit she'd put on after her shower, she walked slowly out onto the terrace, gave Oliver's shoulder a gentle squeeze of hello as she passed, then stood with her back to him at the railing overlooking the beach. When several minutes passed and still she didn't speak, Oliver took the first step.

"You got back okay. I was worried."

She turned to lean against the wooden rail. "You shouldn't have been." But it touched her nonetheless. "I took a drive." He nodded, and she felt a tinge of remorse that she'd left the beach without a word. His thoughts were back there, too.

He dared a faint smile. "I had trouble finding my towel . . . without your breasts to mark the spot."

"Oliver . . ." she pleaded.

"Sorry." He nodded once, then schooled his expression to the proper degree of sobriety. "Couldn't resist that."

"I'm sure."

"I did miss you, though," he said, suddenly and fully sincere. "It was fun lying like that . . . talking. . . ."

Hadn't she had similar thoughts? She looked down at her bare feet and crossed her ankles. "Uh, that was what I wanted to talk to you about."

Far more jumpy than she might have imagined, Oliver grew instantly alert. He held up a hand and shook his head. "Listen, Leslie, it was no big thing. I wasn't out chasing you or anything. I mean, I'd been to that beach the day before, and when I saw your car I thought I'd look for you. I didn't mean to pester. Hell, I was only teasing about your breasts. . . ." His voice trailed off when he caught her amused expression. "What's so funny?"

"You are. When you get defensive, you're adorable. But that's beside the point. I was just wondering if—well, there's this quiet restaurant in Gustavia . . . very classy . . . and I thought, well, I don't really feel like going alone what with everyone else coupled up, as you said." She paused for a breath, wondering why he didn't come to her aid rather than sitting there with a bewildered look on his face. "What I was wondering," she began again, "was whether you'd like to have dinner with me."

"Yes," he answered instantly.

"I mean, you can think about it. I . . . I can't offer anything afterward. Just dinner."

A broad smile illuminated his face. "That's fine. Dinner will be just fine."

She took a deep breath and smiled. "Good. I'll make reservations for eight-thirty?"

"Great."

She nodded, feeling awkward again. Pushing off from the railing, she headed for the beach. "See ya then."

THE EVENING turned out to be worth every bit of her hemming and hawing in issuance of the invitation. She'd wanted stimulating company; stimulating company was what she got. Looking particularly handsome in a navy blue side-buttoned shirt and white slacks, Oliver proved to be an absolutely charming dinner partner. Ever solicitous to her whim, he deftly steered the conversation from one topic to the next. Not only was he conversant in the fine points of Wall Street, he was easily able to match Leslie's knowledge of politics, as well. He got her to talk more about her work, showing genuine interest and a flair for understanding the tenuous link between parent, child and teacher. Only when once or twice on impulse Leslie shot a personal question at him did he pull back. She assumed it was standard practice—the refusal to allow a client past a certain point. And though she was curious as to what made him tick, she appreciated the reminder about the nature of their relationship. With such an attentive and attractive man sitting elbow to elbow with her in the intimate confines of the small French restaurant, it was far, far too easy to forget....

TUESDAY WAS A DAY for remembering, a quiet day, a restful day. Leslie saw Oliver only in passing, and then but once, at noontime. They exchanged quiet smiles and hellos. He explained that he wanted to pick up something for his sister back home and asked for her advice. Stifling the urge to ask all about his sister, she suggested a small boutique in Gustavia, from among whose selection of hand-blocked prints and clothing she was sure he'd find something. Then he was off, with nary a word about the evening before.

Just as well, she told herself again. Just as well. She'd come here to be alone. Alone was what she'd get.

Unfortunately, alone became lonely at some point around dinnertime. With no sign of Oliver, she grilled a piece of fresh fish, sliced and marinated vegetables, made herself an exotic-looking drink, which was little more than rum and coke dressed up in a coconut shell with an orange slice across the top, and ate by herself on the beach. It was there that, long after the sun had set, Oliver found her.

"Leslie?" he called from the terrace. "Leslie?"

"Here, Oliver!" she answered, her heart suddenly beating more lightly. "On the beach!"

A random cloud had wandered in front of the moon. It took him a minute to find his way down. Only when he stood before her on the sand did the silvery light reemerge. "You're eating here...in the dark?" he asked, spying the tray behind her.

She looked up from where she sat, knees bent, arms crossed around them. She wore a gauzy blouse and skirt, the latter ruffling around her calves. "It wasn't dark when

I ate. I've just been sitting here thinking." For a minute she feared he would simply nod and, finding her safe, return to the house. To her relief, he hunkered down beside her.

"Mind the company?" he asked, suddenly cautious.

"No," she breathed softly. "As a matter of fact, it's kind of lonely here. The company would be nice."

"You should have called. I'd have come."

"You weren't here."

"I've been back for at least an hour and a half."

"Where all did you go?" He wore shorts and a shirt and looked devastatingly handsome.

"Oh—" he gazed out at the sea "—I was in Gustavia, then rode around for a while."

"Find something for your sister?"

"Uh huh."

"Have you eaten?"

"I grabbed something in town."

She nodded, feeling superfluous, then took a fast breath. "Hey, if you've got something to do. I don't want to keep you...."

"You're not. I was the one who offered, remember?" His voice lowered. "You look pretty. Very... feminine."

Her blush was hidden by the night. She shrugged. "It's nice to wear something like this every so often." Last night, her dress had been as soft, but more sleek—to lend her an air of confidence and sophistication. Tonight she looked and felt vulnerable.

Attuned to her mood, Oliver kept his voice on a gentle keel. "It must be appreciated. I'm envious of those men you date at home."

Her heart skipped a beat. "You don't need to be. There aren't an awful lot of them."

"But you do date...."

"Only when necessary."

He frowned. "What do you mean?"

"Just that," she returned frankly. "There are certain...social obligations to be fulfilled. Birthday parties, openings, receptions—that type thing. It's sometimes easier being with someone than without."

For a moment, only the gentle lapping of the waves broke the silence of the night. When Oliver spoke again, his voice held a deadly calm. "Was that what you felt last night?"

"Oh, no!" she exclaimed without pretense. "Last night was something different! Last night...it was...I wanted it...." She stared wide-eyed at Oliver until at last he reached over and took her hand in his. Only then did she relax.

"I'm glad, Les. I enjoyed myself last night. More than I have in a very long time."

"A very long time?" she teased. "Doesn't say much for all those other women."

His fingers tightened around hers instants before his taut voice rang out. "There haven't been all those other women, Leslie. I think it's about time we clear that up. I'm not a gigolo."

"I never said you were," she countered weakly.

"But you've thought it. And don't deny it, because my thumb's on your pulse, keeping track of your lies."

"That's fear you feel. You're frightening me." Instantly his grip eased, though her hand was as much a prisoner as ever.

"Have you ever thought I was a gigolo?"

"I, uh...."

"Yes or no."

"Yes. Well, what was I to think? You were my birthday present. My brother *bought* you for the week. For *me.* Isn't it pretty much the same thing?"

To her relief, Oliver's voice had gentled again. "I suppose. If it were true. But it's not."

"What's not?" She felt a glimmer of hope. "Tony didn't hire you?"

"Tony called me, explained the situation and proposed I come. Aside from free use of this house, everything has come from my own pocket."

Leslie's mind had begun to whirl, her relief nearly as overwhelming as her embarrassment. Not knowing what to say, she blithely lashed out at Tony. "That cheapskate! I mean, I know that you probably do very well modeling, but I'd have thought that if the plan was his the least he could do was foot the bill!" Taking Oliver off guard, she tore her hand from his and tucked it tightly into her lap. She was sitting cross-legged now, the folds of her skirt gathered loosely between her legs. "I'm not sure whether to be more angry for his having gypped you or undersold me!"

"You weren't sold, Leslie! That's what I'm trying to tell you! I needed a vacation. Tony simply suggested a spot. As for the practical joke, well, that was to be frosting on the cake."

"Frosting, indeed," she mumbled. "All along I've assumed this was nothing more than a business proposition for you. But you speak very comfortably of Tony—do you know my brother?"

Taking a deep breath, Oliver settled on the sand facing her. "I met him about a year ago. We play tennis every now and again."

"Was it Tony who set up the Homme Premier thing?"

"No. As a matter of fact, it was sheer coincidence that the ad ran in his magazine."

"I see." Lowering her chin, she scowled at her skirt. She did see—more now, at least, than she had before. Yet while one part of her was elated to learn that Oliver Ames wasn't the horrible playboy for hire she'd thought him to be, the other part was mortified.

"Les . . . ?" came the soft voice opposite her. "What is it?"

"I feel foolish," she whispered. "Really foolish."

"But why?"

She looked up then, her eyes round and luminous. "I thought you were a gigolo." She paused, offering a spitting aside, "God, that word's disgusting!" before resuming her self-castigation. "You must think I'm a perfect ass . . . what with some of the things I said."

"Actually," he grinned, "they were amusing."

"At my expense!"

"At mine. I was a good sport, don't you think?"

"I think you could have told me the truth. Good sport, hah!" Swiveling on the sand, she turned away from him.

"Hey," he crooned, reaching out to take her arm. "Come on. There was no harm done. Besides, you really didn't say very much that didn't apply to a model as well. I've never thought less of you . . . for any of it."

She wanted to believe him, but simply shook her head. "I felt so humiliated when I first arrived, thinking that Tony was really paying you to keep me company."

"Sweetheart, nobody pays for my time in chunks like that," he drawled, then cleared his throat when Leslie eyed him questioningly. "I'm a free agent. I don't like to spend more than one day at a stretch on any given job. This is no job. Believe me, if I hadn't wanted to come here, I wouldn't have. Likewise—" his hand caressed her arm "—I could have left at any time."

Trying to assimilate this altered image of Oliver, she felt confused and unsure. A model. Just a model. Was that so awful? It was still a world away, and in many ways the epitome of all she'd fought for years. Illusion. Grand pretense. Wasn't that what advertising was all about? But then there was this man—his face, his smile, the vulnerability about him that mirrored her own. . . .

Turning her head, she looked up at him. Then, without thinking, she rolled to her knees, put her arms around his neck and held him tightly. Only after several seconds did she feel his arms complete the circle.

"What's this for?" he whispered hoarsely.

She closed her eyes and hung on a minute longer, drinking in every bit of his closeness before finally loosening her grip and sinking back against his hands. "An apology... and thanks."

"Thanks?"

"For not accepting money to pleasure me."

His voice deepened. "Am I... pleasuring you?"

She could barely breathe, the pull of him was so strong. "Yes. I've enjoyed having you here."

"Now, that's a concession," he said softly, then shifted to lower her to the sand. With one hand he propped himself over her, with the other very gently tucked her hair behind her ear. "You are beautiful, Leslie," he murmured. "Even if there had been all of those other women you'd imagined, I'd still have thought you to be the best."

"Must be the full moon addling your mind."

"You don't think you're beautiful?"

"No. Oh, I make a nice appearance. But beautiful?" She shook her head against his hand, liking the feel of its tethered strength. "No."

"Well, you are. And if you didn't turn all those guys away so quick, they'd be the ones telling you, not me."

"They tell me, they tell me! It's so boring when you know it's all part of the game."

Oliver's body grew tense, his eyes darker. "This isn't, Les. I mean it. To me, you are beautiful. Do you believe me?"

Strangely, she did. "I must be as crazy as you."

"Not crazy. Simply...." He never finished what he was going to say, but instead lowered his head and took her lips in a kiss that was crazy and heady and bright. "Ahh, Leslie," he gasped, pausing for air before returning to take what was so warmly, so freely, so avidly offered.

Reeling beneath the heat of his kiss, Leslie could do nothing but respond in kind. Her lips parted, giving the sweet moisture of her mouth, the wet stroking of her tongue into Oliver's thirsty possession. With the freedom she'd craved—forever, it seemed—she thrust her fingers into the thick hair behind his ears and savored its vibrant lushness as she held him all the closer.

"Mmm, Oliver," she whispered on a ragged breath when he left her lips and began to press slow kisses against the fragrant pulse of her neck.

"You smell so sweet—" he breathed deeply against her skin "—so sweet."

Then he raised his head and kissed her again, moving his lips with adoration, his hands with utter care, his body with the gentleness she'd come to expect of him. He was lean and strong, his long frame branding its readied state on her, telling her of his need, inflaming her own. If this was illusion, she mused, it was divine illusion indeed.

"I need you, Les," he moaned, leaving one of his hard thighs thrust between hers as he slid to his side to free a hand for exploration. "I need to touch you here—" his hands grew bolder, spreading over her waist and ribs "—and here." Claiming her breasts with tender strength, his fingers circled her fullness, sending corresponding spirals of fire through her. "Feel good?"

She closed her eyes and nodded. "Oh, yes—" When his palm passed over her nipple, taunting it into a tight nub, she moaned and strained upward. Then, eyes flying open, she pressed her hand on top of his to stop its motion. "My God, Oliver, there's no end...."

"There *is* an end, sweet. I'll show you."

He held her gaze; she held her breath. Slowly he released first one, then another of the buttons of her blouse and slipped his large hand inside. "I wanted to do this yesterday on the beach," he whispered, fingering her flesh, sensitizing her to his touch.

"I know...." She sucked in a loud breath.

"Nice?" His fingers worked a heated magic, making everything feel so very right.

"Mmm... Oliver?"

He put his lips to the upper swell of her breast. "What, sweet?"

"My breasts..." she managed through a daze of passion, yielding to a nagging force. "You said you were only teasing...that they were more appealing than the others on the beach. Were you?"

He drew his head up to eye her in earnest. "No, I wasn't teasing. I meant what I said, Leslie. Your body affects me in a way no other can." Leaning forward, he nudged her blouse farther aside, then took her nipple into his mouth and kissed it reverently.

She shuddered, sighed, arched ever so slightly closer. "I'm glad. I don't like to be teased...not about a thing like that." Her voice grew stronger. "Not about a thing like...us."

A nearly imperceptible quiver worked its disquieting way through Oliver's long, taut limbs. He stilled for an instant, then slowly, reluctantly disengaged his mouth from her breast and gave a final kiss to the hollow of her throat before setting his fingers to the task of restoring order to her blouse. "We have to talk," he murmured against the warm skin of her cheek. "We have to talk."

Very slowly, Leslie realized that the source of her pleasure was gone. With uncertainty coming fast on the heels of passion, her limbs felt like rubber. When Oliver lifted her to a sitting position, she docilely sat. Her eyes were wide, her voice breathy. "What is it?" she asked, fearing she'd done something dreadfully wrong.

"We have to talk."

"You've said that . . . three times."

"I also said I'd leave you alone. I haven't done that."

Hearing the self-reproach in his voice, Leslie was fast to shoulder the blame. "What happened just now was more my fault than yours. I was the one who threw herself into your arms."

"That's beside the point," he grumbled, then shoved a hand through his hair and took several steadying breaths. "Listen, maybe you're right. Maybe it is the full moon." Standing, he reached to pull her up. "Come on. Let's go inside. I could use a drink." One-handedly scooping up the tray that held the remnants of her dinner, he motioned for Leslie to precede him.

She did. It took everything she was worth, but she did, and with each step she came closer to the understanding of what had nearly happened. Even now her breath came in shallow bursts, her legs shook, the knot deep within clamored for more. But her mind, ahh, her mind delivered a batch of far different messages.

Passing through the kitchen, she made straight for the living room, seeking shelter in a deeply cushioned rattan armchair to weather the storm. For there was bound to be a storm of some kind, she knew. It had been building from the moment she'd arrived last Friday, had been denied outlet moments before, now ached for release.

Through troubled eyes she watched Oliver approach the bar. As attractive as he looked in his jersey and slacks, their fine fit fairly broadcast his tension. His shoulders were rigid, his back ramrod straight, his legs taut. He poured himself a brandy, shot a glance over his shoulder, poured a second drink, then crossed the room and handed her one. While he tipped his snifter and took a drink, she merely watched the swirl of the amber liquid in her own glass, her lips tight in self-disdain.

Legs planted firmly, Oliver stood before her. "Leslie, I want to tell you—"

She gave a violent shake of her head. "Please, no excuses."

"But there's something you should know."

Refusing to look at him, she continued to shake her head. "It must have been the moon. I don't usually forget that easily."

Embroiled in his own quandary, he swallowed more brandy, then stalked to the window. "This whole thing was crazy from the start. I can't escape it! Damn it, I can't escape it!"

"What happened just now was nothing more than sheer physical need," Leslie ranted on, no more hearing Oliver's words than he did hers. She lowered her head and put two fingers to her brow. "I can't believe I let that happen. I thought I'd learned. It was dumb. Really dumb!"

"All game playing—here, back there," Oliver growled. "I thought I could get away from it but I'm only in deeper." Whirling around, he stepped quickly forward. "Leslie . . ."

She sat with one hand over her face, helpless to stop the tears that flowed. Legs tucked beneath her, body curled into itself, she was unhappiness personified.

"Oh, Leslie," he groaned from somewhere deep in his throat. Within seconds he knelt before her, gently releasing the snifter from her fingers and setting the glass down on the floor. Immediately she added her other hand to her defense. "Don't cry, sweetheart." He tried to pull her hands from her face but she fought that further exposure.

"I don't cry. What's wrong with me?" she whimpered between shuddering gasps.

Oliver slid his arm across her back and drew her forward. "I don't know that, sweetheart. You'll have to tell me." He curved his fingers around her neck, twining his long fingers through her hair. "Talk to me, Les. Tell me what you feel."

"I feel . . . I feel . . . very confused. . . ."

"About us?" he whispered.

"About . . . everything. . . ." When she dissolved into another bout of quiet sobbing, he pulled her down beside him on the floor, holding her close. With his back braced against the chair, he rocked her gently, stroking her arm and the silk of her hair as he let her cry herself out.

At long last she sniffled and grew quiet. "I'm sorry," she hazarded a shaky whisper. "Now I've made your . . . shirt wet."

"It'll dry. Do you feel any better?"

She nodded, sniffling again. "I don't usually do things like this."

"We all need the outlet every once in a while," he crooned, only then looking down to wipe the tears from her cheek. "Feel like talking?"

She thought about it for a long time, hiccoughing every now and then, blotting her lower lids with the fingers of one hand. Finally she looked up at him. "I don't think I can," she whispered.

"You can tell me anything. . . ."

But she shook her head against the warmth of his chest. "I can't tell you something I don't know myself."

"You can tell me your thoughts."

"They're all jumbled up."

"Maybe I can help unjumble them."

Again she shook her head. Somehow, with the expenditure of tears, she'd purged herself of much of her tension.

Now she felt . . . tired. "It's something I've got to work out, I guess."

"You're sure?"

With a sad smile, she nodded, then caught her breath. "But—Oliver?"

He smiled down. "Yes?"

"Can we sit here . . . like this for a little while? Just . . . sit here?"

He lowered his cheek to her head and gave her a tight squeeze. "Sure thing, Les. I'd like that."

They said no more for a time. Leslie nestled against him, finding quiet solace in the support of his arms, reassurance in the beat of his heart near her ear. Though her thoughts were indeed a jumble, she made no effort to unscramble them. There was too much to be savored in the utter simplicity of the moment. Just Oliver and Leslie. No past or future. Just . . . now.

Slowly her limbs began to slacken, and her breathing grew soft and even. Relaxation was a blissful thing, she mused as she snuggled closer to Oliver's warmth. Closing her eyes, she took a long, deep breath. Then something struck her.

"Oliver?"

"Hmm?" His eyes, too, were closed, his limbs at rest.

She tipped her head up. "Oliver?"

He opened his eyes. "What, sweet?"

"I still can't smell it."

"Smell what?"

"Your Homme Premier."

"I don't wear it."

"You don't wear it? Ever?"

"Ever."

"Isn't that against the laws of advertising or something?"

He hugged her more tightly and closed his eyes again. "I thought you were going to sleep."

"I think I was . . . then I thought of that."

"Don't like the way I smell?" he mumbled.

"I *love* the way you smell," she murmured, burrowing against his chest. "All warm and fresh and . . . manly. . . ." As though to make her point, she took a deep, long breath and sighed. "Mmmmmm. So very . . . you. . . ."

"I hope so," Oliver whispered, hugging her a final time before setting his head atop hers.

Leslie's next conscious thoughts were of the sun, the living room carpet beneath her cheek, the stiffness of limbs that had spent the night on the floor . . . and Oliver's hand on her rump.

5

IT WAS THE LAST that brought her fully awake. Squirming to a sitting position, she watched as that hand slid from her hip to the floor. Oliver was dead to the world. His tall form was sprawled prone on the rug with head turned away, his breathing slow and deep.

Stretching first one way, then the other, Leslie winced, then struggled to her feet. Her skirt and blouse were badly wrinkled, but then she'd spent the night in them. Putting a hand to her head, she tried to recall what had happened. Inevitably, her gaze returned to Oliver, and it all came back.

With sad eyes she studied his passive form. She was half in love with him, she supposed. Half in love with a man who prized his freedom, who resented being tied down for more than a day, who was no doubt the heartthrob of millions of women in America. It was a sad state of affairs.

Distractedly she made her way to the kitchen and up the stairs, finally sinking down on her bed. What other ads had he made? For what products? Wearing . . . what?

She knew the course of those ads. Not only would they appear in *Man's Mode*, *G.Q.* and *Esquire*, they'd appear in *Vogue* and *Cosmopolitan* as well, plus a myriad of lesser publications. His face, his body would be seen and savored by so very many eyes. In turn, he'd have his choice of the most exquisite of those admirers. Why, then, of all the places on God's green earth, was he here? And why, oh, why was he leading her on?

Rolling to her back, she stared wide-eyed at the ceiling. After all, what could he see in her? There was nothing slick or glittery about her; she'd made sure of that. Nor, despite what he'd said about her breasts, did she have a body to attract a man of his stature. So he wasn't a gigolo, as she'd originally thought. Still, he was the image of glamour, the striking playboy, the model. She, on the other hand, had chosen a different track to follow, a more quiet, private one. And she couldn't switch from it . . . any more than he could from his.

Realizing that no amount of deliberation could alter the facts, she dragged herself from the bed, showered and pulled on a clean sundress, then set out to grocery shop in Gustavia. By the time she returned to the villa, Oliver was on the beach. For a long time she stood on the terrace, unobserved, watching him. He lay absolutely still, a unified mass of bronze flesh broken only by the thin navy swatch at his hips. He loved nudity, he'd told her once. She'd love to see him strip. . . .

Frustrated by the single-mindedness of her thoughts, she whirled away, made herself a tall glass of iced tea, picked up her book and settled in a lounge on the terrace. It wasn't that she wanted to see Oliver when he left the beach, she told herself, simply that she felt like sitting on the terrace. This was, after all, her house. . . .

By a quirk of fate she dozed off. When she came to, it was with a start. Disoriented at first, she stretched and looked around, then jumped again on encountering Oliver's worried brown eyes.

"Oliver! You frightened me!"

Perched near her legs on the edge of the lounge, he smiled sadly. "We seem to have a way of doing that to each other. Are you all right?"

"I'm fine." Her hand went automatically to her wrist and, finding it bare, she frowned. "What time is it?"

"I'm not sure." He squinted upward. "I think about one." Then his gaze returned intently to hers. "*Are* you all right?"

The deeper meaning to his question didn't escape her this time around. Slowly beginning to relax, she offered a soft and helpless smile. "I think so."

Reaching out to take her hand in his, he made study of her small, slender fingers. "About last night, Leslie—"

On elusive butterfly wings, those very fingers slipped from his and touched his lips. "Shh, Oliver. Please. Don't say anything." Her smile grew pleading. "It's not necessary. Really it's not. I think we both got . . . carried away by—" she rolled her eyes to the palms overhead "—the atmosphere of the place. There's no harm done."

"I know, but still, there's so much I want—"

"Please," she interrupted more urgently. "Please don't. Things are . . . nice just as they've been. Why upset the apple cart?"

His chuckle was harsh. "To get to the rotten apple?" he mumbled, thinned his lips in frustration and shook his head. Then he, too, raised his eyes to the palms. "The atmosphere of this place—such a simple explanation. . . ."

"If there are others," she stared soberly, "I don't want to hear them." The last thing she wanted was glib words of excuse, or worse, of affection. It was obvious that Oliver Ames had one way or another gotten himself into an uncomfortable situation. She was simply trying to offer him an easy out. "Nothing's happened here that I haven't wanted to happen. I have no regrets."

"None?" he asked, his voice a bit too low, his eyes too dark.

She had the good sense to look away. "Well . . . none that can't be remedied." When she faced him again, her smile was forced. "Anyway, it's already Wednesday. I've got no intention of living with regrets for the rest of the week. Before I know it I'll be back in New York." Her voice cracked. "Let's not spoil things by analyzing them to death. Okay?"

A strange look appeared on his face, and he grew even more intense. His dark eyes held hers relentlessly, delving deep, finding secret paths to her soul, leaving her raw and exposed. She felt as though she'd been taken apart piece by piece and thoroughly possessed. When her heart beat faster, his gaze fell to her breast.

"Oliver?" she whispered. "Okay?" Her sense of bravado was a bygone thing.

Slowly his eyes returned to hers. "It's okay, Les. I see your point." Patting her knee, he stood up. "I'd better get dressed if I'm going to bike downtown."

"Take the car if you'd like. I won't be using it."

"No, thanks. I think I prefer the bike. Don't dare ride one at home." He threw her a cynical smile. "Wouldn't want to risk damaging the goods. The camera doesn't take kindly to gross blemishes."

He'd left before she decided just whom he'd been mocking—the camera, himself or her. But it didn't matter. Nothing did. As she'd told him, there was no point in endless analysis. And before long she would be back in New York. Strangely, this thought disturbed her more than any other.

Alone on the beach that afternoon, with the knowledge that Oliver was in town, she yielded to impulse and stripped off her bikini top. Her tan was really coming along, she mused, as she studied its golden hue while spreading lotion liberally over her skin. Would anyone see it? Not on her breasts. No one but herself—and she'd remember. . . . And grow warm just thinking about lying on the beach—beside Oliver.

It was a lovely memory, even if it had nowhere to go. Where were they now? Back to square one, each going his own way, leaving the other in peace. Funny how "peace" could take on such different meanings....

FOR LESLIE, a special kind of peace came that evening when, out of the blue, Oliver appeared at the door of the den. "Hi, Les."

She looked up with barely suppressed pleasure at the sight of the tall, casually lounging figure. "Hi."

"Whatcha doin'?"

"Crossword puzzle." She slapped her pencil against it. "Lousy puzzle. I'm really stuck."

"Need some help?"

"Oh, no." She held up a hand and pressed the paper to her chest. "I can do it. It may take me several days, but I'll get it if it kills me."

"You like word games?"

Most likely they bored him to tears. "I do," she said pertly, tipping her chin up in challenge. Wearing cutoffs and an open short-sleeved shirt, Oliver looked disgustingly virile. She needed something to dilute the effect of him; a challenge was just the thing.

"Are you any good?" he asked, eyes shining.

Leslie gave a modest shrug. "I've never won any championships, but I think I can hold my own."

"Got Scrabble?"

"Uh huh."

He tipped his head almost shyly. "Are you game?"

"Are *you*?" she countered in surprise.

"Sure."

They played Scrabble until midnight, broke for several rounds of Boggle and some coffee, then returned to the Scrabble board. Whether it was the lateness of the hour or the pleasure of being with Oliver, Leslie didn't know. But when, sometime around two, giddiness set in and the choice of words took a decidedly suggestive turn, she played right along. After all, it was a game, only a game.

SOFT. SENSUAL. LIBIDO.

"Good one, Oliver!"

BED.

"Come on, Les. You can do better than that."

"I'm trying. But I haven't got any vowels."

"Here. Let me give you a couple."

VIRILE.

"Very smooth."

CARESS.

"Not bad. I thought you didn't have any vowels."

"I just picked them. Go on. Your turn."

WARMTH. FLOW. WAIF.

"Thirty points, Oliver. You're good at this."

SPA. SIR. KEYS.

"Pure, Leslie. Very pure."

SEX.

"Oliver! That's a nothing word!"

"I wouldn't say that. It's got an *x*. That's worth eight points."

"But you didn't even get it on a double or triple score. You blew it."

"I'll say," he muttered under his breath. "Your turn."

AROUSE. GROAN. RAPE. BREAST.

"I don't know, Ol. This is getting pretty bawdy. Hey, you can't use *breast*. You've got two blanks in there that aren't really blanks. The other two are already on the board. That's cheating."

"Come on, Les. Where's your sense of humor? *Breast* is a great word!"

"It's bawdy. Try again."

BAWDY.

"That's not fair. I gave it to you."

"Uh uh, Les. You didn't have the letters. I don't like that gleam in your eye."

"Hold on to your socks. *Bawdy* is nothing. Look at this."

QUIVER.

"Triple word score, plus double letter on the *v*. Twelve ... twenty ... twenty-two ... that makes sixty-six points. So you can keep *bawdy*, even though the *y* does run off the board."

For the moment she'd taken the upper hand. Then, in the last move of the game, Oliver struck.

LOVE.

No double or triple word score. Not even a double or triple letter score for the *v*. Nothing but the emotional clout of a simple four-letter word.

Strangely and mutually subdued, they called it a night after that.

DESPITE ITS POIGNANT ending, the camaraderie they shared that Wednesday night carried over to Thursday. By silent agreement they spent the day together, starting with Leslie's mushroom omelets for breakfast, moving down to the beach for several hours of sun and surf, finally doubling up on the motorbike for a shopping expedition into Gustavia.

"You're sure you're up for this?" Oliver asked, strapping a helmet on her head before donning his own.

"Of course. I've taken the bike out myself many times."

"The roads are narrow."

"I'll hang on tight. Hey, are you sure *you're* up for it?"

Taking in her knowing grin, he returned with a pointed stare. "I will be soon," he growled, tossing his leg over the bike, reaching an arm back to settle her snugly behind him, then setting off.

To Leslie, nothing could have been more exhilarating. Wearing shorts and a T-shirt, she felt the sun's rays in counterpoint to the breeze whipping her skin. And Oliver—so firm and hard and strong between her thighs, against her stomach and her breasts— She held on for dear life, her arms wrapped around his lean middle, her hands flattened on his ribs.

"Okay?" he called back once, rubbing her hand with one of his own in a warmly endearing gesture.

"You bet," she returned, closing her eyes as she pressed her cheek to his back. To have a viable excuse to do this was . . . was ecstasy.

To her delight, the ecstasy continued long after they left the bike at the quai and began to stroll along the streets. Oliver kept her hand tucked firmly in his, holding her close to his side as they ambled idly in and out of shops in search of nothing in particular. Indeed, they chanced upon a kind of euphoria; they were a couple among many couples, yet were oblivious to all but each other.

Twice, as they browsed, they stopped at small cafés to sit and talk and further savor the atmosphere of the town. The few purchases they made were Leslie's—a bottle of imported perfume, a small enameled box and, on a whim, a soft pink pareo made of an original hand-blocked fabric that had appealed to her instantly. She knew that the three items would have special meaning for her, given the circumstances under which they'd been bought. Her only regret was that the bag holding them came between Oliver and herself during the airy ride back to the villa.

"How about a swim?" Oliver asked as he parked the bike next to the car.

Leslie smiled and stretched. "I don't know. I feel really lazy. I think I could go to sleep. What with late nights and fresh air and walking. . . ."

"Come down to the beach with me, then. You can sleep while I swim."

To her amazement, that was precisely what she did. She remembered seeing Oliver dive into the waves, watching him swim for a minute . . . then nothing. Once she stirred, finding the warm body near her in her sleep and snuggling closer. When she awoke, Oliver was there, sleeping beside her, his arms cradling her ever so gently. Turning carefully, she raised her head and looked at him. His face was the image of peacefulness. In turn, her own glowed.

"Oliver?" she breathed in a whisper.

"Mmm?" He didn't move.

"You awake?"

"Sure," he murmured in a sleep-slurred voice. "Just have my eyes closed."

"Is that all?" she teased.

"Sure. Late nights don't bother me. Do it all the time." He smacked his lips lightly together once, twice, then his head lolled to the side. His eyes still hadn't opened.

Capitalizing on a rare opportunity, Leslie made a free study of his chest. She loved the smoothness of his skin with its soft mat of hair. She loved the way his nipples hid amid dark whorls of chest hair, camouflaged in apt reminder of a dormant sexuality. She admired the fluid span of his collarbone and the way the muscles of his shoulder had bunched to accommodate her head. She was fascinated by the more vulnerable skin on the underside of his arm and the silkiness of hair there. She raised her fingers to touch, momentarily resisted the temptation, then yielded.

"Hey!" Oliver came alive at once, capturing her hand with unerring aim. "That tickles!" One eye opened, deep and brown. "You must be bored."

"Oh, no."

"Restless?"

"A little."

"Hungry?"

"Mmm."

The double-entendre sizzled between them for a breath-taking minute. Then Oliver snatched her to him and hugged her tight. "My God, Les!" he exclaimed softly as he crushed her to his bare skin. She felt the tremor of his arms and knew an elementary satisfaction that was in no way lessened when he set her back.

"Let's clean up and go into town for dinner," he suggested in a deep voice. "I'm in the mood for something . . . hot and spicy."

"Creole? That's funny. I would have thought you'd prefer soft and subtle and classic."

The sudden smokiness of his gaze sent corresponding spirals smoldering through her. "Later," he crooned. "Later."

It was a promise that was foremost on Leslie's mind. When she bathed, it was with special care to leave her skin soft and aromatic. When she styled her hair, it was with attention to even the smallest wisps. When she made herself up, it was with the lightest hand, no more than the most subtle emphasis on eyes and cheekbones.

Come time to dress, there was no question of her choice. Padding from the bathroom into the bedroom wrapped in a towel, she took the exquisite pink pareo from its bag, shook it out, studied its gentle floral print for a minute, then turned to the mirror. Loosening the terry knot at her breast, she let the towel fall to the floor. Her eye slid from her naked body to the print, then back. With careful concentration, she straightened the fabric, held it up to herself and began to wrap it around the pliant lines of her body, finally criss-crossing the ends at the hollow of her throat and tying a loose knot at the back of her neck.

Then she turned to study herself. It was perfect. Had she picked it out with this in mind? She ran her hands down along her hips, eminently aware of the smooth, unbroken line. Soft pink. Just as the Homme Premier sculptor had requested. Soft pink. Just for Oliver.

When he met her at the front door at eight, he was very obviously affected. For a minute he simply looked at her, devouring every soft inch, every gentle curve. "You look . . . beautiful, Leslie. Absolutely beautiful."

She felt it. She felt beautiful. She felt . . . special. In spite of all their many differences, in spite of the more glossy women he'd surely known in his time, in spite of all the power and grace and raw virility that the man exuded in his fine-tailored slacks and designer shirt, he had a way of making her feel as though there had never been, as though there never would be, another woman for him.

Leslie barely knew what she ate that night, only that she sat at an intimate table for two, elbow to elbow with Oliver, and that he didn't take his eyes from her the entire time. They may have talked of interesting things, but conversation, too, was secondary to mood. Had she tried to classify it she would have used words like loving, needing and expectant. For those feelings permeated her being, blinding her to everything but Oliver.

Somehow, sitting there at a small table in an unpretentious restaurant on the warm, cozy island of St. Barts, she was ready to play the game she'd decried for so long. She was ready to believe that Oliver was as taken with her as she was with him, that they were positively meant for each other, that what existed between them would be right and good and lasting. What he was in real life didn't matter any more than did her own past or future. They were together now and, in the illusion, very much in love. That was all that mattered.

"Dessert?" Oliver murmured, fingers entwined with hers, eyes adoring her lips as the waiter stood nearby.

Entranced by the faint but roguish shadow of his beard, she shook her head. "No," she whispered.

"You're sure?" he whispered back, as distracted as she was.

She nodded.

Within minutes they were in the car headed back to the villa. There, Oliver led her on the long path around the house, holding her hand tightly, turning at times to circle her waist and lift her over a tricky patch of rocks. When at last they reached the beach, he took her in his arms.

It was as if she'd been waiting for just this moment all night, all week, all month, all year. Shorn of inhibition by the aura of love surrounding them, she stood on tiptoe and wrapped her arms around his neck. When her feet left the ground completely and he gently rocked her back and forth, she hung on all the more tightly.

"Ahh, Leslie, this is what I've wanted." Setting her feet back on the ground, he curved his body over hers and buried his lips against her neck. His arms crushed her to him with a fierceness that in itself thrilled her as much as did the feel of his long, lean lines. "So beautiful. . . ."

"Like you," she whispered as she ran her fingers through his hair. Inclining her face, she buried it in that vibrant shock. His scent was clean and rich, pure and unadulterated by fragrant colognes or balms. Breathing deeply, she was further intoxicated. It was only his straightening that brought her away.

His eyes were hot and intense, echoing the silver light of the moon as it shimmied over the waves. He raised a hand to her cheek, tracing its sculpted line, the curve of her jaw, her ear. "I want to kiss you, Les," he rasped. "I want to kiss you everywhere."

If his words hadn't sent fire through her veins, his restless hands would have done the trick. Straining closer, Leslie tilted up her mouth in sweet invitation, then gave him everything when he accepted her offer. There was no teasing, no feint and parry, but rather an all-out meeting of minds, of hearts, of bodies.

Her lips parted before his thirsty advance, moving with and against him just as anxiously. When his tongue plunged inward, she opened to receive him and suck him deeper. She needed to know of his hunger, absolutely loved the feel of his consuming her, indeed wanted him to know every dark niche within.

All the while, his hands charted the outer landscape of her femininity, sliding around and across her back, over the gentle swell of her hips, the firm contour of her bottom. He lifted her, pressed her more closely, set her down and began again.

Deep within, a gathering of fire had begun. Never before in her life had Leslie known such an intensity of need. But then, Oliver's body was perfect. Arching against him, she felt its every contour. Her hands scoured him, mapping the breadth of his shoulders, the tapering length of his torso, the slimness of his hips, the solidity of his thighs. Around the latter her fingers splayed, sliding up and down as the sinewed cords beneath his slacks grew more taut. She felt the tremor that buzzed through him and found satisfaction that she could have caused it. But her satisfaction was quickly burned to a crisp beneath the flame of a hunger that flashed through her own limbs. When Oliver's voice came, thick and low by her ear, she quivered all over.

"You're not wearing anything under this, are you?" He drew back only to see her face. In the moonlight it had a pale silver glow and looked all the more fragile.

"No," she whispered, eyes strangely innocent.

"For me?"

She shrugged shyly. "I wanted to feel . . . sexy. I did."

"Do you now?"

"Oh, yes," she breathed.

"And . . . if I took the pareo off, would you still?"

Her pulse had taken such a giant leap that she could only nod. It was what she wanted, what her entire body craved. Somehow hearing his intent was all the more erotic. She reached back to the knot at her neck, only to have his warm hands pull her arms away.

"Let me," he murmured, dipping his head to kiss her slowly, languorously, before turning his attention to the knot. His eyes held hers while his fingers worked, gently pulling at the ends of the cloth, steadily loosening them.

When she felt the fabric slacken at her chest, Leslie felt a moment's hesitation. There was nothing at all glamorous about her body. And though he'd seen most of it already, there was something very. . .special about that part he'd now see for the first time. But it was too late to go back, she knew. If the determined look on Oliver's face hadn't told her so, the soft tendrils of excitement skittering in the pit of her stomach would have.

Slowly he drew his hands forward, unwinding the fabric and letting it fall to the sand. As though sensing her need for support, he instantly put his hands on her shoulders, rubbing them gently as his eyes fell to delight in her.

"Oh . . . Les . . ." he managed brokenly.

She caught in her breath. "Is it . . . am I . . . ?"

Only then did he look back to see the unsureness on her face. While one hand tightened on her shoulder, the other slid up to her neck. "You were worried?" he asked in surprise.

"I'm not gorgeous. . . ."

Helplessly drawn by the golden sheen of her skin, his gaze fell, to journey with his hand in a slow descent. The texture of his palm was the slightest bit rough in contrast to the butter-smooth skin of her breasts. His fingers seemed that much stronger than her waist, her hips, almost able to circle her thighs. But when they feather-touched the golden curls he'd never seen before, his hands were all male and dynamite.

In response to their tender force, Leslie reached out to clutch his shoulders in support. "Oliver!" she whispered hoarsely.

"You were worried?" he repeated dumbly as his hands flowed down and around and back up. Everywhere they touched she felt ready to explode. Again she moaned his name.

Framing her face with his hands, he tipped it up to his. "You're magnificent, sweetheart. Every inch of you. So warm—" he brushed his lips to her nose "—and soft—" he licked the line of her cheekbone "—and full where you should be full, and moist just there...." His lips became pulsing things then, capturing hers with a frenzy that spoke more eloquently than anything else might have done. And Leslie surrendered to their argument, giving herself up to the fire of the moment, choosing to believe she was indeed as magnificent as he'd claimed.

For a minute, held and holding breathlessly on to him, she savored the feel of his clothing against her skin. It made her feel naked and naughty and sensual. Yet when she burrowed her head against the column of his neck and opened her lips to the heat of his skin where his shirt fell open, she wanted more. Naked and naughty and sensual were very lovely narcissistic things to be. But what she felt for Oliver went far beyond narcissistic.

As she kissed the bronzed hollow of his shoulder, her hands worked feverishly at the buttons of his shirt, releasing one after the other, finally tugging the material from his pants and brushing it away. Then, with a sigh of delight, she set her hands loose on the playground of his chest, feeling as though in being able to touch him at will she'd been given the greatest gift of all.

"That's right," Oliver moaned, pressing his hands to the small of her back to keep their lower bodies close despite the inches that separated them above. "I've wanted you to touch me for so long—to feel your hands on my body. . . ."

"Tell me what you like, Oliver," she whispered as she spread her fingers wide and ran them up his sides. When her thumbs grazed his nipples, he jerked. Returning to them, she circled their tips, tormenting them with the pads of her thumbs until he moaned again.

"Like that," he gasped, his eyes closed, his chest laboring in the effort to breathe. She found that to please him, to bring his body alive, was a joy in itself. Growing bolder, she bent her head and replaced her fingers with her lips. With the tip of her tongue she danced along his flesh, dabbing the hardened nipple with a sensual moistness, grazing it with her teeth. This time in response his groan was one of sweet agony. Crushing her bottom with his hands, he ground his hips to hers.

His voice was a low, unsteady rasp, his eyes wild with fire when he tore her head up. "I don't know how much more I can take, Leslie," he warned. "I've needed you so badly all week—and now . . ."

Setting her back, he attacked the buckle of his belt. It was released, along with his zipper, in an instant. But as he would have thrust the fabric down, Leslie reached out.

"Wait!" she cried, then at his stricken look realized his misconception. "No," she whispered, stepping closer, "it's just that I want to do it." Arching against him, her hands at his waist, she stretched to reach his lips. Her breasts strained against his chest, creating a heady friction that gave even greater heat to her kiss. Then, offering him her tongue by way of exchange, she slid her hands beneath the band of his briefs, sought and found what she wanted, and stroked him tenderly. Fully aroused, he was thick and hard. She found herself breathing as heavily as he was, needing to touch him, yet needing so much more.

Oliver moaned again, and a shiver shook his limbs. Setting her aside almost roughly, he thrust slacks and briefs down over his legs and cast them aside, then caught her again.

At the contact, she cried aloud. It was new, rich and electric.

"Oh, Les . . ."

"Yes, yes . . ."

"Come here!" The last was a command ground out from his chest moments before he slid his hands down the backs of her thighs and lifted her, spreading her legs, fitting them snugly around his hips. Then, poised on the brink of her, he dropped smoothly to his knees and gently lowered her backward. Only when she was fully cushioned by the sand did he retrieve his hands. With one he propped himself up, with the other he reached down to unerringly find her warmth.

"Please, Oliver..." she pleaded, moving against his hand in frustration.

"Do you want me?"

"Oh, yes!"

His fingers caressed her longingly. "You're ready. . . ."

"I've been ready for so long—I don't think I can stand much more. . . ."

"I can't," he grated hoarsely. Planting his other hand near her shoulder, he moved his hips against hers.

They looked into each other's eyes then, aware of the moment as of no other before. To Leslie, it was right—right in every way, form and fashion. Not only did her body want Oliver, but her mind and her heart did as well. Regrets would be nonexistent, regardless of what the future held. For the moment to come promised to be the culmination of something very special to her as a woman. Pulse racing in wild anticipation, she grasped his hips and urged him in.

Ever wary of hurting her, he rocked slowly, surging forward by degrees, conquering her by inches. Her mouth opened in silent exclamation at the beauty of it, the slow filling, the exquisite heat. When at last he was fully buried within her, he dropped his head back and let his breath out in a soulful rush.

"You have no idea, Leslie...."

"But I do," she cried, lifting her hips and hooking her ankles together at his waist. "I do," she breathed, tightening herself, closing her eyes with the sweet, sweet pleasure of knowing that Oliver was deep inside.

On arms that trembled, he lowered his head to envelop her mouth. Then he began to move his hips, slowly at first but with growing speed and power as the flight of passion caught him up.

Leslie was with him every step of the way. Her lips answered his hungry nips, her hands roamed in greedy caress through the damp sheen of sweat rising on his skin. She felt his strength and the rock-hard boldness moving within her and, coaxed by instinct, caught the rhythm of his fire.

In those instants what existed between them was raw and primal and devoid of identity other than that of an all-consuming and mutual need. Labels would have been useless; Oliver was no more the glamorous male model than she the private preschool teacher. The pleasure they brought each other was direct and intense, unsullied by anything either of them might have been or done or wanted before in their lives. There were just the two of them, making love at that moment; nothing else was of consequence.

"Oliver!" she cried from a daze of passion, her body alive with a fire frightening in its intensity.

"That's it, sweet," he urged, plunging ever deeper, "more...oh, yes...there..."

She cried his name again, strained upward, then dissolved into spasms of ecstasy. In the next instant Oliver, too, stiffened, then let out an anguished moan of joy as his pleasure went endlessly on.

At last, totally spent, he collapsed over her. Then, when her gasping grew as loud as his, he quickly levered himself up on his elbows to relieve her of the worst of his weight. His gaze its most tender, he looked down at her.

"Does that smile mean that you're happy?"

Her throat felt suspiciously tight. She nodded.

"I'm glad," he said softly, brushing his lips against a corner of the smile in question. "You are beautiful. That was beautiful." He paused for a breath between each brief burst of words, then slowly slipped to her side, leaving one thigh firmly over hers. "Well, what do you think?" His tone verged on the giddy, yet she knew that deep down he needed to know that he'd pleased her. She also knew that it had very little to do with ego, and she was enchanted.

She brushed the dark wave from the dampness of his brow, then repeated the gesture when it fell right back down again. "I think," she began with mock deliberation, "that for a professional lady-killer you do just fine."

"I'm glad," he murmured, "because if my past has been worth anything, it's been to make me better for you."

"That's a sweet thing to say."

"It's what I feel, Leslie." He was suddenly serious. "You do know that it's never been like that before, don't you?"

Because she wanted to believe him, she nodded.

"You also know that I'm now very sandy."

"You ain't the only one." Before she could say another word, Oliver was on his feet, dragging her up with him. "What are you doing?" she cried, then pulled back on her hand. "Oh, no, Oliver Ames, it's chilly in there this time of night! You're not getting *me* in there."

"It's only the air that's chilly," he chided, dealing with her resistance by sweeping her into his arms.

"Oliver! You're supposed to be limp and sleepy. You can't do this!"

"I'm doin' it." His feet were making definite tracks, and not toward the house.

"But, Oliver!" She held tightly to his neck when she heard the splashing at his feet. "Oliver!" He bounced farther into the waves. "Come on, Oliver!" When the water touched her bottom, she strained upward, only to slide helplessly down when he released her legs.

Even the placid light of the moon couldn't hide the mischief in his eyes. His hands went to his neck. "Let go of me, Leslie," he murmured silkily.

She shook her head and locked her hands all the more tightly. "No."

He spread his hands beneath her arms. "Let go. . . ."

"No."

Then he tickled her. On a reflex of self-defense, she lowered her arms . . . and tumbled helplessly into the waves. Never once did he totally release her, though. His hands were there at her waist to lift her as soon as she'd been fully submerged.

"That was a dirty trick!" she sputtered. Tossing her wet hair back from her face, she scowled, but he pulled her against him once more and she melted nearly on contact.

"Now you can hold on again."

"Uh uh. You'll only tickle again."

"I promise I won't."

"Yeah, yeah."

"Really."

She wanted to believe. "Really?"

"Uh huh."

She hesitated for only a moment longer. Then, sensual slave that she happily was, she locked her arms around his neck once more. The fit of their bodies was perfect. "Only problem is that you've still got sand on you, and now it's back on me."

"Oh?" He frowned, as though stymied by the problem. Then, with an innocent shrug, he twirled and fell backward into the sea, dunking them both.

This time she came up laughing. When Oliver grasped her around the waist and hoisted her higher against him, she looked adoringly down at him. "That was nearly as dirty a trick as the other."

"But we're clean," he murmured between nips at her chin, "aren't we?"

Her legs floated around him naturally. "Uh huh."

"Are you too cool?"

"In your arms? Never."

He tipped her back and looked at her then. The moonlight set his features in relief, giving them a masterful air in counterpoint to the tenderness of his voice. "Why is it that you've always got the right answers?"

"They're not necessarily right," she replied lightly, "just honest."

"You like honesty?"

"I need honesty."

"Spoken with the same vehemence I've heard from you more than once before." He paused. "What happened, Leslie?"

Her legs slipped slowly downward. "What do you mean?"

"You've been hurt. Something happened. I want to know."

"You don't really," she said, trying to make light of it.

"I do." His expression echoed his words. "I want to understand why you feel so strongly about some things. Why you put that certain distance between you and your family. Why you seem leery of men."

"I don't know, Oliver. It's really irrelevant . . . and very embarrassing." He would think her a positive fool!

"Then—" he swept her up in his arms, turned and started for shore "—you'd better talk quickly so that the darkness can hide your blush. I intend to hear about it . . . tonight!"

"Or . . . ?" Her arms were around his neck once more.

"Or else."

"Or else what?"

"Or else . . . I'll hold you prisoner, stake you spread-eagled out in the sun tomorrow morning, and let you fry until you talk."

"Mmm, sounds very provocative."

Out of the water now, he stopped dead in his tracks. "Primitive is the word."

She gave a playful growl. "Primitive turns me on."

"Leslie, you're not being serious—but you won't get away with it." He let her feet fall to the sand, holding her waist until he was sure she had her balance. "Now pick up your things, and let's get up to the house. We've got some talking to do."

She picked up her sandals and let them dangle from one hand. "Oliver?"

He was searching the night sand for a second sock, his body lean and glistening in the moonlight. "Mmm?"

Inching closer, she wrapped an arm around his waist. His skin felt slick and smooth; her flesh slid easily over it. "Wouldn't you rather make love?" she asked softly, her expression more heartfelt than seductive.

He popped a kiss on the tip of her nose. "That, sweet angel, will be your reward. Now up!"

6

ACTUALLY, they didn't make it beyond the upper terrace. Stubbing her toe on the corner of a lounge chair she hadn't seen in the dark, Leslie needed consolation. Much later Oliver was to tell her that she'd simply wanted to make love on every level. But he hadn't complained at the time. Rather, there had been a kind of poignant drive to his love-making that had surprised her, given the satisfaction they'd so recently found on the beach. It was almost as though he feared what he'd learn when they talked.

He wasn't deterred, however. After they'd reached Shangri-la and beyond, had lain savoring the sensations, then recovered enough to languidly leave the lounge and pick up their clothes once more, he ushered her into the den. He left her only to go in search of robes, returned to gently clothe them both, then folded his long frame into the chair opposite hers and leaned forward.

She simply stared at him.

"Okay, Les," he began, undaunted. "Let's have it."

"Aren't you exhausted?"

"Nope. Who was he?"

Leslie tucked her legs beneath her and wrapped her arms around her middle. "It's not important."

"I think it is."

"It's *my* past. I don't ask you about yours."

He took on the same mocking expression she'd seen more than once before. "That's because mine is so lurid and filled with such an endless stream of women that I wouldn't know where to begin."

"Well," she prevaricated, "maybe mine's the same. Maybe I have a hidden past. Maybe I'm not as pure as I let on."

He chuckled and sat back, momentarily indulging her. "Funny, I never thought of you simply as 'pure.' Maybe pure honey or pure wit or pure sensuality. Never just . . . 'pure.' Besides—" he came forward again, his dark eyes narrowed "—you were the one who informed me—albeit in a very sexy voice—that you didn't sleep around."

She recalled the moment exactly, the Friday before, when she'd first arrived from New York and had been sick and very threatened by his presence. How far she'd come, she mused, then abruptly realized she hadn't. If she stopped to think, she'd know that she was still very threatened indeed, though by something quite different now.

"So, Les," Oliver went on, reaching forward to brush his thumb against the furrows on her brow, "tell me about it." His voice was quiet, patient. "Tell me about honesty. Too many times I've heard bitterness, then just now vehemence, in your voice when you've mentioned it. You need it, you say. Why?"

Quiet and patient, yes. But there was also an unmistakable trace of cynicism underlying his tone. Disturbed, Leslie tore her gaze away. "It's not relevant to anything, Oliver."

Though his stance remained casual, long bare legs set nonchalantly, hands now crossed over his stomach, his gaze was sharp. "It's relevant to us . . . and to what's happened twice now. And it matters to me. I need to understand you."

It was the last that hit home. She mulled the words over again and again. *I need to understand you . . . need to understand you.* Perhaps it was nothing more than a continuation of the illusion born earlier that day and brought to fulfillment on the beach. But she wanted so badly to believe that he cared that at long last she yielded and spoke, softly, slowly, eyes downcast, arms clutched tightly about herself.

"It's really very simple," she began. "I grew up a Parish, always a Parish. Living in an exclusive area, going to a private school, my friends were pretty much...people like me, people who'd had most everything they'd wanted in life." She lifted her eyes to find Oliver sitting back, listening thoughtfully. "Oh, I had friends. A couple of good ones I've kept. But at some point I became disillusioned with most of them. They seemed shallow. Boring. Quick to manipulate when it suited their purposes. Maybe it was natural for me to rebel. I was the youngest Parish and felt I had gone through life in the shadow of the others. I was seventeen and feeling my oats. Having always had the material things I'd wanted and knowing that they'd always be there for me, it was easy to turn my back on them."

"You became a flower child!" Oliver asked, faint amusement lighting his features.

She blushed. "Not really. Just a free thinker. I did little things to proclaim my individuality—like going vegetarian and boycotting the senior prom and donating my graduation money to Oxfam and biking across the country with three friends."

Again his eyes lit. "Bicycling?"

She lowered hers. "Motorcycling."

"And the three other kids?" he asked more pointedly.

"My best friend from school . . . and her twin cousins."

He caught the drop in her voice and interpreted correctly. "Male?"

"Yes." She raised a defensive gaze and went quickly on. "Not that anything happened between us. I mean, we were all good friends, but that was it. We didn't cause trouble, either. Our idea of adventure was in living as cheaply as we could. We camped out a good part of the time, stayed in our share of sleazy places. Just knowing how appalled our parents would have been enhanced our joy." She sighed. "We did see the country, I have to admit." Then she qualified the statement. "I mean, we'd all seen the country before, but never like that."

"Sounds like fun," Oliver ventured wryly.

"It was! It really was. We enjoyed mocking everything we'd always had. Then the other three went right back to it when the summer was over."

"And you?"

"I went on to college. Berkeley." When he winced, she smiled. "It wasn't so bad. Actually, I'd already gotten much of the rebelliousness out of my system, so I was pretty receptive to learning. I felt confident and in control and loved the idea of being three thousand miles away from all of the other Parishes."

"They didn't keep close tabs on you?"

"Naw. They trusted me."

He arched a brow. "Should they have?"

She thought for a minute, then nodded. "My intentions were good. I was idealistic, bent on making a very serious, independent way in the world. I would never have done anything to disgrace them." She paused, then frowned. "Not knowingly, at least."

Silence sat between them for a time, broken only by the gentle murmur of the night surf on the beach as it accompanied the softest of breezes through the open glass doors. Leslie let herself be momentarily lulled, then, eager to get out the worst, she went on.

"I had a great freshman year. I loved school and did well." She cast him a sheepish look. "It was an awakening to find myself among so many people who were legitimately serious and independent. In many ways, it was humbling. I guess I withdrew a little, letting the place itself speak for my rebellion while I got reacquainted with the person I was inside. I liked myself. I thought I'd found a nice blend between 'way out' and 'way in'...." Her voice trailed off as her eyes reflected a distant pain.

"Then what happened?"

As though she'd forgotten his presence, she came back with a start. With a shrug she looked down at the pleats her fingers were nervously folding into the terry fabric of her robe. "I met a guy. A med student." She tossed her head to the side, keeping her eyes downcast, safe from Oliver's intent study. "He was tall and good-looking and bright and funny...and very high on life and himself." Her voice took on a gently mocking tone. "He was going to be a doctor. You know, heal the world?"

"I know the type," Oliver injected, but Leslie was too immersed in her story to hear the dryness in his tone.

"Anyway," she sighed, "we started to date and things got pretty heavy. We couldn't see each other often. I was busy studying, and his schedule was ten times worse. I think it was the time we spent apart that aided his cause more than anything. I was young and starry-eyed and spent those times away from him imagining all the wonderful things he was going to do." She lowered her voice to a self-conscious murmur, "All the wonderful things we were going to do together. He was talking about the Peace Corps. That fit right into my scheme of things—noble, stoic, commendable. I spent those days alone dreaming about how, after graduation, we'd both go to South America or South Africa. He'd doctor; I'd teach. It was perfect." She paused to recall that particular illusion, then shook her head in dismay. "Things didn't quite work out as I'd dreamed."

Oliver propped his elbows on his knees and prodded gently, "Why not?"

She looked up then, vulnerable and in pain. "He was married."

"Oh. And you didn't know."

"Of course not!" she cried, doubly hurt. "I'd never have knowingly had an affair with a married man! For all my ballyhooing about rebellion, I'd been pretty conservative about sex; it was enough for me to have had an affair in the first place! I honestly thought that he was busy studying all the time. I mean—" again the mocking tone "—between classes and rotations, a med student has to be the most put-upon person in the world. Hmmph," she mused aloud, "no wonder they go out into the world and keep patients in their offices waiting for hours. Revenge, I'm sure. Simple revenge."

Oliver let her anger gradually seep away before he spoke. "Not all doctors are that way, Les. There are ones who do serve time in the Peace Corps, or who keep ungodly hours as staff physicians well after their med-school days are over, or who go into private practice and make a point to see all their patients on time. How they are as doctors can sometimes be very different from the way they run their private lives."

"I'm not so sure about that," she retorted bitterly, "though I'll concede you the point. For all I know Joe's become an excellent doctor. And for that matter, I may have been as much at fault for what happened between us as he was." At Oliver's puzzled look, she explained. "Idealistic young thing that I was, I accepted everything on faith. He explained that when he was free he wanted to get away from it all. So he always came to my place, rather than the other way around. Sucker that I was, I believed him."

"Did you love him?" came the quiet follow-up.

"What I knew of him, yes. He was truly charming—great bedside manner, if you'll excuse the pun." Her lips thinned.

"We'd been seeing each other for nearly six months when one day I thought I'd surprise him and bring a home-cooked dinner to his apartment. I knew his address in Palo Alto, though I'd never been there before." She swallowed hard, trying to accept all over again what she'd learned that day. "It was a lovely dorm not far from the medical school. Prettier than most—you know, small balconies with hanging plants and a baby swing here and there. When I went into the lobby to buzz him, I understood why. It was a married students' dorm. 'Dr. and Mrs.' all along the roster—the Joe Durands right up there with the rest. I turned around with my shattered dreams and went home."

By way of offering comfort, Oliver took her hand, but it lay limply under his gentle massage. "Did he ever follow you?"

"Oh, yes," she spat out with a harsh laugh. "He hadn't known I'd come and didn't know anything was wrong. He assumed his little game could go on indefinitely. When he showed up several days later, I'd had time to cool off and gather my thoughts. I was really quite . . . good."

"I'm sure," Oliver remarked tightly.

"I was," she insisted, raising her eyes in a burst of courage. "It was actually funny. I threw myself into his arms and told him how much I'd missed him, how much I loved him. After he tossed back those same hollow words, I told him about my brainstorm. It had occurred to me, I told him, that he'd be able to save all kinds of money if he moved in with me. I could cook for him and do his laundry and take care of him in between my own studies. After all, why not, since we loved each other so much?"

"That was mean," Oliver scolded, though he couldn't completely hide the glimmer of admiration in his gaze.

"It was intended to be," she rejoined without remorse. "I was brokenhearted at the time. I felt used and dirty. I had

to score some points, and since I didn't have the heart to resort to blackmail, I simply wanted him to squirm."

"Did he?"

"Oh ho, yes," she answered, neither pride nor pleasure
in her tone. "He hemmed and hawed about how he'd never
get any studying done if we lived together, and he'd feel all
the more guilty about having to put me off when he did need
to work. I insisted that it wouldn't bother me and that it
would be better watching him study than not seeing him at
all."

The fire in her eyes spoke of an inner strength. Respect-
ing it, Oliver grew more grave. "How did he handle that?"

"Very predictably, actually. On the pretense of being
overcome by my offer, he took me in his arms and tried to
put off the whole discussion by making love."

"You didn't—"

"No. I brought my knee up hard, and then told him to go
home and *try* to make love to his wife."

Oliver jacked forward as though in physical pain himself. "You really did that?"

"You bet I did," she breathed, "and I haven't regretted it
for a minute. I was hurt and angry. The look of surprise,
then disbelief, then sheer terror on his face was the small
satisfaction I got out of the affair. That . . . and the determination never to be made a fool of again." With the last of
her venom trickling into thin air, she spoke more gently and
with an awareness of Oliver once more. His face was racked
by pain; she was touched by his sympathy. "It's okay,
Oliver," she said, forcing a smile. "It's over, and I sur-
vived. In hindsight, I guess I was most disappointed in myself—disappointed that I'd been fool enough to be so
completely taken in. I really did love a part of Joe. I thought
I'd found someone different—someone down-to-earth,
someone more concerned with doing and living than claw-

ing up the social ladder." Her voice grew sad. "I was wrong. His greatest fear, when he discovered I knew the truth, was that I'd blow the whistle on him and somehow hurt his chances for a future in Boston. Not Kenya. Boston." She sighed, her tone a mere whisper. "Boy, was I wrong."

For the longest time, Oliver simply sat and stared at her, his chin propped on his fist, his face a mask of dismay. When she could no longer stand the silence, Leslie pushed herself from her chair and paced to the window.

"So now you know what a clever lady I am," she called over her shoulder. "Now you know why I'm wary."

With the sound of his bare feet muffled in the carpet, she didn't hear him approach. When his arms slipped around her to draw her back against him, she resisted. But he was insistent. And in the end she needed his support.

"I'm sorry," he murmured so sadly that Leslie turned in his arms to face him.

"You're sorry?" she asked, bemused by his almost anguished expression. "It wasn't your fault!"

"But still . . . in some ways I identify with . . . your Joe."

"He's not my Joe, and that's ridiculous. Aside from the fact that you both wear pants, you're nothing at all like Joe. He was a two-timing liar. You're not. You've never made promises or said things you couldn't see through. You've never made any attempt to deliberately sweeten the image of what you do, even when I've thought the worst." Her ardent claim did nothing to ease his pain.

"But you know so little about me," he began, his voice heavy and low.

"I know the essentials," she pointed out quietly. "And Tony knows you. If there was something grossly unsuitable about you, he would never have suggested you come. Besides, I know that you were kind enough not to laugh at me just now."

"Did anyone laugh?" he asked, brows lifting in a touching challenge. Was he truly a knight in shining armor, prepared to defend her virtue?

"No one laughed," she murmured, "because no one knew. And if anyone finds out," she warned only half in jest, "I'll personally knock you off that white steed of yours."

Attuned to the analogy, he grunted. "Better to fall from a horse than to be kicked in the balls. Hell, you're a dangerous woman."

"Only when I'm pushed. I don't really want to be dangerous."

Oliver's expression took a soulful twist as his arms tightened around her back. "Oh, Leslie," he murmured, his gaze clinging to each of her features in turn, "I wish...I wish...."

"Shh." She pressed a finger to his lips. His entire body felt tense; she began to rub his shoulders and back in an attempt to loosen him up. "Please don't say anything. Life here is so ... basic. So simple." Her voice dropped to a whisper. "It's like lying bare on the beach. Unadorned and lovely."

"But there's still New York—"

"Next week," she vowed more strongly. "Not now."

"Then where's the honesty you claim you need?"

"What's honest in New York, New York can have. I just want to enjoy what's here. Now." Her eyes grew beseeching. "Can you understand that, Oliver?"

"Oh, sweetheart, only too well," he murmured with a sudden fierceness. Then his lips sought hers, transmitting that fierceness through her body in the name of passion. His kiss was long and possessive, enduring even as he swept her off her feet and headed for the bedroom. Only when the large bed took her weight did he raise his head. Trembling as he leaned over her, he sighed her name several more times and with reverence. "Leslie, Leslie, let me love you the way you should be loved...."

Stunned by the aching depth of his plea, Leslie could find no words to express what she felt. Oliver Ames had to be the most gentle, most compassionate man in the world. Opening her arms, she reached up to him. For just a minute he held her, embracing her with the same fierceness with which he'd kissed her, then gently pressing her away. With unsteady fingers he untied her robe, and spreading it to either side, proceeded to worship every bare inch of her body with his hands, then his mouth, then his tongue. Helplessly she writhed at the havoc he caused, loving every minute of it, loving him all the more. For there was something supremely tender about his lovemaking this time, something that went far beyond the gentleness he'd shown before. It was as though in this abandoned adulation he sought to apologize for what another man had done, to make amends, to tell her what an exquisitely feminine wonder she was.

And she believed. She believed. How could she not, with the warmth of strong, manly fingers stroking her hips, with the wetness of a long, sensual tongue adoring her breast, with the length of lean, sinewed flesh branding her cherished? If she'd thought to protest that it wasn't Oliver's apology to give, her need for his loving was far too great to deny him his penance. His entire goal seemed to be giving her pleasure; yet she reveled in the sound of his own moans and sighs, in the quaking of his limbs when he finally drew back to remove his robe.

Then, wanting to absolve him of guilt for all time, she opened her thighs and welcomed him. The ensuing fire was purgative, cleansing, propelling them onward to a climactic point where it seemed their souls would fuse forever. When, after wave upon wave of glory washed over their straining bodies, they finally cooled, exhaustion took its inevitable toll. Deliriously happy and at peace, Leslie fell asleep in her lover's arms, awakening only when morning had fully established itself over the island.

"HAPPY BIRTHDAY, sweetheart."

She snuggled closer, eyes closed, a smile on her face. "Mmm. You remembered."

The arms around her tightened. The voice by her ear was a deep, lazy hum. "Of course, I remembered. Thirty years old...oops, what's this?"

She felt the hair being lifted from her neck. "What's what?"

"This line."

"What line?"

One long finger sizzled around her throat. "This. Must be your age. They say the neck is the first to show it, love."

Leslie tipped her head back, arched a brow and opened the violet-hued eye beneath it. "Is that so?" she asked smartly.

Oliver nodded, trying his best to keep a straight face. "Uh huh. I should know. In my business, the face is everything. We worry about important things like lines around the mouth and receding hairlines and sagging chins."

"Do you now?" she teased. "And what'll you do when your day is done?"

"Oh, I've got no cause for concern," he stated outrageously. "Men don't get older; they just get more dignified-looking. It's women who have to worry. Say, Les, I wouldn't scowl like that. It'll only bring out lines on your forehead." He ducked in time to avoid the playful swat she aimed at his head, then grabbed her and kissed her soundly. She protested for only an instant before surrendering to his morning pleasure. When he came up for air, his eyes were dark and earnest. "Somehow," he said softly, stroking the delicate lines of her face, "I don't think you have to worry about wrinkles. You sure as hell don't look thirty. I may not have known you five or ten years ago, but I'd guess that you're one of those women who's getting better, not older."

"Oliver Ames," Leslie scolded gently, "this sounds like a living advertisement. Next thing I know the cameramen will pop out from behind the drapes."

"There aren't any drapes."

"Then . . . from under the bed."

"Heaven help anyone who was under this bed last night. Poor fool would have a concussion."

She shook her head and sighed through a grin. "You are incorrigible."

"Better incorrigible than late for breakfast. Come on," he announced, dropping her onto the sheet as he rolled out of bed, "I'm hungry." Then he looked down at her. "On second thought, you stay put. For the birthday girl, breakfast in bed."

The birthday girl, however, was suddenly and acutely aware that she'd never seen Oliver nude in the daylight. Beneath the bright sun streaking through the skylights, his body looked very strong and very male.

"Les?" He leaned over her. Startled, she raised her eyes. "You do want breakfast, don't you?" he whispered.

She swallowed once and realized how silly he'd think her if she said she just wanted to look at him, to touch him. "Sure."

As though reading her thoughts, he sat back down on the sheets. Taking her hand in his, he pressed it to his hip, moving it gently over the strip of flesh that all the world had seen. "Maybe I'm feeling my age, after all," he teased. "You gave me quite a workout last night." Leaning forward, he kissed her forehead. "We'll have breakfast and then go . . . exploring. How does that sound?"

The deep velvet of his voice sent shivers of excitement through her, as did the smoothness of his flank. She grinned. "I'd like that." Slipping beneath the sheet, she watched him leave the room and closed her eyes, awaiting his return.

Return he did, bearing a tray filled with all sorts of breakfast goodies. They ate to their hearts' content, then explored as he'd promised. It was nearly noon before they finally climbed from bed, showered together, then headed for the beach wearing nothing but oversize towels, which they proceeded to spread on the sand and lie upon.

"This is indecent," she remarked, eyeing the solid length of Oliver's naked body stretched beside her, "but I love it."

He opened one eye. "You're very daring for a conservative lady. Topless on the public beach, nude here. Say, you never did finish the story of the flower child." He closed his eye and flipped onto his stomach, propping his chin on his hands in time to see her bob up.

"Wait," she said, "if you're going to switch on me, you need more lotion." She had the bottle in her hand and was kneeling at his hips, grateful for the excuse to touch him. He shivered when she drizzled a line of cream down his spine. "Wouldn't want your butt to get burned."

"God forbid," he muttered, burying his face in his arms to endure the agony of the hands working so diligently over his skin. It was a full minute after she'd finished and lain down again before he thought to look up. Shifting in a vain attempt to make himself comfortable, he cleared his throat. "Your story."

She was on her back, arms and legs restful, eyes closed, face to the sun. As an afterthought, she rubbed the lotion lingering on her hands over her stomach and breasts, then fell still. "Not much more to tell."

"Did you transfer back east to finish school?"

"And jeopardize my independence? No way."

"It didn't bother you to be out there with memories of that fellow all around?"

"I was so angry at the time that I was thinking only of the discomfort he'd feel knowing I was there. When the anger faded, I realized that there wasn't an awful lot left. Yes, I was hurt and embarrassed and more than a little disillusioned. But I knew that it'd be worse to fly back home with my tail between my legs. Besides, I liked Berkeley and what with the course load I took on, I had plenty to keep me busy. I graduated a semester early and taught for six months before going back to grad school. By that time I'd accepted what had happened with Joe."

"So you came home."

She nodded. "I'd done a lot of growing up during those three and a half years. Not only was I the wiser for my experience with Joe, but I realized that I was a strong enough person to hold my own among the Parishes. And, as it happens, I love New York."

Eyes closed, he groped for her hand, finding it, enveloping it in his. "Look who sounds like an ad now? And I thought you didn't like crowds."

"I don't . . . when it comes to going to work or the bank or the dry cleaner or the supermarket. But I love museums and the theater, and there's nothing more delightful than bundling up and strolling down a packed Fifth Avenue at Christmastime. That's why I live outside the city but within easy reach. If I don't feel like reaching, I don't. I have the choice." Oliver's respectful chuckle brought her head around. "What about you? Doesn't it bother you—living right in the thick of things?" He'd previously told her that he lived in the city, though he hadn't elaborated either on where or on what kind of place he had.

He shrugged. "For the convenience of it, I'd put up with most anything. Besides, I have a small place in the Berkshires. Great for weekends."

She wondered what he did on those weekends, whether he had someone to play Scrabble with and...do other things with. But she didn't ask. She didn't feel she had the right. After all, there had been no lofty words of love or proclamations of undying devotion. She didn't want them. They could be so very shallow. *No*, she mused, *better to assume nothing than to pin false hopes on something that would probably never materialize.* It was far safer this way. Safer, if discouraging....

"You're awfully quiet," Oliver whispered.

She tossed off his concern with a shrug. "Just...thinking."

"About what?"

"About . . . how beautiful it is down here and how much I wish I could stay another week." Though roundabout, it was the truth.

He was up on an elbow. "Can't you?"

Feeling his gaze, she shook her head and smiled, but didn't open her eyes. "The centers await." She gave an exaggerated sigh. "Ah me, the price of success. For us lady executives, the day is never done. They depend on us," she drawled. "They need us. Oh, to be a lowly errand girl—hey, what are you doing?" She opened her eyes with a start to find Oliver on his haunches by her hip.

"Lotioning you up." His hands were already at work spreading the cream he'd gushed on.

"But I'm already lotioned!" Feeling her body's instant reaction to his touch, she twisted to the side. Oliver simply straddled her hips to hold her still. "Oliver..." she warned, lying flat, looking up at him. His hands slid over her skin in a pattern of sensuous circles, teasing by sheer impartiality. "Oliver!" she whispered more urgently. "This is ridiculous! The oldest trick in the book—seduction by suntan lotion!"

"Guess I'm not terribly original then," he murmured, slithering his hands over the peak of her breasts again and again.

"My God!" she moaned. She bit her lip and arched helplessly into his touch.

"No, sweetheart, just me." Planting his hands on either side of her shoulders, he stretched his full length over her. His eyes held the lambency she'd come to know, the depth she'd come to love, the vulnerability that could touch her every time. "Just me . . . needing you again."

Leslie coiled her arms around his neck. "I don't know about these male model types. They're insatiable."

"Only with you," he murmured, seeking the honey of her mouth as he nudged a place for himself between her thighs.

And she believed . . . again. She believed because she had to, because the intense love that swelled within her came part and parcel with trust. If she was wrong, she'd be later damned. But for now she had no choice. No choice at all.

"THIS IS POSITIVELY decadent," Leslie remarked. "I don't think we've been properly dressed for two days."

It was Saturday morning, and they'd just emerged from an early-morning swim. She blotted her towel over her face, then glanced up to find Oliver just standing there, dripping wet, looking down at her. His towel hung, forgotten, in his hand, but she, too, forgot it in the face of his strangely uncertain expression. She'd seen that expression more than once in the past two days. It was not quite haunted, not quite pained, not quite worried, not quite fearful, yet it held a bit of all of those emotions and more, thrown together to produce something that cut to her heart, then twisted and turned.

"Are you all right?" she asked softly. She took a step forward, then was stopped by a sudden sense of foreboding. Shaking her head, she moved forward again. "Oliver?"

He blinked and inhaled. "Sorry, Les. I missed that."

Very gently, using her own towel, she began to dry his chest. "Didn't miss much. I was only being smart."

"Again?" His cockeyed smile was a relief, as was the mischievous eye that warmed her length. "You know, we really should get dressed," he suggested, tugging her against him. "It's been nearly two days. Think we'll remember how?"

At first she thought he was mocking her. After all, hadn't she just commented on their seemingly perpetual state of undress? But he looked so innocent and sounded so sincere. Where had his mind been then? She'd noticed his tension of late, a tension coming at odd moments such as the one past. What was he thinking?

It was getting more difficult. Each day of bliss made it worse. *Think of today, only today,* Leslie told herself. But it didn't work. There was tomorrow, and the tomorrow after that...and so on until she was back in New York. Would she see Oliver then? Could she possibly reconcile her far slower life-style with his faster one? Did she want to? Did he want her to? All she knew was that she wanted Oliver. Very desperately.

"Hey, what's this?" he asked with exquisite tenderness as he dabbed a tear from the corner of her eye. Without awaiting her answer, he closed his arms about her and hugged her tightly.

"I don't think I like the idea of getting dressed," she said in a soft, sad voice.

"Neither do I, but we'll have to sooner or later. You know that, don't you, Les?" His deeper meaning was as glaring as the sun upon open waters.

"Oh, yes."

He drew his head back to look at her. His jaw was tight, his expression closed. "You also know that I'm not letting you go, don't you?"

His vehemence surprised her as much as it pleased her. "No, I didn't know that," she whispered.

"Do you mind?"

She shook her head. Mind? *Mind?* The first hint that he wanted to see her back in New York . . . how could she possibly mind? True, there'd be mammoth hurdles to clear. True, she might stumble and fall. But . . . what if she took it one day at a time, much as she'd tried to do here? Wouldn't it be better than nothing at all?

"Of course I don't mind," she answered, eyes misty, a smile on her lips.

"Good. Then what say we get dressed and go into town. There's something I want to pick up."

"Sounds fine."

"And brunch on the quai, a drive around the island, the afternoon on the beach?"

"Um hmm."

"And dinner . . . a last night out?"

She swallowed down the knot that was so very quick to form. "You bet."

He kissed her then, each eye in turn, then the tip of her nose, then her mouth. Sucking in a shaky breath, he hugged her tight, then, head down, moved back and took her hand. Leslie could have sworn he was as affected by the moment as she, but how much of what she saw was a product of what she wanted to see, she didn't know. Wishful thinking was a dangerous thing. Dangerous . . . though irresistible.

IT WAS A BUSY DAY, this, their last full one on St. Barts. By unspoken design, they kept their minds occupied with the pleasure of what they saw, said and did. It was as though each feared the thoughts that, given idleness, might creep in and begin to fester.

Gustavia seemed more alive than ever. They walked, then brunched—then, to Leslie's horror, stopped at the jewelry shop Oliver had obviously visited earlier that week, to pick up a beautiful gold necklace he'd purchased. It was a serpentine chain whose central links had been removed to make way for a single amethyst. The stone matched her eyes perfectly. Only when he lifted the chain from its box and started to put it around her neck, though, did she realize he'd bought it for her.

"I can't accept this, Oliver," she breathed. "It's...it's too much!"

"Not too much. Just right. It was made for you, your birthday present. I'm sorry it's late." He deftly hooked the clasp, then straightened the chain and stood back to admire the way it nestled against her skin.

Leslie raised a trembling finger to touch the warm amethyst. "But you didn't have to— There was no need...." Then, embarrassed, she scowled. "Tony didn't put you up to this, did he?"

For a minute she thought Oliver would hit her. His eyes grew dark, his features fierce. "No, Tony didn't put me up to it. I thought of it all by myself."

"I'm sorry," she said quickly, reaching out to grasp his arm, "that wasn't what I meant." In pain, she looked down. "It's just that it's so beautiful . . . and the thought that went into it.... I...I wanted, needed to know the thought was yours." Dropping her hand, she turned away. "I guess I'm not very good at accepting gifts. So often they've either been too easily come by, or given with an ulterior motive."

"Oh, sweetheart," he moaned and turned her to him. Placing his hands on her shoulders, he lowered his head to look at her. Her eyes lifted slowly as he spoke. "I want you to have this just . . . because."

"Just . . . because?" she echoed timidly.

"Just because you're you and I'm me, and together we've had a pretty wonderful week. I want you to have this so that when we get back to New York—" his features stiffened imperceptibly "—you'll be able to touch your throat and remember what we've shared."

"I could never forget," she murmured, entranced by the goodness he exuded. "Never, Oliver."

"I hope not," he rasped, then crushed her against him with a kind of desperation that was to remain with them through the rest of their stay. It poked its head through the palm fronds when they played on the beach that afternoon. It was propped between the salt and pepper shakers when they had dinner out that evening.

Later that night their lovemaking was slower and more intense than it had been. It was an expression of all the things they'd meant to each other during the week—of fresh lemonade, wine and cheese and Scrabble, of gentle and intimate talk about nothing in particular, of loving and living and counting one's blessings for the moment, of a gold chain with an amethyst at its heart. Particularly when they awoke again at dawn to desire and to each other was there a desperation in it, a kind of grasping and seeking and holding to something that might never come again. For that was precisely what Leslie feared. With the north would come the cold and the real world and all the differences she could only imagine to exist between herself and this man who'd made such a thorough conquest of her heart.

As a couple boarding the small island-hopper Sunday at noon, they were subdued. Transferring to the larger jet on St. Martin, they were distracted. Arriving in New York in the dark to subfreezing temperatures, they were visibly tense. Only when Oliver put Leslie in a cab headed for her home on the island, though, did she come close to breaking.

"Oliver?" She raised a frantic gaze to his, prepared to blurt out her love, prepared to plead, prepared to do most anything to prolong the inevitable parting.

"Shh. I'll call you. Okay?"

Don't call me. I'll call you. Her heart plummeted to her frigid toes. "Okay." She flashed him a plastic smile, swallowed hard, then turned and let the driver take her home.

7

OLIVER STOOD at the curb for what seemed hours after Leslie's cab had pulled away. With his eyes he followed it as it dodged other vehicles and slowed, then entered the airport's exit road and sped forward, finally disappearing around the bend that would take it to the parkway and on to her home.

A part of him was in the cab. He wasn't sure how or when it had happened—whether he'd first fallen in love with her honest smile or her ready wit or her breasts in the sun or her mushroom omelets. Hell, it might have been the lavender leprechaun, stuffed-up and sneezing, for whom he'd first fallen. But he'd fallen. No doubt about that. He'd fallen hard. And, damn it, he didn't know what to do!

He'd made a mess of it with his whimsy of shaking the image and existing solely as a man. It had backfired! He'd simply been pigeonholed differently.

Leslie knew him as a model. Oh, yes, it had had its moments, and it was certainly flattering. Only trouble was that she loved him. He was sure of it. Leslie, who believed in, who needed honesty above all, was in love with a man who had deceived her from the start.

"Hey, fella, we're holdin' up the line. You wanna cab or not?"

Snapped from his brooding, Oliver looked down at the body sprawled from the driver's seat toward the passenger's window, at the face scowling up at him. With a curt nod he opened the back door, picked up his bags and tossed them in, then followed them. After giving his Manhattan address to the cabbie, he slouched against the door, his fist pressed to his mouth, and stared blindly into the arena of headlights and taillights they entered.

Was it deceit? Or simply evasion? He'd never lied, but had told only half the truth. He did model, though it was purely a hobby and something he did far less frequently than he'd let Leslie believe. If only he *could* model more often! But his practice was more demanding than it had ever been. Demanding, challenging...rewarding. Even now he wondered what bizarre messages he'd find awaiting him when he got home. Then his thoughts turned to Leslie, and he lost interest in bizarre messages.

She'd been as upset as he when they'd left St. Barts. A healthy tan notwithstanding, she'd looked as pale as her hand had felt cold. They'd said little to each other. He knew she'd hoped for something, but he'd been stymied.

He'd tried. He had tried. Even if she hated him when she learned the truth, she'd have to admit that he'd tried. And every time, she'd hushed him, saying she hadn't wanted to know, that it wasn't important. So why hadn't he pushed? He'd always been strong and convincing, never one to let a woman deter him when he'd had something to do or say. But...he'd never been in love before. And Leslie was a woman like no other he'd known.

The cab swerved. The cabbie swore. From his slouched position Oliver muttered an oath and thrust a hand through his hair. New York looked ugly, all dark and gray and spattered with mud from the snow that must have recently fallen. So different from the sunshine and heat of St. Barts. Damn, but he felt cold inside!

Seeking warmth, he wearily dropped his head back and conjured up memories from the week now past. It worked for a time. As the cab sped onward, snaking in and out of the parkway traffic, he thought of the villa, the beach, bubbling Gustavia . . . and Leslie through it all. The times he'd spent alone at the start of the week had mysteriously fallen from mind. The images that remained were of time they'd spent together—living, laughing, loving.

But Oliver Ames, more than most, knew that one couldn't exist wholly in a world of memories. In addition to past, one needed present and future. Present and future. The present was a dingy cab fighting its way across town now, through congested Manhattan streets. The future was a confrontation he feared as he'd never feared anything before. So much was at stake. So very much.

The cab lurched through the Sunday-evening traffic, forging steadily onward until at last it came to an abrupt halt at the door of his building. Oliver dug his wallet from his trousers' pocket, thinking how strange it felt in his hand after a week without it. He tugged out several bills and paid the cabbie, then hauled himself and his belongings from the cab.

The doorman was on the spot. "Good evening, Dr. Ames. Would you like a hand?"

Oliver dipped his head in response to the greeting, held up a hand in refusal of the offer, then headed through the door that the attendant had opened. Eighteen floors later, he was in his own apartment.

Leaving his bags by the door, he easily found his way in the darkness down the two steps into the sunken living room, where he collapsed in a sofa and dropped his head into his hands. Then, propping his chin on his palms, he studied the dark.

He missed her already. It was so quiet here. Not that she made much noise, but just knowing she might be in another room would have lightened the atmosphere of the place.

What was he going to do? For three days now, since
Thursday, when they'd spent the day together and then
made love and he'd realized just how deeply he was in over
his head, he'd been trying to decide. He could call her right
now and blurt out the truth, counting on her love to master
her anger. Or he could make a date for tomorrow night or
Tuesday night, and then tell her the truth. He could send her
a letter of confession and follow it up with two dozen long-
stemmed roses. Or he could storm over to her place and
confess it all in person. As a last resort, he could always ab-
duct her, break the news, then hold her prisoner until she
forgave him.

Damn Joe Durand! It sounded as though Leslie had been
leery enough of deception before Joe had come along, but
his shoddy treatment of her had cemented her feelings. Now
Oliver had inadvertently stepped in the muck Joe had left,
and his feet were stuck. He felt like such a heel! A heel!

Eyes wide, he threw his head back, then gave a savage
push, and left the sofa. Flipping on the lights by the door,
he grabbed his bags, strode angrily down the hall to his
bedroom, tossed the cases onto the bed, then stood glaring
at them.

"Damn!" Crossing to the bedstand phone, he picked up
the receiver, held it midair for a minute, then scowled at it
and slammed it down. He stormed back down the hall,
paused overlooking the living room and stood, hands on
his hips, frowning.

He lived in the lap of luxury in this coop with its prestigious East Side address. Maybe she wouldn't be surprised
at it; after all, she'd assumed him to be a successful model,
and they reportedly did well. Rubbing a tired hand against
the taut muscles at the back of his neck, he slowly descended the steps and perched on the arm of a chair.

He liked this place. He'd certainly worked hard enough for it. Plush carpeting, cushiony upholstered sofas and chairs, lacquered coffee tables and wall units bearing unique mementos from one trip or another—a far cry from the cramped duplex his parents had rented all those years. He thought of the pleasant garden condominium he'd recently helped them buy, and smiled. They were comfortable; they deserved it.

In its idle wandering, his gaze tripped over loose pillows of the same rich browns and beiges and grays as the rest of the room before falling on the ancient brass spittoon he'd picked up in Wales. It was a planter now, bearing a small fig tree. Standing, he walked over to finger the oval leaves. It wasn't doing well—it needed sun and warmth. He snorted. *He* needed sun and warmth, but his sun and warmth was Leslie. Did he look as despairing as the poor fig tree in front of him?

The jangle of the phone startled him. His head flew toward the kitchen. It was his private line ringing, not the business phone he kept in the den. In two strides he'd covered the distance and snatched up the phone.

"Hello?"

"Oliver, you're back! It's Tony. How did it go?"

"How're ya doin', Tony?" Oliver asked, trying to cover up his disappointment. For a split second he'd hoped it would be Leslie.

"Not bad . . . but tell me about *you*." His voice grew cautious. "She wasn't angry, was she?"

"As a matter of fact," Oliver began with a sigh, "she wasn't thrilled at first. But she came around."

Tony grinned. "I knew she would. You've got charm, friend. I knew you could handle her. It was a good week, then?"

"Great. You were right. The villa's gorgeous. So's the island. Bright sun every day. It never rained."

"Come on, Oliver. This is the guy you sweat with on the tennis court twice a month. I don't want a camp letter. I want some of that gut-spilling you guys love to provoke. Was it a good week?"

"It was a great week."

"And?"

"Any more is private."

"She's my sister, Ames. I wouldn't have sent you down there if I hadn't had hopes that you two might hit it off."

"Hit it off...." Oliver smirked, rather amused by his friend's impatience. "You mean ... *make* it?"

"I mean like each other." Tony grimaced. "The woman's impossible. I've tried again and again to introduce her to men I think she'll like, but she's just not interested. My happening to know the man in the Homme Premier ad was a bolt out of the blue."

Oliver shot a glance at the ceiling. "So it was a fix-up after all. Strange, I thought it was supposed to be a joke," he remarked grimly. Of course he'd known better than that. Tony Parish was transparent, at least when he, too, was sweating it out on the courts. But it didn't bother him to string Tony along. He needed someone to blame for the mess he was in.

"You didn't hurt her," Tony came back more quietly.

"No. I didn't hurt her. At least not yet."

Once more, deadly calm. "What are you talking about?"

Oliver rested one hand low on his hip and hung his head. "We had a wonderful week together. It was...unbelievable."

"So?"

"So—" he took a breath "—I think your sister's fallen in love with a man she believes to be a very glamorous male model."

"Male model? Didn't you tell her the truth?"

"That is the truth . . . albeit only a tiny part."

"And you didn't tell her the rest?" came the disbelieving voice.

"No."

Tony swore softly, then began to pace within the limits of the telephone cord. "You picked a great one to lie to—"

"I didn't lie."

"Then you picked a great one to be evasive with. Jeez, I don't believe it. I was sure you'd tell her everything within the first day or two. You're almost as straitlaced as she is!" He paced another round. "Do you have any idea what my sister thinks of deception? She's pretty opinionated on that score. Do you?"

"I didn't, then. I do now."

Tony had paused in his ranting long enough to hear the dejection in Oliver's voice. "Are you all right?" he asked, cautious again.

"No, I'm not!" Oliver exploded, his own frustration needing outlet. "I've got to figure out some way of telling Leslie what I do without having her positively despise me for not having told her in the first place. I'm *not* all right. It's become an emotional issue; she's apt to hate me."

The voice on the other end of the line was instantly contrite. "And that matters to you?"

"Damned right it matters! Not that I'd particularly want you for a brother-in-law knowing that you concocted this cock-and-bull scheme in the first place . . . !"

Satisfied, Tony sat down in his chair. "She was the one with the idea, Oliver," he said indulgently. "I simply set it into motion."

"Same difference. Damn, it's hard."

"Can I help?"

"Don't you dare. As a matter of fact, don't you dare repeat a word of this conversation to Leslie! I may have made a mess of things, but it's my mess, and I'll be the one to clean it up."

"She's got fire in her."

He gave a wry nod. "Tell me."

"Think you can handle her?"

"I'll handle her."

"Okay, pal." Tony was smiling broadly. "And Oliver?"

"Yeah?"

The smile grew more mischievous. "Good luck." If anyone could handle Leslie Parish, her brother mused, Oliver Ames could. Despite this minor and surely temporary misunderstanding, things had worked out well indeed.

Oliver wasn't in quite as optimistic a frame of mind when he hung up the phone. Love did strange things to otherwise rational people. It made them lose perspective and overreact. That was what he wanted to avoid.

Back in the living room, he opened the bar and poured himself a drink. Its warmth was the first he'd felt since . . . since he'd made love to Leslie so early that morning. Just that morning—it was hard to believe. He remembered every sweet moment; even now could feel the fragile shape of her in his hands. She'd been so honest and giving in her lovemaking. She'd lived true to her word. Not for a minute, though she hadn't said it aloud, had she hidden from him the fact of her love. And not for a minute did Oliver believe that he was vainly imagining it. He hadn't asked for love, hadn't gone looking for it. But feeling the all-consuming need he had to be with and share with and do for Leslie, seeing an identical desire written on her face time and again, he knew. Leslie loved him. He loved her. All that remained was for him to tell her what he'd done and why.

Bidden in part by determination, in part by the sheer need to hear her voice, he returned to the kitchen and lifted the phone. Information quickly gave him her number. As quickly he punched it out. The phone rang once, then a second time.

"Hello?" She sounded breathless, as though she'd come running.

"Leslie?"

A smile lit her voice. "Hi," she said softly.

"You got home all right," he ventured likewise.

"Uh huh. And you?"

"Okay. I'm . . . cold."

"I know the feeling." It was only incidentally related to the abrupt change in temperature to which their bodies had been exposed in the past few hours. "Your house was okay? No problems?" She lived in a small Tudor home on a wooded lot, she'd said. He worried about her being so alone.

"Just quiet." Her voice fell to a whisper. "And lonely."

"I miss you," he murmured in lieu of taking her in his arms and kissing her loneliness away.

"Me too." She paused then and, sensing that she wanted to go on, he gave her time. "Oliver," she began again and timidly, "when will I see you?"

The utter smallness of her voice cut him to the quick. He could imagine how she'd fought asking. She'd want to be so sophisticated and cool and unclinging. He hated himself for having forced her hand, though he found solace in this further evidence of her love.

"That's why I'm calling, sweetheart. I'd like us to spend next weekend together. Just the two of us at my place up north. I could pick you up Friday night and have you back Sunday. How about it?"

"I'd love to, Oliver." Her voice glowed. In turn he smiled.

"I wish it could be sooner. Friday sounds so far off. But this week will be crammed...after last."

Her laugh was a light, airy sound that made him float. "What is it this week...say, what *do* you do, other than cologne?"

His bubble threatened to burst. "Oh, clothing and stuff. Have you spoken to Tony?"

"Not yet. I'll have to give him a call to thank him for my...birthday present." Her voice lowered. "Thank you again."

"For what?"

"For...taking care of me when I was sick, for making the rest of the week so wonderful, for the necklace."

"Are you wearing it now?" Closing his eyes he pictured her as she'd stood before him last night, wearing nothing but the moonlight and that strip of gold with its amethyst eye.

"Yes. I'm wearing it," she murmured shyly.

"I'm glad." He smiled, then realized that he could sit forever saying small nothings to her. But he wanted to tell her he loved her—and he feared doing that. "Well, then, how does six on Friday sound? We can stop for dinner on the way."

"Sounds perfect."

"I'll be looking forward to it." His voice was suddenly lower and faintly hoarse.

"Me too."

"Take care, Les."

"You too. And Oliver?"

"Yes?"

"I...I...thanks for calling."

"Sure thing, sweetheart. See you Friday."

For several minutes after hanging up the phone, he sat where he was, basking in the glow that lingered. She was a wonder...so thoroughly lovable. And she'd had more courage than he. She'd nearly said it. I love you. Why couldn't he say the words? He admitted them freely to himself, had even implied them to Tony. Was it that he'd feel hypocritical telling Leslie he loved her while he knew he'd been less than forthright on other matters? Was it that he feared she might not believe him in *this* when he finally did confess to his deception?

The glow was gone by the time he stood up, replaced by a shroud of concern. He'd tell her this weekend after they arrived at his place. They'd be isolated and, aside from his own car, more or less stranded. She'd be stuck with him. She'd have to hear him out. And he'd have the whole weekend to prove his love one way or the other.

That decided, he returned to the front hall and picked up the thick pile of waiting mail. An hour later he retreated to the den, pushed several buttons on his telephone console and sprawled out on the dark leather sofa with an arm over his eyes to listen to the phone messages for the week.

An hour after that he was ready to return to St. Barts.

LESLIE, TOO, had gone through her mail and then taken to the phone, but in a more active capacity.

"Tony?"

"Les! How are you?"

"Great." Silence. She was grinning like a Cheshire cat. "Thanks, Tony. It was a super birthday present."

"Liked it?" he asked smugly.

"Uh huh."

"I thought you would. He's quite a guy."

"Uh huh."

"So." It was like pulling teeth, in addition to which, he felt decidedly duplicitous. "Will you be seeing him again?"

"Uh huh." Her pulse sped at the thought. "He's got a place in the Berkshires. We're going up this weekend."

"Great!" he exclaimed. So Oliver had decided to make his pitch in the Berkshires. Secluded. Romantic. *Good luck, pal.*

"How's everything here, Tony?"

"Fine. Busy. Dad's still in Phoenix."

"Still? I thought he was due back last week."

"He was...."

She smiled. "But the golfing was too good."

Tony chuckled. "Something like that."

"And the kids are well?"

"Raising Cain in the other room. You mean you can't hear the noise?"

"Why aren't they in bed?"

"Because it's back to school tomorrow. And the law of adolescence says that one positively cannot be awake and aware on the morning following a school vacation. Heaven forbid they should be in condition to learn."

She laughed. "Perverse little things, aren't they? So why isn't their father laying down a law of his own?"

"Because he's talking with you."

"Oh. Good reason. Well, then I won't keep you long. I want to give Bren and Diane calls anyway. They're both doin' all right?"

"Brenda's fine. The kids had a ball skiing. She and Larry have about had it with lugging skis and poles and boots back and forth to the slopes, but otherwise Vail was to their liking." He paused, frowning. "Diane's the one who's got me worried."

"What's wrong?"

"I'm not sure. She's been behaving really strangely. She took off by herself last Monday and Tuesday, had Brad worried to death until he finally found a note buried at the bottom of the mail."

Leslie, too, was worried. Diane had always been a little high-strung, and it was obvious that she hadn't been happy of late, but she'd never disappeared before. "Where was she?"

"In a hotel."

"In the city?"

"Uh huh. Just sitting by herself. Thinking, she said. I couldn't get much more out of her. When she came home Tuesday night she was pretty subdued."

"How have things been going for her at the office?"

Tony sighed. "According to Gaffney, things have been tough. She's difficult to work with and getting worse all the time. Demanding and unpredictable. Very temperamental. Why don't you give her a call, Les? Maybe you can find out what's bothering her."

Leslie gave a facetious grunt. "I know what's bothering her. It's Brad."

"Come on. Brad's not that bad."

"Tony, he's fooling around, and you know it!"

"What else is new?"

"Diane knows it, too. Discretion has never been one of his stronger points."

"Yeah, but a lot of the time it's just talk—"

"Which can be nearly as hurtful."

"Come on, Les. I can't believe that Diane would be threatened by talk. Brad wouldn't go out of his way to humiliate her."

"You're sure of that?" she asked skeptically.

Tony hesitated, then gave vent to his own frustration. "Of course I'm not sure! The guy may be a great businessman, but we've never been terribly close. I can't know what he'd do. All I do know is that if Di doesn't shape up, he may have just cause to wander."

"That's an awful thing to say, Tony, particularly since he's the thing preventing her from shaping up! Okay, I'll grant that Diane's had other problems. But can you imagine how she must feel when she hears about each of Brad's little . . . diversions? *Your* wife was a wanderer. How did you feel?"

"A low blow, Les."

"And well aimed. How did you feel?"

He pondered her question, then spoke with uncharacteristic seriousness. Gone was all pretense of the invincible male. Left was a man whose home life had fallen apart. "Angry. Hurt. Confused. Embarrassed. Insecure."

Much the same way Leslie had felt when she'd discovered that Joe Durand was married. Much the way she couldn't help but feel at the thought of Oliver with . . . other women. . . .

"Thank you for being so honest," she said more gently. "Now try to think of Diane living with, or trying to live with, those same feelings."

There was a meaningful silence. "Isn't that something she's got to work out with Brad? We can't give her much more than emotional support."

"Exactly. Let me call her. Maybe she'll talk to me. Sometimes just being able to air things helps."

"You know, Les," Tony breathed over the phone, "you're a good person."

"I'm her sister."

"There was a time way back then when you wanted nothing to do with the Parishes," he reminded her softly. "We thought we'd lost you to the West Coast."

"I needed breathing room, Tony. I still do. I guess I'm just fortunate in that I've found plenty of it."

She heard a riot of sounds in the background, then Tony's voice aimed away from the phone. "Leave him alone, Jason! If you boys don't.... Mark, go upstairs!" The voice returned. "Listen, hon, I've got to run."

"So I hear. Go ahead, Tony. I'll call Di. And...thanks again for Oliver."

Her brother smiled warmly. "My pleasure. And many happy returns."

Mirroring his smile, Leslie hung up the phone. Memories of Oliver warmed her for the moment. Then, unable to shake her concern, Leslie did put in a call to Diane. A disgruntled Brad announced that she was in her room reading and had left orders not to be disturbed. Reluctant to force the issue and possibly increase the tension between husband and wife, Leslie simply left word that she'd call the next day.

It was easier said than done. Round and about her own hectic schedule, she tried to reach Diane at the office three times. Each time she was out. It was not until after dinner that evening that Leslie finally made contact. What ensued was the most unproductive conversation she'd ever held with another adult human being.

"Di?" When there was no sound of recognition, she identified herself. "It's me. Leslie." When there was still no sound, she prodded gently. "Are you there?"

"Yes."

"How are you?" When again there was silence, she babbled on. "I tried you last night after I got back from St. Barts, but you were reading."

"I'm okay."

"Are you sure? You sound awful."

"Thanks."

"I didn't mean that in offense. Just concern." Silence. "Is everything all right there?"

"Yes."

She dared. "Brad's okay?"

"Yes."

"Hey, I'm not interrupting dinner, am I?" There had to be some excuse for her sister's curtness. Perhaps she and Brad were in the middle of a fight, and Brad was standing right there.

"No."

"Listen, maybe we could meet for lunch one day this week."

"Maybe. I'll get back to you."

"How about Wednesday?" Leslie blurted. Tomorrow sounded obvious.

"I don't know. I'll have to get back to you."

"Will you?" Even in the best of times, Diane was notoriously bad at returning calls. It was one of the things her business associates were always yelling about.

"Yes."

"Try to make it Wednesday."

"I'll call you."

"Please, Di. I'd really like to talk." Leslie tried to make it sound as though she were the one with the problem. The subtle suggestion went right over her sister's head.

"I said I'd call you," Diane snapped back impatiently.

"Okay, Di. Talk with you then."

Diane hung up the phone without another word, at which point Leslie promptly called Brenda. Between them they were no closer to knowing what to do about Diane.

"Maybe something happened at the office?" Leslie suggested in trying to explain Diane's sudden turn for the worse.

Brenda sighed. "Possible. Not probable."

As Leslie had talked with Tony, she now raised the issue of their sister's shaky emotional state with Brenda. "So what do we do?" she asked. Of the three other Parishes, Brenda was the only one she'd ever leaned on. Capable and serious in business matters, Brenda had a level head on her shoulders. Ironically, the errors she'd made in her personal life were attributable to this very compulsion for order.

"We keep the lines of communication open. You'll have lunch with her Wednesday—"

"Wait a minute. I was the one who proposed Wednesday. Diane refused to commit herself. I'd put money on the fact that she won't even call me."

"Then you'll call her again. Try tomorrow night. Bug her until she caves in."

"I'm telling you, Bren, she really did sound like stone."

"I know. But she'll be all right."

"Maybe she needs professional help," Leslie ventured cautiously, though she could have predicted Brenda's response. None of the Parishes were fans of psychiatry, though Brenda was worse than the others. A computer person at heart, she believed there to be a sane, systematic, physical explanation for just about everything that happened in life. When her first marriage fell apart, she considered it a victim of the occupational hazard of being a full-time working mother. There simply had not been hours enough in her life to accommodate a demanding husband. Larry, her second, was a warmer, more easygoing man who was very satisfied to take Brenda when she was free. In turn, Brenda seemed free more often, though she'd never admit to the deep emotional need she had for Larry. He, saint that he was, was confident enough not to demand such a confession.

"A shrink?" Brenda asked with obvious distaste. "I doubt it. No, there has to be something more immediate that's causing her to clam up and act strangely. You're right. She's always been shaky. Which is all the more reason why something's got to have triggered her now."

"Well," Leslie sighed, discouraged, "I'll try to get her out with me. I'll let you know what happens."

As though her mind's computer had filed one document and called up another, Brenda's voice lightened. "Hey, you haven't told me about your trip."

Her trip. Mention of it brought an instant spot of warmth to her heart, an instant glow to her cheeks. "It was great." How much did Brenda know? Had Tony told her about his little "joke"?

"Lots of sun?"

Brenda's what-else-is-new tone said it all. She knew nothing. And Leslie wasn't about to enlighten her until she herself felt more sure of Oliver. On St. Barts he'd been unswervingly attentive. Back here, though, even in spite of a weekend date, it remained to be seen whether his seeming affection would hold up. Once he got back out in that faster, glittery world of his....

"Yup," she answered with feigned lightness. "Lots of sun. I got a great tan."

"And rest?"

"That, too."

"Good. Okay, then, you'll keep me posted on Di?"

"Uh huh. Bye-bye, Bren."

Leslie hung up the phone thinking of Oliver. She'd been thrilled to hear from him earlier, after having spent the first agonizing hour at home convinced that he'd never call. Life on St. Barts had been so simple. Life in New York—ah, that was another matter. Theoretically, if she loved Oliver and he loved her, nothing could be simpler. But she could only guess at Oliver's feelings. He was a model and hence, to a certain extent, an actor. On St. Barts she would have sworn he loved her, but that had been part of the illusion she'd chosen to live. Back here, she just didn't know.

The weekend would only be telling to a point. He'd have had five full days to compare her with his other life. If he called on Thursday offering a lame excuse to cancel the weekend, she'd know. But even if the weekend went on as proposed and he was as wonderful as he'd been on St. Barts, would she be able to know for sure that he wasn't simply reliving his vacation fun, simply lusting his way through the weekend, using his home in the Berkshires as a substitute for the villa on St. Barts? Would she ever really know his feelings? More important, could she trust him fully enough to believe them? When she was with him, trust was automatic. But at moments away—at times such as these, of which there would be more and more—she doubted.

FOR LESLIE, the week was a trying one, filled with highs and lows and very little in between. While it was wonderful getting back to work, wonderful being at work where her mind could be occupied, her free time was quite the opposite. She thought of the restlessness she'd felt so strongly before she'd ever left for vacation, and she realized—as she had on St. Barts—what ailed her. The house was quiet. Meals alone were not really meals at all. Despite a backlog of paperwork, evenings dragged. And an empty bed—an empty bed was cold and forbidding. At times she was so very hopeful, so very buoyant and in love. At other times she was as down in the dumps as Diane appeared to be.

Ironically Diane's depression was the only thing that, in Leslie's free hours, gave her respite from her own love woes. As predicted, she didn't hear from Diane. Giving her the benefit of the doubt Leslie waited until Wednesday morning to call, striking out at the office, finally reaching her at home. No, she wasn't sick. No, she couldn't make it for lunch. No, she couldn't talk just then. Leslie hung up the phone more convinced than ever that something very definitely was wrong. On Wednesday night, with nothing better to do but brood about Oliver, she got in her car and drove to Diane's.

Brad answered the door. He was a man of average height, average looks, above-average business acumen and super-average ego. Beyond that, he was thoroughly charming in a thoroughly contrived way.

He smiled broadly. "Leslie! What a surprise. We weren't expecting you. How are you?" He stood aside to let her in out of the cold but left the door conspicuously open.

"I'm fine. How are you, Brad?"

"Very well. Hey, nice tan you've got there. You must have been somewhere warm."

Diane hadn't told him. Well, Leslie reasoned, there was nothing so awful about that. Diane would have no cause to keep Brad informed of the details of her family's comings and goings. "I spent last week at the villa. It was beautiful. Is Diane in?"

He shot her his most regretful smile. "She's in but she's sleeping."

"Sleeping? It's so early. Is she all right?"

"Fine. She's fine. Just been working hard, and I think it's tiring her. She's been concentrating on some new designs for the fall line."

"I see." It wouldn't pay to say that Diane had been out of the office every time Leslie had called. "You're sure she's not angry with me? I've been trying to talk with her since I got back, and she's been practically incommunicado."

Brad gave a loud laugh. "That's Diane," he said, then feigned a conspiratorial whisper. "It's the prima donna in her. I'm sure she's not angry. She'll get back to you as soon as things clear up a little."

On the surface the words were innocent. Delivered by Brad, however, who stood with his hand on the open door, they bore deeper meaning. Leslie felt distinctly unwelcome.

She shifted her stance and fingered her keys. "Well, then, I won't disturb you. You will call me if there's any problem, won't you?"

"What problem could there possibly be?" Brad asked, throwing his arm around her shoulder in a spurious show of affection that successfully turned her toward the door. *Not as subtle as usual,* Leslie mused, then reminded herself that she'd never been a great fan of Brad's. Even before he'd launched his playboy routine, she'd found him far too pretentious for her taste.

"Well, if there's anything. . . ."

"She'll be fine. Take my word for it."

He sent her on her way with a brotherly kiss on the cheek. Once in her car, Leslie quickly wiped it off and pulled out of the drive, reluctantly concluding that she'd done her best. Yes, she was still worried about Diane. But if Diane didn't want her help and Brad didn't want her help, she could only butt in so far. Besides, she was suddenly in the mood for thinking about Oliver.

As she drove home, she thought of how much more handsome he was than Brad. While she lingered on her living-room sofa over a cup of tea, she thought of how much more sincerely he came across. When she climbed into bed with a book, she thought of how he, and he alone, electrified her senses. Finally, despairing of concentration, she turned out the light and, setting doubts aside, gave herself up to dreams of how beautiful the coming weekend would be.

UNFORTUNATELY her dreams were to remain unfulfilled. Leslie had barely stepped foot in the house after work on Thursday when the phone rang. She nearly panicked. Her relief at finding that it wasn't Oliver calling to cancel on her was short-lived.

It was Brad, in a state of panic himself. "You've got to get over here, Leslie! I don't know what to do!" Gone was all pretense of composure. He sounded frantic.

Leslie's stomach lurched. "What is it, Brad? What's happened?"

"She spent the day in her room. When I got home a little while ago I found that she'd been on a silent rampage."

"What are you talking about?"

"Her scissors. She's taken her scissors to the sheets, the pillows, the drapes, the clothes . . . it's a mess!"

Images of destruction had begun to form in Leslie's mind's eye. "Calm down, Brad," she said, trying desperately to stay that way herself. "What's she doing now?"

"That's the problem. Now she's in the dining room breaking dishes. She just stands there throwing them on the floor. When I try to stop her she aims at me! You've got to come over, Leslie! I can't seem to get through to her. Nothing I say registers. I don't know what to do!"

Nerves in a bundle, Leslie hung her head and pressed her fingers to her temple. "Okay, Brad." She thought aloud. "You stay there. I'll be right over. Did you call Tony?"

"What can Tony do? He's about as understanding as a bulldozer!"

Though on the surface brother and brother-in-law had always gotten along, Leslie could understand that Brad was, in his way, intimidated by Tony. "Okay. I'll take care of it. You watch Diane and make sure she doesn't hurt herself. I'm on my way."

Pressing the cut-off button, she punched out Tony's number. Since he'd taken over as president of the company, he'd also taken over as head of the family. It was the handing of power down a generation, with the senior Parish happy to hold no more than a purely titular position.

Leslie impatiently tapped her foot as the phone rang repeatedly. The receiver was finally lifted just as an angry voice finished its statement, "...always the one who has to!" The voice lowered. "Hello?"

"Mark?"

"It's Jason."

"Jason. This is Aunt Leslie. Is your dad home yet?"

"Yeah. Just a minute."

"Thanks."

She raised her eyes to the ceiling, praying he'd hurry. When she heard a rustle at the other end of the line, she readied herself.

"Leslie?"

"Tony! Thank heavens you're there."

"You sound hassled, Les. What's up?"

"It's Di. Brad just called. She's gotten worse."

"How...worse?"

"Violent."

"Violent? *Diane?*"

As calmly as she could, Leslie related what Brad had told her. "I'm going over there now. Brad doesn't have the foggiest as to what to do. Not that I do, but she needs *something.*" When Tony remained silent, she prodded. "What do you think? Should we call someone? I mean, I'm not thrilled with the idea, but I'm nervous. It's fine and dandy to overlook strange behavior in the hopes it will go away, but when strange turns violent, it's scary."

Tony hesitated for only a minute. "I agree. Listen, I'll get on the phone. You go on over and see what you can do. I'll meet you there as soon as I can."

"Thanks, Tony," Leslie said, then quickly hung up and reached for the coat she'd discarded just moments before.

Tony was good at this type of thing—identifying resources, sifting through to find the cream of the crop. She felt assured that he'd come up with a qualified professional to treat Diane.

The scene at Brad and Diane's was gut-wrenching.

"Where is she?" Leslie asked the subdued Brad who answered the door. His face was pale, his hair disheveled. He bore a look of shock; she couldn't help but wonder how he'd managed to be so ignorant of Diane's mental state that he hadn't seen this coming. Then she chided herself for her insensitivity. The man's wife was falling apart. Cad he might be, yet he had a right to be upset.

"She's in the den," he said grimly.

Leslie glanced toward the dining room. Even from where she stood she could see shards of fine white china littering the oak floor and overflowing onto the rug. She frowned and looked around, listening. "She's quiet?"

"She ran out of plates. And steam, I guess. She's just sitting there crying."

Thrusting her coat toward Brad, she headed that way without a word. On the threshold, she faltered. Diane sat, a petite form in a long white robe, curled in an oversize armchair in the corner. Head bent, one hand to her face and another tucked against her waist, she was a pathetic figure.

"Di," Leslie whispered in agony, leaving the door and quickly crossing the room. She knelt before her sister's chair and placed her hands on its arms for support. "Di, what is it? Di?"

Diane's sobbing was quiet and internal, far different from the violent behavior she'd exhibited earlier. When she continued to cry, Leslie coaxed her gently.

"Diane, it's me. Leslie. I want to talk. Come on. Say something."

Very slowly Diane raised tear-drenched eyes. Time seemed to fly back to the day she'd been eighteen and had lost the most important gymnastic competition of her life. She looked crushed.

"Leslie?" she murmured in a small, high voice.

As though Diane were one of her preschoolers rather than actually two years older than her, Leslie reached up to tuck a long brown wave of hair from her cheek. "What is it, Di?" she asked gently. "What's bothering you?"

"Oh, Les," Diane began with a new rush of tears, "I've . . . made a mess of . . . things. I've really . . . blown it."

Leslie took her hand and held it firmly. "No, you haven't. Everything can be put to rights."

Diane was shaking her head even as Leslie spoke. "No. No. You don't understand. It's . . . everything. I'm lousy at the office. They override every decision I make. I'm lousy here. He finds his pleasure everywhere else—"

"No, Di—"

"It's true!" Diane cried, eyes suddenly flashing. "I hate him! I hate all of them!"

"Shh. You don't mean that—"

"I do!"

For a minute Leslie just rubbed the back of her sister's hand. If Diane were indeed four years old, she'd know what to say. Even now her temptation was to acknowledge that she had simply thrown one hell of a temper tantrum and now just needed a good talking to. But it wasn't that simple. Diane wasn't four; she was thirty-two. And her temper tantrum had involved acts that could easily have been harmful to herself. Then there had been the days of depression beforehand. . . . Where was Tony? Where was help?

"You may feel that way now, Di, but you're angry."

"I'm . . . not . . . angry. . . ." She dissolved into tears again.

Rising from her kneeling position, Leslie perched on the arm of the chair and tried to put her arm around her sister. When Diane resisted, burrowing more deeply into the cushions, Leslie had to settle for her hand again.

"Can I get you anything? A glass of wine? Warm milk?"

Crying softly, Diane simply shook her head.

"How about lying down?"

"I . . . can't. The room's destroyed."

"You could lie down on the sofa here." She started to get up. "I'll get a blanket—"

"No! I . . . don't want . . . to lie down!"

Feeling totally inadequate in the role of therapist, Leslie patted her hand. "Okay, hon. We'll just sit here."

"You don't have . . . to stay. . . ."

"I know."

"I'm . . . such a burden. Now to you, too."

"You're not a burden," Leslie argued ever so softly and urgently. Her face bore a pained expression. She didn't think she'd ever seen such dire unhappiness, such raw despair as she now saw on her sister's face.

Then she glanced up and, in a wave of relief, saw Tony stride through the door. Her gaze fell again to Diane, and she wondered what her reaction would be to seeing him.

"Diane?" Tony said, hunkering down before her much as Leslie had done at first. "Are you all right?"

Diane looked up in alarm. "Tony! You . . . shouldn't be . . . here!" she cried between sobs, wrenching her hand from Leslie's to cover her face with it. "I don't want . . . you to see. . . ."

"Diane, I've brought someone with me. He'd like to talk to you."

Only then did Leslie look up, her expression hopeful in a desperate kind of way. Then she froze. Her eyes grew larger. Hopefulness yielded to confusion, creating such a whir of sounds in her head that she barely heard Tony's words.

"This is Dr. Ames, Diane. He's going to help you."

8

SHOCKED, Leslie watched as Tony straightened and moved aside to let Oliver take his place. Dr. Ames. *Dr.* Ames? The man in question shot her a somber glance before turning his attention to Diane.

"Hi, Diane," he said in a low, gentle voice. "Not feelin' great?"

Diane looked up, first at Tony, then Leslie, her tear-streaked face accusing them of betrayal. "What is this?" she whispered.

Leslie couldn't possibly have answered. She felt numb, as stunned as Diane. Tony chose not to answer. It was Oliver who came to the rescue.

"I'd like to help you."

"But . . . you're a . . . psych. . . ."

"A psychiatrist. That's right." His voice was miraculously calm in light of the anguished expression he sent toward Leslie, who was far too busy comprehending his words to begin to see the pain accompanying them.

A psychiatrist? It had to be some kind of joke. This was Oliver of Homme Premier fame. Free heart. Golden boy. The man she'd once actually thought to be a gigolo. *Her* Oliver. His skin bore its familiar tan, his features their familiar shape. And the silver C behind his ear—it was there as well.

Yet something was different. Was it the tailored slacks he wore, or the blazer or shirt or tie? Was it the air of authority about him? But he'd had that even on St. Barts. Now, though, it was . . . professional.

Stupefied, Leslie raised glassy eyes to Tony, who was looking directly at her. Obviously feeling Diane to be in the best of hands, his concern had shifted. In an instant Leslie realized that he'd known all along. Of course. They played tennis together, didn't they? They were friends. Tony had known just whom to call tonight.

Feeling superfluous at the moment and badly in need of fresh air, Leslie stood abruptly and started for the door. But Oliver caught her arm. His voice was calm, his expression well schooled. Only his fingers, fiercely circling her wrist, betrayed the intensity of emotion within him.

"Why don't you wait in the other room," he ordered softly. "I'll be out to talk with you in a minute."

Releasing her hand he turned back to Diane, to all appearances having done nothing more than offer support to the distraught relative of his patient. Tony knew better. He followed Leslie out, leaving Oliver to deal with Diane.

Feeling on the verge of suffocation, Leslie ran to the front door and opened it. She stood gasping the cold air when Tony reached her.

"Leslie?"

She shot him a look of bewilderment, then looked back out at the driveway, a bleak winter scene.

"It's all right, Les. There's really nothing so terrible about a psychiatrist."

"A psychiatrist?" she echoed dumbly. "I can't believe it. He's a model. A handsome model."

"No, Les. He's a handsome psychiatrist who happens to model on the side."

"But I . . . he can't . . . I never. . . ." She shook her head in confusion and slumped sideways against the door.

"Come on in, Les. You'll catch cold."

"I've already had my cold. He took care of me. A doctor...damn!"

"It's really no big thing—"

"No big thing?" she exclaimed, turning the force of her upheaval on Tony. "That's easy for you to say! You weren't the one who spent the week with the guy! You weren't the one who believed his lies!" And he certainly wasn't the one who'd fallen in love. In deep pain, she turned her head. "He didn't tell me," she murmured. "All that, and he didn't tell me...."

Watching the agony his sister endured, Tony felt hamstrung. It would be so simple to tell her of Oliver's pain, but he'd promised his friend that he'd keep out of it. It was bad enough that the revelation had been forced upon them tonight; for that, too, Tony felt responsible. Too late he wondered if he might have been able to keep Leslie away from this house; unfortunately, at the time, he'd been more concerned with seeing that Diane was all right. Brad seemed useless. Even now he stood at the door of the den, his eyes downcast, his charm nonexistent.

"Come in from the cold, Les," Tony said again.

She looked up, uncomprehending at first, frowning in puzzlement. Then, as though suddenly given direction she pushed off from the doorjamb and moved into the house, but only to put on the coat that Brad had dropped on a nearby chair.

Tony eyed her cautiously. "Where are you going?"

With her coat hanging open, she dug her keys from the pocket and turned to the door again. "Home." She felt numb and simply wanted time and space to consider what she'd learned.

"Wait, Les! You can't leave!"

"Why not?"

"Diane. Diane needs you."

"Diane's got capable help. He *is* capable, I assume," she snapped sarcastically.

"The best. But she'll need our support, too."

"You stay here. And Brad's here, for what that's worth. I only know that I wouldn't be much good to her tonight." She was already outside and halfway down the steps."

"But Oliver said to wait—"

"Tell Oliver," she yelled on the run toward her car, "that I don't take orders from anyone! Least of all *him!*"

"Leslie . . . !"

But she had slammed the door and started the engine before he could say any more. He stood helplessly and watched as she whirled her car around and gunned from the drive, praying that she'd have the sense to slow down before she got herself killed. Glancing at his watch, he calculated the amount of time it would take for her to drive home. Then, vowing to call to make sure she was all right, he quietly closed the door and turned back toward the den.

Oliver had drawn a chair up close to Diane and continued to talk to her in a slow, soft reassuring manner. At Tony's return, he stood, squeezed her shoulder and walked to the door, where he gestured with his chin toward the hall. When Tony joined him there, he spoke in hushed tones.

"I think she's gotten the worst of it out of her system. She's tired and confused. I'll give her something to help her sleep." He glanced up briefly when Brad joined the conference, then swung his attention back to Tony. "Is there someone who can stay with her?" He frowned and looked around. "Where's Leslie?"

"She's gone home," Tony ventured hesitantly, at once aware of the way his friend's jaw tensed at the news.

Oliver thrust his fingers through his hair. "Swell," he muttered under his breath, then turned to Brad. "Your wife is upset. She'll need to rest and then talk with someone. I'll stay with her until she falls asleep. Can you get her to my office tomorrow morning?"

Unbelievably, Brad grew nervous. "You don't think she should be, uh, hospitalized?"

"No, I don't," Oliver decreed, his voice low and taut. "Hospitalization at this point would only upset her more."

"But what about what she's done?" Brad countered. "What if she wakes up and turns violent again?"

"She won't. She's let off the worst of the steam…and she's got our full attention. Now she needs our understanding and support."

"She doesn't want *me* to do anything for her," Brad went on in a sulking tone. "I tried before. She wouldn't let me near."

"That's because you're very much a part of her problem," Oliver stated with a decided lack of sympathy for the man who'd been so blind to his wife's worsening mental state. Tony had filled him in on the history of the Weitzes' married life, and though it wasn't Oliver's job to pass judgment, he couldn't deny his anger. Any more than he could deny his need to get out of this house and go after Leslie. "Tony tells me you've got a housekeeper."

"Some help she is," Brad grumbled. "She's been hiding in the kitchen through all of this."

"Can I see her?"

"I guess so." With a parting glance of irritation toward the dining-room door, Brad stalked off toward the kitchen.

"Nice guy," Oliver couldn't help but observe.

"Yeah. But Diane loves him. At least she did."

"She still does or she wouldn't have gone off the deep end like this."

Tony grew more alert. "Has she, Oliver? What's the prognosis for this kind of thing?"

Oliver shrugged. "I've only talked with her for a few minutes. But between that and what you've told me, I think she's got very workable problems."

"You can help her?"

"In time." He frowned, his eyes clouding. "I just hope I'm the one to do it."

"Why not? You're the best."

He snorted. "Be that as it may, I happen to be emotionally involved with your *other* sister, and that fact could complicate my treating Diane." Hands in the pockets of his slacks, he crossed the hall to stand by the front bay window.

Tony was quickly by his side again. "Come on, Oliver. Don't make me go to someone else in a matter as sensitive as this."

Something in his voice, a note of urgency, pricked Oliver's curiosity. "Your family isn't big on psychiatry, is it?"

"Why do you say that?" Tony returned defensively.

"Because, among many families in your social stratum, psychiatrists have become standard fixtures. I'm surprised that none of you thought to call in someone earlier."

"We didn't want to interfere. We thought it was a matter between Diane and Brad. It wasn't until today that we realized how bad things were. Leslie's been trying to see Diane all week, but she'd put her off each time...." When Oliver simply continued to stare expectantly at him, he scowled. "All right. We're not big on psychiatry. My mother was pretty unhappy during the last years of her life. We don't talk about it much, but I think we all agree that the guy she was seeing didn't do her much good."

"She was seeing a psychiatrist?" Leslie had never mentioned this. "Why?"

"Depression. Anger. Loneliness."

"With a husband and four kids?"

"It was the husband she wanted, and he was never around. What with business trips and all...." He'd said enough, without elaborating on the "and all." "The kids could only fulfill certain needs. She had a slew of others that were never addressed."

"How did she die?"

"She didn't commit suicide, if that's what you're thinking. She had cancer. I think she just . . . gave up. Not much difference, I suppose."

Oliver was given no time to comment, for Brad returned with a shy-looking woman in tow. Introductions were made, at which point Oliver spoke kindly to the woman, asking her to check in on her mistress at intervals during the night. Diane was not to awaken alone. She was to be made comfortable and given food or drink or anything of the like that she wanted. And he was to be called if there was any further problem.

Returning to Diane, Oliver gave her a sedative and helped her upstairs to a bedroom at the opposite end of the house from the one she'd torn apart. All the while he talked quietly with her, demanding little, letting her speak as she wished. The housekeeper brought the glass of warm milk he'd requested; he supported Diane while she drank. Then, denying the gremlins that thudded impatiently inside him, he sat by her bedside until the sedative took effect, leaving only when he was sure she was asleep.

LESLIE WISHED she were out of it. Her mind was in a turmoil from which neither the sobering drive home nor her arrival at her own warm, familiar house nor a glass of her best and most mellow wine could rescue her. She picked up the mail, looked through it, put it down. She turned on the television, ran the gamut of channels, switched it off. She went to the refrigerator, stared at its contents, shut the door without touching a thing.

Wiping a single tear from her eye, she climbed the stairs to her bedroom and lay down in the dark. She felt hurt and tired, stretched taut by the emotions that gathered into a tight knot deep inside.

When the phone rang, she simply glared at it. Then it rang a second, a third and a fourth time and she realized it might well be Brenda calling in concern about Diane.

"Hello?" she began cautiously, prepared to hang up if it was Oliver.

It was Tony. "Thank goodness," he breathed. "You got home all right."

"Of course I did," she answered in quiet relief, then growing irritation. "What could have happened?"

"The way you were driving, I wasn't sure."

"I'm all right."

"Are you?"

"Relatively speaking."

"He wasn't pleased that you'd left."

"Tough. How's Diane?"

"He took her to bed."

"Oh, great."

"He *brought her upstairs*. He gave her a sedative and said he'd talk with her until she drifted off."

"Then what?"

"Then he'll probably go after *you*."

Leslie scowled in frustration. "Then what does he have planned for Diane? One sedative and a good-night talk is hardly going to solve her problem."

"He'll see her in his office tomorrow."

"That's good of him."

"It is, given the fact that he's booked solid, and that he's got serious reservations about treating her, what with his relationship with you. Come on, Leslie. Ease up."

"Relationship with me," she muttered to herself. "*What* relationship? A relationship based on lies is nothing!"

Tony started to argue, then caught himself, fearing he'd only make things worse. "Listen," he said in his most placating tone, "Oliver will explain everything, I've got to run. I'll catch you later."

"Sure," Leslie murmured, hanging up the phone and lying back in the dark again. She didn't know how much time passed, only knew that she couldn't motivate herself to do anything but lie there and wonder how she'd managed to get hurt again. It hurt. It did hurt. As the numbness slowly wore off, the sting had begun.

When the front doorbell rang, she wasn't surprised. She'd known he would come. The male mind was very predictable when it came to bruised egos, and she'd bruised his with her refusal to hang around at Diane's house. No, it hadn't taken psychiatric wizardry to anticipate his move.

She lay in the dark listening. The bell rang again and again. When he began to pound on the thick wood, she simply turned onto her side and huddled in a tighter ball. When the back bell rang, again followed by knocking, she flipped onto the other side. She heard the vague echo of her name and found perverse satisfaction in his annoyance. His ego certainly was bruised; small solace for the tatters to which he'd reduced hers!

To her amazement, he gave up after several minutes. She grew more alert, listening closely for any sounds of his prowling outside. But what could she possibly hear? Her bedroom was on the second floor. It was the middle of winter. Snow blanketed the ground, providing a natural cush-

ion for footsteps, while thick storm windows blocked out
not only the cold but extraneous noise as well.

It was spooky, she had to admit, lying here, wondering
if she was being stalked. She sat up to listen. Slipping quietly from the bed, she stood at the door. Everything was
still. Had he left, the coward? Had he tossed in the towel so
easily? Then it had been illusion, what she'd imagined he'd
felt on St. Barts. Illusion and deception—all she detested.

A sound caught her ear and brought her instantly alert.
A door shutting. In the kitchen? Then she heard footsteps
and nearly panicked. Someone was in her house. Someone
had broken in. The alarm...what had happened to the
alarm? Had she actually forgotten to reengage it after she'd
come in? Everything had been locked, she was sure of it.
Hand on her thudding heart, she stood rooted to the spot,
thinking she should call the police, waiting, waiting....

"Leslie! Where are you? I know you're here!"

Her heart continued to thud, despite the wave of relief
that swept over her. The footsteps came and went as he
passed from area rugs to hardwood floors and back. He
searched the living room, the dining room, the library, the
den. On stocking feet she walked quietly from her bedroom door to the top of the stairs. Though the lower floor
was bathed in light, she stood in darkness, waiting.

When Oliver reached the stairs and looked up, he saw her
instantly. Hand on the end curl of the wood banister, one
foot on the lowest rung of the steps, he stared up at her for
a moment.

"Come on down, Leslie," he said evenly, his manner
tautly reined. "We have to talk."

"How did you get in?" Her voice was as tight as his.

"Through the garage. The lock on the inner door was easy
to pick."

"That's breaking and entering, Oliver. Another of your surprise talents?" She hadn't moved, finding small comfort in the advantage of her raised position.

"The fact is," he snarled, whipping off his overcoat and throwing it over the bannister, "that it was a lousy lock. You should be better protected than that. I'm surprised no one's broken in before."

"Someone has. I have an alarm system."

"It did one hell of a job just now."

"It wasn't on."

"Swell! Your insurance company would be real pleased! So you're one of those who feels that the little sticker on the front window is enough to scare away a thug?"

"It didn't scare *you* away. What would you have done if the whole system had gone off, and you'd found yourself surrounded by cops? It's hooked in to the police station, you know."

"I would have told them the truth. And I certainly would have had your attention."

"Oh, you've got my attention, all right," she spat. "You've had that since the first time I found you in my bed. Thing is that I could get you for perjury."

Oliver simmered. "Come downstairs, Leslie. I can't talk standing here like this staring up into the dark. I'd like to see your face."

Her fingers tightened on the wood railing. "Why? So you can gauge my reactions and gear your words accordingly? So you can analyze my frame of mind and plot your counterattack? So you can—"

"Leslie! Get down here!" he thundered, then swore softly and lowered his voice. "Please. It's been a long day for both of us. I'm tired and no more wild about this turn of events than you are."

"I bet you're not," she bounded on, driven by the anguish festering within. "I bet you'd have liked to have kept the charade going a while longer. Fun."

Oliver shot her a withering stare, reached up to loosen his tie, then turned and headed for the den. In her mind's eye, Leslie saw him approach the bar, remove a glass, open the small refrigerator below, extract the same bottle she had earlier and uncork it. Only when she heard the refrigerator door close with a thud did she very slowly start down the stairs.

He met her at its bottom holding two glasses, his own and the one he'd refilled for her. Head high, she took it from him without a word and padded softly into the living room. It was a larger room, not quite as intimate as the den and, for that very reason, never a favorite of hers. On this occasion, she mused, it would serve just fine. She needed the space. She also needed four-inch spikes; she felt suddenly much smaller and more insignificant than she had before. It took all her courage to settle calmly into the armchair and tip her head at its most arrogant angle toward Oliver.

She waited in silence, determined to do nothing to put him at ease. For ease was the last thing she felt. Looking at Oliver, vitally aware of his very presence in her home, she felt as though she were being torn apart. Strange, when Joe had come to her apartment that last time, she'd felt angry and strong and vindictive. Now, though, angry and vindictive were simply for show, while strong was nonexistent. What *did* she feel? She ached—inside, outside, everywhere.

Oliver took several gulps of wine, then tugged his tie looser and unbuttoned the top collar of his shirt. Anchoring one hand in the pocket of his slacks, he looked down at her. "I was going to tell you this weekend," he said quietly.

"Were you." It wasn't a question, rather a statement whose blatant mockery was quickly punished by the piercing arrow of his gaze.

"I would have told you as soon as we arrived in the mountains, once I'd isolated you from the world so you wouldn't be able to run out of the house and barrel off in your car. That was a dumb thing to do, Leslie!"

"That's strange." She gritted her teeth against the hurt. "I thought it was pretty smart. I wasn't needed there. Diane was well taken care of."

"And what about us?"

"We were well taken care of, too."

"Well taken care of...as in finished?" he asked, his voice grating. "Not quite."

She sipped her wine without tasting a drop. Then she took another sip, a larger one in search of the inner warmth that totally eluded her. She drew her legs up under her and wrapped her arms about her waist. "I think so," she murmured. "You've ruined everything."

"Only if you decide that I have," he countered firmly. His jaw was clenched, his shoulders rigid. "I'm not Joe Durand, Leslie. I did nothing immoral. And I didn't set out to hurt you. That was the last thing I wanted to do."

"You lied."

"I never lied."

"You said you were a model. Not a psychiatrist. A model."

"I am a model. You've seen my work. I pose every so often just for the fun of it. And I never said I *wasn't* a psychiatrist. I just—" his voice lowered "—didn't say that I was."

"And that's not lying?"

"Technically, no."

"Then you're splitting hairs, Oliver. You let me go on believing that . . . that . . . oh, what the hell." Eyes moist, she looked away and took a fast drink of her wine.

"Go on."

And give him the satisfaction of seeing how badly she ached? "No."

"You disappoint me," he taunted. "You're a woman of strong opinions. You mean to say that you've suddenly gone private with them? Where's the woman who asked point-blank why I'd choose to spend a quiet week at her Caribbean villa rather than live it up at a nearby hotel?"

"Maybe she's wary of the answers. Maybe she knows not to trust them anymore." Finding small satisfaction in seeing Oliver wince, she once again sank into a dark, brooding silence. Bowing her head, she didn't see him set his wine down on the nearby coffee table. Only when his hands settled on the arms of her chair did she grow aware of the large body bent over her.

"That's bull," his voice rumbled near her ear. "Her pride's been hurt, and she's vulnerable and in love—"

Leslie snapped her head up. "She is not!"

"No?" he hummed, his lips near her cheek.

Momentarily unable to function, she closed her eyes. He was close and warm and beckoning. His smell, clean and natural even at the end of the day, titillated her senses. All week she'd waited to be with him. She wanted him so badly. . . .

"No," she whispered, reinforcing the lie. If he could do it, so could she.

"I love you, Leslie," he murmured, his own eyes closed, his own senses absorbing her closeness. All week he'd waited to be with her. He wanted her so badly. . . .

"No!" she screamed, taking him by surprise and bolting past him. Oblivious to the slosh of wine over her hand, she ran to the fireplace and turned to face him. "No!" she cried, suddenly shaking all over. "I don't want to hear it. You had plenty of time to say it before. You had plenty of time to say everything before. Now it's too late. I can't believe any of it!"

"Leslie—" He started toward her.

"Don't come hear me!" she yelled, cringing against the marble. When he continued forward, she tried to escape to the side, only to have her shoulders caught in the vise of his hands. "Let me go! I don't want you touching me!"

"You'll hear me out!" he growled, then grunted when her foot hit his shin. Rather than releasing her, he slid his hands to her upper arms for better leverage, then with one hand relieved her of her endangered wineglass. "Childish, Les. Really childish."

"You must be used to it," she gritted, trying to push against his arms and free herself. "You're the expert on temper tantrums." She twisted and turned, but to no avail. Even when she brought her knee up, she was thwarted. Anticipating her ploy, he easily blocked the move.

"You told me about that little trick once before. Remember? You shouldn't have tipped your hand."

"I didn't think I'd need to try it on you. Let...me...go!"

"No way," he growled, all but carrying her to the sofa. "You're going to hear me out if it kills us both."

"And then where will Diane be? Where will your other precious patients be? Where will the adoring public in love with the Homme Premier man be?"

Having shoved her into an upholstered corner, he stood over her, his hands on the sofa arm and back, barring her escape. "I don't give a good goddamn about anyone but you. And you will listen to what I have to say! Now, do I have to restrain you, or do you think you can try to behave yourself?"

"I am behaving myself," she said quietly.

He stared at her suddenly still form for a minute, then straightened. Taking a long, ragged breath, he walked to the far end of the room, turned back toward her, and tucked both hands in his pockets.

"When Tony suggested I spend a week on St. Barts, it sounded like a super idea. I was tired. I needed a vacation. When he told me about you and his little joke, I wasn't deterred. It sounded like fun, entirely harmless. Tony said you were the independent sort and that you'd probably go about your business as though I wasn't even there. Other than sharing laughs that first day, I didn't expect a thing."

"Got slightly more than that, didn't you," she murmured morosely.

"Slightly. I didn't expect an adorable purple elf with a whopper of a head cold bouncing into my bedroom to wake me up."

"Adorable?" She screwed up her face. "As in puppy? Something you trick into fetching slippers solely for the sake of a stale biscuit?"

His tone softened. "Adorable as in fresh and pretty."

"Come off it, Oliver! I was sweaty and hot." The last thing she needed was his sweet-talking, given her peculiar susceptibility to it.

"Sweaty and hot, then fresh and pretty...and needing my care." He came several steps closer. "You don't know what that does to a man in this day and age, to feel needed."

She eyed him skeptically. "You're needed all the time! Look at the way Diane needed you, not to mention the crew of unhappy people who must have brooded around Manhattan while you were away."

"Professionally, fine. I was talking personally. And on a personal level, it's nice to feel needed once in a while."

"Polishes that image of the macho protector?"

His lips thinned. "The image of the macho protector is nothing compared to the one you're trying to project of the hard-bitten independent woman. Sarcasm doesn't become you, Les."

She had no smart retort. He was right. She didn't care for her tone any more than he did, and the fact that she was merely lashing out in anger did nothing to sweeten the bitter taste in her mouth. She dropped her gaze to the fingers clenched in her lap and listened as Oliver went on in a softer tone.

"You saw me as the man from the ad. To tell you the truth, I kind of enjoyed it." When she raised her head and took a breath to protest, he held up a hand. "No, no, Leslie. I'm not making fun of you. It was from a selfish standpoint that I enjoyed it. It was a new image for me. Believe it or not," he said less surely, "I needed that."

"I don't believe it," she said, but without sarcasm. She was puzzled. It didn't make sense. "What could possibly be wrong with being a psychiatrist?"

"Do you like psychiatrists?"

"No . . . but my situation is different. And my bias is strictly emotional. From an intellectual point of view, I respect the fact that you've had to make it through med school to get into psychiatry."

"Thank you," he drawled with a touch of sarcasm of his own, then grew more firm. "But most people don't think of that when they meet me. They think of how eager I must be to hear their problems, how good I must be at reading their minds, how neurotic I must be myself. When a psychiatrist meets people, they usually fall into two categories. There are those who treat him like he's got the plague, who are aloof, who won't go near him for fear that he'll see something deep inside that they'd rather hide. And there are those who flock to him and tell him everything." His face contorted. "Do you have any idea how boring that can be?"

"Don't you like your work?"

"I love my work . . . *when I'm working.* Not twenty-four hours a day. Not when I want to relax. Not when I go to parties or dinners or the theater." In vehemence, his brows drew together. "It's damned frustrating to be constantly labeled. In the first place, I don't identify with many of my more eccentric colleagues. In the second place, *I'm a man.*" His voice had risen steadily. Suddenly, as though a bubble inside him had popped, he spoke more softly. "At any rate, that was why I didn't jump to correct your misconception when you assumed that I was a model. It was my vacation. What better way to escape reality than by taking on a new identity?"

His manner was so sincere that Leslie could almost believe him. Almost . . . but not quite. He'd seemed so sincere about everything before. She'd believed then—and felt humiliated now.

"But you let me say so many things," she argued with a surge of embarrassment, "things about women and action and—" she tried to remember them all "—and aging. I even implied that your parents might be ashamed of your work."

To her relief, Oliver didn't laugh. "And everything I answered was honest. My parents are proud of what I do. And I do model, Leslie. Even though it's a hobby, I get a significant amount of money for it. I don't stick around long enough to see the glamorous side. You imagined that; I simply did nothing to disillusion you." He took a deep breath and walked to the fireplace, where he stood with one elbow on the mantel, one foot raised on the hearth. His gaze raked the cold, ash-strewn grates. "Modeling is an escape for me. To spend an afternoon doing something as light as that is refreshing. I need it from time to time."

His voice seemed to hover in the air, then drop into a chasm of silence. Leslie tried to find fault with his reasoning, but couldn't. Oliver tried to find reasoning for his fault, but couldn't.

"I should have told you everything."

"You should have. Why didn't you?"

He looked at her then, his expression one of vulnerability. Not wanting to be affected, she lowered her eyes. But his words came to her nonetheless, accompanied by a note of urgency. "Because at first I enjoyed the role I was playing. Then, as the week went on, it grew stale. And about the time I realized that you were something very special to me, I got wind of your obsession with honesty."

"So why didn't you say something?"

"*I was scared!*" he bellowed, feeling angry and frustrated and embarrassed, just as Leslie had felt.

She wanted to doubt him. "You? Scared?"

"Yes," he answered somberly. "Me, scared. I wanted you. I needed you. You seemed to be everything I'd waited thirty-nine years for. I felt as though we'd gotten off to such a good start. I didn't know what to do. On the one hand, I didn't want you to know I was a psychiatrist. It's so...complicated sometimes. A model—that's simpler. On the other hand, I knew you'd be upset if I didn't tell you." He took a breath, then threw up a hand in frustration. "It was the old story. With each day that passed, it got more difficult. The longer the deception went on, the more I feared confessing to it. And in the end, the joke was on me. By the time we were ready to return to New York, I knew I loved you...and though I hated myself for having deceived you, I didn't know how in hell to correct the error without the risk of losing you completely."

He swallowed hard. His hand gripped the mantel until his knuckles were white. Gazing at Leslie, he hated himself all the more for having put that look of misery on her face. Somehow, some way, he had to convince her of his love.

"I tried to tell you, Leslie. Several times as the week went on, I tried to tell you. But you wouldn't let me, and I was happy enough not to push. There were times when I wondered if you knew. Once when you kiddingly called me Dr. Ames, another time when you begged me not to analyze things to death." His voice grew deeper. "Do you remember that time? We were on the terrace...." He started to move toward her but she quickly rose from the sofa and crossed the room to stand at the window with her back to him. In tailored wool slacks, a sweater and blouse, she looked every bit the successful businesswoman, every bit the caring teacher, every bit the woman he loved.

"I remember a comment you made," she began in a distant voice, her mind, too, back on St. Barts, "when I thought Tony had paid you to give me a good time. You laughed and said that nobody paid you for your time in chunks like that. I suppose I should have wondered what you meant, but I assumed you were talking of modeling. Deep down under all that wariness, I was so ... so anxious to believe." She shook her head in dismay. "What is it about me?" she asked herself. "After Joe, I swore I'd never be taken in. One week with you...and bam, I'm blind all over again."

Oliver came up from behind and stood at her side without touching her. "Love is blind," he said, casting a sad smile her way. "Haven't you heard that saying?"

She gave a meager excuse for a laugh. "Yeah. Dumb, isn't it?"

"Not dumb at all. I let love blind me to your need for the truth. I let it convince me to leave well enough alone." His voice took on a husky timbre. "I do love you, Leslie. And if you weren't so hurt and angry I think you'd admit that you love me, too."

"But I am hurt and angry," she argued, the proof of her words in her large violet eyes, which were open and pleading. "I feel . . . betrayed."

"Aw, Les," he moaned, "I haven't betrayed you." He reached out to touch her cheek, but she flinched and he let his hand drop. "Everything about me is the same as it was. Psychiatrist and model, they're one and the same. If you could love the model, why not the psychiatrist?"

"I didn't love the model!" she cried, grasping at the one illusion that might save her from the power Oliver had. For she felt it now—the need to touch him, to hold him and be held, to find oblivion in the fire of his passion. "I got...carried away by the romance of the island. That was what it was. Nothing more."

His gaze narrowed knowingly. "Is that why you were so quiet during the trip home? Is that why you so readily agreed to spend the weekend with me? Is that why you gave yourself to me with such abandon, why you'd do it again if I took you upstairs now? You 'don't sleep around.' Remember?"

Leslie's heart began to knot up. Whether it was his skill as a psychiatrist or simply that of a very perceptive man, he asked pointed questions. "You're good in bed," she heard herself say in a voice far cooler than the caldron heating within. "And I needed the escape. Maybe you weren't the only one trying to flee an image," she said, the words coming fast as the ideas formed. "Maybe I needed to shake the image of the down-to-earth schoolteacher for the week. Maybe I did have a ball. Maybe I was truly sorry to see my vacation end. Maybe my acceptance of your invitation for the weekend was nothing more than a wish to escape for two final days. Maybe I was playing a role, too."

She'd hit home. Oliver stood suddenly straighter. "I don't believe you."

"That's a shame. Funny...it seems to be a hazard of trips such as ours. When two people play for a week, it's hard to know afterward what's for real." Given strength by self-deception, she turned and headed for the front door. "I think you ought to leave," she said without looking at him. "The game is over."

"Not by a long shot!" Oliver exclaimed, coming from behind to whirl her around. "I don't believe a word you say. I know you, Leslie. I can see inside."

She pulled her arm from his grip. "Then you've got a double problem. Because if you want me to believe that, I'll have to believe all those stereotypes about psychiatrists. And if I do, I won't want to be around you. I've got secrets, just like everyone else. And I don't like the idea of being transparent." She took the few remaining steps toward the door and stood with her hand on the knob for support. Her legs felt like rubber. "Now are you going to leave, or do I call the cops and report a breaking and entering?" She crinkled up her nose in echo of her heart. "Wouldn't be good for the image, Ol. Either of them."

For a minute he stood staring at her. Though he hadn't believed a word she'd said, his claims to that effect had only hardened her. There had to be another approach, one that would be more successful. Unfortunately, he couldn't think straight. His insides were being chewed up; every bit of his energy was needed simply to keep his cool. Almost as an afterthought he remembered his overcoat on the bannister. Head down, back straight, he retrieved it, then returned to the door as Leslie opened it.

"This isn't the end, Leslie."

"I think so," she whispered, suffering behind a mask that barely hid her pain.

He simply shook his head. Daring to touch her because he needed to so badly, he lifted a hand to her face. When she tried to draw back, he anchored his fingers all the more firmly in her hair. "No, Les. What we had on St. Barts was unique. Most people go through a lifetime in a futile search for it. I'm done searching. All I have left to do is to prove that you are, too." He let his thumb drift ever so gently along her cheek to her lips. She wanted to pull back, to shake it off, to do anything but admit to herself how much she craved him. But she was rooted to the spot.

Again he shook his head, this time with a smile to match the tenderness of his touch. "We found a special something down there, and I'll be damned if I'm going to let it go."

For a split second, she thought he would take her in his arms. Her eyes widened. She swallowed hard. But while she was still trying to decide whether or not to fight, he dropped his hand, stepped away to put on his overcoat and left.

She stood in the doorway until his car was out of sight, then went upstairs and cried herself to sleep.

9

IT WAS A LONG two weeks before Leslie heard from Oliver again, two weeks rehashing all that had been said and done between them, two weeks of soul-searching. At first she'd been constantly on her guard, wondering when or where he'd show up . . . for she was sure he would show up. She'd seen that look of determination in his eye when he'd spoken of the special something he'd found, and her feminine intuition told her to beware.

At the start there was anger, anger that Oliver had deceived her, anger that she'd fallen for his ruse. And there was the hurt of betrayal. Yes, they had had a special something, but it had been built on delusion and was now destroyed.

The pity of it was that she'd wanted it, too, that special something. She couldn't deny it any more than she could deny that the mere thought of Oliver set her heart to beating with a vigor it lacked at other times.

Oh, yes, she'd wanted it. Before she'd ever gone to St. Barts she'd been aware of a lack in her life. She'd been restless and searching. Hadn't she debated going back to school, or worse, joining the corporation? But either of those options would have been stopgap measures for an ailment that went far deeper. She loved her work as it was. What was missing was a man, a home, children of her own. She wanted a relationship, a closeness, a warmth. She wanted love. She was thirty now; hadn't she waited long enough?

A special something. She had, indeed, found it on St. Barts. Illusion though it might have been, it had been divine while it lasted. Somehow in comparison the rest of her life paled dramatically.

By the end of the first week much of the anger and hurt had filtered away, replaced by an overwhelming sadness. She wanted to believe everything Oliver had told her that last night at her house, but she couldn't. She was afraid...afraid of trusting, then of being hurt all over again. What they'd once had had been so good; she felt as though she were mourning the loss of a limb or an ideal or a dearly beloved friend.

And she was lonely. So very lonely. Even during the hours she spent at one or another of the centers, she ached. There was some solace in the fact that Diane appeared to be responding to Oliver's ministrations. Though Leslie was unable to shake the vision of destruction at the Weitzes' house, regular phone calls to Tony, then to Diane herself, assured her of progress on that front. It was Brenda, however, who systematically homed in on Leslie's own malady.

"You sound down, Leslie," she commented during one evening's call.

"I'm worried about Di. You know that."

"And that's all?"

"Isn't it enough?"

"What about Oliver?"

Leslie stiffened, startled. "What about him?"

"Tony told me—"

"He had no business doing that!"

"He's your brother. He's worried."

"I told him I'd be all right."

"You don't sound it."

"Please, Bren. I don't want to argue."

But Brenda was insistent. "Is he very special . . . this Oliver?"

Very special? Ironic choice of words. For an instant Leslie wondered whether Brenda wasn't in cahoots with the man himself, then she chalked it up to coincidence. "Yes," she sighed wearily. "He is."

"Then give, Leslie. Give a little."

She'd already given her heart. What was left? "Brenda..." she warned.

"I'm trying, I'm trying," Leslie grumbled, and indeed she was; she was trying to envision her future, but it remained a muddle. Thoughts of Oliver tore at her endlessly. *Classic withdrawal*, she told herself. Persevere, and she'd be fine. But the ache persisted, and by the end of the second week she'd begun to despair.

Then the kitten arrived. She'd just gotten home when the doorbell rang. For an instant she stood frozen, wondering whether this was the time Oliver had chosen to pop back into her life. But it was a delivery truck on the drive, leaving a small brown-wrapped box in her hand when it drove away.

An F.A.O. Schwarz package? She had no idea. Then she peeled back the wrapping and unearthed the sweetest hand-sized toy kitten she'd seen...since...since she was seven and her own just like it had gone to the laundry and never returned. Her vision blurred as she stared at the tiny silver button in its ear. Steiff. And its name. Jigs. She smiled and sniffed and shook her head. Then, hands trembling, she reached into the box and extracted the card buried therein.

"Not a puppy to chase and fetch, but a kitten to purr and stretch and thrive on attention. I'd even indulge it its occasional bristling. All my love, Oliver."

Collapsing on a nearby chair with the kitten pressed to her heart and her head buried against her arm, she burst into tears. How could he remember such a small thing as that? How could he do this to her?

But he had. He'd sent her a teaser, then nothing. Another week passed without a word. Staring at the kitten each night, picking it up in her hands and holding it, knowing that Oliver had to have done the same when he'd bought it, she felt all the sadder, all the more lonely.

Predictably, with time, she grew used to thinking of Oliver as a psychiatrist. Unpredictably, given her annoyance that he should be something other than what she'd been led to expect, she grew curious. From model to psychiatrist—it was quite a switch. When she'd been on St. Barts she'd imagined what his life as a model was like. She'd never asked for details, feeling foreign enough, intimidated enough, to be wary of asking. He'd volunteered little. As she reflected on it, she realized that those few times she'd asked him questions he'd deftly turned the conversation around. At the time she'd simply thought him to be all the more modest, all the more attentive to her. Now she realized that his attentiveness had probably been not only habitual probing, but a diversionary tactic as well.

To think of him now as a psychiatrist conjured up quite a different picture of the way he spent his days. Rather than being in a studio, perhaps wearing a terry robe that he'd shrug off when it was time to climb into bed for the shooting of something akin to the Homme Premier ad, he'd be in an office, dressed in conservative slacks and shirt, tie and blazer, much as he'd been dressed when he'd come to Diane's house that night. Tony said he was skilled; indeed Diane appeared to have gotten a temporary handle on the more erratic of her emotions. Tony said he was busy. Leslie pictured him behind his desk, leaning far back in a chair, his long fingers steepled against his lips as he listened intently to his patient's words, interjecting questions or suggestions, concentrating fully on that one individual until the end of the hour, when, like clockwork, the guard would change.

To each patient he would seem all-attentive, fully engrossed. That would be part of his skill, making the patient feel wanted. Just as Leslie had felt wanted, and needed, and loved.

No sooner had she chased that thought from her mind than her curiosity went to work again. She wondered what time he went to work in the morning, when he got home at night, what he did evenings and on weekends. He'd obviously been free enough to invite her away. But certainly he had a social life, and most certainly it would be of a different class from that of a full-time model. Ironically, she assumed it would be similar to the kind of social life her family knew. Oliver appeared to be successful. He lived in Manhattan, had a place in the Berkshires, had been able to easily swing a trip to St. Barts, not to mention the beautiful gold necklace she wore, yes, every day. No doubt he lived well. No doubt he was part of that same social world she'd sworn off so long ago. . . .

As the days passed, she was prone to abrupt mood swings, high one minute and low the next. She'd miss Oliver with all her heart, then be glad he was gone. She'd be relieved he wasn't a model, then sad it should be so. She'd be proud to think of him as a psychiatrist, then furious at the way he'd so skillfully manipulated her mind. She'd be angry then contrite, indignant then forgiving. But through it all she was confused. Her future seemed more in limbo than ever before. She simply didn't know where she wanted to go, and the unsureness of it all gnawed at her constantly.

By the end of the fourth week, the unbuttoned ear of the small stuffed kitten had begun to show the imprint of her thumb. Much as she wished it weren't so, Oliver was never far from her thoughts. With March nearing an end, spring wouldn't be long. And spring, well, spring was a time for birth and brightness and love.

Had he had that in mind the day he sent the vase filled with violets? Violets...not drooping as she'd been that first day she'd arrived on St. Barts, but fresh and moist and gay. Had he known how desperately she'd needed word from him?

Her hand shook as she read the card written in the now-familiar bold scrawl. "I couldn't resist. I'll never see a violet without thinking of you. Care for them . . . please?" It was signed, "Love, Oliver."

She was more rattled than ever. Though ecstatic to receive his gifts, she was terrified to read too much into them. Worse, she was appalled at how much she wanted to read into them. She was wary and elated, distrustful and optimistic, and very much afraid of being hurt again.

Determined to view the violets as nothing more than a token, she put them in the center of her bright kitchen table and tried to go about her business as usual. She went to work each day at one of the centers, invariably brought paperwork home to do at night, had a pleasant if uninspiring dinner-date with a college professor she'd dated from time to time, spoke to Tony and Brenda, met Diane for lunch.

And the violets remained on her table. She gave them fresh water. She misted them. She recut their stems. She withered a little as each delicate face fell, dried up and had to be removed from the bunch. With no more than four or five flowers left, the vase began to look as lonely as she felt.

Then, on a rainy Wednesday evening that just happened to be April Fool's Day, Leslie came home from work to find a puddle of water accumulating in her basement frighteningly close to the furnace. Tired and discouraged, she was trying to get the sump pump going when the doorbell rang.

Struggling frantically, she poked and pinched in vain. Then the bell rang a second time. Swearing at the stubborn machine, she brushed off her hands as she ran up the stairs.

The house, a brick Tudor, had an inner door, a small foyer, then a thicker outer door with multiple locks. Dashing through the first door, she stood on tiptoe at the second to peer out its single window. She was saved! Flipping the locks, she opened the door.

Standing in the cover of the meager overhang was Oliver. His hair glistened; his raincoat was wet. Collar up, he was hunched over as though trying to protect himself from the rain.

Without a pause she stood aside to let him step quickly in out of the rain. His breathing came fast; he must have dashed from the car.

"Hi," he said, shaking out his sleeves. "Man, is it pouring! Listen, I'm sorry to barge in on you like this, but I was worried you wouldn't see me unless I took you by surprise—"

"Thank heavens you're here, Oliver! Do you know anything about sump pumps?" She reached up to help him out of his coat.

"Excuse me?"

"Sump pumps!" She hung the coat to drip on the tall brass coat stand, then led the way into the house and directly toward the basement door. "Do you know how they work . . . or what's wrong with them when they don't?" She was taking the stairs at a clip, calling back over her shoulder to the bemused figure following her lead. "I can't get the thing to work and my basement's beginning to flood and if the water keeps coming in the furnace is going to be knocked out and then I'll be without heat and—"

"Keep still for a minute while I take a look."

Oliver hunkered down and peered into the small hole of the compact piece of machinery that was barely above the water line. Shrugging out of his blazer and handing it to her, he rolled up his shirt sleeve, then reached in to locate a part here, to jiggle a part there, to fiddle with still a third, while Leslie looked on.

"I can't believe this is happening!" she exclaimed. "I have a service that comes in twice a year to check both the furnace and the pump. They assured me both were fine. What do you think?" she asked, anxiously clutching his blazer. "Should I call the plumber?"

"I think," he grunted, reaching lower to tug at a lever that momentarily resisted him, "that the guy simply had the thing turned off. It's stuck. Wait.... There." Sure enough, with a final forceful tug, Oliver had the pump started. Removing his hand from the water, he shook it, then stood.

"It wasn't turned on," Leslie stated as though any fool should have known it right off the bat. With an expression of exasperation, she shook her head. "Terrific April Fool's Day prank.... Here, let me get you a towel." She would have escaped up the stairs had Oliver not caught her hand.

"The towel can wait. I can't." He drew her toward him.

The basement was gray, lit by a sole bare bulb hanging over their heads like mistletoe. Leslie looked up at Oliver then, and in an instant was hit by the fact of his presence. *He was here.* He had come. Or was he nothing more than a tall, dark and handsome April Fool's Day mirage?

"Heeey, don't look so stricken," he whispered. "I'm only going to kiss you." And kiss her he did, with one large hand curved to her throat, the other arm around her back holding her closer.

Leslie was stunned. In a matter of seconds, every one of the emotions with which she'd been wrestling for five weeks declared war. She loved him, she didn't. She needed him, she didn't. She trusted him, she didn't. She wanted him, she didn't. But . . . she did.

His lips felt wonderful on hers, bringing back thoughts of warmer, more carefree days on a distant Caribbean isle. His arms were strong, his body large and hard and just right to lean upon. Any thought Leslie might have had of denying her physical attraction to him was negated by the helplessness of her response. She needed to feel the hungry movement of his mouth, needed to respond to him for just that minute, just that minute . . . until sanity slowly returned. Only then did she put her palms to his chest and exert the gentle force that would speak for her.

Oliver instantly released her lips and buried his in her hair. Both of his arms circled her now, hugging her tightly for a minute. "Oh, Leslie, I've wanted to do that night after night," he whispered, then loosened his hold as she'd requested.

Looking up, Leslie met the same warm brown eyes that had so enchanted her on St. Barts. In self-defense, she averted her gaze and hugged his blazer tighter while she dug her free hand into the pocket of her slacks. Clearing her throat, she started for the stairs. "I'll get you that towel," she murmured, running ahead.

Oliver indulged her, though his hand had begun to dry on its own. She was nervous. Hell, so was he. God bless the sump pump for giving him entrée into the house; he hadn't been in the mood for picking locks tonight. It was dark and rainy and he'd had a long and trying day, not the least of which related to his anticipation of this visit. He'd planned it this way . . . almost. He'd guessed that she'd be better left alone for a while to quiet down, to put things into perspective. The kitten, the violets . . . they were simply reminders that he'd been thinking of her. Now came the test.

"Here you go," Leslie said as she handed him the towel. Then, not knowing what else to do, she stood back against the kitchen counter and waited for him to speak.

Unsure as to how he'd be received, Oliver was in no rush. He wiped his hands, rolled down his shirt sleeves, picked up his blazer from the chair over which Leslie had laid it and put it on.

Leslie's pulse raced as, arms hugging her waist, she followed each step of the dressing process. Damn, but he was handsome. Had he been this good-looking on St. Barts? His hair seemed darker; but of course it was wet. And the silver streaks seemed to have acquired several companions at his sideburns; or was that simply the reflection of her kitchen light? He looked leaner, which puzzled her, since she'd have thought that clothes would have made him look heavier. Perhaps it was the flattering fit of his gray slacks, the length of his legs, the thinning effect of the navy blazer he was slipping on. Beautiful material. Well tailored. But then, with his broad shoulders and tapering physique he was the perfect mannequin.

"There," he said with a final tug to his shirt cuffs. "Thank you."

"Thank *you*. I might have had a flooded basement had it not been for you."

"You'd have called a plumber," he said dismissingly. "It was a simple enough problem to solve."

"Well," she sighed, rubbing her hands together, "thanks anyway." She looked up at him, then away, intimidated by the intensity of his gaze. She didn't know what to say. She didn't know what she wanted to say. Oh, yes, she was glad to see him again. Even now, mired in confusion, she felt more alive than she had in five weeks. Why was he here? What did he want? At one time she might have believed that he wanted to be with her. Now she was wary.

"How've you been, Leslie?"

"Okay." She looked up shyly. "Thanks for the kitten. It's adorable. And the flowers." Her gaze wandered to the table where now only the empty vase stood. "They were beautiful."

"So are you."

Frowning, she absently rubbed at a small chip on the edge of the Formica countertop. Seeing her discomfort, Oliver instantly changed tactics.

"Listen," he said, clearing his throat, "I thought maybe we could go out for a bite."

"It's pouring."

"I don't mind if you don't. It's been a long time since lunch. Didn't I pass a place about ten minutes back down the road?"

She nodded, biting her tongue. She could fix dinner here. But she wouldn't. Oliver Ames in her cozy kitchen would be far too much for one Leslie Parish to endure.

"How about it?"

She shrugged. "I don't know."

"Have you eaten already?"

"No."

"Then come on." He cocked his head toward the front of the house. "Keep me company. We'll just get something to eat . . . and then talk. I'll drop you back here afterward." When she hesitated still, he tipped his head and eyed her teasingly. "You're not frightened of me, are you?"

"Frightened of you? Are you kidding?" She was scared to death, though quick to point out to herself that technically she hadn't lied. She could play that game, too.

"Then why not dinner?"

Because being with you may be as painful as being without you. On the other hand. . . . She sighed her resignation. "Why not."

Within fifteen minutes they were seated across from each other at the steak-and-sandwich place Oliver had selected. Leslie remained quiet, letting Oliver take the lead. If he wanted to talk, let him do the talking for a change. She'd done her share on St. Barts.

As though understanding her silent request, he began to speak soon after their orders were taken. And if he'd been hesitant to discuss himself during their time on the island, he was no longer. Indeed he seemed to want her to know everything. In turn, Leslie couldn't help but respond to his openness.

"I always wanted to be a doctor," he began quietly, almost shyly. "From the time I was a kid. It wasn't until I was nearly done with medical school that I decided on psychiatry."

"Why?"

"Why did I wait that long?" He gave a self-conscious laugh. "Because I think I wanted to see myself in a more—" he frowned as he searched for the word "—flamboyant field. I'd had my heart set on surgery. I was going to be a surgical pioneer, improving on existing transplant processes, experimenting with others."

"What happened?"

"My surgical rotation was a disaster. Not only was I clumsy with a knife, but I also discovered that I wasn't terribly sorry about the fact. Scalpels are cold, impersonal, sterile tools. The major tool the psychiatrist uses is his own intellect—I kind of liked that. I felt there was that much more of a challenge in psychiatry. Perhaps not the glory of a transplant surgeon. But a good feeling right here." He tapped his chest in the region of his heart.

"Has the good feeling persisted?"

"For the most part. Sure, there are some patients who are either beyond my help or, for one reason or another, resistant to it, but I've seen progress."

"Diane seems better," she began on impulse, then caught herself. "I'm sorry. I know you can't talk about her."

"That's all right. It wouldn't be violating doctor-patient confidentiality for me to say that things are beginning to move. She's opening up." His brow furrowed. "She calls me often, which is normal for someone just making that transfer of trust. I don't want her growing too dependent, though. I'd been seeing her three times a week; I've just cut it back by a session."

"She sounds okay when I speak with her."

"She is. She really is. And she'll be fine."

Leslie nodded, thinking how ironic it was that Diane might trust Oliver so completely while she had to remain on her guard all the time. Maybe she was the one with the problem, she mused, then reminded herself that it was the truth. To sit with Oliver like this, loving him so very much yet trying to remain detached, was pure hell.

"You enjoy private practice, then?" she asked, needing to keep the conversation going as a detour from her thoughts.

The waitress brought a carafe of wine, from which Oliver proceeded to fill their glasses before answering. "I do...."

His slight unsureness caught her ear. "You don't sound sure."

"I am," he said more firmly, but he continued to study the swirl of rosé in his glass. "I'm not sure I see myself doing it forever." When Leslie remained silent, he went on. "I'm on the Bellevue—N.Y.U. staff; I spend two mornings a week there seeing patients. In some ways I prefer that kind of practice."

Leslie was puzzled. In the social circles in which she'd grown up, private practice would certainly have been far more prestigious, not to mention lucrative. "Why?"

"The patients. The problems. They're more diverse, often more extreme. I'm needed—and appreciated—that much more. Those patients could never afford the hourly rates I usually charge." His was a straightforward statement, devoid of either pride or arrogance. Perversely itching to find the latter, Leslie prodded.

"If you don't find private practice as rewarding, why do you do it at all? Bellevue is a teaching hospital; surely they'd take you on full-time."

"They would."

"Then why not?"

His eyes held hers levelly. "The money. I want the money private practice can offer."

So he was like the rest, she decided, though she felt no elation at having discovered his fault. "That's noble," she murmured.

"Not noble. Just practical." His eyes pierced her shell of cynicism. His voice held conviction. "I want a wife . . . and a family. I want to be able to support them well, to have a nice home, to travel, to take them to fine restaurants and the theater, to buy them gifts. I've been saving money for the last ten years, investing it, reinvesting dividends. The way I figure it, another seven or eight years should do it. Then I will be able to accept a full-time position at a hospital, either Bellevue or another, without denying my family . . . or myself."

For a minute Leslie had nothing to say. He'd been blunt. And honest. She couldn't believe that he would have risked evoking what he knew to be her distaste for the calculated amassing of money had what he said not been the truth. To her amazement, she respected him.

"Tell me about your family, Oliver," she said with a new note of interest in her voice.

And he did. He told her of his parents and sister, of their modest roots and the relative comfort they'd finally achieved. Over thick steaks and hearty salads, he told her of his college years, inspiring laughter and sympathy in turn.

That weekend, over dinner at a more elegant restaurant in the city, he told her more about his work, outlining a day in his life, amusing her with the zaniest of his cases.

The following Tuesday, as they sat, heads together, in a dim theater waiting for the movie to begin, he told her about his experience as an expert witness in criminal cases and about the book he hoped to write.

The Saturday after that, strolling arm in arm with her through a sprawling suburban shopping mall, he told her about his few good friends, his addiction to tennis, his dream to one day charter a boat and cruise the Mediterranean.

And the next Monday he insisted on taking her to the reception her sister Brenda was throwing to commemorate the debut of the Parish Corporation's home-computer system. Leslie hadn't wanted to go. Receptions such as these, to which only the shiniest of brass and the biggest and most promising of clients were invited, bored her to tears. Between Brenda and Oliver, however, she hadn't stood a chance. As it happened, with Oliver by her side through the entire ordeal, it wasn't all that bad. Indeed, the only awkward moment came when, as a couple amid several hundred, they ran into Diane and Brad. Diane seemed stunned, then embarrassed, then plainly nervous in their presence; Oliver handled the encounter with grace and tact. As for Leslie, she pushed the confrontation from her mind the instant they left the hall.

All in all, she was so in love with Oliver that she was ready to burst. He'd been so open, so gentle, so very obviously honest that she simply couldn't doubt him any longer.

She was also extremely frustrated. Through the warm, casual getting-to-know-Oliver days, he never once repeated his words of love. After each date he'd drop her back at her house with a tender smile, perhaps even an affectionate hug, an extension of the hand-holding and elbow-hooking they did all the time. But though he had to have known she'd be more than willing, he didn't kiss her. Though her body seemed to ache endlessly for him, he showed no inclination to make love. And his words, other than to say that he'd call, were noncommittal.

Oh, he did call. Every night he called just to talk, to hear how her day had been, to tell her about his own. There were times when he was tired, when she could hear the fatigue in his voice, when it was her pleasure to be able to hear out his tale of woe, to commiserate, to soothe.

But he didn't say he loved her. And, fearing the breach of that last bastion, she said nothing.

"Hi, sweetheart."

"Hi."

"Good day?"

"Mmm. Busy. Three kids got sick and had to be sent home. Two of them needed rides to relatives without cars, so guess who drove. I did interview that woman for next fall, though. She's lovely."

"Think she'll be good with the kids?"

"She seemed it. I let her cover for me while I played chauffeur, then when I got back I was able to watch her in action. She's very warm."

"What's her background?"

"She just got a degree in special ed."

"No work experience?"

"Yeah. Six children of her own. Hey, how're *you* doing?"

"Not bad."

"Come on. You can do better than that. I thought the head banger at the hospital quieted down?"

"He did. A new one's into tap dancing."

"Tap dancing? You've got to be kidding."

"I'm not. Listen, babe. About the weekend. Should we, uh, should we try for the Berkshires again?"

"Do you want to?"

"Yes! But only if you do."

"I do."

"Good. Six on Friday?"

"Make it six-fifteen—I'm superstitious."

"Six-fifteen. I'll see you then."

"Sure thing. Bye-bye."

THEY NEARLY MADE IT. It was five-thirty when he called. His voice was as tense as she'd ever heard it. She instantly knew that something was very wrong.

"What is it, Oliver?"

"I've got a problem here. I may be late."

"You're at the office?" She could always pick him up there.

"No."

"At the hospital?"

"No."

He'd been so forthright in the past weeks. His evasion only fueled her concern. "What's wrong?"

In other circumstances, Oliver would have simply named a later time when he'd pick her up. But he knew all too well that his tenuous relationship with Leslie was based largely on openness. "It's Diane, Les," he offered quietly. "She's acting up again."

"Oh, no! What's she doing?"

"It's all right, sweetheart. She's just being . . . difficult."

"You're there now?"

"Yes. Listen, this may take a while. Why don't I call you when I have some idea what's happening."

"Oliver—"

"Please, Les," he begged, "no more questions now. I've been looking forward to tonight since . . . since St. Barts. And if you think I'm pleased with Diane's sense of timing, you're crazy." She heard his desperation. "Let me call you?"

"Okay."

"And Leslie!"

"Mmm?"

"I love you."

"I love you, too."

There was a pause, then Oliver's broken, "I'll call."

With tears in her eyes, Leslie hung up the phone. He'd sounded awful. What could possibly have happened? *I love you,* he had said. And she'd answered him with total openness for the first time herself.

Likewise, for the first time, she felt no confusion at all. Suddenly everything Oliver had said and done made sense. She believed him. She trusted him. And she knew precisely what she wanted to do.

Within half an hour she arrived at Diane's. To her dismay, the driveway was packed. She recognized the Weitzes' cars, Tony's car, Oliver's car . . . was that Brenda's car? She bit her lip as she pulled in behind one she didn't recognize. What was going on?

A frazzled Brenda opened the door. "Leslie! What are you—"

"What are *you* doing here?"

"I'm . . . I'm trying to help out."

Leslie strode past her into the hall and dropped her coat on a chair. Keeping her voice low, she looked around.

"Where are they? What's she done? Why wasn't I called?" At the sound of raised voices in the living room, she headed that way.

"Leslie, please—" Brenda tried to stop her but it was too late. No sooner had Leslie appeared on the threshold than every eye turned her way.

What she saw, perplexingly enough, was what looked to be a very orderly family gathering. There was sign of neither destruction nor tears, though the level of tension in the room was up near the danger mark. Diane, wearing a look of placid arrogance, sat regally in a high-backed chair, while her husband stood behind her, a hand on either sculpted post, an indignant expression on his face. One end of the sofa was occupied by a man Leslie had never seen before. To her eye, his hair was too perfect, his three-piece suit too flashy, his entire bearing too glossy; she disliked him instantly. Tony stood by the fireplace in a state of obvious agitation. And Oliver stood by the window observing the group from a more detached position. His composure was, for show, well intact. Only Leslie recognized the grim set of his lips, the shadow of worry on his brow, the stiffness of his casual stance.

It was to Oliver that she spoke, her voice a whisper. "What's going on here?"

"You shouldn't have come—" he began somberly, only to be interrupted by an irate Diane.

"And why not? The rest of the family knows. And *she* should know. More than anyone, perhaps. After all, she's the one who's been mooning over you. I think she's got a right to the—"

"Diane!" Tony broke in. "That's enough!"

Diane fumed, her eyes blazing. "She'll know when it hits the papers anyway. She's your sister. Don't you want to make it easier for her?"

"Make what easier?" Leslie asked, her stomach tied up in knots. "What are you talking about?" Her wide-eyed gaze swung back to Oliver for a minute. His lips were tight.

Brad's were not. "It seems that your boyfriend has made good use of his high-priced time to seduce my wife."

Leslie stared, aghast. *"What?"* She was aware of Brenda coming up from behind to give her support, but shrugged off the hand at her shoulder.

It was Tony who took over, speaking more quietly. "Diane is threatening a malpractice suit against Oliver. She claims that he forced sexual relations on her for the sake of therapy."

"That's the stupidest thing I've ever heard," Leslie stated with amazing calm. "Oliver wouldn't do a thing like that."

"And I'd lie?" Diane cried, rejoining the fray. "See. He's got you as brainwashed as he had me. Only I'm not so crazy about him that I can't think straight."

Leslie swallowed hard and tucked her fists in her pockets. "That's a whole other issue. What does Oliver say to all this?"

Oliver's voice came deep and firm. "He denies it."

"Well, he can deny it in court," Brad countered, then cast a nod toward the slick man on the sofa. "We've retained Henry to represent us."

Leslie shook her head in disbelief. "You're serious! I'm amazed. You should know better, Brad. My God, it's not as though Diane's been the most stable—"

"Leslie!" Oliver cut in sharply, then lowered his voice. "Please."

The eyes that held hers said far more. *She's sick. Go easy on her. Besides, she hasn't got a case. Trust me. I love you.*

With the ghost of a nod, she walked to a free chair and sat down. She'd be quiet, but she'd be damned if she'd leave.

"Okay," Tony said with a tired sigh. "Where were we?"

Brad spoke up, looking down at his wife with a warmth that made Leslie nauseated. "Diane was just going through things chronologically. You were saying, sweetheart—"

"But what's the point of all this?" Brenda burst out, her gaze sliding from Brad to Diane and back. "I don't understand what you want. You're going to sue for damages? Neither of you needs the money."

Brad's jaw was set at a stubborn angle. "It's the principle of the thing. He's hurt our marriage and seriously threatened Diane's peace of mind."

"Now wait a minute." Oliver came forward. "Your marriage was on the rocks before I ever came on the scene. And as for Diane's peace of mind, it was nonexistent even then. Why do you think she spent an entire day cutting your bedroom to shreds?"

"That's beside the point," Brad went on in the way of the injured innocent. "What I'm concerned about is what happened *after* she started seeing you."

"But a judge and jury will take in the entire picture," Oliver pointed out calmly. "They'll ask about your marriage. They'll hear testimony about Diane's emotional state. Are you sure you want to put your wife through that?"

"For the satisfaction of seeing you lose your license to practice? Yes."

"That won't happen, Brad. Your allegations are absurd. You haven't a shred of evidence—"

"Other than my wife's testimony. Henry tells me that judges today lean heavily in favor of a woman who's been raped."

"She wasn't raped," Oliver scoffed impatiently. "Scandal is all you'll be able to create. Headlines. Innuendo. But no case."

Diane spoke softly. "Headlines and innuendo will be enough." She turned her smile on Leslie and crinkled up her nose. "Won't want to be seen with a guy who's got an atrocious reputation and no job, will you?"

"You're crazy," Leslie murmured.

"Di," Brenda said, "don't you think you're carrying this a little too far? I mean, headlines and innuendo could be harmful to the corporation, too."

"Not if I'm the injured party."

"But you're not," Tony injected, growing as impatient as Oliver, "and Brenda's right. This is foolish—"

"It is not!" Diane screamed. "You weren't the one who was—who was violated!"

Tony's tone mellowed to one of sweet sarcasm. "And you were truly violated?"

"Yes!" She tipped up her chin. "He took advantage of me! Maybe he takes advantage of every pretty girl who comes along. I don't know. That's something for the authorities to investigate." She arched a brow. "All I know is what he did to me."

"What did he do to you?" Brenda asked bluntly. "Tell us, Di. Tell us everything."

"He seduced me in the name of psychiatric treatment."

"Sounds like you got that from last month's *Post.*"

"He did. He seduced me."

"Seduced—what does that mean?"

"Brenda . . . !" Diane protested in a whine.

"Seduced. Explain."

For the first time, Diane seemed to waver. "He . . . he . . . made love to me."

"Where?" Brenda shot back.

"Now just a minute," Henry the lawyer spoke up. Leslie thought his voice was as phony as the rest of him. "I don't believe my client has to answer your questions."

Brenda came forward, her hands on her hips. "Your client happens to be my sister. And the man she's accusing is a man who means one hell of a lot to my other sister. I'll ask whatever questions I want." She turned back to Diane. "Well? Where did you two make love?"

Diane shifted in her seat, keeping her gaze far from Oliver. "He made love to me, and it was in his office."

"On the desk?" Brenda came back as sweetly and sarcastically as Tony had moments before.

Diane scowled. "No." Her voice wavered. "There's a sofa there."

"Do you lie on the sofa during your sessions?"

"No. I . . . I sit in a chair."

"So how did he get you to the sofa?"

Diane grew petulant, reminding Leslie of a child who'd been caught in a lie and was trying to lie her way out of it. "He told me I'd feel better if I were to lie down."

"So you did."

"He was the doctor. Yes."

"And he just told you to take off your clothes?"

"Wait a minute—" Brad cut in, only to have Tony cut him off in turn.

"Let her answer. This is getting interesting."

"It's getting personal," Brad argued.

Tony's nostrils flared. "Isn't the whole thing personal?" Sucking in a loud breath, he turned to Brenda. "Go on."

Without pause, she resumed her relentless prodding. "What did he do . . . after you stretched out on the couch?"

Diane looked at the carpet. "He . . . he told me. . . ." She waved a hand and winced. "You know."

"I don't. Tell me."

"He said. . . ." She scowled in frustration. "You can imagine what he said, Brenda! What does any man say when he sets out to seduce a woman?"

Brenda pursed her lips. "I've only known two men in my life, and neither of them has tried to seduce me on a psychiatrist's couch. So my imagination's no good, Di. Tell me what he said."

Diane seemed to hesitate. She frowned, then gripped the arm of the chair. "He said sweet things."

"Like what?"

If Brenda's patience was wearing thin, Diane's was exhausted. With a sudden fury, she glared at her sister. "He told me it would be good for me, that it was a vital part of my treatment! He told me that he wanted me anyway, and that he'd make it good!" Her anger took on a touch of sadness. "He said that Brad must have been crazy to pass me by and spend time with women who couldn't possibly hold a candle to me."

Tears in her eyes, she bolted up. She was oblivious to the contorted expression on her husband's face. "He told me that I was still young and beautiful. That he loved me," she blurted defiantly. "And I loved him. He was kind and considerate and caring." Standing rigidly, she sent Leslie a gloating stare. "He's a good lover, Leslie. Very skilled and gentle. Not selfish like Brad," she spat.

Then, as the others watched in varying stages of anger, dismay and pity, she sank into her chair and let her head loll back. Astonishingly, her voice gentled along with her expression. She seemed to enter a dreamlike state. "His skin was smooth here, rough there. And he was lean and hard. He wanted me. He did. And I wanted him." She closed her eyes and breathed deeply. "I think I'll always remember that smell...."

Leslie sat forward. "What smell?" she whispered, entranced by her sister's performance.

Diane opened her eyes and sent Leslie a patronizing smile. "His cologne, Homme Premier." She shook her head. "He's so handsome. It's not every girl who's lucky enough to have a model as a therapist."

"He doesn't wear cologne," Leslie stated quietly.

"Excuse me?" Henry asked, twisting to study her.

She looked him in the eye and spoke slowly, with confidence. "I said that he doesn't wear cologne. I know. I spent a week with him at the villa on St. Barts." Rising smoothly, she walked to where Oliver stood and slipped her arm around his waist. Together they faced the gathering. "I know him far better than Diane ever will. Oliver doesn't wear Homme Premier...or any other cologne, for that matter. He never has. And if I have any say in the matter—" she looked adoringly up at him "—he never will." A slow smile found its way to her lips as a foil for the tears in her eyes. "He smells far too good on his own." Then, at the urging of his arms, she turned fully into his embrace. "I love you," she mouthed.

The moisture that gathered at the corner of his eye only enchanted his silent echo of the words. Then he smiled, and Leslie knew that everything would be fine.

10

FASCINATED, Leslie stood staring at Oliver's sleeping form. He was magnificent. Dark wavy hair, mussed by loving, fell across his brow. His jaw bore the faintest shadow of a beard. His nose was straight, his lips firm. Lying amid a sensual array of sheets that barely covered one leg, and that part she now knew so well, he was the epitome of health, good looks and raw masculinity.

Again and again her gaze returned to the taunting strip of flesh at his hip. It would always excite her, even now that her fingers had repeatedly conquered its velvet smoothness. With a sultry half smile, she let her eye creep back up, over the broad and sinewed expanse of his lightly haired chest, to his face.

"Where've you been?" he murmured sleepily, holding out an arm in invitation for her to join him.

Flipping off the bathroom light, she was across the room and in his arms, stretched out against him, in seconds. "I was just looking at you," she said softly, "remembering the very first time I saw you."

"On St. Barts?"

"In *Man's Mode*. You were so beautiful. Tony must have thought I was crazy. I kept staring at that ad, at the expression on your face." She nestled her chin atop the soft hair on his chest. "You wore such a look of vulnerability; you seemed lonely and in love. I wanted to reach out to you then!"

"Took you long enough," he chided, giving her a squeeze.

Her voice was mellow. She kissed his warm skin, then laid her ear against it. "I know."

"What was it, Les? What finally brought you back to me?"

Surrounded by the night sounds of the Berkshires, she pondered his question. It had been long after dark when they'd arrived, so she'd been unable to see the beauty of the hills. But the sounds—the rustle of wind through the forest, the murmur of nocturnal life along its mossy floor, the occasional hoot of an owl—gave her a sense of well-being.

"I think I never really left you," she confessed, experimenting with the fit of her hand to his ribs. "I was so in love with you on St. Barts. I'd never known anything like that before!"

"You should have told me."

"Did you tell me?"

"No. But that was because I knew I'd been deceiving you, and I felt like a louse. The last thing I wanted was to tell you I loved you, then, when you learned the truth about what I did, have you throw the words back in my face. With regard to those three little words, I needed you to believe me."

"I believed you. Oh, I tried not to. But I believed you."

"You said you didn't."

"I lied. I was angry and hurt. I felt so . . . naive. I'd had a complex all along about having to compete with the glossy women I'd assumed you were used to. Then when I found out that you were a psychiatrist. . . ."

"Do you mind?"

"Mind what?"

"That I'm a psychiatrist."

"Of course not. What's to mind?"

In the darkness she could just make out the gleam in his eye. "Psychiatrists are loonies, didn't you know? They're as crazy as their patients. They're—" he curled his mouth around and drawled the word "—strange."

"Not this one."

"You're sure?"

"I'm sure. You must be nearly as rational as my sister Brenda." When he eyed her as though she were the strange one, she explained. "Your plan. It was brilliant. Those weeks you left me alone were awful. I missed you so terribly and kept trying to convince myself that I was better without such a lying devil, but it didn't work. When you sent that little kitten, I was overjoyed." Her voice dropped. "I love the kitten, Oliver."

"I'm glad," he whispered against her brow. His fingers idly traced the line of her spine. Her skin was warm and smooth; he'd never get his fill of touching her. "I had it all worked out. I figured I'd give you time to cool off and even miss me, then I'd let you get to know the real me. Then I'd bring you up here and start the seduction all over again." He paused. "But it was going to be slow and considerate, not fast and furious. I think I miscalculated somewhere along the way."

"There'll be other times for slow and considerate. Tonight I needed fast and furious. How did you know?"

"I couldn't control myself! I mean, it's tough for a man to be so turned on by a woman and not be able to go through with it."

"But you never even kissed me!" she protested, eyeing him in surprise. "You never gave the slightest indication that you wanted anything more than a squeeze or a hug."

"That was all part of the plan," he scoffed. "Let me tell you, you were gonna get it one way or the other over the weekend. Maybe it was good that Diane pulled her little act. She certainly brought things to a head."

His words gave them both food for thought. Leslie rubbed her cheek against his chest. He pulled her more tightly against him. Their voices were soft and intimate.

"Oliver, will she be all right?"

"I think so. I gave Tony a name of a colleague of mine who's very good. He'll be better able to treat Diane than I ever could."

"Why did she do that?"

"Ironically, it was probably her seeing us together at Brenda's reception that did it. It's not an uncommon phenomenon for a woman patient of a male doctor—in any kind of therapy—to think she's in love with him. She sees him as the source of her health, her confidence, her general well-being. I'd already begun to feel that Diane was growing too dependent on me; I told you that."

"I remember."

"I had just cut her sessions back from three a week to two. That may have bothered her. Brad was obviously still bothering her. He's a bastard." The aside was muttered under his breath. "A good deal of the time she feels she is unwanted and unloved. When she saw us together and, from what Brenda says, looking very much in love, she was jealous. Furiously jealous. Jealous of you. Furious at me. And Brad—well, with her cock-and-bull story she thought she'd be giving him the message that someone did want her, even if he did not."

"I feel so badly for her."

He drew soothing circles on her back. "So do I. She's very unhappy. I told Tony that I thought she and Brad should separate. Even her original outburst didn't faze Brad; Diane says that he's still seeing some little sweetie, and I think I believe her."

"Poor Diane. And we've got so much."

He hugged her, his arms trembling. "We do."

They lay together in silence for several minutes, each simply enjoying the presence of the other.

"Oliver?"

"Mmm?"

"How did you get to Diane's tonight? I mean, I'm surprised that she'd have wanted to give you a chance to defend yourself."

"She didn't. But she needed some sense of power, so she called Tony to tell him what she'd planned. He called me, then Brenda. He knew their lawyer was going to be there and hoped to nip the whole scheme in the bud."

"Why wasn't I called?" Leslie asked in a small voice.

Oliver planted a gentle kiss on her nose. "We didn't want you to be hurt. Diane's claim was pretty ugly."

"But it was false!"

"I knew that, but the words would have been hurtful enough. Besides, if we were successful, you'd never have been any the wiser to her threat." He paused then, hesitant. "Leslie?"

"Mmm?"

"Did you ever believe her?"

She brought her head up in surprise. "Believe Diane? Of course not. Were you worried?"

"That you'd believe her, a little. After what I'd done to you on St. Barts, I wasn't sure how far your trust would go."

"Were you worried that she would bring the case to trial?"

"I wouldn't be honest if I didn't say yes. She was right in a way. Headlines and innuendo could have easily damaged my career. Not destroyed it, but damaged it badly. Even if a person is found not guilty by a jury, the stigma of having been accused in the first place remains. It's a sad fact, one that our system of justice can do little to change." He grew quiet, pensive, his breathing even, close to her ear. Hooking his foot around her shin, he drew her leg between his and pressed his hips more snugly to him. Then he held her still, appreciating the beauty of the moment. "Thank you, Leslie," he said at last, his voice intensely gentle.

"For what?"

"For trusting me."

She laughed shyly. "It's nothing. You're an easy one to trust," she pinched his ribs, "even when you are lying through your teeth."

"I don't lie!" he stated with such vehemence that she realized he would always be sensitive about what had happened on St. Barts. She couldn't deny her delight; somehow she had managed to find the most straightforward man in the world.

"I know," she apologized gently. "I was only teasing." Then she grew more thoughtful herself. "A little while ago you asked what had brought me back to you. It was several things, I think. Time, for one. I was able to sort things out, to put things into perspective. I realized that what you'd said made sense. And I missed you so much I was very willing to give you any benefit of the doubt.

"When we started to see each other and I got to know you, I saw that what you'd said was right. Model or psychiatrist, you were the same man underneath. You were so open then, making up for all you hadn't said on the island. And right about that time I was beginning to feel like a hypocrite."

"You? A hypocrite?"

"Mmm." She breathed in his natural scent and was buoyed up by it. "For all my talk, I really wasn't any more honest with you—or myself—than I'd accused you of being. I did love you. I loved you back on St. Barts. When we made love, well, I played games with myself. I told myself that the only thing that mattered was the moment, that I didn't care about the past or the future. But I did. I should have been more open about my feelings then. I should have let you speak when I knew you wanted to." She raised soulful eyes to his. "It was my fault that you didn't tell me about yourself. But I was afraid—afraid of what you might say, afraid that it might burst the bubble of illusion we'd created. It was such a lovely bubble. I didn't want anything to happen." She looked down. "So you see, I was pretty bad myself. I created an illusion and clung to it as it suited me. But I was fooling myself to think that I could return to New York and forget you. I realized that during the cab ride home from the airport."

Oliver skimmed her cheek with the side of his thumb and brought her chin up. "I love you, lady. Do you know that?"

Seeing it written on every plane of his face, she smiled and nodded. "You know," she whispered through a veil of happy tears, "I feel sorry for all your female patients. If you'd been my therapist, I'd have certainly fallen in love with you."

"If you'd been my patient," he growled, rolling slowly over to pin her to the bed, "I'd sure as hell have been guilty of some mighty unethical thoughts."

"Only thoughts? No acts?"

"Nope."

"I'm not pretty enough? Or rich enough? Or thin enough? Why not?"

"If you want to know the truth, that sofa happens to be the most uncomfortable thing I've ever been on!"

"Oh? So you have . . . tried it out?"

He nipped her shoulder in punishment. "I've sat on it. I've fallen asleep on it once or twice."

"Have you ever *made love* on it?"

"No. Maybe we'll try it sometime."

"Aw, I don't know, Oliver. That might feel . . . unethical."

"But you're not my patient."

"I know, but. . . ."

"Tell me you're tired of me already."

"Are you kidding? It's just . . . well . . . even though Diane won't be suing you, I think I'll always remember her threat. I'd feel guilty making love in your office. Your patients have problems so much more serious than ours. . . ."

Adoring her sensitivity, Oliver felt choked up. When he could finally speak, his voice was a husky murmur. "You're amazing, you know that?" Before she could answer, he sealed her lips with his own in a kiss so gentle and loving that she could have wept for all she did have. "It doesn't bother you, then," he mused against her mouth, "that I'm a psychiatrist?" He was thinking of her mother and what Tony had told him.

She sent her tongue in search of the corner of his lip, then smiled. "I'm proud of you."

"You will have to meet my parents," he quipped, recalling an earlier discussion about pride.

She remembered too and blushed. "I did wonder for a while there what kind of parents would be proud to have a gigolo for a son. Now that I know better, I'd love to meet them."

"And you'll marry me?"

"I'd love that, too."

He sucked in his breath, then let it out slowly as he raked the length of slender flesh beneath him. "You are beautiful. Not too thin. Not too rich. Just right. When we get back to the city I'm going to buy you a silky white negligee. I'd love to be able to take it off. . . ."

"Oliver!" she exclaimed, delighted by the very definite effect the simple thought of it had on him. "You must have this thing for nudity. What would Freud say about that?"

He moved more fully on top of her. "I don't give a damn. Freud was nothing but a constipated old—"

"Shh...." She put a finger to his lips, then let it wander to his hairline, into the thick waves, around his ear to trace that silver arc. "I like nudity, too. Knowing that you were naked beneath that sheet in your ad nearly drove me crazy. Oliver?"

He managed a muffled, "Uh huh?"

"Will you stop...doing that for a minute so...I can speak?"

"Doing what?"

"Moving like that." He'd begun to shift against her on the pretense of kissing her eyes, then withdrawing, kissing her nose, then withdrawing, kissing one earlobe, then the other. In essence his entire body was rubbing her in all the right places, and she'd begun to sizzle.

He stopped instantly, propping himself above her. "There. Better?"

Was frustration better? "Not really...except for speaking."

"So...what were you going to say?"

"I wanted to, uh, to ask you a favor."

"Shoot."

She raised her hands to his shoulders and followed their progress as they slowly descended over his chest. When her palms felt the unmistakable tautness of his nipples, she stopped. "It's about your modeling. When we're married...."

"What is it, sweetheart?"

She shot him a glance, then retreated. "I know it's silly of me to even think of this—"

"Out with it, woman, so we can get on with it!"

"I don't want you posing nude! I don't think I can stand it! I don't want other women seeing your body! I want you all to myself!" Running out of breath, she lowered her voice. "I told you it was silly."

"It's not one bit silly, Leslie," Oliver returned gently. "It's sweet and loving and possessive, and it pleases me tremendously."

"Really?" she asked timidly.

"Really."

"Because I love your body." She slid her hands from his chest and ran them down his sides to his thighs. "I do love your body." Lifting her head, she pressed her lips to the turgid spot that her palm had just deserted.

"It's yours!"

"Just like that?"

"Just like that. There's just one little catch."

"Uh oh. Here it comes." She shut her eyes tightly. "Okay. Tell me."

"I want *your* body. That's a fair exchange, isn't it?"

"I suppose."

"What do you mean, 'you suppose'? You're supposed to be ecstatic."

"But...what about my mind? Don't you want that, too?"

"Your mind? Oh. That. Uh, well, let's see. We could always put it in a little box on the nightstand—hey, that tickles!"

"The ad was right, you know. You *are* a rogue."

"Any objections?"

She smiled and spoke with confidence, serenity and love. "None at all, Oliver. None at all."

THE FOREVER INSTINCT

Barbara Delinsky

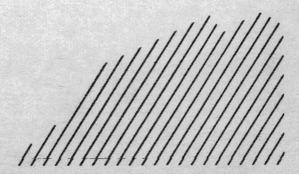

"It's too late, Jordanna," Patrick whispered

"It's too late to turn back now." He didn't touch her. He didn't have to. His brand was intangible but potent.

At the sound of a snap, then a zip, Jordanna's gaze shot up. He was in the process of wrenching wet denim from his legs, and she couldn't look away.

In only a pair of darks briefs, Patrick looked totally masculine, every bit as perfect as she had feared. Swallowing hard, she tried to think of something sensible to say. Nothing came.

"You should have fought me but you didn't," he murmured, squatting down beside her. "So now I know that you want me. And I know, too, that I'll have you...."

1

SHE RECOGNIZED HIM instantly. His face was the same, if more mature, with tiny time lines etched into his brow and at the corners of his eyes. Flecks of silver whispered through his thick sable hair. Though thinner than he'd been when she'd seen him last, he was every bit as tall and broad of shoulder. And his intensity hadn't lessened.

"Jordanna Kirkland," he stated, dredging her name from the depths of the past as he soberly stared at the woman whose arrival at the campground had coincided nearly perfectly with his own.

Letting her frame pack slide the length of her leg until it stood on the ground, she struggled to contain her shock and its attendant rush of memories. "Lance."

"It's Patrick now. Patrick Clayes." Dragging his eyes from hers, he extended a hand to each of the other four members of the group in turn. "I'll be your guide."

"Larry Earls," said the first, slim, pale man.

"Donald Scheuer," was the response of his taller, more heavyset companion.

"John Kalajian," the third said with a nod, an attractive professorial type.

"Bill Wennett," declared the last, the hint of arrogance in his voice echoing his cocksure stance.

All looked to be in their early forties and, from the similarity of their dress and gear, friends. It wasn't quite what Jordanna had expected when Craig Talese had so gallantly offered her his place on the trek.

Scrupulously avoiding Patrick's gaze, she looked from one man to the next. She had their undivided attention. "How many others will be joining us?" she asked quietly, assuming the women to be lagging somewhere behind. The names Scheuer and Wennett were ones Craig had mentioned; she was with the right group.

John looked at Larry; Donald's gaze met Bill's. Then all four looked with dawning dismay at Patrick, who finally spoke. "I was told there would be five of you. I guess this it."

"There *were* supposed to be five of us. Who's she?" Bill demanded, turning an imperious eye on Jordanna.

She raised her chin a fraction of an inch. She'd learned to deal with high-handed men long ago. "Patrick had my name right. It's Jordanna Kirkland."

"Where's Craig?" Larry asked.

"He got an emergency call from San Diego. His daughter is ill. He flew out last night."

"So he called *you*?" Donald said in disbelief.

"Yesterday," she stated.

"And you decided to join a group of men for five days in the wilds?" This from Bill again, with unmitigated disdain.

She stiffened her spine. "I had no idea I was joining a group of men. That must have been Craig's idea of a little joke." It fitted. Though as her accountant he was second to none, he was forever ribbing her about what he called her "male instinct" in the world of business.

"It's a lousy joke," Larry muttered. To Jordanna he seemed more threatened than angry at her presence.

Not so Donald. Anger punctuated his every word, though his attention jumped from one to the other of his friends in search of support. "More than that. It's impossible! This was supposed to be a fun week with the guys.

Totally uninhibited. There's no way we can have that with her along."

Jordanna's lips quirked at the corners. "Don't let me stop you. You can be as uninhibited as you want. I've seen a lot in my time. You won't shock me."

Donald ignored her. "What in the hell did Craig have in mind?"

For the first time since announcing his name, John spoke up. His voice was quiet, his manner philosophical. "Maybe he wanted to knock a hole in the last bastion of male chauvinism. You know how he's always after us." His pensive gaze slid to Jordanna. "Jordanna Kirkland . . . as in Willow Enterprises?"

Time reversed itself. It was as though she were once more standing before the skeptical bank board that would decide whether to grant her that crucial loan to bolster her fledgling business. As she'd done then, she now donned her most serene and confident expression. "That's right."

"You're its president?" John queried.

"And founder," she added, her pride present if understated.

Donald cursed, but he had the grace to do it softly. There his civility ended. "So she's the one he's been raving about all this time?" When John nodded, he scowled. "Then the joke's on us. Man, how could he do this?"

"Must be his warped sense of humor," Bill countered, looking as disgusted as his friend.

"I'll say."

"Kind of funny, when you think of it," John mused, only to draw three irate glances. He shrugged and held up a hand in self-defense. "Just kidding, guys. Just kidding."

"But what are we going to do about it?" Larry asked.

"She can't come, that's all there is to it," Donald said sharply.

Bill seconded the motion.

John had the good sense to keep his mouth shut.

By this time Jordanna was incensed. "What do you mean, she can't come?" she demanded. "She's here, in case you hadn't noticed. She's traveled six hours to get here, not to mention the time it took to make arrangements to be out of the office for the week. She's reimbursed Craig for the money he chipped in with you guys and she has her gear packed, and—" her eyes stopped flashing long enough to eye the foursome solemnly "—she's probably in far better shape for this hike than any of you."

Bill gave her the once-over, very slowly, then raised a brow and drawled, "Wouldn't surprise me in the least." His eyes narrowed. "But you have to wonder why a woman would want to go off into the woods with five men."

Jordanna didn't flinch. "You're being offensive," she stated quietly, then turned her head toward their guide for the first time since the fray had begun. And for the first time, she felt a true surge of anxiety. The four other men didn't daunt her in the least. For the past ten years, she'd fought their type. Though self-centered, they were predictable; though unpleasant, relatively harmless. Lance Clayes was something else. He was the link to a past she'd just as soon forget.

The way he was staring at her didn't help. She saw what he saw, fragments of those days of glory. And she saw something more. In the instant before he shuttered his gaze, she saw curiosity, perhaps a touch of respect, but also an undeniable flicker of heat. It unsettled her as the men's outward hostility had not done.

Slowly Patrick straightened, his dark brown eyes now harder as they held Jordanna's. "You're determined to come?"

"Yes."

"Do you know what you're getting in for?"

"I've read the trip description."

"And you think you can keep up?"

"I know I can."

"Have you ever backpacked before?"

Taking a calculated risk, she tipped her head toward the others. "Have they?"

The silence from the four was answer aplenty. If they'd been experienced backpackers, they would no more have hired a guide than have chosen to wear spanking new hiking boots. Not that hers were any more broken in, but they were softer, a gentle offshoot of the traditional heavy leather clods, more sneaker than boot. Indeed, part of her mission was to test their wearability; they wouldn't hit the market for another four months.

Patrick ran his tongue around the inside of his cheek, carefully choosing his words. "I was told you were all beginners," he said, shifting his gaze to the men.

Jordanna answered with a self-confidence none of the others could muster. "We are." She'd learned early on that being forthright about her weaknesses enhanced her strengths. "But we're determined." She ignored four scathing looks. "And ready to go." Innocently she scanned the faces of the men, then spoke with mock sweetness. "We were to be off by one, weren't we?"

"Yeah," Bill grumbled, turning to lift his pack.

"Hold on," Patrick cautioned as he loped off toward the Jeep parked near the other cars on the fringe of the campground. "I've got the supplies here," he called over his shoulder. "We'll have to divvy them up." With a minimum of effort he hauled first his own pack, then three open cartons filled with food and equipment from the back of the Jeep. "Bring your packs over. It'll be easier."

The five did as told, then watched him apportion supplies among the six packs. It was with mild dismay that Jordanna watched the proceedings, praying that she'd have enough room in her pack for everything he gave her. She'd followed Craig's instructions to the letter, had even rushed out and bought as many books as she could find on backpacking, several of which had included step-by-step guides for filling a frame pack. Three times she'd loaded and unloaded the nylon-duck bag that sat so innocently atop its aluminum frame; each successive time the bag had looked less innocent. How something so roomy when empty could hold so little when filled was beyond her. But she'd persevered, discarding an additional item or two of clothing with each round of packing, until she'd finally found the right combination.

Mercifully, she'd had no trouble placing numerous bags of freeze-dried food in the top of her pack, or stuffing other goodies into side pockets. There were raisins, nuts, freeze-dried coffee and Tang, each carefully packaged in plastic bags for a minimum of bulk and weight. The latter was crucial. When every compartment was securely closed, and her sleeping bag and Ensolite pad rolled and fastened at the top of the frame, she had a substantial load to challenge her fitness.

For a second too long she eyed the pack. "Problems, Jordanna?" Bill goaded. "Look too heavy?"

"I can handle it," she answered calmly.

Donald joined his friend and ally. "You're sure?" He shook his head, his mien patronizing, to say the least. "You can change your mind now before we get going. Once we're on the trail it won't be so easy. It'd be unfair to ask one of us to walk all the way back here with you."

Jordanna simply smiled. "We'll see who tires when," she said softly, then turned to her pack and contemplated the simplest way to put it on. The problem was taken out of her hands when Patrick easily lifted it and held it out. Turning, she slipped her arms through the straps, then, head down, fumbled with the hip belt. When she straightened, he was before her to adjust the shoulder straps.

Given the silence among the rest of the men, she wasn't sure whether to be grateful or annoyed. Patrick's assistance did nothing either for her own peace of mind or for the image of competence she was trying to project. In a way it was patronizing. Yet when she met his gaze there was neither smugness nor any semblance of a leer. Rather there was a dark intensity, a hardness reminiscent of the Lance Clayes of old. A muscle jumped in his jaw. Underdog or not, he was a man of determination.

"You can manage, can't you?" he asked quietly enough to spare her embarrassment, yet firmly enough to suggest his own doubt.

Jordanna was only marginally aware that the others had begun to don their packs. Her attention was riveted to Patrick. "Of course I can manage," she said, wondering why her voice didn't sound as firm as her conviction.

"The pack's heavy."

"I'm strong."

"We'll be going a long way, some of it over rough terrain."

"I've been running better than thirty miles a week for the past four years."

He showed no sign of being impressed, but simply continued to stare at her, into her, through her.

"I can do it, Lance—"

"Pat."

"Pat. Even if his sense of humor *is* a little off, Craig would never have suggested I come if he hadn't had faith in me." She took a breath, then stated baldly, "His job's at stake."

"What does he do?"

"He's my accountant."

For several seconds longer, Patrick studied her. His expression grew strangely wary. "You're a successful woman, Jordanna. Why are you here?"

"Can't successful women go on backpacking trips?" she countered, trying to make light of his query and the very powerful presence behind it.

"Sure they can," he asserted softly. "More often, though, they choose a week of leisure at one resort or another." His gaze clouded. "It's odd. Jordanna Kirkland. Peter's wife—"

"Peter's *ex*-wife," she corrected in a half whisper. "We've been divorced for nearly ten years. Our paths rarely cross. And who I was then has no bearing whatsoever on my presence here today."

He considered her quiet vehemence for an instant before silently turning away. Perplexed, Jordanna watched him hoist his own pack to his back. She sensed there would be far more to say about the past before the five days were done, and she wondered if she would be wise to turn back while she could. Patrick's presence shook her; she felt oddly unbalanced. If only she had an inkling as to the thoughts running through his mind . . .

Then she caught herself and brought her chin up. On principle alone she was determined to see the week through. She had decided to come; she had spent the past thirty-six hours making arrangements. And neither four reluctant men nor one Patrick Clayes was going to stop her.

Standing idly, waiting for the others to adjust their packs, she surveyed the surroundings only her peripheral vision had previously absorbed. In the parking area stood just four vehicles, two for the four buddies, Patrick's Jeep and her own rented Chevy. It seemed they'd have the woods to themselves—not surprising given the fact that it was early November. The foliage seekers had long since retreated to the warmth of their homes for the winter.

Two trails led into the woods from the parking area. Having studied the trip description long hours into the night, Jordanna knew they'd be taking the Basin Trail and making a large, rugged loop covering nearly twenty-two miles before returning on the Wild River Trail.

"Okay, listen a minute," Patrick began, gathering them all around for preliminary instructions. "First off, we travel as a group. The trails are well marked and hard to miss, but I don't want to risk losing any of you. We'll stay on the beaten path. No bushwhacking. Zero-impact hiking is what it's all about. When we disband Friday night, there should be no sign whatsoever that we've ever been here. Side trips through the bush will only destroy the natural beauty of the place. None of us want to do that," he stated positively as he looked from one to another of his charges. To Jordanna's relief, his gaze touched her but briefly.

"Our walking time this afternoon will be roughly two hours, though with stops here and there we probably won't reach the Blue Brook shelter until dinnertime. It's a perfect walk for beginners. But—" he paused, a warning look on his face "—if anyone has trouble, *any* trouble, I want you to yell. If your pack is killing you, it might need a simple adjustment. Same with your boots. At the first sign of blisters, we stop to apply moleskin. At the first problem with a knee or an ankle, we put on an Ace bandage. Since none of you have backpacked before, there are bound to be aches and pains, but—within limits—I want you to speak up. This is a pleasure trip. We don't need martyrs. We're not looking for heroes. A problem dealt with early on can be easily handled. Down the road it may be a little harder. Understood?" He cast a glance from one intent face to another. When each had nodded, he eased up. "Any questions?"

Jordanna had a million questions. Where do we sleep? How do we cook? What if it rains? Will there be bears? But like the others, she shook her head, confident that the answers would be forthcoming in time.

"Let's go," he said. "I'll lead the way. John, you take up the rear. We'll switch around once you all get the hang of it."

Without further ado, he set off. Jordanna watched his retreating form, admiring the way his gear seemed an extension of his body, wondering how long he'd been backpacking. Judging from the spring in his step, he loved it.

"Jordanna?"

John's quiet call drew her from her momentary preoccupation. With a start she realized the others were already on the trail. Flashing him a buoyant smile that she hoped would cover for her lag, she moved quickly ahead.

Though the air was brisk, it wasn't cold. Having checked the long-range forecast, Jordanna knew that there were no major storms expected. Chills she could easily withstand; the clothes she wore were designed to be lightweight and warm. Snow, though, she could do without. She was no glutton for punishment.

The path was of crushed stone leading southward past several deserted campsites before entering deeper woods. She concentrated on walking steadily and shifted her pack once to a more comfortable position. She was grateful she hadn't skimped in selecting her gear; her shoulder straps were well padded, her hip belt substantial enough to evenly distribute the load. Amazing what she'd learned about backpacking in such a little time, she mused. She only hoped her cramming would pay off further along. Going to bed at 2:00 A.M. hadn't been the smartest thing to do, particularly since she'd awoken at six to shower and dress and head out from New York. She would be tired tonight. But then, evenings on the trail were probably going to be quiet and early ones.

Few words were spoken as the six walked on, each seeming too awed by the silent splendor of the woods to shatter its effect. They had left all civilization behind. Even the path was now of packed earth strewn with leaves. Larry, the photographer of the group, paused to take pictures from time to time. When he stopped to adjust his pack, Patrick assisted him while the others rested, occasionally sipping from canteens or flexing cramped shoulders.

On the move once more they came to a wetter area of ground, where a plank walkway had been constructed.

"Someone was thoughtful," Larry observed.

"We'll run across these from time to time," Patrick explained, tapping his booted toe against the first of the planks. "But they're not first and foremost for our benefit."

"Then whose?" Bill asked irreverently.

"The earth's," Patrick answered. "Walkways like these retard soil erosion. Without them, some of the trails would be impassable, not to mention devoid of vegetation." Without awaiting further comment, he went ahead. The others followed. What had been the symphonic rustling of dead leaves underfoot became a more percussive series of thuds as they progressed.

Head down now, Jordanna studied the planks, then the soggy ground to either side as her professional instinct went to work. She wondered how her hiking shoes would hold up on wet ground. Had Patrick's words not run fresh in her ear, she might have been tempted to step off into the muck. But his words had hit their mark, and besides, she was hemmed in front and rear by men who would delight in any slip she made. A soggy shoe was not the most auspicious adjunct to a hike. Perhaps at the end of the trip, she decided, when no great harm could be done, she'd experiment.

On dry ground once again, they climbed steadily along what Patrick announced to be Blue Brook until they reached a footbridge. There, at his direction, they lowered their packs for a rest. At first Jordanna was startled. They'd been walking for barely an hour. Only when she set her pack on the ground and straightened did she understand his motive. Though she thought herself in the best of shape, there seemed to be tiny muscles in her back that she'd never felt before. Stretching carefully, she eased down onto a nearby rock to savor the sight of the gurgling brook below.

The men talked among themselves. She sat apart, perfectly comfortable with the distance. Solitude was a treat for her, given the number of people who rushed in and out of her working life. If the others left her to her own musings during the trek, she wouldn't mind in the least.

"Everything okay?"

She looked up to find Patrick shading her from the sun.

"Fine," she answered quickly, her gaze darting back to a gentle cascade splashing into a pool. "Its really beautiful."

His eyes followed hers. "It's just the beginning. This season is the best. Minimum people, maximum nature."

Something in his tone said that he appreciated solitude as she did. Looking up, she studied the rugged planes of his face. He was unfairly handsome; time had served him well. "Do you—" she swallowed involuntarily and began again "—do you do this often?"

He continued to stand beside her, legs braced wide. His dark hiking pants were well worn and fitted him comfortably. She sensed pure muscle beneath. "Backpacking? Whenever I can."

"Guiding," she corrected, tutoring her thoughts away from his thighs. She wondered if he earned his living as an outdoorsman. Scanning her memory, she couldn't recall having heard about him in recent years. But then, she realized, the mind did strange things. For years she'd blotted out anything and everything to do with football. She might have seen something in the paper and never taken it in.

Eyes trained upstream, he didn't spare her a glance. "Nah. I only take groups out once or twice a year, usually in late fall or early spring. When I go myself, it's into more remote areas, ones I've never seen before."

"You're an explorer then?"

"Mmm." As though loath to say more, he abruptly turned and wandered to a nearby boulder. Lithely hiking himself upon it he wrapped his arms around his knees to enjoy the scene a while longer.

Staring after him, Jordanna wondered just what path he had taken in life. His playing days were over; forty-year-old quarterbacks were not exactly in demand. If he'd turned to coaching, he'd hardly have been able to take off a week at the height of the season. On the other hand, he might well have entered broadcasting, where his presence on the weekend would suffice. He was eloquent; his initial speech to the group had proved that. And if the private type, he was hardly shy. Yet in the old days he had avoided the press. Peter had been the one to court them with every bit of charm he could manage, and that was considerable, she remembered with a scowl.

But she didn't want to think of Peter. Or Lance. *Or* the old days.

With a deep breath she lowered her gaze. Her fingers idly slid through the dried brush by her side, but the startling image in her mind's eye was of a softer, more vibrant brush, that of the dark hair peeping through the open neck of Patrick's shirt as she'd seen it moments before. Stunned, she frowned, then reached for a dead leaf and crushed it along with the unbidden image. Refocusing on the enchantment of the stream, she let her mind trip pleasantly until, at length, Patrick hopped down from his perch and retrieved his pack in silent example to the others. With the wave of his hand, they were off again.

Bathed in the relief of having donned her pack alone, Jordanna felt fresh of mind and decidedly confident. Eyes alert, she took in everything from the pines swaying rhythmically above to the solid firs more stoically enduring the intrusion of humanity. The cliffs that banked the far side of the stream were granite slabs slicing neatly into the water, where, over ages, they were gentled by the crystal-clear flow.

When the path took a turn upward, her legs were tested for the first time. She welcomed the exertion, enjoying the stretch as she always did in her early morning warm-ups. She found something intrinsically refreshing in the reminder that her body was far more than a machine to be taken for granted. Being well oiled took work. She liked testing her limits and even now lengthened her stride until she clearly felt the muscles of her thighs and calves. This appreciation of the physical was but one of the ways Willow Enterprises had benefited from its founder.

As if in reminder, she touched her cheek, then reached back into a lower side pocket of her pack for a small tube of cream. Makeup was her specialty; indeed, cosmetics for the sports-minded woman had been the first order of business after Willow Enterprises' founding. Its product line was extensive, and though it included the colorful creams and shadows desired by the fashion-conscious woman, its pride was a more practical line of moisturizing agents. The dab of cream now in her palm was one of these. She smoothed it across the backs of her hands and around her fingers, then applied the excess to her cheeks and chin in a motion that might have been a simple soothing of flesh had any of the men noticed. Five days in the wilds without benefit of other makeup would put the cream to the test, as would the sun, even weak as it was, its protective qualities.

Without missing a step, she comfortably kept her place in the casual line, breathing deeply of the scent of fall. Clusters of birches, their yellow leaves now pale and withering, had sprung up to share the forest with beeches and firs. High above, the cry of migrating geese echoed amid the breeze.

"You look more spring than fall," John commented, startling her as he drew abreast of her.

She glanced down at her outfit, a stylish, lightly padded jacket cuffed at the waist and wrists, with matching pants that tapered, then zippered at the ankles. She was lime green from collar to heel.

With a soft chuckle, she concurred. "It was a choice of this, bright yellow, soft pink or lavender. Somehow I thought the green would blend better with the woods."

"Isn't that a jogging suit?"

"Pretty much so, though we're marketing it as an all-purpose sports outfit. The principles are the same. Loose and light but insulating. Actually, this jacket is warmer than a regular running shell. I'm really comfortable." She looked far more so than any of the men, she admitted to herself with a certain amount of smugness. Their hiking jackets and pants were a sight heavier. Only Patrick with his anorak looked fully at ease.

"Not bad," John decided, then fell back several steps once more.

Jordanna did feel comfortable, surprisingly so. She'd packed a heavy wool sweater, but she was counting on multiple layers of lighter coverings to keep her warm. Walking was one thing; despite the growing chill in the air as the afternoon wore on and the sun paled and dipped, she actually felt tiny trickles of perspiration on her back beneath her pack. When the day's walk was done and they sat idle, ah, that would be a different matter.

"How's it going back there?" Patrick called from the front of the line. Three other heads swiveled around with his.

"Just fine," Jordanna assured them all with a smile.

"Blisters?" Donald suggested.

"Nope."

"Sore shoulders?" Bill hinted.

She shook her head. "Sorry. Of course, if you guys are tired—"

Just as abruptly as they'd looked back, all three faced forward again and moved on. Only Patrick lingered for a moment's study of her serene expression. Then he too whipped around and was off.

The remainder of the afternoon's trek was pleasant. Tuning out the men's chatter, Jordanna derived from the outdoors the gratification she sought. The gentle sounds of the wild, the random rustle of tiny woodland creatures, the sweet scent of spruce—all were a soothing balm against the memory of the city's bustle.

Her body held up well; she smiled to herself when, behind her, John began to grunt as the trail climbed toward a ridge. When at last they reached the shelter where they'd be spending the night, she silently congratulated herself on a job well done.

Half an hour later she began to wonder if her congratulations had been premature. It had been one thing when they were walking, single file for the most part, and she could easily lose herself to the joy of the forest. Stationary now, idly studying the three-sided log shelter, she let herself think for the first time of the awkwardness such closeness could present to a woman among five men.

They'd all lowered their packs and were relaxing while Patrick set up the camp stove to heat water for hot drinks before dinner. A stream just north of the shelter was their water supply; he'd shown them the way before he'd set to work. Now there was little to do but relax until the business of making dinner began.

As had happened during the afternoon, the men talked among themselves, ignoring Jordanna as much as possible. She studied them as she sat on the ground, then reached into her pack to change into a pair of soft moccasins. She wore two pairs of socks, a thin inner pair and an outer pair of thicker wool rag. Her feet were toasty, though she still felt chilled. Digging in the pack again, she pulled out a heavy wool cap and tugged it on over her stylishly cropped thick chestnut hair.

She had settled back once more when Patrick suddenly moved from the stove to his own pack. As she watched, he shed his jacket and unbuttoned his shirt. She held her breath when the shirt came off to reveal corded shoulders and a lean torso. When he bent to fish into the pack, she was held by the play of his muscles, sinewed and firm, flexing grandly as he reached forward. Then he straightened and, as though physically touched by her gaze, slowly turned his head to look at her.

Jordanna felt a strange thudding in her chest. She tried to look away, but his dark eyes were locked to hers. Then, as slowly as he'd turned his head, he began to approach, stopping only when he was within arm's reach of her. His long-sleeved, insulated shirt hung limply from his fingers. With catlike grace, he lowered himself to his haunches.

"Anything wrong?" he asked softly.

She quickly shook her head and dropped her eyes, not altogether prudently, to the soft pelt of fur on his chest. He had to be cold, yet he looked warm and alive, making her, to her dismay, feel the same.

"You're sure?"

She swallowed hard and nodded. But her eyes clung to his flesh. Her fingers curled into her palms.

"You'll catch a chill," she whispered.

"Are you worried?" he returned in that same soft voice. It held a touch of silk this time, its smoothness shimmering into her.

"You're our leader," she managed. "It wouldn't help us if you got sick."

"I've got an iron constitution."

"So I see," she said, then willed the words erased. The flush that rose to her cheeks had little to do with the brisk early-evening air.

Then she caught sight of a pale scar at his shoulder and, without thinking, reached up to touch it. Patrick's flinch was involuntary but quickly controlled, and he held steady while her fingertip traced the mark.

"Battle scar?"

He hesitated a minute. When he spoke, his silken tone held grains of sand. "Of sorts. Throwing a football for years can do great things to a man."

"When . . . ?"

He cleared his throat. "My last year. It made the decision to retire that much easier." His voice was devoid of bitterness, indeed of all emotion, in keeping with his eyes.

She nodded dumbly, unaware that her finger remained on his skin until he grabbed her hand and pressed it to his flesh, inching it downward and around the muscled swell of his chest. His flesh was firm beneath her palm, his heartbeat much more steady than her own. When her fingertip grazed his tight nipple, her gaze shot to his.

"Have a thing for jocks?" he asked on a velvet note of mockery. When she grabbed her hand away, he readily released it.

"That was unnecessary," she scolded unevenly.

He gave a one-shouldered shrug, then looked down and slid his arms into the shirt. "It'd make sense. Peter... me...."

"You're almost as crude as Bill."

His eyes met hers as he raised the shirt, lifted his arms and eased his head through its collar. Jordanna suspected the leisurely way he stretched into the knit was deliberate; extended, his body looked all the more powerful. His summer's tan lingered attractively, only slightly paler beneath his arms amid the soft, dark hair that sprouted there.

"Bill doesn't know you," he said, his voice muffled through the shirt.

"Neither do you!" she exclaimed, indignation rising to displace all thoughts.

Without hurry, he smoothed the shirt down over his chest. "I know who you are."

"So do I. I'm Jordanna Kirkland of Willow Enterprises. Period."

His voice lowered and grew harder. "You're also Peter Kirkland's ex-wife."

Jordanna studied him closely, her eyes growing sharp. "That bothers you, doesn't it?"

"Why should it bother me?" he asked with a nonchalance that didn't extend to the telltale flex of his jaw.

"Because you and Peter were rivals from the start. Because Peter bested you once too often." Goaded by instinct, she barreled on. "Because maybe, just maybe, you find me attractive."

His back suddenly ramrod straight, Patrick stared at her for a minute. Then, with neither admission nor denial, he rose and returned to his pack. As abruptly, Jordanna shifted to lie against her own, facing away from the rest. Throwing an arm across her eyes, she took a deep, calming breath and willed the image of a lean, sun-bronzed chest to self-destruct. When it refused to do so, she forced her mind back to New York, burying her thoughts in Willow Enterprises as she'd done now for ten long years.

She wasn't sure if she dozed off, but when John came to offer her a cup of coffee, she opened her eyes with a start and sat up.

"Thanks," she said, mustering a weak smile.

"Tired?"

"A little. It's been a long day."

He hunkered down beside her to nurse his own hot brew. "You drove all the way from New York this morning?"

"Uh-huh."

"Then you must be dead. We all came up yesterday and slept late this morning."

She threw a cursory glance toward the others. "Have you families?"

"Three wives and seven kids among us. Bill's a bachelor."

"How do you know each other?"

"We were college friends."

This time her smile was more natural. "You're kidding! And you've stayed close all this time?"

"Actually, no. We went separate ways after graduation—Don to dental school, Bill to business school, Larry to work with his dad, Craig to get his CPA."

She took a sip of her coffee, savoring its warmth as it slid down her throat. "And you?"

"I went on for a Ph.D. in math. I teach now."

"Math," she mused. "Interesting." Then she frowned. "But how did you all get back together?"

"At our tenth reunion. We discovered we still had a lot in common, including an itch to get away for a week now and then." He laughed softly. "The first time we tried it, we went as couples to the Caribbean. None of the wives got along, and Bill's girl was an absolute pariah."

Jordanna's brows met in a sympathetic frown. "That's a shame."

"No, it was great." When her frown deepened in confusion, he explained. "What we *really* wanted, the guys, I mean, was a week away from *everything*—wives, girlfriends and kids as well as work. So we started planning trips like these." He rocked back on his heels and rolled his eyes toward the darkening sky. "We've sailed in the Bahamas, skied in the Rockies, eaten our way through a cruise, lost our share in Las Vegas."

"But never backpacked before."

"Nope. Never that."

"How did you get hold of Patrick?"

"We didn't. Larry's travel agent did. She knew that he took groups out from time to time and gave him a call. That was last spring."

"You booked him that early? You must all be football freaks." Though she couldn't quite hide the scorn in her voice, John attributed it to a typical female disdain for the sport. His response was indulgent.

"As a matter of fact, one of our trips did combine four days in L.A. with the Super Bowl."

Her moan was not at all feigned. "Oh, God, then I'll have to listen to shoptalk all week?"

"No. That was a stipulation of Patrick's before he'd be our guide."

"What do you mean?"

"He won't discuss football. Apparently it's a standard rule of his." John grew more thoughtful. "I guess he'd had it by the time he retired." He shook his head wistfully. "Man, he was some player."

She scowled. "They didn't call him Lance for nothing."

"Mmm. He really shot that football down the field." As though suddenly realizing that Jordanna knew more than she let on, John eyed her curiously. "You knew him. You know football." When he paused, Jordanna held her breath. "Kirkland. You can't be related to . . . ?"

There seemed no point in prevarication. Patrick had said it twice now; it was simply a matter of time until the others overheard. "Peter. I was married to him for three years. We've been divorced for ten."

"No kidding?" A broad smile split his face. "Hey, that's great! Not the divorce part, I mean. But the marriage. You must have been with him during the best of his playing years! That's exciting!"

"Not really," she stated. "As a matter of fact, it was pretty boring."

"You couldn't have thought so if you married him."

She sighed and looked down. "You're right. I didn't at first. But I learned pretty quick how . . . ah, it's not important." She raised her eyes to focus on Patrick, who seemed busy around the stove. "We should give him a hand," she mumbled, pushing herself to her feet. She had the fleeting image of jumping from the frying pan into the fire, but only knew that she had to let John know there were some things *she* wouldn't discuss.

Patrick looked up at her approach, his expression blank. It was a help.

"What can I do?" she asked, rubbing her cold hands together.

"You can dig the beef stew out of your pack. This water's nearly boiling."

By the time she returned with the packets, the other men had gathered round to watch the proceedings.

"You mean those little things are gonna fill us?" Donald asked, eyeing Jordanna's booty with dismay.

The small nearby lantern illumined Patrick's smirk. "You'll be filled. Believe me. I've allowed two portions for every man."

"Then we can divide up Jordanna's extra?" Bill asked, grinning at what he thought to be irresistible cleverness.

"Not on your life," Jordanna responded. "I'm eating."

"You'll get fat," Larry cautioned.

"Working as hard as you guys? No way."

Bill turned to Donald. "I think she should do the cooking. Woman's work and all."

"No wonder you're not married, Bill," Jordanna scoffed. "No woman in this day and age will have you."

Larry gave half a guffaw, then gulped when Bill scowled at him.

Patrick held up a hand. "Children. Please. Let's try to restrain ourselves. Everyone chips in when it comes to cooking. John and Donald, go on up to the stream and fill the extra pots with water. We'll put them on to heat while we're eating so we'll have something to clean up with later. Bill, I think the pudding's in your pack. I'll need it in a minute. Larry, you've got the plates and utensils. Jordanna, come over here and make the stew." He frowned. "And don't look at me like I'm the devil incarnate. You cook tonight and you're done for the week. Fair?"

The rebellion that was on the tip of her tongue instants before simply vanished. "Just tonight . . . then I'm done for the week?" she asked with a bargaining half smile.

"Uh-oh," Donald groaned, "she's a bra burner. The executive woman. She hates to cook."

Donning her most beatific smile, Jordanna knelt beside Patrick. "You instruct. I'll cook."

That was precisely what she did. Dinner was surprisingly good and decidedly filling. Patrick was patient, if all business, which pleased her no end. She'd begun to imagine that being near him for the week might be an ordeal above and beyond those memories she fought, but, during dinner at least, he treated her like one of the guys.

Later that night, well, that was something else.

2

EXHAUSTED, JORDANNA fell into a deep sleep shortly after dinner. Burrowing snugly into her sleeping bag in a far corner of the shelter, she was comfortably warm and dead to the world. The men talked and laughed, but she heard nothing until the middle of the night when, disturbed by an unexpected sound, she awoke with a start.

It took her a minute to remember where she was. Groggy, she looked around, then sat up and studied the darkness. When the noise came again, her head jerked toward the vague forms on the opposite side of the shelter.

Someone was snoring. She put a hand to her chest to still the thudding of her heart, then scowled and looked away. Peter had snored. More nights than she cared to recall she'd awoken to urge him onto his side. Then she'd lain awake for hours brooding, unable to fall back to sleep.

So now she was suddenly wide awake. The snoring persisted, a deep shudder that grated as she sat. She tried to make out who it was, but couldn't tell one sleeping bag from another in the dark—not that she would have been able to do anything had she known who the culprit was.

Annoyed at having been awakened, she drew her down-covered knees to her chin and glared out at the woods beyond the shelter, then back into the shadows. As her eyes slowly adjusted she deciphered one sleeping bag set apart from the others, lying roughly halfway between hers and theirs. It had to be Patrick's.

At least he wasn't the snorer, she mused, studying his dark cocooned form. Strange how he'd set himself there; perhaps not so strange in light of his job. He was the quarterback, calling the plays, ready to deal with any problem that might arise in the middle of the night. She gave a derisive snort. Perhaps he was afraid that one of the men might approach her. How touching. Her white knight, sound asleep.

With lips pressed tightly together she struggled to her feet and, sleeping bag and all, shuffled from the shadowed shelter out into the pale moonlight. Only when she'd gone far enough to reduce the snoring to a dull hum did she stop. Sinking down inside the sleeping bag, she sat cross-legged on the ground, her back to the shelter, her eyes on the nightscape.

Cast now in silver rather than gold, the woods were as beautiful as they'd been by day. She tipped her head back to study the branches overhead, then slowly returned her gaze to the ground. At a movement in the brush, she froze, watching wide-eyed when what appeared to be an opossum sauntered across her range of vision, leading with its pointed nose, trailing with its tail, disappearing into the woods with an indifference to her presence that she accepted with pure relief. Though adventurous, a physically active woman, she knew little about creatures of the wild. For an instant she wondered what else might wander about in the night—deer, fox, *bears*—then she quickly thought of Patrick and found solace knowing he was near. He seemed levelheaded and skilled when it came to the outdoor life; she admired him for that. Thoughts diverging, she also admired him for the ease with which he'd handled the group on this first day of the hike, for his deep, rich voice, for the firm tone of his body....

Her mind drifted and she was back in the colosseum stands, eyes glued to the teams in formation at the five-yard line. The crowd roared on either side, but beyond its thunder, her sole concentration was on the quarterback whose hands were ready, awaiting the snap. He turned his head to one side then the other, shouting coded commands to his team. Then he had the ball and ran back to pass, his padded shoulders bunched and broad, his hips sleek and lean. Jordanna had always responded to seeing him that way. Poised on the brink of action, he was, in her mind, the quintessential male.

Moments later, when having failed to find a receiver, he'd barreled over the line to make the touchdown himself, he was lost to her. Arms raised in triumph, he'd belonged to the crowd, his adoring public and his own monumental ego.

Shaking her head in an attempt to chase these unbidden images from her mind, she hugged herself more tightly. Peter had been physically magnificent, both on the field and off. Emotionally, intellectually—those were other matters.

And what about Patrick? He was good-looking, she admitted reluctantly, too good-looking. And he affected her, which bothered her. She'd been unaffected by a man for years and had wanted it that way. Given the debacle of her marriage and the subsequent demands of the career she'd molded for herself, she had no time for men.

Her physical response to Patrick surprised her. Even now she could recall the feel of his skin beneath her hand, and her palm tingled. Was she sex starved? Or simply a masochist? *Did* she have a thing for jocks?

Moaning softly, she buried her face against her knees. Then she heard a footstep behind her and whirled to confront a dark form looming above. When she would have cried out in fright, a large hand clamped over her mouth.

A long arm curved around her middle. Strong thighs lowered to frame her hips.

"Shh. It's just me." The whisper faded. Slowly the hand from her mouth was withdrawn, fingers trailing across her lips in reluctant departure.

"Patrick?" she whispered, twisting to look up into his moon-shadowed face, in doing so dragging her head to his shoulder. His arm remained around her sleeping bag in the vicinity of her waist.

"Yes," he whispered. "Are you all right?"

Her pulse was racing. "You frightened me!"

"I heard you get up. I thought you had to go to the...well, when you didn't come back I got worried."

"I'm fine," she whispered, but wondered if it were true. Her nerve ends continued to jump. She made no move to free herself from his embrace, though. It was surprisingly comfortable, not binding, yet warm and supportive.

"Couldn't sleep?"

When she would have cast a glance toward the shelter, she found she couldn't take her eyes from his. "One of the men was snoring." The dim sound persisted. "It woke me up."

"Don't like snoring?" Given the lightness of his tone, she could have sworn he was teasing her.

"No."

"Peter didn't snore?"

Not teasing. Goading. Straightening, she freed herself from his arm and inched forward on her bottom until she sat a solid foot away. She stared into the woods. "Peter snored."

"And you didn't like it."

"No."

For several moments there was silence. Then Patrick flipped to the side to sit on the ground by Jordanna's hip, facing in the opposite direction. She didn't look at him.

"Why are you here, Jordanna?" he asked at last, his voice still low but now hard and direct.

She knew he wasn't talking about the woods in the middle of the night. "You've asked that before. It's getting boring."

"I'd still like to know."

She did look at him then, but his profile was shadowed. "Why?"

"Curiosity."

"Curiosity killed the cat." She spoke to herself as much as to him. There were far too many questions on her mind.

His jaw flexed. She saw that much. "I'm not planning on dying just yet," he stated softly but firmly. "I've fought too hard for too long. Which brings me back to my question. Why have you come?"

She refused to be put on the defensive. "Why do *you* think I've come?"

"It's occurred to me," he began without hesitation, "that you knew I'd be leading this group."

"*Are you kidding?*"

"Shh!" He tossed a glance toward the shelter. "You'll wake the others."

Though she lowered her voice to a whisper, her incredulity remained. "You think I came because of *you?*"

"It's been done."

She threw her head back vehemently. "Omigod, I don't believe it! Another one! Pure ego!" Then she raised her head and stiffened her spine. "If I'd known you were going to be here, I'd *never* have come!" Her eyes flashed angrily, uncompromisingly.

"You hate me."

"What?"

He spoke more slowly, his eyes just as uncompromising in their hold on hers. "You hate me."

"I barely *know* you. How could I hate you?"

"You were the one who pointed out that Peter and I were rivals."

"What's that got to do with hate?"

"You were his wife. It'd be natural for you to side with him."

"Peter never hated you."

"No," he mused grimly. "I suppose you're right. Since he always came out on top, he'd have no reason to hate."

"But you do?"

"Hate? No. Resent . . . perhaps. It wasn't pleasant playing second fiddle to Peter Kirkland all those years. . . . But we're getting off the point."

"Which is?"

"Why, in your words, you'd never have come on this trip if you'd known I'd be along."

With a deep breath, she squeezed her eyes shut and lowered her head to her knees once again. "To be blunt, Patrick," she began, speaking slowly, as though with great effort, "I don't need the memories."

"Ahh. You've sworn off jocks."

Her head shot up. He was goading her again. "I was never *on* jocks," she stated ardently. "I was in love with Peter Kirkland, the man, *not* the jock."

"Could you separate the two?" he asked pointedly.

Her whisper was less steady. "I thought I could. At first."

"But not in the end?"

"We're divorced. It's over." She turned her head away. "And none of your business."

Undaunted, he gave a magnanimous sigh. "Well, that's a relief, at least."

"What is?" she murmured against the rim of her sleeping bag.

"That you're not into jocks. But you are into men?"

She whirled around. "I can't believe you said that."

"Why not? It's a simple question."

"It's crude."

"Like Bill. Ah, that's right. I remind you of Bill."

He didn't. Not in the least. And whether he was teasing or goading this time, she didn't know. "Why are you doing this?" she whispered. "Why don't you . . . go pick on someone your own size?"

"I like your size better." When she tried to rise, he shackled her arm through the bag and stayed her escape.

"Go talk to one of the men," she muttered.

"They're sleeping."

"Why aren't you?"

"Because you're not. Because I heard you get up. Because I was worried. And curious."

He inched closer. She could see that his hair was mussed, that his jaw was tight, that his gaze had dropped to her lips. When again she tried to pull back, he swung around to much the same position he'd been in when he'd captured her.

"Let me go, Lance," she whispered, struggling to steady the suddenly erratic beat of her heart. He was behind her, his warmth blanketing her back, his arms circling her front, holding her more gently than she wished. For, had he been rough, she might have fought. But this gentleness, this warmth was strangely seductive. Or was it the night? Or the allure of the woods? Or the fact that it had been a long, long time since she'd been held by a man?

"It's Patrick, Jordanna," he murmured against her hair. "Lance no longer, exists; you needn't fight memories with me. It's Patrick. And he's a man. And, damn it—" his voice lowered "—he does find you attractive."

When she should have been turned off by his begrudging admission, she was only further intrigued. Suddenly she wasn't thinking of Lance or the past, but of Patrick and the way his firm man's body seemed to shield her from all else. She was thinking of his chest, with its soft, dark hair, of his fingers, smelling faintly musky as they'd brushed her lips, of his eyes, deep brown and warm when he willed them so.

Cupping her chin, he tipped her head to the side, resting it in the crook of his shoulder in an open spill of moonlight. His face mere inches away, he looked at her then, studying each of her features in turn as she lay, mesmerized, in his arms.

"I was curious," he began in a soul-stroking murmur, "about what it would be like to kiss you."

Only in that instant did Jordanna allow herself to admit that she was curious about the very same thing. Patrick Clayes was strong, eminently masculine, thoroughly appealing. When his head lowered by inches until his lips were a hair's breadth from hers, she held her breath, waiting, waiting to see if the frisson of excitement shimmering through her veins was an illusion.

It wasn't. His mouth whispered a kiss first on one corner of her lips, then the other, and her heart beat faster. Having expected a more forceful approach, she was both startled and charmed by his gentle evasion. The excitement she'd felt was joined by a strange languor. Her limbs went weak. She closed her eyes to better savor every soft nuance of his touch.

His lips moved slowly, stringing the gentlest of kisses along the line of her mouth until she thought she'd scream in frustration. He was goading her. Or was he giving her time to demur? But she wasn't the demurring type. She knew what she wanted. It wasn't the sanest thing, but she did know.

Her lips parted, met seconds later by the fullness of Patrick's kiss. Like his voice it was rich and velvet smooth, like his skin, warm and alive. He moved his mouth with the same riveting gentleness with which his arms held her, drawing a response from her most feminine depths.

When he suddenly drew back, she was bereft, but only until she caught the smoldering gleam in his eyes. "Jordanna?" he whispered unsteadily.

In answer, she reached up, threaded her fingers through the thickness of his sleep-mussed hair and drew his head down until their lips met once more. This time she found the force she'd expected before, but far from brute, it was electrifyingly wonderful, satisfying the very need she felt. Raising a hand to her throat, he caressed its smooth line as his tongue sampled the more varied textures of her teeth, her gums, her seeking tongue. He was as breathless as she when they separated.

"You're so soft," he whispered against her temple as his hand continued to stroke her neck. He slid a finger beneath the crew neck of her thermal shirt and traced a gentle arc along her collarbone. "How come you're so soft?"

"My cream," she said unsteadily, her sole concentration on that finger that seemed, with each slow sweep, to inch lower. Her breasts were taut, upthrust, aching to be held.

"Your cream?" He looked down at her.

She swallowed hard under his lambent gaze. "Moisturizer. I'm an addict."

His hand came to a rest over the hollow of her throat. "For business?"

"For me. I like taking care of myself."

He dropped his hand, but left his arm around her back. "Is that a hint?"

"I hadn't meant it to be," she said, sobering now that the lure of his touch seemed a dream, "but I suppose it's true."

"You're independent."

"Yes."

"No leaning on a man?"

"Not anymore." Left unspoken was direct comment on her marriage. Patrick seemed willing to let the matter ride.

"Surely you've been involved with men since Peter."

"Why surely?"

He studied her for several moments. Then he let out a sigh of resignation and, as if he'd forgotten her question, spoke on a different track. "You're a beautiful woman, Jordanna. I always envied Peter. You made him look good."

She sat up slowly. "Funny, I thought it was the other way around."

"No way. He may have had the trophies, but you had the class. Your business is proof of that."

"You know about my work?"

He donned an endearingly sheepish expression. "Only what I overheard the guys saying tonight."

She scrunched up her face. "You mean that while I slept they were *talking* about me?"

The gentle fingers he placed on her lips quieted her more so even than his soft, "Shh. They needed to let off steam. A couple of them are still pretty miffed that you insisted on coming along."

"Tough," she spat, but in a whisper. "They're a bunch of—"

"Uh-uh. Be generous. They feel awkward. That's all."

"Do you?"

"What do you think?"

"I don't know. I don't know you at all."

"Are you sorry . . . that happened?"

She knew he was referring to their kiss, and could be nothing but truthful. It was her way. "No," she answered softly. "I'm not sorry. Are you?"

"No." He paused. "I wish like hell you weren't Peter's girl. . . ."

"I'm *not*! Why do you keep bringing *Peter* into this?"

"Because he's there, damn it!" Patrick growled, surging to his feet.

"Weren't you the one who said Lance didn't exist anymore? Weren't you the one who said there were no memories to fight?"

"Then it looks like I was wrong," Patrick muttered, raking a hand through his hair in frustration. "I lived in Peter Kirkland's shadow for years and I'll be damned if I'll take his castoffs." Turning on his heel, he stormed off, not toward the shelter but into the woods.

Mouth agape, Jordanna stared at his vanishing form. Only when night had swallowed him completely did she clamp her mouth shut. Her trembling limbs spoke of her fury, her wide eyes broadcast hurt. Oh, she was no novice to cutting statements, but coming from this man and on the tail of his spectacular kiss . . . it stung.

The worst was that he was gone, and there was absolutely nothing she could do by way of reply. She felt frustrated, impotent. She'd been wronged and was helpless to correct the situation.

As the quiet minutes passed, she cooled down, but the hurt lingered after she'd returned to the shelter. When she finally fell asleep it was nearly dawn. Patrick had not returned.

"JORDANNA?"

A gentle hand shook her shoulder, then tentatively rubbed her back.

"Wake up, Jordanna."

She heard his voice from far away and pulled the sleeping bag more tightly over her head. It was too early, pitch-black, and she was tired, so tired.

"Come on, Jordanna. Everyone else is eating breakfast."

She slitted open an eye and searched the darkness, saw nothing, attributed the voice to a dream. Then she realized where she was. And remembered what had happened. On pure reflex, she recoiled from the hand on her shoulder and sat up, slowly lowering the sleeping bag to her shoulders.

To her chagrin, the sun was shining, which was unfair when she felt tired, disgruntled and stiff. Sure enough, the men were grouped around the small camp stove. She squinted at them, hoping Patrick would simply evaporate. When he remained squatting by her side, she turned to glare at him.

"You can leave now," she said coolly, clutching the sleeping bag to her breasts. "I'm awake." Twisting away, she dug a hairbrush from her pack.

"Jordanna?"

Her hand hovered, fingers gripping the brush handle.

"Look at me, Jordanna."

Very slowly she turned her head, her face a mask of tension.

"I'm sorry for what I said last night. It was wrong of me."

"You meant it. Why apologize?"

"I didn't mean to imply that you were one of Peter's cast-offs."

"Then why did you say it?"

Looking down, he snapped a dried twig between the fingers of one hand. "I was feeling threatened. I lashed out. It was juvenile." He sought her gaze again. "And cruel."

"You're right. It was both of those things, plus another—it was *wrong*." Eyes flashing, she stared him down. "I was the one who divorced Peter, not the other way around. I was the one who was fed up, who wanted out, who wanted something more than he had to offer. I cast *Peter* off, if you want to know the truth." She grew more skeptical. "And whatever would you have to feel threatened about?"

His eyes were a deep, deep brown that invited drowning. "You. The pleasure I felt when I kissed you."

Fighting his appeal, Jordanna looked away and briskly worked the brush through her hair. "It was just a kiss. Nothing threatening about it."

Strong fingers seized her chin and turned her face his way. "It was a *super* kiss. Don't tell me you didn't think so."

She felt positively belligerent. "Of course it was a super kiss. You're a pro, Lance. But it was *only* a kiss. Nothing to be threatened by." She was goading him without remorse. "Now, will you please let go of me?"

Patrick's features darkened. Very slowly he dropped his hand. "I hurt you, Jordanna, and I'm very sorry for that. If lashing back at me makes you feel better, go ahead." He sighed on a note of what Jordanna almost thought to be defeat. "You can use the stream to wash up and change. I'll keep the guys here for a while so you can have some privacy." Pushing himself to his feet, he turned and headed toward the others.

Determined to let him go his way, Jordanna busied herself with digging everything she'd need from her pack. Under cover of her sleeping bag, she tugged on yesterday's running suit, then, as Patrick had suggested, headed for the stream to clean up and put on the fresh things she carried.

The air was cold, the stream a challenge. Holding her breath, then expelling it in involuntary little cries, she threw handful after handful of water on her face. The diversion was welcome. By the time she'd dried and moisturized her skin, sponged off her body and gotten dressed again, she was tingling all over. And confused.

She ate breakfast quickly, packed up her things and set out with the others, all the while wondering why she wasn't furious with Patrick. She should be, but she wasn't. Hurt as she'd been by the insult he'd hurled in the dark of the woods last night, she did believe that he was sorry. His apology had been forthright, his manner sincere. And he was obviously as bothered by the past as she was. Knowing well the arrogance of Peter Kirkland, she could begin to understand the bitter pill Patrick had had to swallow for years. She could begin to understand—and forgive—and that confused her all the more.

As though made to order, the day's route was demanding in terms both of strength and concentration. Once the group was twenty minutes into the hike, Jordanna's legs weren't the only ones to protest.

"Whew," John breathed, calling to Patrick from the end of the line. "Is it uphill all the way?"

Patrick looked back with a knowing smirk. "For a while. Problems?"

"Nope! Nope!"

"Why're you huffing and puffing like an old man?" Donald teased, directing his words to John, though catching Jordanna's eye and winking at her in a show of friendliness that surprised her. "*We're* all doin' fine."

"Speak for yourself, Don," Larry groaned, collapsing onto a rock and tugging at his boot. "I think yesterday's blister just woke up."

Patiently Patrick helped him put moleskin on the offended spot. "We'll take it slow," he avowed as they started off again. "But you'll earn your stripes today."

Jordanna was grateful. Unsure as to how to act with Patrick, she welcomed the hard work he drew from them all. As the morning progressed, they followed the Black Angel Trail to Rim Junction, where five different trails met in an intersection as confusing as any Jordanna had ever seen. There were no street signs, no service stations or churches or McDonald's to distinguish one trail from the next.

But Patrick knew. At his direction they headed south onto the Basin Rim Trail. It was this trail that took them through stands of spruce and across ledges to the foot of Mount Meader.

"Doesn't look so tough," Bill observed, eyeing the wooded crest when they were still a distance away.

"Gettin' bigger," Donald commented sometime later.

"Man, this looks rugged," was John's accurate summation when they began the ascent.

It was rugged. Many of the rocky inclines called for teamwork in the scaling; packs were passed from hand to hand, freeing bodies to concentrate on handholds and steady footing. To Jordanna's relief, Patrick kept his distance, seeming determined to let her hack it on her own. And she did. Ignoring muscles that clamored for a rest, she kept pace with the men through the steep climb. By the time they stopped for lunch on the scenic lookout ledges near the summit, though, she was grateful to crumple on a rock and lie back against her pack.

She wasn't the only one. Four men collapsed on the ledges nearby. Only Patrick had the strength to move around from pack to pack, gathering and distributing Slim Jims, Triscuits and nuts.

"Is this exhilaration?" Larry asked, doubt written all over his pale face.

"Sure," Bill said, reaching for the plastic container of peanut butter Patrick offered. "You're just out of shape. I told you to build yourself up before you came."

"I did. I did."

"How many knee bends?" Donald asked, squirting a blob of jelly from a plastic tube.

"Enough," Larry mumbled.

As always, Jordanna was slightly apart from the others. Patrick sank to the ground by her side. "You're doin' fine," he observed casually.

"It's fun," she replied cautiously.

"Not mad at me anymore?"

She thought for a minute. "I think I walked it off."

"That's good."

Unwrapping a Slim Jim, she bit off a piece. "I like the exertion."

"Not tired?"

"I didn't say *that*." After listening to the men's talk with half an ear, she spoke again. It was time she explained herself. "Backpacking is an adventure I've never had the opportunity to take part in before. When Craig called, the time seemed right. Things were only mildly chaotic at the office for a change. I needed a vacation. Winter will set in before long, and I'll be stuck inside."

"You don't ski?"

"No. Do you?"

His lips twitched. "I tried. I wasn't too good at it."

"A professional athlete? I can't believe that."

His eyes went cold for an instant. "I *was* a professional athlete. Past tense. And being good at one sport doesn't imply skill at all others."

"I didn't mean that," she said softly, then corrected herself. "Well, maybe I did. You were supercoordinated on the field. You're a pro here in the hills. I guess I assumed . . . well, I'm sorry. I didn't realize you were sensitive."

He popped a cashew into his mouth. "I'm tired. That's all. It was bad enough in my playing days having to constantly compete with . . . the other talent on the field. Now people expect me to compete with the man I was then." He raised his eyes to hers. No longer cold, they were nonetheless earnest. "I can't. I don't want to." As though unconsciously punctuating his words, he flexed his shoulder, rubbed it, then dropped another nut into his mouth.

"Does it hurt?"

"Not competing?"

"I was thinking of your shoulder, but I guess the question could apply to that too."

"Both. On occasion."

"Does your pack bother it? Your shoulder, that is."

He crinkled his nose, looking almost boyish. "Nah. Well, maybe once in a while. It's okay."

Again they sat in silence, taking their turns with the peanut butter and jelly, then the Tang. Jordanna found herself thinking of what he'd said and feeling touched by what appeared to be nicks in his armor. Peter had had no nicks. He'd been perfect. Bright and shining. Invincible. And, as time passed, totally obnoxious.

"What do you do?" she asked, searching for fodder to further delineate Patrick from his archrival. When he looked up questioningly, she gestured broadly. "Job-type thing."

He hesitated for a minute. "What do *you* think I do?"

The sudden twinkle in his eye evoked even greater indulgence on her part. "Oh, no. You're not getting me into trouble with that one."

"Come on," he coaxed, seeming fully at ease. "If you were to imagine what a football-playing has-been would do, what would it be?"

Ironic she mused, how he could still feel such bitterness toward Peter, yet toward his career's demise, none at all. It gave her courage. "When I first saw you yesterday, I wondered if you were either coaching or broadcasting. But you're so determined that the days of the Lance are over that I'd have to rule those out. Which also rules out the probability of living off endorsements." As Peter did, she was going to say, but prudently caught herself. Her eyes narrowed on Patrick in speculation. "You could be selling cars or clothes or real estate." She arched a brow. "Some former greats own restaurant chains." Her gaze fell to the remains of the Slim Jim in her hand, then skipped to the Triscuit Patrick was about to dunk in the peanut-butter tub. Gourmet fare? "Forget that. No restaurants."

He chuckled. "No restaurants. Try again."

"You're very good with people," she reflected as her gaze encompassed the men nearby. "Management? Personnel? Wait. I'll bet you're a psychology professor."

"You were closer before," he said softly. "I'm in business."

"Oh?"

He nodded. "Venture capitalism."

"Oh."

He laughed aloud at her comical change of expression. "What's wrong with being a venture capitalist?"

She scowled. "Nothing. I suppose."

"Come on. Out with it."

She took a breath. "I went to a bunch of investors when I was first setting up the business. They turned me down cold."

"Maybe they didn't think you could make it."

"Obviously." She gave a sly smile. "They must be choking on their Scotch now."

"We don't *all* drink Scotch...."

"True," she admitted, realizing she probably sounded as bigoted as those she accused. Relenting, she shrugged. "You must do some good."

"I think so. In the six years my group's been at it, we've set up several dozen new businesses and put any number of others back on their feet from states of near bankruptcy."

"Have any of those businesses been women-run?" she asked skeptically.

"Several." His eyes held meaning. "We don't discriminate. If a woman's got it all together, we'll take her on."

"Your investors agree?"

"They trust us."

"I see."

"Come to think of it, we've never gone wrong with a woman. Those few disasters we've had have been male-run all the way."

"Perhaps there's a double standard at play," Jordanna mused, unable to help herself. "Women have to work twice as hard. They have to be twice as good. Isn't it possible that to be accepted by your group she's got to be far superior to everyone else out there?"

Patrick was undaunted by her not-so-subtle accusation. "I'd like to think that *anyone* we decide to back is far superior to the rest of the field. It's my money and my partners' *and* that of the investors we corral to join us. But—" he gestured dismissively "—it's not only the money we put up. It's the working together. The management. That's where the real challenge comes in."

She eyed him warily. "It does excite you, doesn't it?"

"Yes."

"And I suppose you do it well."

"I hope so. I'd like to believe that much is part of my personality," he said gently. "It's the competitive instinct. Football or business—I wouldn't do it at all if I couldn't do it well."

Nodding, she sat back to munch on the cashews he handed her. A fast glance at the other men was enough to assure her that she and Patrick had privacy of sorts. "You've never married?"

"The same theory applies. I refuse to do it if I can't do it well." He gave a lopsided grin. "I've never found the woman who, shall we say, inspired that forever instinct." Shifting and stretching out on the ground, he pillowed his head with his hands and closed his eyes.

Jordanna's gaze raked his supine form. Long, well-formed legs lay beneath denim made soft and supple by wear. The broad chest she'd so admired pulled his navy turtleneck taut; both were framed by the open zipper of his Goretex shell. His cheeks were lean and clean shaven, a far cry from the day's stubble sported by the four other men. His hair was thick and full, clipped close only at the sideburns and neck. Long, dark lashes dusted cheekbones that were high, strong and tanned.

Clamping her eyes shut against the involuntary flutter in her middle, she slowly settled onto her back to follow his lead and absorb the sun's warm noontime rays. Only with the passage of several moments did she open one eye to steal another look.

Patrick was waiting for her. He rolled to his stomach, bringing himself within inches of her. "I wondered if you were falling asleep," he murmured. "You look tired."

Tipping her head more fully his way, she opened the other eye. "I seem to have had a minimum of sleep the past two nights."

"Two? Then there was a wild farewell Sunday night with a special someone?"

Her smile was soft. "Not quite. I was up late cramming for this trip."

"Cramming?"

"Reading everything I could about backpacking. Thank heavens for bookstores open on Sundays."

He returned her smile with one that was heartstoppingly gentle. "You're quite something, ya know that?"

"Not really," she said, and meant it. Though she was proud of what she'd made of her life, she was far from cocky. And she'd never before found a man confident enough to compliment her with such honest admiration.

"You're blushing. It's pretty." At his whisper-soft words her color rose all the more. "You've aged beautifully, Jordanna. I swear you look even better than you did when you were with Peter, and you were gorgeous then. How old are you? Thirty? Thirty-one?"

Enjoying his attention, she propped her ear on her palm. "Thirty-two."

"You married young."

"I was nineteen and dumb." Her grin took the sting from her words. Patrick lifted a finger to trace its soft curve.

"Funny, our meeting this way...you and I, away from all that...."

She nipped at the tip of his finger. "It is funny."

"You're a great kisser."

"So are you."

His lips twitched playfully. "But it'd be *really* dumb if we got involved with each other."

Her eyes glowed a seductive amber-in-hazel. "*I'll* say."

"How about a fling? You know, a three-night stand with sleeping bags zipped together?"

She winced. "Patrick! With *them*?" The grimace she tossed toward the others was comical.

"Of course not," he whispered back. "I could drag you by the hair into the woods—"

"Caveman tactics, hmm?"

"If need be. You turn me on, Jordanna."

"The feeling's mutual."

"But dumb."

"Really dumb."

He sighed then, a long, slightly wavering exercise of the lungs. "We'll have to try to remember that," he croaked. Then he cleared his throat, pushed himself up and raised his voice to call to the others. "Okay. Let's clean up this mess and get going. As the man said, we've got miles to go before we sleep. . . ."

THE AFTERNOON'S TREK was as rugged as the morning's. With much panting they reached the summit of Mount Meader, then wound down along the Meader Ridge Trail. One spectacular view followed the next—narrow ridges playing up distant mountain ranges, contortions of rock where long-gone glaciers had carved out the landscape, spruce-covered hillsides, craggy ravines. Larry had a field day with his camera. The others enjoyed each pause to make mental pictures of the sights.

Seeming to have accepted her presence, the men included Jordanna in their talk from time to time. She came to realize that complaining was part of their fun. In truth they enjoyed the hike and its views as much as she did.

On the more tedious stretches of the trail, they walked in silence. Part of the path was boggy. Much of it now was downhill. As a runner, Jordanna knew the perils of the downhill trek. When Larry and Donald in tandem cursed their quads, she smiled knowingly.

They stopped for a break in the middle of the afternoon, then followed an old logging road through a forest of white birch. At last they reached Wild River.

"This is it?" Bill gawked in dismay.

Jordanna joined the man to stare at the dark bed of mossy rocks. "It is wild, isn't it?" she quipped, surprising herself with her own good humor when her shoulders, her back, her legs ached.

"We're upstream from the water," Patrick explained. "Come on. Campsite's not too far ahead."

By the time they reached the dry, flat area he had in mind, Jordanna was as happy as the others to shed her pack for the night. There was no formal shelter this time, simply an abundance of woods surrounding an open area with a rough circle of stones for a fire.

As had happened the day before when the sun set, the air grew rapidly cold. Sweat that had gathered during the trek dried. Jackets were momentarily shed for the donning of additional layers beneath.

Under Patrick's patient tutelage, the tents they'd carried were unfurled, erected and anchored. As Jordanna did her share of the work, so she did her share of speculation. Three two-man tents. Interesting. By the time she stood admiring one such finished product, the other two tents were spoken for. She looked at Patrick. He looked at her. Then, with mirrored shrugs and the faintest tugging of smiles, they tossed their packs to the front of one remaining tent and turned with relish to the prospect of a hot dinner.

As had happened the night before, Jordanna's eyelids began to droop long before she finished the coffee in her mug. The men had begun to play poker. Excusing herself as unobtrusively as she could, she crawled into the tent, stripped down in her long underwear, climbed into her sleeping bag and fell promptly asleep.

This time it wasn't snoring that woke her, but a pair of warm male lips caressing her brow.

3

THE SENSATION was pleasurable, one of a delicious warmth in contrast to the cold night air. For long moments Jordanna succumbed to its allure, smiling in the state of half sleep from which she had no desire to emerge. She didn't want to think, she didn't want to analyze the source of such simple bliss. Wakefulness was her enemy. But it could only be held off so long.

"Patrick," she murmured sleepily, "what are you doing?"

"Warming my lips," he breathed against her eyes. "It's damn cold out there."

"Not much better in here. My nose is freezing."

Instantly his warmth touched the afflicted feature. "Better?" he whispered, his breath coffee scented and very, very close.

Her eyelids flickered. Withdrawing a hand from its shelter deep inside her sleeping bag, she felt for his jaw. It moved slowly beneath her palm as he breathed soft kisses from the tip of her nose to its bridge.

"Funny, you don't feel cold," she mumbled, her grogginess dissipating by the second. His cheek was warm, as was his brow and, her fingers discovered when they slid into the thickness of his hair, his scalp. Moreover, his very nearness sent a wild shaft of heat through her body.

Suddenly she was wide awake . . . and aware of the folly of letting him kiss her further. Clutching a handful of his hair, she drew his head back. "Isn't there a law against this?"

"Against what?" he asked, his voice the embodiment of innocence.

"Messing with the clientele."

"I love messing with the clientele."

Her fingers tightened. "You do this *all the time*?"

He twisted his head to alleviate the pain of her grip. "Ahh. Ease up." When she did, he rubbed the offended spot and spoke gruffly. "Of course I don't. What do you take me for?"

"I could take you for the same kind of rutting stallion Peter was," she said without thinking, then regretted it moments later when Patrick came down full length on top of her, pinning her body to the ground, her hand to the corner of the sleeping bag by her shoulder.

"I'm not Peter, Jordanna," he said in a dangerously low voice, then repeated it again very slowly and with feeling. "I'm not Peter. We may have shared a profession, a playing field on occasion, a podium from time to time and any amount of newsprint, but that's where the association ends." His grip tightened on her wrist. Even in the dark his eyes held hers, which were wide and stunned by the force of his reaction to her careless barb. "I don't know what kind of husband he was, or lover, and I don't give a damn. I do know that he was loud and brash and had a corner on the market for conceit—"

"Hey!" A muffled shout from without broke into his harangue. "What's going on over there!"

It was joined by a second, aimed snidely at the first. "What do you *think*'s going on?"

And a third, more indulgently. "They're talking football. Let them be."

"But I'm trying to sleep," complained the first.

"Could've fooled me," grumbled his tent mate. "You've been thrashing all over the—"

"Damn tent's too small!"

"Shut up, all of you," came the fourth, last but not least. "You're making more noise than the lovers!"

Jordanna could contain herself no longer. "Lovers?" she cried indignantly. "*Lovers?* Are you all mad?"

Patrick's fingers sealed her lips as he raised his head to address the shrouded night. "You guys better get some sleep. Jordanna and I just had a minor disagreement. We'll keep it down."

There were several vague grunts, followed by silence. Jordanna held her breath, abundantly aware of Patrick's hard length pressing her to the ground. Even the padding of her sleeping bag seemed insignificant against his commanding form. She had mixed feelings when he rolled onto his back atop his own sleeping bag.

The silence was thick, the tent suddenly minuscule. Jordanna listened to the sound of Patrick's breathing and wondered what had happened to those other sounds of the night. There seemed no breeze, no stirring of woodland creatures across the carpet of dried leaves, no distant trickle of the stream. Only Patrick. Breathing far more steadily, she cursed silently, than was she.

Unable to stand the kind of suspense that hung in the air, she turned her head in his direction. "Pat?" she whispered.

When at last he gave a quiet, "Mmm?", she breathed a sigh of relief. She knew he wasn't asleep, but she wasn't sure whether he'd admit it.

"Pat, I'm sorry." The simplest part of what she had to say came fast. Now she began to struggle for the right words. "I...well...I didn't mean to compare you with Peter. It...it kind of came out all by itself." She looked toward the roof of the tent, then threw an arm across her eyes. When Patrick remained silent, she realized he wasn't going to help her. She stumbled on. "I really... I really haven't been with that many men. I mean, I don't sleep around and I guess you make me...feel vulnerable...." She swore softly and turned onto her side away from him. Scowling into the darkness, she wondered how she'd managed to make such a mess of something so small. What had he said—that he loved messing with the clientele? Of course he'd been teasing her. Of course?

"I was only teasing," he whispered as if on cue. With a sudden movement, he reached out and slid an arm beneath her to roll her back toward him. Jordanna's initial resistance owed more to the strangeness of the intimacy than to genuine reluctance; after several seconds, she relaxed against him, letting her cheek rest in the crook of his shoulder while his arm held her fast. "Not all men bed-hop, Jordanna. There are those of us who are somewhat fastidious. It's as intimate, as private, as special an act for me as it is for you, you know."

She hadn't thought about it that way and now that she did, particularly hearing the words on Patrick's lips, she felt a shimmer of electricity sear her in passing. In part to fight that unbidden awareness, she resorted to gentle mockery. "Are you trying to tell me you're a virgin?"

His chuckle was priceless and worth the risk she'd taken that his good humor had returned. "Not quite. But I don't sleep around either. I may never have married, but I've been lucky enough to have had some truly fine relationships with women. I've learned from them. I've learned a lot." He slanted his head down; his lips brushed her brow as he spoke. "Among other things, I've learned that respect is critical to any meaningful relationship. Self-respect, as well as respect for one's partner. No, Jordanna, I don't mess around with the clientele." His already low voice dropped to a nearly inaudible level. "At least, I never have before...."

"I heard that," Jordanna whispered through a gentle smile. "And thank you for saying it. It's a relief to know that I'm not the only one acting out of character."

Again came the chuckle that tickled her pink. "Not by a long shot, angel." His arm tightened momentarily around her. "Must be something about this backwoods air that plays havoc with the hormones."

"Guess so," she murmured softly, then moved her hand along his chest. Above the waist, he wore nothing more than a thermal shirt like hers, but she was further bundled in her sleeping bag. "You must be freezing!" she exclaimed, moving her hand in a larger arc. "Don't you want to get into your sleeping bag?"

"Not . . . particularly."

"Why not?"

Again his breath played against her brow. "Because that'll be one more layer between us. *Your* sleeping bag's bad enough." Shifting deftly into his side, he brought his face opposite hers. "Let's zip them together. Come on. What do you say?"

Jordanna's shiver was not from the cold. "I say that we'd be crazy to do that."

"We'd be warm."

"Too warm."

"Listen," he began, reaching out through the darkness to stroke her hair with an ease that belied the urgency in his voice, "I know you're not loose. And I know I'm not either. But, damn it, something's happening here. I take one look at you and—bam—I forget who we are, where we are, and the only thing I want to do is to take you in my arms and...."

"And?"

"Make love to you."

Jordanna's insides quivered. She couldn't deny anything Patrick said, for her body clamored likewise. Unable to help herself, she placed her fingers against his lips, ostensibly stilling him while in reality very slowly exploring his lips in the way of the blind. "You shouldn't say things like that, Pat. They're nearly irresistible."

"They're meant to be," he whispered without remorse. "So, how about it? Should we warm each other?"

"No."

"Mmm." With a soulful sigh, he released her. "Dumb."

"Uh-huh."

For long moments they lay in silence. Finally, Patrick raised himself enough to slide into his sleeping bag. It seemed forever until he made himself comfortable and lay still. "Damn tent," he muttered, squirming again. "Whose brilliant idea was it to sleep here?"

"Yours."

He cleared his throat. "Right."

Again they said nothing for a stretch. Jordanna was so acutely aware of the body next to hers that she had to concentrate on breathing steadily. Patrick turned away onto his side, lay there for several minutes, then flipped back.

"I can't sleep," he announced, sounding so much like a little boy that Jordanna couldn't help but laugh.

"Of course you can't. You must be running plays over and over in your mind."

"I am not running plays."

"Then why don't you try lying still?"

"I'm trying. I'm trying. It's all your fault, you know."

"*My* fault?"

"I can't sleep with you lying so close."

"What would you like me to do? Move outside."

"No. Move over."

"There's no room!"

"That's the point." Suddenly he was up on an elbow. Though Jordanna couldn't see a thing in the dark, she felt his every move. "How about a goodnight kiss."

She tipped her head his way. "What good'll *that* do?"

"It'll settle me down."

She laughed again. "I think your reasoning's screwed up."

"No, no," he returned earnestly. "I keep wondering if it'll be as good the second time round. If it's not, I'll be cured."

"And if it is? Then what?"

"Maybe I'll get it out of my system."

"You're a dreamer, Patrick Clayes."

He thought about that for a minute. "Mmm. I suppose so. How about you? Do you dream?"

"On occasion."

"About what?"

"Now you're really getting personal."

"Come on. Tell me. What do you dream about?"

"Work. Success."

"And . . . ?"

"That's it," she lied. "Very simple."

"Very dry. Very boring. Surely you fantasize. About men. Love. Sex."

"Do you?"

"About men? Not quite. About love and sex? All the time."

"Tell me," she coaxed, turning the tables. "What are your greatest fantasies?"

"Oh, I dream about a woman, *the* woman."

"What does she look like?"

"I don't know," he murmured. "It's not her looks that make her so special. It's her warmth. Her individuality. Her caring. That's it. Her caring. She cares for me above and beyond anything and everything else in life."

"A pretty self-centered fantasy, isn't it?"

"Hell, no. I care for her the same way. It's just that, well, I've never really had anyone who cared for me that much . . . and it matters."

"What about your parents? Surely they loved you."

"Oh, yeah. They did. Me and my four brothers and three sisters."

"Eight kids? Wow, that's great!"

"Not when you want that little bit of individual attention. I was the baby. My older siblings were stuck looking after me more often than not. And I do mean *stuck*. They weren't terribly thrilled about having a constant tagalong. When I took to playing football, we were all relieved."

"You started playing young?"

"I was seven when I began tackling kids on the street. I began throwing the ball a year later. When I was nine I joined a peewee league. You know the rest."

But she hadn't known the first, and it was enlightening, to say the least. It certainly explained his drive, not to mention the frustration he must have felt coming in second to Peter Kirkland all those years.

"Your parents must have been proud of what you made of yourself."

"I suppose. But we were never close. I resented them for years."

"Do you still?"

"They're dead."

"Oh, Pat, I'm sorry."

He paused then, growing more pensive. "I am too. It took a lot of growing up for me to begin to understand that they did what they had to do." His voice hardened. "But I'll never do that to a kid of mine. I want two kids. That's all. And I'll give them everything I've got."

"You'll spoil them rotten."

His laugh was gentle once more. "Which is why I need a good woman to keep me in line. So, angel, how about it?"

"How about what?"

"That good-night kiss," he whispered from close by her lips. "Now that I've spilled my gut, you owe me."

"Why do I feel I've been manipulated?" she returned, her breath suddenly in short supply.

"Not yet. If you want—" he curved his fingers around her shoulder and turned her toward him "—I'd be glad to comply."

"Patrick . . ." she whispered in warning.

"Just a kiss. One kiss." Without awaiting her reply, he closed the tiny distance between them, molding his mouth to hers as his arms completed a circle of her back and drew her on top of him.

Jordanna simply couldn't resist. She found him far too attractive to begin with and, now that he'd let her into his private domain, felt all the more drawn to him. For the moment it didn't matter that he'd been Peter's rival all those years, or that there were four men within easy hearing distance. The tent was their shield, the night further fortification. She gave herself up to his kiss because he touched something raw within her, something that all the protestation in the world couldn't deny.

His lips opened searingly over hers, caressing her warmth, partaking of her essence. Again and again he drank of her, draining her until the thirst was mutual and acute. His tongue thrust deeply, scorching hers, matching its length, then drawing it into his own mouth. When his arms left her back to frame her face, she bolstered herself on her palms. Only then did his lips release hers to lie half open against her cheek.

"Well . . . ?" she whispered tremulously.

"Better than the first. I think…we're in…trouble." The slight adjustment he made in the positioning of his hips elaborated on the problem.

"I think I'd better get back on my side of the tent," she mumbled, but when she made to do so, he slipped his hands beneath her arms and held her still.

"No. Not yet."

"We've been over this before, Pat. It's not sane."

"But it sure feels good," he rasped, then took her mouth again with the sureness of a magnet drawn to its kind. And Jordanna was helpless, riveted to him by the seeking spirals of desire curling through her veins. "Tell me it doesn't," he dared, when at last he came up for a breath.

"It does. It does," she cried. "But that's not the point."

"You're damn right," he said with another meaningful shift of his hips. "It's lower and deeper and—"

"Shh!" She brought a hand to his mouth, then gasped when his own took advantage of her move and slid to encircle her breast.

He moaned softly. "Oh, God, Jordanna. You're so firm. So full." His hand gently kneaded her, his thumb finding then teasing the tautness of her nipple.

She sucked in a deeper breath and, closing her eyes, arched her back. Her one supporting arm trembled, but she could no more have removed herself from him than she could have denied, at that moment, the very obvious proof of her arousal.

"Come here," he growled, hauling her higher until his lips touched the fullness of her breast. Through the fabric of her shirt he nibbled at her flesh. His tongue dampened the thermal cloth, sending a fiery heat through her skin toward her most feminine core.

Lost in a world of exquisite pleasure, Jordanna sighed his name. She lowered her head and buried her face in his hair, breathing deeply of its clean male scent. Through vague remnants of lucidity, she wondered how anyone could smell so clean after traipsing through the woods for the better part of two days, then realized that what struck her senses was the sheer maleness of Patrick Clayes. Chemistrywise, he could do no wrong.

Intentionwise, not so. Suddenly, he was a whirlwind of action, setting her down on her back and fighting with the darkness for something she couldn't fathom.

"What are you *doing*?" she gasped, twisting as his hands searched on either side of her.

"The damn sleeping bag's in the way," he growled, sitting up and continuing his struggle. "We've got to get them together—"

Miraculously she found his hands and anchored them to her chest. "No!" she cried, then lowered her voice to a husky whisper. "No, Pat. Please. Don't."

He was breathing heavily. She all but felt the ragged rise and fall of his chest a foot above her. "Why not? You felt what I did."

"But it's wrong," she went on breathlessly, holding his hands all the more tightly, fearful of what might happen should he touch her again. "It's wrong. We have too much to fight, you and I. You heard the guys before. They said we were talking football. Well, we were, in a way. Your past *is* football. So is mine, in a sense. The only difference is that where football for you was a saving grace, for me it was hell. Pure hell."

Though his hands, remained coiled steel in hers, Patrick went very still. "You've got to be kidding."

"Oh, no, I'm not. That game—"

"Not about football," he snapped. "About stopping."

"That too," she whispered on a breath of despair.

"Good Lord, do you have any idea—"

The sharp squeeze she gave his hands stilled his words. "I do. I know what you feel. And I'd be lying if I said I didn't feel the same. Frustration isn't a man's prerogative, y'know." When he fell back onto his sleeping bag, she released his hands.

"Ah, hell. Another lecture on sexism."

Jordanna stiffened, curling her now empty fingers into the material of her sleeping bag. "I don't give lectures on sexism. I state facts."

"Well, so do I," Patrick countered, rearing up once more and leaning close. "And the facts are, one, that I need you, and, two, that you need me."

"You've forgotten several others," she stated in a pained voice. "Three, neither of us goes in for casual affairs. Four, we've got to be able to live with ourselves in the morning. Five, we have another three days of trekking through the woods with a group of men who'll make the most out of any relationship we have. And six, come Friday night we go our separate ways." She lowered her voice. "Not to mention the facts that, seven, I'm Peter Kirkland's ex-wife and you're through with taking seconds, and, eight, that I've had my fill of athletic egotists."

She stopped then, breathless and spent. Patrick was as speechless.

When at last he spoke, his words were preceded by a weary sigh. "Well, I guess you've covered everything. Good night, Jordanna." Turning away from her, he lay perfectly still.

It took Jordanna far longer to quiet her rampaging nerves.

WEDNESDAY MORNING dawned bleak and overcast, a fitting backdrop to Jordanna's mood. Awakening to find herself alone in the tent, she snatched up her things and headed for the stream. She was relieved to find the campsite quiet.

The last thing she needed was a smart comment from one of the men about something that might have been overheard in the night.

Head down, brows drawn together, she distractedly followed the path. When she reached the edge of the stream, she put down her things, then straightened, moaning aloud when the muscles of her back protested the simple movement.

"What's wrong, Jordanna?" came a deep voice from the side. "Feeling stiff?"

Her gaze spun to focus on Patrick, who leaned indolently against the peeling trunk of a tall birch. "Playing Peeping Tom today?" she snapped, to cover her surprise. Not that she shouldn't have guessed he might be here. After all, he hadn't been in the tent, and he hadn't been in the campsite's clearing.

He stood his ground, holding her gaze. "Just answering nature's call," he announced bluntly. "What's your excuse?"

"I might say the same, but I guess it'll have to wait." Turning back to the stream, she knelt, gingerly submerged her hands in the cold water, then pressed them to her face.

"Not a morning person, I gather?" he asked, from closer this time. When Jordanna didn't answer but simply kept her cold fingers pressed to her eyes, he spoke again, more gently this time. "If it's any solace, I've just walked off some of my own black mood. I didn't think anyone else would be up this early."

"What time is it?" she murmured, dipping her hands in the water again and reapplying them to her face.

"Seven."

She moaned softly. "Must be force of habit...." She quickly splashed her face several times in succession, gasped against the cold, then reached to the side and pressed her towel to her face. When firm hands began a gentle massage of her shoulders, she stiffened only momentarily before relaxing under the patient ministration.

"That's it," he coaxed softly. "That's it. Just let go."

With a shuddering breath, she dropped her head back, then forward again. "I'm so tired," she murmured, any annoyance she might have felt toward Patrick forgotten as his deft thumbs kneaded the taut lines of her neck.

"You've kept right up with the rest. You should feel proud of that."

"But I'm so tired. I swear I could sleep for a week."

"All you need is a good night's rest. That's three in a row now without, hmm?"

"Mmm."

From his haunches, Patrick slid his knees to the ground and eased Jordanna back into the cradle of his thighs. His mouth was by her temple, his arms overlapping below her breasts. "The soreness will wear off once we get going. It always does."

"I don't know. The thought of lifting that pack doesn't thrill me."

"I could take some of your load."

"And let the others think I'm giving in? No way."

"You know, you can only fight being a woman up to a point. It's a biological fact that a woman's body has a lower proportion of muscle than a man's. It'd be only natural if you—"

"I'm okay," she asserted, but made no move to withdraw from the comfortable haven he offered. It was the most welcome support she'd had in days.

Patrick slid his cheek against her hair. "You're an enigma to me, Jordanna. Do you know that?"

"Me? An enigma? I thought I was pretty straightforward."

"That's part of the fascination. You're so in command at times, then at other times, like now, so much more vulnerable. I don't think I've known anyone with quite so many facets, and I get the strange feeling that I haven't seen half."

Her chuckle was soft and short. "Neither have I. I constantly surprise myself." Most surprising was the way she was yielding once again to Patrick's appeal.

"Tell me you like the theater."

"Living in Manhattan? Of course."

"And P. J. Clark's?"

"Hamburgers on paper plates with super steak fries and an occasional celebrity or two? You bet."

"And alfalfa sprouts?"

"Nice and crunchy. Sure."

"And the late, late show on TV?"

"As long as it's a two-tissue romance."

She had barely realized her confession when the snap and rustle of footsteps on the woodland floor heralded new arrivals.

"Oh, Lord," Donald moaned, but there was a teasing note to his voice, "they're still at it."

"And here we thought they'd be holed up in that tent for another hour at least," Larry quipped.

Coming to stand before the stream, John glanced down. "Guess we won't be throwing the water through the flap after all."

Neither releasing Jordanna nor looking up, Patrick grinned against her hair. "Try that, bud, and you're apt to find something wet and wriggly in your boot."

Jordanna withered into Patrick. "Oh, God, are there snakes around here?"

His response was flush by her ear. "None that you'll see. But I know where to look and if need be—"

"He's serious, guys," she called out loud and clear. "Better watch it with the water. For that matter, better watch it with the wisecracks. If he's offended, there's no telling what the man might do."

A groggy Bill emerged from the path and came to a standstill looking disgruntled toward the duo by the stream. "What're *they* doing?"

"Come to think of it, we never did find out," John stated.

"What *are* you doing?" Larry asked more directly.

Jordanna dropped her gaze to the stream and in so doing missed the look of utter blankness on Patrick's face. "Doing? Us?" He squeezed her middle when she began to snicker. "Ah, we're . . . we're washing. That is, I was showing Jordanna how to wash." He lowered his voice in a conspiratorial manner. "You know how it is with city women. They're kind of slow—ah!" Jordanna's elbow caught him in the ribs. He released her as he would a hot potato and stood. "And ornery first thing in the morning. You guys can have 'er!" With that, he turned on his heel and headed back toward camp.

Taking his departure with good grace, Jordanna reached for her tube of moisturizing cream. Though she would never have opted for an audience had she had a choice, pride held her rooted to the spot.

"Whaddya say, guys?" Bill asked good-naturedly. "Who wants her? John?"

"No, thanks. She's too good on the trail. I can barely keep up. My ego's taking a bruising."

"Larry?"

"Are you kidding? She probably earns twice what I do."

"Don?"

"Marie would kill me. Hey, how about you, wise guy? You're the only bachelor around here."

While Jordanna very placidly massaged moisturizer onto her face and hands, looking for all the world as though she were alone by the stream, Bill made pretense of mulling a possible purchase, narrowing his eyes, stroking his stubbled jaw. "I dunno. She is kinda pretty." Jordanna tipped her head to the side. "Nice neck. But she's awful skinny."

"The word is slender," Jordanna corrected with just the right amount of haughtiness, "and if I were five pounds heavier you'd probably be worrying about cellulite."

"Got a sharp tongue," Bill went on. "And she can't cook." He gestured dismissively. "Clayes can have her back. Not a bad match, actually. He cooks and cleans, she earns the money, and in their spare time they—"

"Talk football," John interjected propitiously. "They've got a lot in common." He shook his head. "Kirkland and Clayes . . . whew!"

Suddenly, Jordanna had heard enough. Gathering her things quickly together, she rose and headed for the path. "Thank you, gentlemen," she mocked on the move. "I can't remember when I've awoken to such clever repartee."

"But that was only the first act . . . !" Donald called after her.

Without missing a beat, she raised a hand. "I'm sure you'll enthrall one another with the second and third. What *I* need right about now is a strong cup of coffee."

It helped, as did the relative silence in which she was allowed to eat breakfast. Though the sky remained overcast, her mood slowly improved. She felt anger neither toward the men, whose earlier teasing had been without malice, nor toward Patrick, whose nocturnal ardor had been replaced by a more objective civility.

If he found her an enigma, she found him no different. But the confusion she felt regarding her feelings toward him were thrust to the back of her mind by the urgency of the day's activities.

With breakfast done, the tents disassembled and packs reloaded and donned, the troop set out on what was to be an easier trek than the day before had been. That was fortunate. Jordanna wasn't the only one whose body had felt the strain; her voice was but the softest in a chorus of furtive moans when Patrick led them upstream toward Eagle Link.

They stopped often as much to admire the scenery as to pamper themselves. Jordanna found Patrick to be a wellspring of information regarding not only the history of the forest through which they passed but the wildlife and plant life as well. She wondered at the dedication behind such a store of knowledge; neither a football stadium nor a business office would have given him any of it. Then she remembered what he'd said about either doing things well or not doing them at all, and she surmised that somewhere in his library was a shelf or two filled with books on the great outdoors.

As the morning progressed, they moved slowly along, joining the Wild River Trail, winding westward. More than once the sky darkened, but the threatening downpour held off. More than once Jordanna gave a sigh of relief.

"You've got rain gear, haven't you?" Patrick asked, catching one of her fearful glances skyward.

"Oh, yeah. I've got it. That doesn't mean I want to wear it."

He glanced at the wool sweater peering from the open neck of her jacket. "Are you warm enough?"

"Mmm. Pretty toasty."

His gaze dropped. "How about your feet? Those things don't look half as sturdy as my boots."

"These *things*," she returned with a half smile, "are phenomenally comfortable. *And* warm. I think I'll give them a good report. No blisters. No frostbite."

Patrick drew back an overhanging branch to allow them passage. "But if it rains? Will they keep you dry?"

"Well, uh, that's up for grabs." She frowned in annoyance. "It wasn't supposed to rain." Then she scrunched up her nose and sent him a pleading look. "Do you think it will?"

Patrick laughed aloud. "Your face. It's amazing."

"Will it rain?" she repeated, reluctant to get into a personal discussion.

He shrugged. "We'll see. In time."

It didn't, though as a precaution, they munched on trail snacks of raisins and candies, saving lunch for early afternoon when they reached Perkins Notch, where they'd be spending the night. When, after lunch, Patrick set out to lead the men to Red Brook for trout fishing, Jordanna opted to stay behind.

"Are you sure you don't want to come?" Patrick asked quietly while the others gathered their reels and rods.

She gave a soft smile. "I'm sure. Fishing has never interested me."

"We're all going. You'll be here all alone."

"That's what I'm hoping," she quipped lightly, then took a deep breath and looked around the campsite. "I thought I'd take it easy. Maybe read. Maybe sleep. I could use the solitude." She arched her brows. "And the shelter, should it start to pour."

"Don't even think that," Patrick advised, chucking her on the chin and turning. "Be good," were his parting words as he loped off toward the others who were waiting. "We'll be back by sundown. Have the home fire waiting." There were several chuckles from the others as they moved off.

Jordanna simply stood and looked after them until the path swallowed them up. Then, propping herself against the trunk of a gracious pine, she put her head back against its knobby spine and closed her eyes.

It was quiet. She needed that. A far cry from her midtown Manhattan office, she mused, wondering for the first time how things were going, whether everything was running smoothly in her absence, what emergencies might possibly arise and how they would be handled when she was, for all practical purposes, incommunicado.

Opening her eyes, she focused on the spot in the woods where Patrick had disappeared. He'd looked so hardy wearing his old faded jeans and boots, his wool jacket, his down vest. She liked him. That was part of the problem. She actually liked him.

Quite unbidden, the image of Peter Kirkland formed in her mind, reconstructing itself from the memories she'd so firmly tried to relegate to oblivion. She'd liked him too...at first. No, she'd loved him. She'd been smitten by his charm, his physique, his sheer charisma. Too late she'd learned that he'd been smitten by the very same things. Increasingly he'd believed in his own press as the months of their marriage had gone by.

It amazed her that she'd lasted three years. With a shudder she recalled the parties they'd gone to, she willingly at first, then with increasing reluctance when she'd found herself alone for much of the night with nothing to bolster her dignity but the fact that she was Peter Kirkland's wife. She was an appendage, nothing more. In time she'd begun to resent that fact.

Miraculously, given the cloistered nature of so much of her life, she'd grown. Or rather, she'd had time, and time aplenty, to analyze her existence and its shortcomings. She'd needed something to do, some identity of her own. Peter had not taken kindly to that conclusion.

"Are you crazy? You don't need to work. I make more than enough to support us. And I need you here. You're my wife."

"But I'm stagnating, Peter. You're off traveling half of the season. And when you're here you're either at practices or meetings or press conferences or . . . or . . . God only knows where." She'd begun to have her suspicions, but she'd kept them to herself. "I need something of my own. Something to sign *my* name to."

"Seems to me you sign your name to a whole load of charge cards."

"I'm bored! Can't you understand that?"

"Frankly," he'd returned with typical arrogance, "no. You've got me. You've got this house—"

"And what am I supposed to do? Clean all day? Spend hours preparing a gourmet meal, never knowing whether you'll come up with a last-minute meeting that you've just got to attend?"

His eyes had hardened then, taking on an ugly gleam. "Jordanna, you're being selfish. I'm the focal point of the team. I have to be there. You know that."

"No, I don't! If you're so important, you should be able to call the shots. Tell them your wife is waiting. Tell them you've got a prior engagement. Tell them to find someone else for a change."

"Someone else won't do. They want me. And I like it that way."

"I know," she'd muttered in defeat. "That's half of the problem. But what about me? What about *me*, Peter?"

"You can cook. You can clean. You can be waiting here for me when I get home. I'd think that would be enough."

"Well, it's not!"

He hadn't even heard her. "Besides, what would people think if my wife went out on her own? And what could you possibly do? You're not trained for anything—" he'd grinned smugly "—besides being my wife." He'd put his arm around her rigid shoulder. "Come on, honey. One superstar is enough for the two of us. Come here. Give a kiss."

Flinching in disgust, Jordanna snapped herself from the past. It was done. Over. Peter Kirkland had charmed her once too often, once too shallowly, once too condescendingly. He'd used her as he had his cleats, valuing them for one purpose and one purpose alone, and that was to make Peter Kirkland run faster. Somehow, she mused, she suspected he'd loved his cleats more. . . .

And now there was Patrick. Every bit as good-looking. Nearly as successful. Little boys. That's what they were. Running into each other. Tripping over each other. Squeezing the life out of that poor misshapen ball.

But she did like Patrick. She couldn't deny that fact. Much as she wanted to think him as egotistical as Peter, she couldn't. But then, what did she have to judge him on? Three days and two nights in the woods of New Hampshire? Okay, so he could cook. So he seemed more than willing to do it. Hell, he was the only one who knew how to work the portable stove!

Still, there were other things that puzzled her, not the least of which was his refusal to discuss football, his insistence that those days were over. While Peter was still milking his jock-high image for every penny it was worth, Patrick was off leading novice backpackers through the woods...when he wasn't in an office ferreting out new ventures to back.

Strange. It was strange. Too bad Patrick hadn't been the one she'd met when she'd been nineteen.

With a sigh, she pushed herself to her feet and, thrusting her hands in her pockets, wandered back along the trail they'd taken earlier, to No-Ketchum Pond. The land by the edge of the long, narrow pond was boggy, a floating mass of roots and moss she was careful to keep her distance from. No-Ketchum Pond. She smiled at the name and at Patrick's explanation of it, even as she prayed the men were having better luck with their fishing at Red Brook. The thought of fresh trout for dinner was infinitely appealing.

As was the thought of taking a nap, she decided with a yawn. Pulling her collar higher against her neck, she returned to the shelter, set her sleeping bag atop one of the board bunks, climbed in and closed her eyes. When next she opened them, it was dark and raining and she was still alone.

4

SLIPPING FROM HER sleeping bag, Jordanna walked to the edge of the overhang and stared out at the pouring rain. Like the shelter they'd used Monday night, this was enclosed on three sides. Here the fourth was partially fronted by the same weathered spruce logs as well. No tents tonight, she mused distractedly. At least she'd be spared the temptation... and its frustration.

Tucking her hands deep in her pockets, she pondered the gloom, then looked back toward her pack. She had a flashlight. No—the lantern. It was there, under cover of the eaves, perched beside the small stove, which Patrick had unpacked earlier. Kneeling quickly, she lit it, feeling vaguely reassured by its amber glow. Then she sat beside it, knees to her chest, waiting, waiting, for the men to return.

With each passing minute, she grew more concerned. Patrick had said they'd be back before dark. Yet it was dark *and* wet, and still there was no sign of them. Loath to imagine a mishap or worse, she directed her thoughts toward making something warm for the men's return. Could she light the stove? She eyed the small contraption. Any number of times now she'd watched Patrick light it. She knew that the first thing she had to do was to fill it with fuel lest they run out midmeal. It was easily done and she had a match in hand when she realized that she'd need water. Unfortunately, the source of pure water was not as convenient to the campsite as it had been on the past two nights.

Resigning herself to braving the rain, which was the least she could do given the soggy state the men would be in when they got back, she donned her rain suit, grabbed two pots and headed out. She'd barely left the campsite, though, when she stopped in her tracks, then returned to leave a note. He'd worry. She sensed it in her gut. And she didn't want that.

Replacing the small pad of paper and pen in her pack, she speared the note onto a corner of the stove within safe but visible distance from the lantern, then, hood up and flashlight in hand, set off again. Only after she'd doggedly struggled through the brush and reached the small spring Patrick had shown them earlier did she realize she might well have simply set the pots out in the rain. But that would have taken too long, she reasoned, and she was here. Somewhat cold, wet around the wrists but here.

Brushing dripping strands of hair from her brow, she filled the pots with water, clamped the flashlight under her arm and began to retrace her steps. One part of her hoped the men would be delayed that little bit longer so that she might have hot soup ready; the other part prayed they'd just *be* there.

She was halfway back to camp and treading cautiously over the wet brush when the sound of something thrashing through the brush brought her to a frozen halt. Eyes wide, she trained her flashlight ahead, then glanced frantically around for a place to escape the big brown bear that surely approached.

The figure that emerged as she stood paralyzed was indeed large and might have been brown, or black—it was hard to tell in a rain-soaked poncho—but, though angry, it was no bear.

"Jordanna! My God, that was a dumb thing to do!" Patrick growled, stomping the last few feet to her and seizing her shoulders as though he would shake her. "I thought I said we traveled in groups. It's pitch-black and pelting rain and the path's poorly marked—"

"I thought you were a bear!" Jordanna breathed, so relieved to find he was not that she couldn't have cared if Patrick had indeed shaken her. Heedless of his dark mood, she sagged against him. Within seconds his arms slid around her back.

"You scared the hell out of me!" he muttered. The gruffness in his voice gave further credence to his words, even as his arms tightened protectively.

Jordanna buried her face against his throat as it lay exposed through the small V of his poncho. "You saw my note."

"Yeah. Just when I'd finished an ordeal of my own. I knew exactly how wet it was. And how dark. The spring's a good ten minutes from camp. You might have gotten lost!"

"I have a good sense of direction."

"You should have waited till we got back. One of us would have gone for water."

"I wanted to have something warm waiting." She was aware of the musky smell of Patrick's neck, unable to draw away even as her initial fright receded. The strength of his body was compelling. She relaxed against him, stealing precious moments of support as she might a forbidden luxury. "I couldn't sit still. I was worried. What kept you?"

He inched his chin against her hood until her forehead was bared to his jaw. "The rain. We found shelter under a grove of trees and kept hoping it would let up. Then the guys started arguing." A hint of humor entered his voice. "Don wanted to move on. Larry wanted to wait. John tried to reason the whole thing out with the two of them."

"And Bill?"

"Bill was really funny. He kept eyeing the sky, then the ground. You could see him calculating his chances. When the other three had reached an impasse, he growled and set off. We followed."

"Good for Bill."

"Not really. He was so hell-bent on being the leader that he missed a step, stumbled on a tree root and fell headlong into the mud."

"Oh, no!" Jordanna tipped her head back. "Was he hurt?"

Patrick's eyes locked with hers in the dark. "Only his pride. Poor guy. He's real big on physical agility and co-ordination. It's a good thing you weren't there; he would have been mortified. He felt a little better when I tripped trying to help him up."

"*You* tripped?"

"I do sometimes. I'm not perfect." His message went far beyond a simple slipping in the mud. As Jordanna melted beneath his gaze, he raised a hand to brush her wet cheek. "I'm human. I've got faults. Not the least of which is this insane attraction to you." His voice thickened. "So help me, it's a good thing those guys are around. If not I would have stayed at the shelter making love to you all afternoon."

Jordanna felt the warmth of his breath by her lips and couldn't demur when the hand he left on her back lowered, pressing her intimately closer. "It's a good thing the guys *are* around," she whispered, totally intoxicated by that same insane attraction. "I just might have let you."

"God, Jordanna!" he rasped, using both arms again to crush her against him. "Don't say things like that."

"Why not?" she murmured against his neck. "You say them."

"Yeah, I'm a man. I'm the lusting beast here. Since I can't exactly hide my physical state, I've got a right to speak my mind. But you're a woman. You're supposed to be the sensible one. You're supposed to tell me how crazy it is, how it would never work. You're supposed to push me away from you when I say things like that."

"I can't. I've got buckets of water in my hands."

Patrick held her back to stare disbelievingly at the objects in question. "Damn it!" he exclaimed, coming to life. "Let me take those!"

"It's okay," she reassured him quickly. In truth, she wanted him to hold her again.

But he grabbed the pots and tossed his head toward the path. "You lead the way with the flashlight. I'll be right behind you."

Lest she protest too much and make an utter fool of herself, Jordanna turned and began to pick her way along the hidden path. It took all of her concentration, which was a lucky thing. Otherwise she might have dwelled on her physical attraction to Patrick, and she didn't want to do that. She wanted to relax, to get the most out of her vacation, to fully appreciate her time in the fresh outdoors.

The rain continued at a torrential pace. The path was mucky and dark. It was colder than she would have believed possible without downright snow, and her hiking shoes were not terribly dry when she and Patrick finally arrived at the shelter. Fresh outdoors? She wondered, as she headed directly for her pack and dry clothes.

Any dissension the men might have experienced during their return from Red Brook had been long since forgotten. Having already changed into dry things—leaving their wet ones strung on a makeshift clothesline, which offered Jordanna privacy of sorts—they were gathered around the stove in lively discussion of their admirable fishing skills. Jordanna listened with one indulgent ear, the other waiting to hear Patrick's voice. When it was noticeably absent, she wondered if he too was changing clothes. On the other side of the line? She shot a glance through the legs of a pair of pants but saw nothing. And heard nothing. Between the patter of the rain on the roof overhead and the men's constant chatter, she would have been unable to hear the swish of a shirt leaving his chest, the rustle of denim leaving his legs.

But he wasn't changing. Not yet, at least. Only when his tall form ducked between two sodden shirts did she realize that his pack was on her side of the shelter. Sitting cross-legged on the floor trying to assess the damage to her shoes, she looked up in surprise.

Patrick took one look at her and halted abruptly. "Uh. I'll come back later."

"No. No. It's all right."

"Jordanna...." His voice held taut warning, carrying with it an instant reminder of his words in the woods. Glancing down, she realized that she wore nothing but her long underwear. Though she was suitably covered from neck to ankle, the clinging fabric did nothing to hide any of her curves.

As casually as she could, she swiveled on her seat and reached toward her pack for a dry shirt. "It's all right," she repeated, her voice less sure. Her pulse was suddenly racing, and she knew well its cause. For a minute she heard nothing but the sounds of her own ferreting, a ferreting that seemed to produce nothing but a mess in her pack. The light of the lantern played off the roof to cast her in the palest glow. It was enough for her to see what she was doing. Enough, she knew, for Patrick to see her too.

She had finally managed to find the warm pullover she'd been seeking when a pair of wet denim legs planted themselves directly before her. Seconds later, Patrick was on his haunches and she raised her eyes.

"You look so damned sexy," he whispered, making no attempt to hide the reluctance of his admission. It should have been a warning. But it wasn't. The reminder that their mutual attraction shouldn't exist did nothing to still the excitement his raking gaze sent through her limbs.

She sat still, afraid to move for fear he'd look away. It was improper. It was unwise. But she wanted him to see her. More, she wanted him to touch her. Her body cried for his touch in a way she had never experienced before.

She was almost relieved when he reached out to stroke her shoulders, then caught her breath when his hands fell to trace the fullness of her breasts, which strained against the constricting fabric, nipples hard and wanting. When his hands moved over her rib cage, she bit her lip in frustration, then held her breath again when he shaped his open palms to the flare of her hips.

Suddenly his touch was withdrawn and he tore at the buttons of his heavy wool shirt. In seconds the shirt was on the ground and his T-shirt over his head and tossed aside. Then he reached for her, bringing her to her knees and flush against him while his hands tugged her shirt up just high enough to allow her breasts to feel his naked warmth.

"Oh, angel," he moaned in a tormented whisper, moving her ever so slowly against his breadth.

Jordanna thought she'd die at the intimate glory of skin on skin. Her limbs trembled wildly. She might have fallen back to the ground had he not held her so firmly. His thumbs found the undersides of her breasts, tipping them higher against him.

"Say something," he urged in an agonized tone.

"I can't. You . . . take my breath. . . ."

"Tell me to go away."

"I can't."

"Scream. Cry rape."

She was breathing in tiny gasps, sliding her hands along the muscled cords of his back in an attempt to know as much of him as possible in the few clandestine moments they had. "You feel . . . so good. . . ."

Suddenly their idyll was interrupted by loud laughter from the other side of the shelter. It was followed by a spate of guffaws interspersed with words enough to assure Jordanna and Patrick that they were, as yet, undiscovered.

Patrick flinched, as though something inside him had snapped. Burying his face in her hair, he groaned. "I'm going to touch you again, Jordanna. Not now. But later." His husky whisper held a shadow of desperation. "I'm going to touch you and kiss you and look at everything I've only been able to lie awake at night imagining. And I'm going to make you want me so badly that you'll never remember there was another man in the world. Then I'm going to make love to you, over and over again, in ways Peter Kirkland never dreamed."

Against the inflammatory effect of his words, mention of Peter's name was chilling. Patrick had intended that. She knew he had. And she wasn't entirely sorry. Something had to bring them to their senses. *What were they doing?* Here, in a rustic shelter, with nothing to separate them from four other men but a line of wet clothes and darkness—here, in a make-believe world, temporarily isolated from a reality in which neither would want the other—*what were they doing?*

"Thank you," she murmured, dismayed and suitably chastised. Belatedly pushing herself from his grasp, she tugged down her shirt and hung her head. Her breasts still throbbed, her body continued to burn where he'd touched her . . . and where he hadn't. She took an unsteady breath. "I guess I got carried away."

"I guess we both did," Patrick growled, surging to his feet and turning his back on her.

Looking up, she watched the rise of his shoulders, the expansion of his back as he took an extended drag of air. She'd felt his body's need, the tautness that moments before had spoken of his heightened state. She could imagine his frustration. Lord knew her own was great enough.

Averting her gaze once again, she sought her pullover and slowly drew it on over the thermal jersey. Then, with a diligence born of confusion, she directed her thoughts toward Peter, picturing his arrogant grin, recalling his preening narcissism, his selfish lovemaking. All were things she'd pushed from mind for years, unpleasant things, things she didn't want to remember. Patrick Clayes made her remember.

Patrick Clayes. He'd been Peter's longtime rival. He was a man who'd strived for glory as Peter had done. She shouldn't want him. Shouldn't want any part of him. But she did.

At the sound of a snap, then a zip, her eyes shot up. Patrick had turned back to her and was in the process of wrenching wet denim from his legs. Though his face was shadowed, she felt his gaze. And she couldn't look away.

He said nothing, simply freed himself of the heavy jeans, tossed them onto a bunk, then approached his pack wearing only a pair of dark briefs.

He was the image of uncompromising masculinity, every bit as perfect of form as Jordanna had somehow feared he'd be. Swallowing hard, she reached for dry pants of her own and leaned back to slip them on. Though the men continued to talk on the far side of the line, it was heartstoppingly quiet in the small space she and Patrick shared.

"Pat?" she whispered, hearing the rustle of clothing as he dug into his pack.

"What?"

"I . . . I'm sorry. I shouldn't have let that go on the way it did."

She waited in a silence broken at last by the rasp of his zipper as he pulled on dry jeans. "I meant what I said," he announced quietly.

When she looked over at him, he was thrusting his arms into the sleeves of a thermal shirt. The snap of his pants lay open; it was all she could do not to focus there. Mouth dry, she pressed her lips together and tried to think of something sensible to say. Nothing came. For a fleeting instant she wondered where the self-confident, wordly-wise woman she'd thought she was had gone. Then time ran out and Patrick was on his haunches again.

"It's too late, Jordanna," he whispered. He didn't touch her. He didn't have to. His brand was intangible, inevitable. "You should have fought me. But you didn't. So I know. I know that you want me. And I'll have you, mark my words. I've been a competitor far too long to turn down a challenge. And when it comes to the prospect of besting Peter Kirkland, no challenge could be sweeter."

Unable to believe the twist of his thoughts, Jordanna was astounded. "I don't believe you said that," she breathed, more hurt than anything. "You'd take me . . . *to best Peter?*"

His expression unfathomable, Patrick stared at her for a minute, then pushed himself up and stalked away under the clothesline without saying another word.

OF THE CHALLENGES Jordanna had herself faced, none was greater than acting calm and collected through a lively dinner with the guys. Though the trout was delicious, she was able to make no more than a minimal dent in the portion Larry had triumphantly presented her. Rather, she pushed it dutifully around on her plate, hoping none of the men would notice. They did.

"Jordanna's not eating," Don observed. "She doesn't like our trout."

"Maybe she doesn't like fish," John reasoned.

"No," Bill countered. "She just doesn't appreciate the effort that went into this particular meal. She should have been out there with us, freezing her butt off at the edge of a godforsaken river."

"The fish is fine," she insisted.

"Then why aren't you eating?" Larry asked.

"I'm not hungry, I guess. You all did do more work than me today. It's no wonder you're famished. It really is delicious. Honest. I've just had enough." She avoided Patrick's gaze for all she was worth.

Bill grinned. "They had a fight. I told you there was something going on behind the clothesline."

"Bill . . ." John warned.

But Donald was on the same wavelength as Bill, fascinated by the way Jordanna had involuntarily flinched at Bill's remark. "Really, Jordanna," he said, lips twitching as he leaned close in a brotherly way, "you've got to be careful of guys like Clayes. They've got one thing on the mind. Must have something to do with the locker-room mentality."

They were teasing her, enjoying her discomfort. She shot a glance at Patrick. His smug grin didn't help. Then again, perhaps it did. "You got it," she quipped. "Locker-room mentality. As a matter of fact, I'm surprised you fellows aren't worried yourselves. I hear homosexuality is—"

"*Homosexuality?*" Patrick yelped.

Larry chuckled. Donald and Bill laughed aloud. Only John looked from Jordanna to Patrick in speculation.

"She got us, didn't she?" Bill mused, then shook his head and laughed again. "I say it again, Clayes. You can have her. She's got an answer for everything, hmm?"

"Almost," Patrick said, his good humor obvious with the gleam in his eye. "Almost."

Only Jordanna—and Patrick—knew she'd lost that round.

Long after the coffeepot had been drained, the men continued to sit around the stove reminiscing about past trips, past adventures. Jordanna sat on her bunk with a book in one hand, a flashlight in the other. She tried to get comfortable, but neither the underpad nor her sleeping bag seemed to provide much of a cushion against the hard wood. She wondered how she'd ever sleep and wished she hadn't napped that afternoon. She was wide awake and alert, though she'd read the same page four times without absorbing a word.

It didn't help that Patrick sat on his bunk not six feet from her, turning page after page of his own book. Nor did it help that each time she dared a glance at him he met her gaze.

There was a purposefulness to him. She felt that quality in the very fiber of her being. And she was all the more confused. When she'd first set eyes on him three days before, she'd instantly associated him with Peter's world, only to find unexpected differences. Patrick was softer, more sensitive, more generous. She'd thought. Until this afternoon.

Strange, she mused, how his words had stirred her at first. She'd never had a man announce his intentions so bluntly, with that hint of fierceness that made it all the more exciting. Lord knew Peter hadn't spared the effort, but then Peter had always gotten what he'd wanted when he'd wanted it.

Turning the page, she stared blindly at the printed words. Oh, yes, Patrick's aggressiveness had excited her . . . until he'd thrown in that remark about taking sweet revenge on Peter. Something had turned sour in her stomach then. The thought had never occurred to her that Patrick might be using her. . . .

A tiny moan of dismay slipped from her throat. She shifted restlessly on the bunk. She felt Patrick's eyes on her and studiously avoided them, feigning intense interest in the book in her lap. When she could take the pretense no longer, she clapped the book shut, snapped her flashlight off, pushed herself from the bunk and wandered to the front of the shelter.

The rain had eased to a drizzle. The air was raw. Wrapping her arms around her middle, she turned back, gave the men a passing glance and returned to her bunk, where she stretched out in her sleeping bag and prayed for the sweet escape of sleep.

It eluded her. An hour passed. The men one by one went to bed. Patrick had long since turned off his flashlight to lie, much as she did, silent in the night.

Another hour passed. The campsite was quiet. The only raindrops to hit the roof now were those dislodged from branches overhead by the breeze.

One of the men began to snore. Jordanna twisted on her bunk, drawing her sleeping bag to her ears in an attempt to drown out the sound. When the tactic failed, she shifted again.

Then there was a hand on her shoulder and an accompanying whisper. "Jordanna?"

She didn't budge even so much as to free her face from the sleeping bag. "Mmm?"

"The rain's stopped. Want to go for a walk?"

"No," was her muffled reply.

312   *The Forever Instinct*

"Why not?"

"After what you said before, how can you even ask that?" She gave a harsh laugh. "You'd drag me to the nearest rock and ravish me. And you'd be right. Peter never did that. He wouldn't dream of taking a week off and going into the woods with me. No press."

"That's what I want to talk about."

She remained silent for a minute. When he didn't continue, her curiosity bested her. "What?"

"Peter. And you."

"No."

Again there was a silence. When Patrick spoke again, his voice held that vulnerability she couldn't ignore. "We've got to, Jordanna. Too much is happening. You need to talk... and I need to hear what you have to say. Come on. We'll just talk. I promise I won't lay a finger on you."

She wanted to say no, then realized how childish it would sound. After all, she couldn't sleep. Evidently, neither could Patrick. And he was right. She'd come to understand the depth of his feelings because of what he'd told her of his past. Perhaps if she explained about her past, Patrick would understand her better.

Very slowly she lowered the sleeping bag from her face. "Just talk?"

"I promise. Please?"

In the end, she agreed only in part because of the gentle nature of his plea. The greater part reflected her own need to share that aspect of her with him. Extricating herself from her cocoon, she reached for her jacket, pulled on her shoes, wool hat and mittens and let Patrick lead the way from the shelter.

The woods were quiet after the storm, its evidence the gleaming of wet branches in the moonlight and the soft squish of the ground underfoot. At a low boulder some distance from the campsite, Patrick spread out his poncho and gestured for her to sit. When she'd done so, he joined her, leaving ample room between them as proof of his promise.

"Tell me about it, Jordanna," he said then. "About you."

She shrugged. "Where do I begin?"

"With Peter."

Nodding, she looked off into the distance. Her mind followed suit. "I was nineteen, just finishing my freshman year in college. I was at a party. He made an appearance with someone else. Naturally, we were all enthralled. He was a national hero, a football star in the big time. I was as curious as the rest. He was a celebrity. And very good-looking."

"How did the two of you get together?"

She frowned. "I'm not really sure. I mean, I was enamored of him from the start. What he saw in me, I wasn't so sure. I was a nobody—oh, attractive enough, I guess, but I'd come from nothing and was at college on scholarship simply hoping to get my degree and some kind of a stable job."

"You wanted a career."

"What I really wanted was a husband. And kids. But having grown up in a household where both my parents worked out of necessity, I assumed I'd be doing the same. I wanted that kind of security." She paused for a minute, trying to express herself as honestly as possible. "I'd be lying if I didn't say I had dreams of marrying a wealthy prince. You know—the Cinderella syndrome."

"But you didn't have a stepmother and three ugly stepsisters."

"No. My mother was—is—lovely. And I was an only child. But young girls have dreams." She paused. "Anyway, by the time I'd entered college I'd pretty much gotten over them. Then Peter came along."

"That party."

"That party. For whatever his reasons, he singled me out. Later he told me that it had been my, uh, my innocence that had appealed to him. I was quieter, more shy than most of the women he'd known." She hesitated. "I was a challenge, he said." She emphasized the word, knowing she'd scored a point against Patrick when he winced. "He asked me out. We became an 'item,' so to speak."

"How did you feel about that?"

"Oh, it was mind-boggling, all right. 'Renowned football hero falls for small-town college girl.' The understatement. It was more like a sack. I didn't have a chance. He knew all the right things to do and say. He had me perfectly psyched. It was seduction in its most perfect form, and I fell for it hook, line and sinker."

"But he did love you."

"Uh-huh." Her voice softened. "He did. That was the one thing I always knew. That was where my true innocence came into play."

"What do you mean?"

"Knowing that Peter loved me, knowing that I loved him, I was totally vulnerable. Carrying on a long-distance affair was devastating. When he asked me to marry him, I was thrilled. He wanted me to be his wife, to be with him always. Giving up school seemed like nothing compared with the prospect of being full-time with Peter." She stopped then, recalling those early days of happiness.

"What happened, Jordanna?"

"Oh, it was wonderful at first. A storybook wedding, complete with a long white train, hundreds of guests, flowers and photographers galore. My parents were proud as punch that their daughter had married a man who could take care of her in the style they'd always dreamed about."

"And you?"

"I was proud too. I was Mrs. Peter Kirkland. I went everywhere with the man I adored. People recognized me, respected me. It was everything I could have hoped for."

Patrick read her pause well. "Except . . . ?"

"I was Mrs. Peter Kirkland. That was all."

"And it wasn't enough."

She lowered her head and spoke very softly. "No. It wasn't. I was bored."

"With *Peter*?"

The barest hint of awe in his voice was revealing. With a wave of insight Jordanna realized that though Patrick might have deeply resented Peter for having stolen the limelight time and again, he nonetheless couldn't deny his admiration for the other man's achievements. In other circumstances, she sensed, Patrick would have revered Peter as many another had done. It was a clue as to Patrick's self-image . . . and the nature of the battle he'd had to fight over the years.

"Perhaps the boredom is too strong a word," she explained cautiously. "Frustration is probably more accurate. I grew frustrated with the kind of life we were leading—running all over during the off-season from one fund raiser to the next, one party to the next, one publicity gimmick to the next. During the season it was worse. Because, despite what Peter had promised, I *was* alone. I didn't go on the road with him—I was too distracting, he said. But he insisted I be at the airport to meet him when the team returned, that I be in attendance at press conferences and on his arm for the inevitable pictures. I was the epitome of the loving wife whose only purpose on earth was to welcome her husband home with open arms.

"All the while I was wondering what had happened to the man who had once upon a time stolen quiet moments for us. There were very few quiet moments after we were mar-

ried. Even when we were home alone Peter's mind was on
the next game, the next endorsement, the next awards presentation, the next interview. He swore he loved me, but in
truth he loved himself. My presence in his life was much like
that of his shiny black Ferrari. He loved that too. It was part
of his image."

"You sound bitter."

"Wouldn't you be?" she responded, the hurt still in her
voice. "Tell me something, Patrick. You say you've sworn
off everything to do with football. Why?"

"Because I've outgrown the sport."

"The sport? Or the life-style that goes along with it?"

He thought for a minute, his dark brow creasing. "Both,
I guess."

"But why?"

"I hurt my knee."

"Beyond that. You were always one to avoid the media.
Why?"

"Because the media twisted things. It created pictures that
weren't terribly accurate. It was shallow—"

"Right! That was my life in a nutshell. Shallow. Shopping expeditions to buy a dress to wear one night. Cocktail
parties with the same boring people over and over again. A
pretty house. A plastic smile for the press." Her voice lost
its edge then, growing low, sad. "There were too many times
when I'd sit at home alone in that pretty house wearing
pretty clothes . . . and no smile at all. It was an empty existence, Pat. At least for me it was."

"What about a family? Didn't you want children?"

"Very much. Not Peter."

"That's strange. I would have thought two kids, a station wagon and a dog would add to the image."

"That was what I thought. But he said that kids would be
too restrictive. That we wouldn't be able to go out as much.

That we'd be tied down. I think," she stated slowly, "that he couldn't bear the thought of sharing my attention. And I don't say that out of arrogance. That was the only conclusion I could reach after months and months of soul-searching."

"Was that when you decided to divorce him?"

"Oh, no. I didn't consider it just grounds for divorce. I rationalized that there had to be another solution to my dilemma."

"Which was?"

"Work." She snorted. "Peter didn't agree. He was against the idea from the start. I'm sure that jealousy was a factor there too. A child. A job. Same difference. Peter simply said that *his* wife didn't work. Wouldn't be good for the image."

Patrick pondered her words before directing the next. "Then what *did* bring about the divorce?"

His gentle voice had a calming effect, the same effect, Jordanna realized, that it had had on her from the start of her dissertation. She'd never talked with another person about her marriage as she did now, yet the words flowed freely.

"It was everything. Snowballing. Things came to a head at a party one night. The team was there, along with the usual hangers-on. I overhead two guys talking about Peter and me. How devoted I was. Remarkable, they said, given Peter's, uh, other interests."

"Other women?"

Jordanna shivered. When Patrick opened his coat in an offer of warmth, she wavered.

"I won't do anything," he assured her softly. "Just help you warm up."

At that moment, Jordanna needed his comfort as well as his warmth. Slowly she slid sideways to rest against him.

"I wondered if it was drugs, at first," she went on meekly. "Or alcohol. Or even some kind of sexual perversion. Anything . . . but another woman."

"Was there one?"

"Not one. Many. One-night stands across the country. Oh, he was careful. Nothing ever made the papers. He swore it was all meaningless, that I was the one he loved."

"He *told* you about it?"

"Sure. He was arrogant enough to think it wouldn't matter. That was when I realized he'd bought it all. He saw himself as the king. And the king could do no wrong." Her chin dropped. When Patrick pressed her head to his chest she didn't protest. "It hurt, Pat. You can't imagine how it hurt."

"I know, angel," he crooned softly. His arm tightened on her shoulder. "I know."

"I tried after that, but it didn't work. My self-image was crushed. I'd had the illusion that our love was all that mattered. But suddenly I couldn't bear sitting in the stands cheering the bastard on. I had no patience for his parties, even less for his teammates who condoned everything he did, probably lived that way themselves. And the nights alone, well, they were nightmares. I was sure that the world knew everything and was laughing at me. It was paranoid, I know, but I couldn't help it. I came to the realization that we defined the word in very different ways. I also came to the realization that I was on the verge of a nervous breakdown. *That* was when I moved out. It was a move of self-preservation, the survival instinct at work."

"You certainly did survive," Patrick murmured, squeezing her shoulder in encouragement. "Look at what you've done."

With a shake of her head, she released her hold on the past. "I do have that. Willow Enterprises has given me my life. I don't know what I would have done without it."

"You might have met a nice, ordinary man and fallen in love again."

"No. Not again. I'm not sure I could trust love the second time around."

"Then you've given up the idea of having a family?"

"The business is my family. I've got wonderful people working with me, and each time we launch another product it's like giving birth to a child."

"Not as warm. Not as loving. Or lasting."

"We can't have it all," she whispered sadly, then caught herself. "The business is a constant challenge. It doesn't give me time to dwell on what might have been."

"And in the future? What then? What happens when you're older and more tired and want to settle back and enjoy life with the resources you've earned for yourself?"

"I'll do it."

"Alone?"

"If that's how it turns out. As long as I have my self-respect, I can live with myself." She wanted to sound positive but somehow the words didn't come out that way. As her thoughts tripped into the future, she felt a strange hollowness. Unconsciously she nestled closer to Patrick.

"Come on. Let's go back to camp. You must be tired."

Strangely, she was. Having poured out so much, she felt drained. Relieved, but drained.

With a nod, she let Patrick help her up and said nothing when his arm remained around her for the walk back through the woods. They reached the shelter to find the men all sleeping. A soft snoring persisted.

"God, I wish he'd shut up," Jordanna murmured under her breath.

"Don't know which one it is or I'd give him a shove."

"How are we going to sleep?"

"I've got one way." Without further word, he worked in the dark to draw the two empty sleeping bags onto the floor and fasten them together. Jordanna watched, knowing what he was doing, reluctant to object if for no other reason than for fear of shattering the warm bond that momentarily existed between them. He'd listened to her story with compassion; that had meant a lot to her. He had to see things from the other side, yet he hadn't sat in judgment. He hadn't proclaimed her the ungrateful bitch Peter had. She felt unbelievably close to Patrick at that moment.

Removing her outer clothes without the slightest hesitation, she slid into the haven Patrick offered. She knew he wouldn't try to make love to her. She knew he was no more in the mood for it than she was. Rather, as she snuggled contentedly against his strong frame, she sensed that he needed her warmth just as she needed his. It was a very private, very personal, very mutual giving. There was nothing one-sided about it.

She didn't hear the snoring from the other side of the shelter. She didn't hear the lonely cry of the wind. All she heard was the steady beat of Patrick's heart. Then, wrapped tightly in his arms, she fell asleep.

5

WHEN JORDANNA awakened the next morning, she was alone with the memory of Patrick's warm body sheltering her through the night. He was long gone, already dressed and at work on breakfast. The other men were just rising.

Her cheeks flushed lightly at the thought of what might have happened had she and Patrick been caught nestled together in their sleeping bag for two. Even now she could hear the razzing. They'd never have heard the end of it.

But they hadn't been caught. Patrick had made sure of that. As the men one by one tugged their clothes from the line, she stole a glance toward the stove. He was on his haunches, immersed in his work. His faded jeans hugged his legs; his plaid wool jacket celebrated the sinewed strength beneath. With his dark hair licking his collar and his large hands deftly manipulating the pot, he looked like a logger, a trapper, a mountain man at ease with himself and the world.

She was envious. And stirred. That the simple sight of him should arouse her was unfair. But it was fact. Had she not been so tired last night, she might have had quite a time falling asleep. He'd been tired too. But if it hadn't been so? Would he have been . . . using her?

Stifling a shiver, she quickly dressed and escaped to the stream to wash. When she returned, breakfast was ready. Momentarily apprehensive at meeting Patrick's gaze, she took longer than necessary in stowing her gear. But she couldn't stall forever. With a deep breath for courage, she headed toward the stove.

She might have been one of the men. Patrick gave her no more than a passing glance as he handed her a cup of coffee. Just as well, she reasoned, accepting the brew and a man-sized helping of hot cereal, which she proceeded to down. She was hungry, and the day ahead would be rugged hiking all the way, Patrick said.

It proved to be so. The trek was tough, if breathtakingly beautiful. Skirting the bog outlying No-Ketchum Pond, they followed the forest trail for a stretch before descending into Perkins Notch. From there they began to climb on a leaf-strewn path, encountering more evergreens as the air thinned. After another descent, they rose again, this time toward Carter Dome, whose summit offered a view of the Wildcat Range and, beyond, the majesty of Mount Washington. It was here that they paused for lunch.

The sun shone brightly. Despite the altitude, the air was surprisingly warm. "Typical New England weather," Patrick explained in rationalizing the contrast from yesterday's storm.

Jordanna was warm in more ways than one. With the morning's hike behind them and a rest period in the works, her mind was free to wander. And wander it did. Though she avoided Patrick's gaze, he was there before her in remembered flashes. A hand on her cheek. Lips teasing her nipple through her thermal shirt. The heat of his hair-roughened chest against her breasts.

"That's it!" Larry cried. "Perfect!"

Stunned out of her reverie, she only belatedly became aware that he'd been taking pictures of her. Her cheeks burned. Scowling, she held a hand up to ward him off. "God, Larry! That's disgusting! Creeping up on a person that way!"

"I didn't creep up. I've been walking around taking pictures of everyone for the past ten minutes. You were preoccupied. You and Pat. You should have seen *his* expression."

Her lips thinned. "Before, or after?"

"Both. Brooding before. Furious after . . . like you." With a grin, he raised the camera again. "Hey, that's great." And snapped, then lowered the black devil. "You're a woman of many faces, Jordanna. Glowing one minute, glowering the next. I should have thought of this sooner." He lifted the camera once more.

This time, Jordanna bolted up and around, right into Patrick. Hands on her shoulders, he steadied her. "Easy, angel," he whispered. "He's just teasing."

"I don't like having my picture taken," she gritted.

"Neither do I, but if you resist, he's apt to want to do it all the more. You're so cool and unflappable most of the time. I think the men would love to see you unsettled."

"Hey, smile, you guys!" Larry called from the side.

Patrick squeezed Jordanna's elbow. In unison, they turned their heads toward the camera's eye. And smiled.

The instant she heard the click, Jordanna's smile vanished. "Was that settled enough?" she murmured for Patrick's ears alone.

"It'll do. See, he's lost interest."

Sure enough, Larry had turned back to the others, all of whom had followed the impromptu photo session, Jordanna now realized, with gusto. Moaning softly, she sat down on the ground again. She was aware of Patrick watching her, wavering, finally returning to his own lunch some distance away, and she wondered why he'd come over in the first place. But of course he'd come to save her from making a fool of herself. Chivalrous.

And why had she been about to make a fool of herself? Because, she realized, Larry had interrupted a pretty heavy daydream. She'd been annoyed and embarrassed. She'd felt utterly exposed. Dangerous man, this white knight of hers. Spawning dangerous thoughts. Very dangerous.

Spearing the single sardine left in her tin, she swallowed it whole.

THE AFTERNOON'S HIKE was as rugged as the morning's had been. Jordanna pushed herself to her limit, ridding herself of unwanted nervous energy. They scaled Mount Hight, then began the torturous climb downward. Her calves ached; her thighs pulsed. Beneath the weight of her pack, her shoulders clamored for relief.

And she began to wonder just why she was submitting to such torture. She'd been a fool to come. One look at Patrick Monday morning and she should have turned and headed straight back to New York. No, on second thought, she should have found the nearest inn and hibernated for the week. She'd needed the rest, the break from routine. But *this*?

Jordanna wasn't the only one to feel the strain. Rest breaks seemed to come more frequently now, prompted for the most part by the men's cries. Once or twice she sensed that Patrick called a halt for her benefit, but if that was the case he made no point of it. Rather, at times, he seemed more like a harsh taskmaster, driving his team on, ever on. She clung to this image. It was a far safer one than that of the eminently virile outdoorsman. Which he was, decidedly. Maddeningly.

The scenery was some diversion. They hiked through forests that had miraculously escaped the logger's ax. Spruce grew tall. Mossy carpets bordered the path. The sun painted dappled patterns on the woodland floor, skittering through graceful birch limbs.

It was late afternoon when they reached Spruce Brook, where they'd be camping for the night. Grateful as she'd never been, Jordanna dropped her pack, then sank to the ground herself. The men had done the same, she noted with some relief.

With a will of their own, her eyes sought Patrick. He, too, was lowering his pack, his back to her. She started to look away, but was held by something in the way he moved. Oh, yes, he seemed as tall and strong as ever. But something marred the fluidity of his movement. She stared, puzzled when he bent to ease the pack to the ground. There was something about the way he straightened, about the way he flexed his back. When he raised a hand to his shoulder, she understood.

An instinct to comfort made her start to rise but she caught herself when he suddenly turned, collided with her gaze and froze. Hand still on his shoulder, he stared hard at her. His message was clear: I'm fine; it's nothing; forget you saw this. Then slowly he lowered his hand, turned away and knelt to open his pack.

Jordanna had no choice but to settle back on the ground again. She wondered how long his shoulder had been bothering him and sensed that his driving them on had been as much for his own benefit as for that of the group he led. Football heroes did that. Injured or not, they played. Pain was part and parcel of the game.

With a quiet snort of disgust, she lay back against her pack, knees bent, and concentrated on healing herself. If Patrick Clayes wanted to martyr himself, let him, she reasoned. Strange, but he hadn't allowed any of them that luxury through the week.

The week. With a jolt of awareness, she realized that the week was nearly done. It was Thursday. Tonight would be their last night in the wilds. Tomorrow they'd complete the circle and head for home. She wondered where the days had gone and felt a twinge of guilt at the begrudging thoughts she'd harbored earlier. Aches and all, it had been a good week. As exhausted as she was now, it was a healthy exhaustion. She hadn't felt as untethered in years.

Turning her head against its makeshift pillow, she peered through her lashes at Patrick Clayes. She wouldn't see him...after tomorrow. That was for the best, she knew, yet she couldn't help but feel the tiniest bit sorry. He excited her. His presence had added something very special to the trip. Pleasure. Anticipation. The same things she felt on entering the office each morning, yet different. Very different.

"You're looking sad. No. Melancholy."

She twisted her head to find John squatting beside her. Trying not to blush, she managed a crooked smile. "I'm just tired."

"That wasn't exhaustion I saw," he chided, arching a brow. His gaze shifted to Patrick, then returned. He kept his voice low. "You like him, don't you."

It wasn't a question. Jordanna cautioned herself not to overreact. "Of course. Don't you?"

"Not in the same way. I like him because he's personable and intelligent, because he's a good leader. You, well, you see things I don't. I'm a man. You're a woman."

"You've got a point there," she murmured, closing her eyes in a gesture of nonchalance that didn't fool John for a minute.

"I hope we haven't embarrassed you. Kidding you and all."

"No problem."

"Will you see him?"

"Who?"

"Pat."

Her eyes opened. "When?"

"After this is over."

"Why ever would I do that?"

"Because you look good together."

She gave a dry laugh and told herself to stay calm. "There's a lot more to a relationship than looking good together."

"You've got a lot in common."

"Oh?" she said noncommittally.

"Football and all."

"I don't have anything to do with football."

"You did."

"Yeah. And I don't want any part of it now."

"Neither does he." John's gaze darted across the campsite to Patrick, who was mixing Tang. "He stuck to his guns. I have to hand it to him. He said he wouldn't talk shop and he didn't." He looked back at Jordanna. "Did he with you?"

"Nope."

"Because you didn't want him to."

"Right."

"And you don't find him attractive?"

"Hey, what is this?" Jordanna asked softly. "An inquisition?" If the questions had come from one of the other men, she might have been offended. Somehow it was different with John. He was the most thoughtful of the group. She was actually curious about what he had to say.

"Of course not. I was just wondering. It's kinda nice, when you think of the possibilities. If you and Pat were to get together—"

"We're not getting together," she interrupted. "Our lives are too different."

"How do you know that?"

"I know."

"I think you're building a wall that may not exist."

Jordanna spoke softly, without malice. "I think you're overstepping your bounds."

"You may be right. But I like you, Jordanna. You're a very strong, together woman. I admire the way you've put up with us all week. And I can understand what Craig's been raving about. You're intelligent. And determined. I can see why Willow Enterprises is a successful concern. I just wonder...."

When his voice trailed off, she slanted him a glance. "Wonder what?"

"Wonder what outlet you give to the softer side of you."

"Businesswomen aren't soft."

"You are. I've seen it. The way you look at Pat sometimes. Like just now. You saw him rubbing that shoulder. It was all you could do not to go to him."

"You saw that?" she asked, momentarily unaware of what she was admitting.

"I happened to catch that look of alarm on your face. When I followed it to Pat, I understood."

She settled back and closed her eyes. "What you saw was compassion for another human being. I've never claimed to be ruthless."

He chuckled. "I don't think you could be ruthless if you tried. Especially not to Pat."

"Maybe not," was all she said. She kept her eyes closed, worked to keep her pose as casual as possible.

"Well," John continued, "you were right before. I probably have overstepped my bounds. The side of Pat we've seen this week is only a fraction of the man. When it comes down to brass tacks, he's probably as shallow as—"

"Are you kidding?" Jordanna exclaimed, opening her eyes and half rising in dismay. But her dismay was never greater than when she saw that John was indeed kidding. With a sly grin and a twinkle in his eye, he moved off to give Patrick a hand.

Bill, it seemed, had a bottle of wine in his pack. He'd kept it tenderly wrapped in his clothes for the week and smugly produced it at the start of dinner. Donald, it seemed, had a second bottle similarly squirreled. When the first was gone, he jubilantly uncorked it. Dinner was a merry event indeed.

Merry, Jordanna thought, as in drowning out those melancholy thoughts that John had rightly accused her of harboring. Or rather, trying to drown them out. Somehow it didn't quite work. Yes, the wine warmed and relaxed her, but never quite erased the fact that Patrick was close. It never quite erased the fact that the tent they'd be sharing that night stood apart from the others, waiting. And it never quite erased the fact that though Patrick might be using her she wanted him nonetheless.

She put if off as long as possible. While the men talked, she sat by, eyes alert, fatigue replaced by an overall tingle. When one by one they headed for their tents, she remained. She ... and Patrick.

"Tired?" he asked quietly. The small lantern cast shadows over his face, lending a more sculpted look to already rugged features.

"No," she answered as softly.

"Want to talk?" She shook her head. "Take a walk?" She shook her head again. "Play gin?"

"Gin?" It sounded safe enough. "Okay."

Patrick dealt. They played three games. He won all three. Jordanna was still busy pondering the lesson to be had when he stood and took her hand. "Let's take that walk."

"No, Pat—"

"Now." His grasp brooked no resistance.

Loath to fight him, she acquiesced, following him quietly into the night woods until he came to a halt at the crest of a rise. Only then did he drop her hand.

"Wise move," she murmured, scanning the darkness. "You know I can't run. I'd get lost." Though the moon was out, its light was shuttered by the thick growth overhead.

Patrick stood with his back to her and spoke without turning. "You'd find your way. You always do."

He was talking of her life, and she knew it. "I try."

"Could you try tonight?"

Her breath caught for an instant. "Try what?"

Slowly he turned. Though the night hid the force of his expression, his tension beamed her way clearly. "Try pretending that we aren't who we are. That the past doesn't exist. That I never played football and that you were never married to my darkest rival."

"For what purpose?" she heard herself whisper, though the beat of her heart was positively thunderous, making his answer no more than a formality.

"For us, Jordanna. You and me. One night. Together."

She wanted to step back, but her feet were glued to the mossy floor. "Oh, Pat . . . I don't know. . . ."

"Don't you want it?" There was neither arrogance nor smugness in his voice, but rather a pleading note that made her ache.

"You know I do," she breathed.

"Then why not? For one night?"

"Because I can't. I can't forget."

"Come on, Jordanna. There's no one here. We're miles away from reality."

But she was shaking her head. "I can't forget!"

"It's not that you can't," he stated then, his voice harder. "You won't. You're afraid."

"Damned right, I'm afraid!" she cried, her composure slowly crumbling. "I'm afraid of everything you were, of everything I was. I don't want that again, Patrick. I told you what it was like. I don't think I could bear it!"

Patrick stared at her in a state of confusion, but when he spoke his tone was even. "I'm not offering you anything you've had before. I thought I'd made that clear."

"You also made it clear that you'd be making love to me to get back at Peter."

"I never said that."

"You implied it."

"*You* inferred it, Jordanna. Let's keep this straight. What I said was that I'd make love to you like you've never been made love to before—"

"Like *Peter* never made love to me."

"That's right. Like Peter never made love to you. You were married to him and it kills me. It kills me to think of you in his arms. It kills me to think of you in *any* other man's arms but mine, but I've got an ego too. And that ego tells me that when I make love to you it's got to be the best thing you've ever felt. I want that. I need that. Don't you see? Any man would!"

"As a challenge, Pat? That was the word you used."

He raked a hand through his hair in frustration. "Of course it's a challenge. Any time a man makes love to a woman it's a challenge. At least it should be. If it's not . . . well, what's the use?"

Jordanna was frightened. He had all the right answers. She wanted to believe him, but to do that would have meant dashing the control she'd held over herself for so many years. It would have meant forgetting. And she wasn't sure she could do that.

Sensing the standoff, Patrick gave a low groan, turned and began to stalk back through the woods.

"Where are you going?" she cried.

"Back to camp," he growled without missing a step.

He was about to round a curve and disappear from sight when Jordanna broke into a run. She had no desire to be left alone to the beavers and raccoons and moose and bears. She had to trot to keep up, his stride was so long. When they reached the campsite she watched him duck into the tent. Her pulse raced in indecision. She couldn't stay outside forever. It was cold. The tent provided shelter, her sleeping bag warmth. Wringing her hands, she waffled. Then, with a helpless moan, she followed Pat.

Having tossed his jacket aside, he was in the process of shucking his jeans. Silently she knelt on her sleeping bag and, head down, proceeded to do the same. When she wore nothing but her long underwear, she quickly slid into her sleeping bag.

Eyes adjusted to the dark, she stared at the roof of the tent. Beside her, Patrick shifted repeatedly in his efforts to get comfortable. Finally, cursing softly, he sat bolt upright and raised a hand to massage his shoulder.

This time Jordanna couldn't look the other way. Rising, she pushed his hand aside.

"You don't need to—" he grumbled, only to be interrupted.

"Shh. It's all right," she whispered. "Let me help."

His muscles were hard, bunched beneath her fingers. She kneaded them gently, persistently, but in vain.

"Take off your shirt," she ordered softly. "My hands keep slipping."

For a minute he did nothing. His head was low, jaw clenched. When at last he reached to pull the thermal shirt from its lower half, she helped him. Then his flesh was bare, warm to her touch. Palms flat, she worked at his muscles, then used her fingers in an attempt to relax them. But the more she toiled, the more tense he seemed. She slid her hands to his neck and attacked those muscles with the same gentle firmness.

Nothing. Nothing but the exhilaration of the feel of his skin. Nothing but the enchantment of his strength. Nothing but a temptation that was driving her insane. Only when she realized that her own tension had grown to match his did she stop. And moan softly. And drop her forehead to his shoulder.

"Oh, Pat," she cried, tottering on the edge.

Slowly he reached up, took her hands and drew them down over his chest. Sagging forward, she buried her face against his neck. He smelled so very male. He felt so very male. And at the moment she felt female from head to toe.

Then he was turning, taking her in his arms, crushing her to him. And she was in his sleeping bag, flush against his strength, offering her mouth for the wild abandon of his kiss.

There was nothing else. Just as he'd said. The past might never have been, for the ardor they shared. He kissed her with a fierceness echoed by her own seeking tongue. And he touched with a thoroughness she needed, not denying her breasts, or her hips, or her thighs, or that warmer, waiting spot between her legs.

She was barely aware that he'd thrust her long johns down to her knees until he levered himself up to do the same. By then she was trembling, arching, needing him more than she'd ever needed another being. Her pants slid to her ankles when she raised her knees to provide him the frame he sought. Then he was inside her, hot, hard and throbbing, stopping her tiny cries at her mouth with the force of his own lips.

Jordanna had never known such raw pleasure. Patrick's ragged gasps were as intoxicating as the rhythmic plunge of his hips. She met him at each thrust, needing to be absorbed, feeling her essence flow toward him even as she devoured all he offered in return. And it was plenty. Amid the fury of their joining, she felt his restraint in the trembling of his limbs. And she knew that he awaited her release as a prerequisite of his own.

When it came, it was blinding, a cataclysmic explosion of inner joy made all the greater by his final thrust, by the cry of exaltation he couldn't contain.

For what seemed an eternal bliss, they clung together until, at last, Patrick collapsed against her. His back was slick beneath her palms, his damp chest melded to hers. The soft sounds of their panting filled the small tent, slowing gradually, reluctantly.

Only after a very long time did he slip from her, rolling onto his side, taking her with him.

"I'm sorry, angel," he whispered, burying his face in her hair. She felt the quivering of his arms as he held her tightly. "I'm sorry."

"Sorry?"

"I wanted it to be so good. So long. I wanted to make love to every single inch of you."

"But you did!"

"I wanted it to be so special."

"It was!" Reaching up, she took his face in her hands. "It was." Her lips brushed his, thumbs replacing them when she drew back. For just a minute she hesitated before whispering God's truth. "Peter never needed me quite that way."

Her words hung in the air until, with a moan, Patrick pressed her head to his chest and hugged her so tightly she had to gasp for breath. "Ahh, angel. I didn't want you to think of him."

"But you do. And I want you to know. What just happened *was* very special to me, Pat. I wanted you so badly."

"And I wanted *you*. You know that, don't you? My desire for you has nothing to do with Peter. It's there. It has been since Monday. I'd have wanted you if you'd been married to the Aga Khan."

"I know," she murmured, slipping her knee over his thigh as she felt him grow against her.

He sucked in a breath. "I want you again."

Her smile lit the dark. "I know."

"Are you pleased?"

"Peter never did," she said in the softest, most vulnerable voice. "Not a second time. I always assumed he was too tired. After a while I realized that he was as self-centered in lovemaking as in everything else. His climax was the be-all and end-all. He owed me nothing further." She traced a small circle over Patrick's breast. "I'm telling you this for a reason, Pat. I'm not one to kiss and tell. But I . . . it flatters me that you want me again." She rushed the words out, feeling vaguely self-conscious. "Especially after what we just had."

"Because of what we just had," Patrick corrected thickly, kissing her brow. "*Because*, angel. It was so good. So right." He paused. "Jordanna . . . touch me. . . ."

Heat shimmered through her veins. She looked into his eyes and saw that need again. Never, she knew, would she be impervious to it. Lowering her hand between their bodies, she circled him, stroking timidly at first, then, when he strained in delight, with a courage born of her own reawakening ache.

"So good, angel," he murmured, eyes closed before the pleasure of her touch.

Mindful of her own gnawing inner void, Jordanna led him to her, releasing him only as he slid into her warmth.

"That's it," he whispered. With his hands low on her hips, he guided her body. "Mmm."

Though this time was slower, the rapture was no less intense. Having freed a foot from her long johns, she curved it behind his knee. "Yes, Pat . . . oh, yes. . . ." Each flex of his hips drove her higher.

"You're . . . uhh . . . you're gonna be black and blue," he panted. "Damned ground . . . ahh, angel. . . ."

"More . . . there . . . oh, God, Pat, it feels . . . so good. . . ."

"And this?" Freeing a hand, he found her breast and rolled its turgid peak beneath his thumb.

"Yes!"

"But I still . . . can't see you . . ." he managed between thrusts. "What I'd really like . . . is to spread you out . . . in the moonlight." Jordanna's soft whimpering gave him but a moment's pause. "Naked on a soft white sheet . . . and I'd look at you . . . and love you. . . ."

She threw her arms around his neck and clung to him. Soft cries came in broken gasps from her throat. Her body was on fire, the core of the heat centered at the point of their union. Her every muscle strained for release.

"That's it, angel," he rasped, his own release imminent. "That's it . . . let it come . . . oh, yes. . . ." He felt her catch her breath, then expel it brokenly. Seconds later, inspired by her abandon, he did the same.

For a long time after, neither spoke. Locked together in the single sleeping bag, their closeness made up for the end of the divine luxury they'd shared. When Patrick's breathing deepened, Jordanna tipped her head back.

"Pat?" she whispered.

"Hmm?"

"Do you think . . . ?"

"What?"

"Did we . . . ?"

"What?"

Embarrassed, she blurted it out. "Did we make much noise?"

The frown he showered on her was tinged with amusement. "Noise?" Though his voice was low, he made no attempt to whisper as she had. "As in grunts and groans and sighs—"

"Shh! You know what I mean. Do you think...any of the men might have heard?"

He laughed softly. "I doubt it. Listen."

Sure enough, when she trained her ears she caught the sound of a distant buzz saw. Then, puzzled, she listened more carefully. "I don't believe it. *Two* of them snoring tonight?"

"Sounds that way. Even if the other two are awake, they'd never be able to hear a thing over that racket. Not that I care, mind you. It wouldn't bother me if those guys knew."

"It *wouldn't* bother you," she scolded. "You're a man. I can just see you strutting around with your chest puffed out—"

He squeezed her tight to cut her off. "Hey, I didn't say that. I'm not the peacock you'd like to think."

There was an underlying note of annoyance in his voice. Instantly Jordanna resented its cool presence in what was an otherwise warm afterglow of passion.

"I know," she whispered, stroking his chest, unruffling his feathers. "I guess I'm just wary. Must be my early training. I'm sorry."

Rolling to his back, Patrick took her hand in his and pressed it to his heart. "No, I'm sorry. Sorry you had to be trained that way. But we're not all like that. You've got to believe me."

She did, and she told him so. When he seemed to relax, she snuggled closer, twining her legs with his.

"Comfortable?" he asked.

"Mmm. I've got the better part of the deal. You make a good mattress."

"My butt's killing me."

"How about your shoulder?"

"It's better. I guess I forgot about it." He shifted until he was more comfortable all over, then kissed her brow. "Good night, angel."

"Night, Pat."

Closing her eyes, Jordanna drifted off to sleep with an ease that would have astounded her. She should have been thinking of what she'd just done. She should have been pondering the ramifications. She should have been wondering what tomorrow would bring. But she wasn't. She couldn't. The moment was too special to be marred in any way. Tomorrow would come soon enough. It always did.

BRIGHT SUNSHINE and invigoratingly cool air—that was Friday's climatic offering. For some strange reason that wasn't really at all strange to Jordanna when she stopped to think about it the weather did little to cheer her up.

Actually, she'd awoken in good spirits, drifting into consciousness on a cloud of erotic memory. Burrowing closer to Patrick had been her first mistake. When she hit empty space, she opened her eyes. That had been her second mistake.

He was gone, as always. Dressed and out of the tent before the rest of the group had stirred. What bothered her was that she wasn't the rest of the group. She was the woman he'd made love to not once, but twice in the night now past. He might have at least kissed her before he'd left. Then again, maybe he had.

Frowning while she tugged on her clothes, she hit the outside air to find the other men digging into breakfast as though they hadn't eaten in a year. The worst of it, though, was not how or what they ate but rather what they talked about. Going home.

It was Friday. Today they'd be going home.

Jordanna silently neared the group, then stopped. She stood listening, unable to advance, unable to retreat, until Patrick's approach broke her paralysis.

"Freeze-dried omelet?" he offered, holding out a plate.

As the first words he'd spoken to her since his tender "Good night, angel," they weren't the most romantic he might have picked. But it was morning. They had an audience. And Patrick's somber gaze was in keeping with Jordanna's mood.

"Uh. . . ." She looked down, wavering.

He spoke gently. "You'll need something. We've still got a full day ahead."

Without looking up, she accepted the plate, helped herself to coffee and sank down to the ground.

"Shave," Larry was saying as he stroked his grizzled jaw. "That's the first thing I'm going to do."

John shook his head. "Not me. I'm heading for the shower before I touch a thing. I must have half the dirt in New Hampshire under my collar. And damn it, Bill, don't give me that bit about washing up more. The water around here's been frigid."

Bill held up a hand. "Suit yourself. Personally—" he grinned and closed his eyes to dream "—I'm dying to sink my teeth into a nice, thick, juicy, rare steak."

"A bed," Donald injected. "That's what I want. A nice warm bed with a mattress that won't bite."

"How about you, Jordanna?" Bill asked. "What's your pleasure, now that the end's in sight?"

Jordanna's insides knotted. It was all she could do not to look at Patrick. "Oh, all of the above, I guess."

"You guess?" Donald teased. "Hey, where's the opinionated lady who arrived here on Monday? She never would have guessed. She would have known. Or—" he sent a sly glance toward Patrick "—are you two planning to stay up here and do the route again?"

Jordanna couldn't help but peer at Patrick then. He looked as grim as she felt. It was only with great effort that she forced what she hoped passed as a smile for the benefit of the other men. "I'd like that, but it's a luxury I can't afford. I've got a business waiting back in New York. Come Monday morning my work's cut out for me."

"Ah, the executive woman," Donald returned in echo of the words he'd used on Monday. Then there had been disdain in his tone. Now there was respect. Likewise, his smile was warm.

Jordanna nodded, her own smile more natural. These men weren't so bad, after all. Come to think of it, they'd been pretty good sports. Her gaze touched one then another of them, giving silent thanks for their indulgence. When, uncharacteristically self-conscious, she looked down, she knew that something *was* different in her now. Was it the soft side John had mentioned yesterday on the trail? *Had* she been burying it all these years?

She had much to think about as they dismantled the tents, loaded their packs and started out on the trail. It was a relaxing hike. Though the scenery lacked the spectacular quality they'd been privy to earlier in the week, it was pleasant. Emptied of food, their packs were lighter. Hardened by trial, their muscles were silent.

Following the Wild River Trail, they stopped for lunch at a peaceful spot overlooking a clear blue pool that would have been a bather's dream had the day been warmer. Jordanna sat quietly munching on the last of her sunflower seeds, wondering where the week had gone, wishing it had been longer. Oh, yes, she craved a bath. And a bed. And a fresh, warm, buttery croissant. But there were other cravings now, ones she hadn't wanted but ones she couldn't deny.

Patrick said little. She would have given any number of pennies for his thoughts, but they were hidden behind a mask of self-control. As always, he was the consummate guide, directing their sights here and there, talking in that exquisitely patient, ever amiable tone of his.

At times she wanted to scream. *What did you feel? What do you think? Where do we go from here?* But she didn't. She knew the answers, at least those that applied to her. She and Patrick would go their separate ways. It was understood. It had to be. Here in the wilderness they might be two creatures without restraint. Back in the city, reality awaited.

And reality drew closer with each step they took. Though the afternoon's walk was undemanding, Jordanna felt a rising anguish. She tried to push it aside, to put the week in perspective, to shift her thoughts forward and muster enthusiasm for her return to work. Somehow that didn't work. Just when she thought she'd mastered her senses, she'd catch sight of Patrick and her insides would twist anew.

Too soon they arrived at the campground from which they'd set out four days before. The men were jubilant, as enthusiastic about the trip as they were about taking off their backpacks a final time. There were heartfelt thanks to Patrick, handshakes all around, even hugs for Jordanna, which she returned with sincerity.

Then Donald and Bill took off in one car, Larry and John in another. And she and Patrick were alone.

Car keys in hand, she slowly approached the Jeep as he slammed its tailgate shut and turned. "Got the tents and all?" she asked.

"Yup."

She nodded, looking out toward the woods. "Well, I guess I'd better be on my way."

"Are you driving all the way back tonight?"

"I was hoping to." Hands thrust in her pockets, she eyed the sky. "I'm not sure. What with all that talk about beds and baths, I might just give in and stop at a motel along the way."

There was silence then. Billowy clouds moved in ever changing formation across the sky. Though they were the object of her scrutiny, she saw nothing of their beauty.

"Jordanna?"

Heart pounding, she met his gaze. "Yes?"

"I know of a nice place. It's about an hour away. I thought I'd spend the night there." He seemed to hesitate. "I'm sure they've got plenty of room. Off-season and all...."

She nodded but didn't speak. Her throat was suspiciously tight.

"Well...I just wanted to mention it...." He turned toward his door, then paused, head down, shoulders tense. When he looked back, his eyes spoke of the same inner pain she'd been feeling all day. Reaching out, he cupped her jaw, caressing her cheek with his thumb. "You'd better get going. I'll follow. I'll feel better knowing you've hit the main road okay."

Tipping her head to the side, Jordanna rubbed her cheek against his palm. "No," she said softly. "You go. I'll follow."

She thought she saw a flare of light in his eyes, but it was gone so quickly she wondered if she'd imagined it. She couldn't have imagined his warmth, however. It was a living thing, searching her depths, seeking and finding her heat.

It was that heat that kept her foot on the gas, her eye on the Jeep ahead of her through the hour's drive to the inn he had in mind.

6

WILDWOOD WAS A grand old inn in southern New Hampshire, set at the far end of its own private road beneath towering elms whose leaves had fallen and majestic firs whose needles had not. Wondering if she'd made the right choice, knowing she truly had no choice at all, Jordanna pulled her rented Chevy to a halt beside Patrick's Jeep in the gravel lot.

He was there to help her out, his expression one of tense anticipation, even uncertainty, if her interpretation was correct. "Let's bring the packs," he suggested quietly. "They'll wash whatever we want." Taking her keys from her, he removed the backpack from her trunk, slung it over one shoulder, secured his own on the other and started up the flagstone path toward the inn's broad front steps.

Jordanna would have protested his carrying both packs, but she caught herself. Divested of sleeping bags and pads, not to mention the food and other equipment that they'd been hauling around all week, the packs weren't heavy. And he was already halfway there, climbing the steps holding the bright white door open for her.

Trotting to catch up, she preceded him into the stately front hall, then stood aside as he approached the registration desk. He didn't look back, didn't ask if she wanted her own room. It would have been a foolish question. After last night, there could be no pretense between them. This elegant old inn with its high ceilings, turn-of-the-century moldings and graceful winding staircase was a reprieve. Jordanna could no more have resisted it than she could have the vulnerable look Patrick sent her when a bellboy materialized to lead them to their room. She answered it with a tremulous smile, quickly averting her gaze and concentrating on following the bellhop.

Their room was large, dominated by ceiling-high windows and a roomy four-poster bed. A heavily sheened mahogany dresser stood against one wall, a similarly finished desk against another. Before the window was a cushiony armchair upholstered in a large floral print of green, burgundy and white; nearby stood a matching lounge chair. The overall effect was of bright airiness and down-home New England charm. Jordanna knew Patrick had stayed there before. He'd chosen well the site for a tryst.

With their packs deposited on a long luggage rack and the bellhop gone, they were somewhat ill-at-ease. Jordanna's eye skimmed the room again, coming to rest on the bathroom door. Though the late-afternoon sun poured into the room, the bellhop had switched on that light in his brief tour.

She dropped her gaze, focused on her muddy hiking shoes, took in the dirty sheen of her pants, then her jacket. Whether it was the utter cleanness of the room or the simple cumulative effect of five days with makeshift bathing, or the fact that Patrick would be seeing her, truly *seeing* her for the first time, she suddenly felt overwhelmingly grubby.

When she looked up, he was craning his neck against the collar of his T-shirt, using a finger to separate it from his skin.

"I think John was right," she murmured awkwardly. "I feel like I've got half the state's dirt under my clothes."

"Me too," he answered. With deft fingers he reached for the buttons of his wool shirt, releasing one after the other until the shirt hit the floor as the first of the must-wash pile.

With a nonchalance she was far from feeling Jordanna began to undress in turn. "They'll really wash all this stuff?" she asked, wondering, as she added her once bright lime-hued jacket to the pile, who in his right mind would want to touch it.

"They always have. I've stayed here several times before."

Nodding, she knelt and concentrated on unlacing her shoes. "These were pretty good. I haven't got a blister."

Patrick's T-shirt hit the pile, then he was bending over to remove his own dirt-encrusted boots. "Ah, but were they warm?"

"Pretty much so."

"And dry?"

She set one aside and went to work on its mate. "Except for the day it rained."

He chuckled but said nothing. Standing, Jordanna reached for the Velcro fastening of her pants, hesitated, then tugged it apart. The sound was deafening to her senses. For a split second she wondered if she'd caught some kind of madness that had been floating around in the woods that week. What she was doing was crazy. It was truly *dumb*. But she couldn't stop her fingers when they grasped the hem of her sweater and pulled it over her head. Nor did she hesitate when Patrick's second boot hit the oak floor with a thud.

Eyes still downcast, she slipped the pants from her legs. They no sooner landed atop the pile when they were covered by Patrick's jeans. Pulse racing against a wave of self-consciousness, she shimmied her long underwear down, dropped the warm cloth and, before she lost her courage, dragged the thermal shirt over her head.

It was then that her gaze met Patrick's. He stood before her wearing nothing but his briefs. His chest was broad, lightly tanned, matted by the dark curling hair she'd only felt before. His torso was lean, tapering to his hips. Well-muscled thighs held him straight, while her own trembled mercilessly. Mouth dry, she watched as his gaze fell.

"Do you never wear a bra?" he asked in a husky whisper. His eyes focused with unhidden appreciation on her full breasts.

She raised her hands to her waist, started to wrap them around herself, sheepishly dropped them. "I...I always do. Working, I mean. But on the weekend when I'm alone.... And I thought it'd be an added restraint while I was hiking...."

"It's okay," Patrick murmured, entranced as he took a step forward. His fingers found the hollow of her throat and traced the lightest of lines southward through the valley between her breasts, then up around one swelling mound. "You're beautiful, Jordanna. Have I told you that?"

Her cheeks were pink and warm. "I think you said something of the sort at one point."

"Well, I say it again. And this time I know what I'm talking about." His gaze fell to the line where her panties began. He looked up once quickly, then as though unable to help himself, looked down again.

Her pulse racing, Jordanna watched his fingertips slip beneath the thin elastic band. With unbelievable grace, he sank to his knees, drawing the silken fabric down until, with a hand on his shoulder for the support she badly needed, she stepped free.

"So beautiful," he murmured again. Sitting back on his haunches, he stared at her. His large hands framed her hips, then slipped behind to gently caress her bottom.

Jordanna's fingers sank into the hard flesh of his shoulders. "I want to be clean for you," she whispered. "I want to be fresh and—"

"You couldn't be more beautiful than you are now. God, Jordanna!" Coming up on his knees, he wrapped his arms around her back and pressed his face into her stomach. "I want you so much I don't think I can stand it."

"You're not standing," she managed in a tremulous whisper. "I'm the one who's standing and I don't think I can much longer." Her knees trembled wildly in rhythm with every one of her nerve ends.

Patrick breathed deeply of her skin, then kissed her navel and forced himself to rise. Against the straining fabric of his briefs, his desire was obvious. "If we don't hurry, I'm apt to take you here on the floor. But I want you soft and comfortable. We've had enough of the ground for a while. And those sheets are too clean and white to even imagine putting these trail-worn bodies on them."

Taking her hand, he led her to the bathroom. There was no sign of a shower. Rather, an ancient porcelain tub stood on its four clawed feet, as beckoning as anything could have been at that moment. Anything, Jordanna mused, except the hard strength of Patrick's body.

Patience, she told herself, though her trembling persisted. Patience.

Propping one arm on the lip of the tub, Patrick turned on the water, tested it, adjusted the taps to ensure the right temperature, then waited for the tub to fill.

Eyes glued to the rising water and hands on his hips, he was more disciplined than Jordanna, who couldn't help but study his body in the bright light. His back was smoother than his hair-spattered chest, his muscles that much more boldly presented. There was the scar that rounded his shoulder, and a small birthmark to the left of his backbone. Helpless, she touched it, then trailed her fingers down the hollow in the center of his back.

If she'd thought him momentarily preoccupied with the bath, she'd miscalculated. Turning, he grabbed her, flattened her against him and began to tickle. "You want it on the floor? Do ya? Hmm?"

"No...don't, Pat...I give! I give!" The words were forced out between laughs. When she tried to evade the devastation of his fingers, he set her back. The humor that had carried his voice moments before was gone.

"Do you, Jordanna?" he asked softly.

Stepping forward again, unwilling to forfeit one instant of his warmth, she threaded her fingers into his hair. "Yes," she whispered. "For tonight, anything...."

Their lips met in a kiss that began gently but escalated until finally Patrick wrenched his mouth away and bent quickly to the tub. "They might not be thrilled if this tub overflowed," he grunted, turning off the taps. "Dirty laundry's one thing. A flood's something else." Straightening, he turned to Jordanna. Eyes holding hers, he lowered his briefs and kicked them off.

Jordanna knew that her breathlessness was not from the tickling he'd given her moments before. Swallowing hard, she let her gaze fall. If what she'd felt, if what had given her such pleasure the night before had been magnificent, the virile display before her was no less.

"Oh, Pat," she whispered with what little breath she could find, "you're beautiful too." Inching closer, she put a hand on his chest, then slowly lowered it until what she'd seen was at her command. The dignity with which Patrick had endured her scrutiny began to disintegrate with his flagrant response to her touch. His arms gently circled her back, muscles quivering in restraint.

"You won't think so in another minute," he growled. "This tile floor's even harder than the wood one out there."

Eyes closed, Jordanna turned in to his chest, kissing him slowly, savoring his textured skin beneath her lips. When her tongue darted out to taste his hard nipple, he jerked.

Taking her face in both of his hands, he forced it up. "The bath?" he suggested.

"Hmm?" She was in a daze of pleasure that had blotted out even the gritty feel of her own body.

"The bath, Jordanna," he repeated, more gently this time as he kissed first one eye, then the other. "I want to be clean for you too, angel. Clean and fresh and smelling of something other than a creature of the wild."

"Creatures of the wild are intoxicating," she said.

"They can be pretty rank."

Her eyes opened. "Were you worried? Last night, I mean?"

"Not then. Well, maybe a little. But when you're out there and you get used to feeling, uh, earthy, things take on their own perspective. Here in this place, it's another ball game."

She smiled. "I do believe you're blushing."

To compensate, he manufactured a scowl. "Would you like a bath, or am I going to take it by myself?"

"I want one." Turning, she dunked a toe, then a whole foot. "Ahh, hot water." Then she was stepping into the tub and sinking down, moaning at the only other pleasure that might have had a chance against Patrick's masculine allure. "This is heaven!"

"How quickly she changes gear," he teased, staking claim on the opposite end of the tub by folding his large body therein.

Much as he might have been ribbing her, he changed gear with alacrity himself. There was nothing seductive about the way they scrubbed themselves, bandying the soap back and forth as though it was the only thing that mattered. When the water was sufficiently dirty, they stood while it drained. Meeting the physical challenge, they bent to the tap, twisting and contorting, laughing in turn, until both scalps were squeaky clean. Then, rationalizing that they had a right to one bath each, they filled the tub again. This time Patrick stretched out and settled Jordanna between his legs. Her head fell back on his shoulder. His arms lightly circled her stomach. For the moment sexual needs were forgotten.

"Nice?" he murmured against her ear.

"Oh, yes," she replied. Clean and warm, her skin tingled. A delicious languor suffused her limbs. "Peaceful. Very peaceful." It was true. She felt wonderfully at home in Patrick's arms. Closing her eyes, she sighed.

"I agree."

"Peaceful?"

"Your sigh. Relaxed. Lazy. Unable to bear the thought of moving an inch."

And so they lay there, steam from the tub wafting over them. Time passed, but they were oblivious. Eyes closed, nestled together, they prized long moments of pleasure. Only when the water began to cool did Jordanna look down to see tiny goose bumps prickling her breasts.

"I'm thinking the same thing," Patrick mused. "It's about that time."

Setting Jordanna forward, he put a hand on either side of the tub and hoisted himself up, stepped out and reached for the thick terry towels that awaited on the nearby rack. Slinging one over his shoulder, he held the other open for Jordanna.

Suddenly the peace of moments before seemed to evaporate, replaced by the sexual tension they'd encountered before in the bedroom. The bath had been a strange buffer, a thing of necessity. But it was done now. And what was to come?

Jordanna knew. She also knew, with a flash of conviction, that it too was a necessity. She needed another dose of Patrick as badly as she'd needed that bath.

Eyes holding his, she rose from the tub and stepped out onto the mat to be enfolded in the towel he held. He patted her face dry with its ends, his eyes flowing from one to another of her features, worshiping each in turn. When he released the towel to reach for his own, Jordanna continued the work herself. The terry was an abrasive stimulant to her awakening flesh; her pulse quickened with each stroke. As she watched Patrick dry himself, she mirrored his movements. It was as though he, rather than the towel, were touching her. In a sense he was; his gaze followed her actions as hers followed his.

Not a word was spoken, but the air hummed with sensual awareness. In a bid to diffuse its frightening force, Jordanna abruptly raised the towel to her head and, bending from the waist, began to scrub at her hair. Most of the moisture had left it as she'd lain against Patrick in the tub. By the time she was finished with the towel, her short auburn crop was barely damp. Wrapping the towel around her waist, she turned to the mirror and began to finger-comb the thick strands. Within seconds Patrick materialized behind her. His hair was in a like state of semidryness, falling loosely in place, looking daringly rakish.

Catching her raised elbows, he slid his hands down until his fingers touched the side swells of her breasts. Jordanna held her breath and watched in the mirror as he cupped, then gently kneaded them. Her nipples grew taut. Grasping them between thumbs and forefingers, he tugged them until her head fell back and she whimpered in desire. He drew her back then, pressing her snugly against him. His own desire was blatant, his breath came unevenly by her ear. When she would have turned in search of greater satisfaction, though, he stepped back to drop his towel on the sink.

Silently he took her hand and led her into the bedroom where the four-poster bed waited. He tugged back the heavy quilt until the sheets lay invitingly, then turned to her.

Heart pounding so hard she felt he had to be able to see it, she tipped her head up at the guidance of his hands. He seemed about to speak. She held her breath, wondering what words could possibly express the unbridled desire in his gaze. When he simply lowered his head and took her lips, she knew there were none. No words to say how much he wanted her. No words to say she wanted him as much. He knew. They both knew.

His lips opened hers with ease, tasting the sweetness of her breath, sampling the delicate texture of her mouth. Not for an instant was he still, yet there was nothing frenetic in his kiss. Rather it was a slow, steady exploration of her every nuance, and it made a statement as to his sensual intent. In that moment Jordanna knew that he planned to do everything he'd once said—to touch her, to look at her, to make love to every single inch of her. Even as she feared the depth of the claim she sensed he'd make, it excited her beyond belief.

He raised his head then, lips moist from hers, and spoke again with his eyes in the deep, sultry voice of silence. Jordanna's limbs quivered at his message. When his gaze dropped to the towel that ringed her hips, she bit her lip to keep from crying out. It amazed her that his kiss, his look could do such erotic things, but while she knew she should have expected it by now, she also knew she never would. It was new and different, this heartwrenching attraction to another human being. With Peter, part of the attraction she'd felt had been inspired by the glamour of his position. She saw that now, and for the first time admitted that, despite her disclaimer to Pat, perhaps what she'd seen in Peter had indeed been his particular status in life.

Patrick allowed none of that. He'd made it clear from the start. His appeal was solely in the man that he was—tall, dark, compelling, dignified and reaching for her towel with an attitude of such intense need that she felt she was the only woman on earth who could possibly satisfy him. It was a heady thought. And Jordanna did have ego needs of her own, very special needs that had never quite been met until Patrick had entered her world.

The towel slid soundlessly to the floor and he was lifting her high in his arms, placing her gently on the cool, clean sheets, coming down on one knee by her side. The setting sun spiked golden arrows over her body, pointing to the concave plain of her stomach, the rounded curves of her breasts, the hollow of her throat, which pulsated with each quick breath she took. Warm and firm, his fingers traced each arrow, inspiring sensations within her that spiraled and converged deep down low in her belly. It was all she could do not to reach for him, so great was her mounting heat, but she opened her palms against the sheet instead and, fingers spread, pressed them flat.

Patrick's touch was devastating. His hands covered every inch of her, shaping each curve, exploring each hollow. Then he bent and began to kiss her, starting at her lips before gliding downward. With each sweet inch, the fire within her burned hotter. When she could bear no more of his delicious torture, she grabbed his arms and urged him upward.

He looked at her for a minute then, and she saw what she herself felt. It was the moment. There could be no more waiting. His knees nudged hers apart, he braced himself on his hands. Then, gaze still locked with hers, he thrust forward.

Jordanna's eyes widened, then closed. His brand was hot and firm, searing her insides with a pleasure beyond words or thoughts or dreams. She sighed softly at the satisfaction of it, then met his movements, stroking his powerful body as the heat rose until, at last, fingers clutching his shoulders, she reached the pinnacle of their joining. All the more heady was the knowledge that Patrick was right there with her. He too closed his eyes against the force of the pounding sensation. His great body stiffened, he sucked in his breath, then let it out in short, ragged gasps. Only in time, when the gasps began to lengthen, did he release his hold on himself and sink down onto her slender form. Head buried near hers on the pillow, he lay still as the last aftershocks of his pleasure shook him. Then he turned his face to hers and placed a slightly breathless kiss on her ear.

"That was...."

Jordanna gave a smug, cat-satisfied smile at the way his words trailed off in suggestion that he too was at a loss. "Wasn't it?"

"Umm." Slipping to her side, he left his arm in firm possession of her waist. "You're something."

She felt like something. It was a delightful feeling. "So are you." She layered her arms over his.

They rested that way for a time, the silence offering a peaceful aftermath to the passionate storm of moments before. All that remained of the sun's light was a pale amber glow reminiscent of the lantern in the woods. Rather than hard ground at their backs, though, there was a welcome mattress. And rather than a sleeping bag and tent to keep their secret, there was new freedom. The knowledge that it was temporary did nothing to curb Jordanna's enjoyment of it. She felt warm and sated and very much enthralled by the dark-haired man whose body seemed so right entwined with hers.

"Angel?"

"Mmm?" She smiled at her automatic response to his nickname. It too was new. To Peter she'd been either baby or honey or sweetie or increasingly, as their marriage became strained, just Jordanna.

"Are you sleeping?"

"Uh-huh."

He gave her a playful squeeze. "That's what I thought." With a burst of energy that startled her, he sat up, stretched over her to switch on the lamp, then grabbed the phone.

"What are you doing?" She laughed, loving the solid feel of his body slanting across hers.

He held her off with an upraised finger and spoke into the receiver. "Yes. This is room 206. We'd like to order dinner. A couple of steaks, medium rare, some baked potatoes, salad, whatever fresh vegetables you've got and a quart of milk." He shot a mischievous glance at Jordanna. "The Black Forest cake will be fine. And some coffee. I think that should do it. Twenty minutes. Right." Then he hung up the phone and slowly slid back to his side of the bed.

Jordanna didn't miss the way his body teased hers in retreat. Her feline smile reflected that appreciation. "Sounds like some meal."

He settled her into the crook of his arm. "We deserve it." He drew the sheet up to cover them.

She nestled against his chest. "I am pretty hungry, come to think of it. I don't want to look at anything freeze-dried for a while."

"What's the matter? Not an outdoors girl after all?"

"Now, did I say that? Seems to me you were the first one to think of steak, medium rare."

"Is that okay?" There was a moment's uncertainty in his voice, but she was quick to set him at ease.

"Perfect."

He kissed her brow. "Mmm. So are you."

"Oh, I don't know. I have my moments."

"At work?"

"Sometimes."

"Tell me about it—your work. How did you get started?"

It surprised her that she didn't hesitate. On one level she hadn't wanted to bring the real world into the fantasy she and Patrick lived. But it seemed so right to want to tell him about her life that the words flowed.

"After I left Peter I went into a kind of blue funk. I wasn't sure where to turn. I knew I wanted to do something. I *had* to do something—"

"Wasn't he giving you support money?"

"Oh, yes. Begrudgingly. And I accepted it . . . begrudgingly. Which was why I was in a rush to find some means of self-support. There was pride involved. *And* a desperate need to do something with my time."

"Did you have Willow Enterprises in mind from the start?"

"Only indirectly. During my time with Peter, I'd met people who suggested that I should start something."

"I can understand it. Classy lady. Influential name. Great visibility. Beautiful to boot."

She raised her head for a minute to scowl. "I didn't see it that way." He returned her head to his chest and left his hand to smooth her hair behind her ear. The gentle intimacy was enough to encourage her to go on. "I looked into lots of things. Had interviews and all. But it seemed I was always at someone else's command. And that was what I'd been trying to escape. So I began to think more and more of starting my own business. When I called the people who'd mentioned it, they were as enthusiastic as ever. Unfortunately, each time I hung up the phone all the negatives crowded back in on me."

"Like what?"

"Like the fact that I'd dropped out of college after my freshman year. Like the fact that I knew nothing about business. Like the fact that starting a business required an investment the likes of which I just didn't have."

"Peter had it."

"Sure he did. And I didn't want a cent. We were getting a divorce, remember?" She took a breath against Patrick's skin and stretched an arm across his waist. His nearness was the reminder she needed that life with Peter Kirkland was indeed behind her. "Anyway, I was hooked. The more I looked for other work, the more I liked the idea of starting something myself. So I began to read. Anything and everything I could find about small businesses. I came to believe that if I could gather the right people around me, they would provide the know-how I lacked. What with my ideas and the contacts I'd made through Peter, we had a fighting chance."

"So you fought."

"Uh-huh. I did. I got a lump-sum settlement from Peter that was enough to start the ball rolling. I rented a small place and hired five women, each of whom had spirit and the right credentials. They became my vice-presidents— sales, marketing, research and so on. We planned everything on paper, then fought dearly for money enough to set the thing up the way we wanted."

"Which was?"

"Solid. And substantial. No cottage industry here. We knew we wanted a class image. From the start we envisioned selling nationwide through the best of the department stores." Pausing, she tipped her head back to meet Patrick's gaze. "Sound arrogant?"

"Not arrogant. Just smart. If you've got the right product and it's marketed the right way, you'd be foolish not to aim high. There's something about a class act that attracts classy people. Basic psychology."

She grinned. "Psychology, baloney! It was common sense. And it worked."

"Sounds like it did. You've done well."

"Well enough to repay the original loans we took. Well enough to go public and expand all the more." Her voice softened in tone but lost none of its pride. "Well enough for me to take out the money Peter gave me and invest it in something in no way connected to the business."

Patrick chuckled. "Good girl. He must've croaked at that."

"I don't know if he even knows, and personally, I don't care. It's what *I* know that counts. It's inside me, Pat. I feel good about myself, about what I've done. I'm a person now, rather than an appendage. It's a very satisfying feeling."

More serious, he studied her urgent expression. "I can see that, angel. I'm happy for you."

She smiled suddenly and pressed her face to his chest to hide her blush. "I get carried away when I talk of the business."

"That's natural. It's your life."

"But I'm usually so busy that I don't think about it this way. It's odd being away from it all and thinking back on it."

"That's what vacations are for. To put things into perspective."

She propped her chin up, humor in her eyes. "Is that so? Funny, I was beginning to wonder if they weren't to pick up strange men and have affairs in the woods."

"We're not in the woods now."

"No."

"Are you sorry?"

"No."

"Good." He captured her lips in a languorous kiss, then, with a growl, pulled her atop him. "I was a fool to think once would be enough. Each time I have you, I want you all the more."

She could feel it, both in her own body and in his. Sliding up over him, she sought his lips again. Her knees fell to the sheets on either side of his thighs. As her tongue filled his mouth, she teased him at that other point where she was so open, so ready. He was addictive; with so little provocation, she needed him again. And as with any addiction, the first and only thing on her mind was to satisfy the craving.

Slipping a hand between their bodies, he found her warmth and stroked her with such knowing care that she had to gasp for air.

"It's no fair, Pat!" she cried, but already he was lowering her hips into his waiting strength. And then all that mattered was the rhythmic surge of their bodies, the lips that clung, the hands that found each other's sensitive spots and drew everything from them. When with joint cries of release it was over, they lay spent, Jordanna's damp body limp above his, which was no more energized.

It was then that room service knocked.

"I don't believe it," Patrick groaned.

Jordanna laughed breathlessly. "I can't move."

"Neither can I."

The knock came again.

"One of us has to get it," she whispered, sliding to his side and drawing the quilt to her chin. There was no doubt as to her choice.

Slanting her a punishing scowl, he untangled his legs from the sheets and pushed himself to his feet. He was halfway toward the door when, hearing Jordanna's laughter, he looked down.

The knock came a third time.

"Coming!" he yelled, racing toward the bathroom, returning as he pulled on one of the terry robes that had hung on a hook. "Pretty funny, huh?" he mumbled, then stopped before the door, donned his most composed expression and reached for the knob.

From her position of maximum concealment, Jordanna watched the waiter who wheeled in their dinner. She was instantly grateful that a young, innocent country girl hadn't been sent. Patrick looked far too appealing with his long, tanned legs extending far below the white robe, whose belt loosely ringed his hips. But, no, the waiter was very definitely a he, and though his tender age suggested he was perhaps as innocent as that country girl might have been, he was obviously well trained. If he suspected what he'd so inopportunely interrupted, he made no show of it. Rather, head bent to his task, he deftly transformed the tray on wheels into a table replete with fresh flowers and the finest of linen and china, not to mention a feast whose aroma was tantalizing.

When the young man left and they were alone once again, Jordanna threw back the quilt and scrambled from the bed. She was suddenly ravenously hungry. Returning quickly to the bathroom, Patrick produced a second robe, held it out for her as though it was the finest of furs, then bent to nip her ear. "I'd let you eat naked, but I don't think I'd make it." He glanced down as she lifted the first of the heavy metal covers. "On second thought, a man cannot live by sex alone. That steak looks great!"

Jordanna had the good grace to set up his meal before uncovering her own. Then they ate greedily, all else forgotten. By the time they were done, nothing edible remained on the table.

Smacking his lips, Patrick sat back in the cushioned chair. "Think we should try the flowers? If they're half as good as the cake was—"

Jordanna's groan interrupted him. Hauling herself back on the lounge, she stretched out and crossed her ankles. "I'm stuffed. Nothing like pigging out."

He sent her a meaningful glance. "We seem to be doing a lot of that lately." As if suddenly endowed with an excess of energy, he bounded up, collapsed the side of the table and pushed the whole thing out into the hall. When he returned, he gestured with his hand. "Move over."

Innocently she looked to either side of her. "Move over?"

"Make room for me."

"Here? What's wrong with your chair?"

"It's lonely. Come on." Swooping down, he lifted her, sank back into the lounge, then fitted her to his side. She had to admit that there was something very nice about being squashed by Patrick Clayes.

"Better?" she asked, looking up at him.

"Much. Are you okay?"

"Fine."

"Like more coffee? I could order—"

"Nothing. I'm really filled."

"How about an after dinner drink. Brandy? Port?"

She shook her head. "Nothing, thanks." Closing her eyes she snuggled closer. "Pat?"

"Mmm?"

"Tell me about your career."

"My work?"

"Football."

He went still for a minute. She felt him looking down at her and tipped her head back.

"You don't really want to hear about that."

"I do." The truth was that she felt open enough, mellow enough to want to know everything about him.

He saw the message in her eyes, the peace there. And he began quietly. "I played through junior high and high school, well enough to get a scholarship to college."

"Had you always intended to turn pro?"

"Uh-huh. Football had been my life from way back when." She nodded, recalling what he'd told her before. "Actually, I'd intended to win the Heisman Trophy. Needless to say, I didn't." Again, she nodded. She knew very well who had won it that particular year.

"No loss," she quipped. "It's only a piece of sculpted metal, and it's a bitch to dust."

Patrick snorted, then grew pensive. "Still, I wanted it. I'll never forget that day in November. I knew there were three of us in the running. According to my agent, I had the east sewed up. Peter had the west. Doug Shoenbrunn had the south. I waited and waited in that office for word, praying that I'd get it, convincing myself that I deserved it. Finally, I just went home. It was two in the morning when my agent called. I was devastated."

"It meant that much?"

"In dollars and cents, not to mention prestige. Almost like an Oscar for an actor. Thank God I didn't have to be on camera when they opened the envelopes. The presentation dinner was bad enough, but at least I'd had time to prepare myself for the loss. It was a blow, I'll tell you. And a harbinger. The following spring, Kirkland was the first player chosen in the draft. I wasn't picked until the third round."

"Why the discrepancy?"

"Go ask 'em. I'd led my team in back-to-back Cotton Bowl appearances and had the best passing record in the NCAA. Who knows what those guys base their decisions on? I sure as hell don't!"

Jordanna could feel the frustration oozing from him and momentarily regretted having raised the issue at all. By way of comfort, she slid a hand inside his robe and lightly kneaded his chest. "You did well, though. Proved them wrong. How many Super Bowl rings do you have?"

Responding to her soothing caress, he lowered his voice. "Just one. The other two I lost to you-know-who."

Relieved at the hint of humor in his tone, she grinned. "I had to polish those too. They were almost as bad as the trophy."

"Polish them? The rings?"

"Uh-huh. He wanted them to gleam when he held them up, which he tended to do very often, if you recall."

"You bet I recall. How not to win friends and influence people. But, damn it, Peter had that charisma. He could do whatever he wanted and still come out smelling like a rose. The world loves a winner. I guess it's as simple as that."

"If the world's love is what you want."

"Mmm."

"And it's not what you want, is it?"

"Not in that sense. Sure, I want to be respected for what I do. I want to be rewarded for it. But with the world's adulation? Uh-uh. I guess I'm like you. What's important is what *I* think. I need self-respect. I want to be able to go to sleep at night feeling good and honest and proud. God only knows how Kirkland slept."

"Like a baby. Says something about his values, doesn't it?"

Patrick hugged her closer and Jordanna knew that he understood and agreed. "Guess so. Anyway, I had my day with football. I've got my MVP awards, my ring, my lame shoulder." She slid her hand to that spot as he went on. "And now it's done. I am grateful; football gave me what I wanted. By the time I retired, I had enough of a name and a kitty to go out and start my own business. It's challenging and rewarding. I'm pleased with it."

"Tell me more, Pat. Are you all alone at the top?"

"I've got three partners. They contribute everything to the group that I can't. In some ways, my story's like yours. I may have a college degree and a smattering of postgraduate business courses under my belt, but nothing like their MBAs from Harvard and Columbia. While I was tossing that crazy little ball around, they were scoring touchdowns on Wall Street. What with their know-how, my money and the additional backing I had access to, we formed the Houghton Group."

Jordanna's hand ceased its gentle massage of his shoulder. She levered herself up and stared back at him. "The Houghton Group? *You're* the Houghton Group?"

The corners of his lips quirked in humor at her expression of amazement. "Sure. It's no big deal."

"Patrick, the Houghton Group has to be *the* up-and-coming firm. I mean, I'm far from an expert when it comes to venture capitalism, but I do read. You name it—the *Wall Street Journal, Forbes,* the *Times*—you've had fantastic write-ups in each of them during the past year!" She looked away, puzzled. "Strange. I don't remember reading your name. I must have been skimming—"

"My name wasn't *in* all of the articles. It's the Houghton Group, angel, not the Clayes Group. I like it that way."

Amazed, but now at the extent of his modesty, she continued to stare at him. He was so different, *so different.*

"Does it matter?" he asked so softly that, lost in her thoughts, she didn't follow at first.

"Hmm?"

"Does it matter who I am and who I'm with?"

"Of course not. It's just . . . fascinating."

He seemed troubled then. "Am I more fascinating now that you know I'm with the Houghton Group?"

And she understood. With a gentle smile, she touched her fingers to his lips. "Yes, you're more fascinating, but not in the way you think. You're more fascinating because by rights you should be arrogant as hell. Yet you're not. *That* is fascinating. It's also very, very refreshing." Stretching, she replaced her fingertips with her lips and kissed him softly. Then she set her cheek against his chest and slid an arm around him. His own locked her there moments before he spoke.

"Refreshing enough to last until Sunday?"

Her heart skipped a beat. "Till Sunday?"

"You don't have to be back tomorrow."

"No."

"Then stay here with me until Sunday. Please. I'd like it very much."

A slow smile spread over Jordanna's face. More than ever before she felt she was her own woman, doing what she wanted, albeit on whim. "I'd like it too," she said softly. "Thank you."

7

PATRICK STOOD at his window, looking down on Park Avenue. Behind him his desk was covered with papers. His secretary sat just outside his door waiting to type the letters he was supposed to have dictated into his machine the night before. But he hadn't dictated. He hadn't done much of anything except think of Jordanna. It seemed to have become a habit of his.

In the two weeks since they'd left New Hampshire, each in his or her own car headed toward his or her own life, he'd tried to immerse himself in his work. He hadn't been terribly successful. Now, as had happened so very many times, he thought back to that weekend. It had been a dream, wonderful and warm, filled with everything he ever imagined and more. Not that they'd strayed far from their room for two days. At first they'd had the excuse of their clothes; it hadn't been until late Saturday that the inn had returned everything washed and neatly folded or hung up. Even then, though, they'd chosen to wear the soft terry robes or, more often, nothing at all.

They'd talked and made love, ordered breakfast in bed and made love some more, had wine and cheese then talked and made love again, ordered dinner, talked, made love. And each time it was better. They'd become the dearest of friends, the most superb of lovers. It had been sheer hell to think of letting her go.

That Sunday, as the hours had passed, a subtle tension had arisen. Both had known what was coming. Their conversation, their lovemaking had taken on a more urgent quality. At last he'd been the one to put it into words.

"We've got something too good to ignore, angel. You know that, don't you?"

She'd looked at him soulfully and had silently nodded.

He'd gone on. "We both need time to think. Once we're back in the city, things will take on a different perspective. It's all been so beautiful here, but far removed from reality. We're going to have to think about us in that other context now."

Again she'd nodded, but her agreement had only fueled his frustration. He'd half wished she'd argued that it wouldn't make any difference, that what they had would exist wherever, that she loved him. But she hadn't argued. She was too sensible for that. She'd been through too much in her life, too much with Peter Kirkland to be blind to the drawbacks of a relationship with Patrick. She had to come to terms with everything if they were to have a chance as a couple in the real world. And he had to come to terms with things too.

Had he? He wasn't sure. All the brooding and debating that he'd done, that he continued to do, had convinced him of one thing. He loved Jordanna. She was everything he'd always wanted in a woman—warm and intelligent and exciting and independent—everything, with one exception. She'd been married to Peter Kirkland.

He couldn't seem to put that thought to rest. It haunted him, as he'd been haunted for so many years living in Kirkland's shadow. And he was furious at himself for being haunted. Too often he pictured Jordanna's naked body, the body he knew so well, in Peter Kirkland's arms, and something angry coiled within him. Then he would relent and want her all the more. If he loved Jordanna, there was no reason why he shouldn't call her, see her, even marry her.

To hell with Peter. To hell with the snide remarks they were sure to get. To hell with the inevitable newspaper stories their relationship was bound to generate. To hell with the world.

But he cared. It bothered him. For his sake *and* Jordanna's. He wanted nothing to mar the beauty of what they'd found.

Had she found it as well? He thought so. Everything she'd said and done during that weekend attested to the fact. He thought back to the last time they'd made love. She'd been more abandoned than she'd ever been, using those soft lips of hers, those slender hands, that agile body to conquer every inch of his flesh. She'd said it in her actions. He thought. She loved him. He thought. But what if he thought wrong?

Turning from the window, he gave a harsh snort. And he thought waiting for the Heisman decision had been tough! Here his heart was at stake, and he was in agony.

HALFWAY ACROSS town, high in her office overlooking Sixth Avenue, Jordanna stared at the papers spread wide on her desk. Hearing a light knock at her door, she looked up to see Sally Frank enter.

"Whaddya think?" Sally asked, expectation in the eyes that darted from Jordanna to the desk top and back. "Like 'em?"

Jordanna pushed herself back in her chair. "They're okay."

"Just okay?"

"I don't know, Sally." Jordanna frowned. "There's something missing. I can't put my finger on it. Some little bit of extra excitement . . . or promise . . . or . . . oh, I don't know."

Sally came to perch on the edge of the desk. "The art department's been working on them for weeks. I thought they were pretty good."

"They are."

"But?"

Jordanna shrugged and raised tired eyes to her friend. Sally had been with her from the start and was the best advertising vice-president she could have hoped for. "I just don't know." She looked off toward the window. "Maybe it's me. I'm not sure what I want."

Sally thought for a minute. "Why do I hear something deeper in that than this ad campaign?"

Jordanna looked back. "Do you?"

"Uh-huh. Come on, love. 'Fess up. What's bothering you?"

"Is something bothering me?"

Sally rolled her eyes. "Always answering a question with a question. Is that the prerogative of presidents, or is it just you being evasive?" Her tone gentled. "What is it, Jordanna? You've been off somewhere since you got back from that trip of yours."

"From Minneapolis?"

"Not from Minneapolis. That was last week and it was pure business. I'm talking about that supposed vacation of yours. You were to be rested and refreshed. Instead you only seem distracted."

"Do I?"

"Come on, Jordanna. This is me. Sally. Your old friend. The woman whose wedding you were maid of honor at. The woman whose kids are your godkids. The woman who cries in your tea every time she has a fight with her husband. What is it, love? *Something's* bothering you."

Jordanna looked at her for a minute, then pushed herself from her chair and walked to the window. Perhaps she needed to talk, to share her thoughts with someone who might be able to help. Lord knew she'd come up with few enough answers on her own.

"I met someone."

"Someone. A man?"

"Mmm."

"Where?" Sally's enthusiasm flared. For years she'd been encouraging Jordanna to date, with far too little success.

"On the trip."

"In New Hampshire? You're kidding!"

"I wish I were."

"Why so glum? I think that's great! So what if he lives somewhere else. You're as mobile as most women nowadays." When Jordanna continued to gaze out the window, Sally bridled her tone. "Uh-oh. He's married."

"No."

"He's a punk-rock superstar?"

Jordanna managed to chuckle. "No."

"Then what? What could be so awful about a man you'd meet?"

"His name is Patrick Clayes."

"Nice name. Good strong sound."

Slowly Jordanna turned. "Doesn't it ring a bell?"

Sally frowned. "No. Should it?"

Slumping down onto the broad windowsill, Jordanna propped herself on a hand by either hip. "It would if you were into sports."

"I'm not. You know that."

"Norman would know the name."

"You bet Norman would know the name. He's a lost cause. Every weekend now it's football. Collegiate games on Saturdays, pro games on—uh-oh. Tell me, Jordanna. Who is Patrick Clayes?"

Jordanna took a deep breath, then let it out with a huff. "Patrick Clayes is—was the quarterback who rivaled Peter for years."

"Ahh. Patrick Clayes."

"You *have* heard of him?"

"No. But I'll take your word that he is who he is. And I take it that bothers you."

"Yes. No. God, I don't know!"

Slipping from the desk, Sally joined Jordanna on the sill. She spoke very softly. "I've never seen you like this, love. Even when things are at their worst here, you're cool. You've always got an opinion, not that I've always agreed with you." When Jordanna sent her a scowl, she got back on the track. "This Patrick Clayes got to you, did he?"

"Yes."

Sally sat back. "There. Now we're getting somewhere. Want to tell me about it?"

"Not really."

"But you will."

"I guess I have to. I don't know what to do about it myself. And you're right. It's affecting my work."

Sally patted her hand. "Okay. Start at the beginning. I take it he was a member of the expedition."

In as few words as possible, Jordanna told her story. By the time she'd finished, Sally had much to consider. "You parted . . . just like that?"

"Just like that. It was the only way. He was right. We were living in a dreamworld."

"But I don't understand why it can't be a real world as well."

"Sally, the man is a football player."

"*Was* a football player."

"Same difference. Do you have any idea what I feel in my gut every time I remember what it was like being married to Peter?"

"Patrick's not Peter. You said it yourself. You kept expecting him to be that way, but he wasn't. He was kind and good and giving." She hesitated. "You're in love with him, aren't you?"

"Yes."

"Does he love you?"

"He didn't say that. All he said was that we'd have to try to cope with our relationship in the context of the real world." She looked at her friend beseechingly. "Don't you see, Sal? He fought being second banana to Peter all those years. How could he possibly become involved with me? I was Peter's wife."

"Sounds like he's already involved with you."

Jordanna quickly waved the argument aside. "That was *there*. We were in isolated circumstances. In a kind of limbo. It was like an island fling or . . . or a shipboard romance."

"But you love him."

"Yes!"

"And you want him to call."

Defeated, Jordanna lowered her head. "One part of me says no. That part of me wishes I'd never met him. I was happy with my life. It was uncomplicated." When Sally snorted, she specified. "In the personal sense, I mean. But. . . ."

"The other part. . . ."

"The other part of me feels empty. It wants to see him. Yes, damn it, it wants him to call."

"Why don't you call him?"

"I can't. I . . . I need time."

"The hell you do. Nothing is accomplished with you sitting here in this office and him—" she swung her hand "—out there somewhere."

"Park Avenue," Jordanna murmured. "His office is on Park Avenue."

"Then that's half the battle. You know where he is. So call him."

"I can't."

"Why not? Hell, you're aggressive enough around here. You wouldn't blink an eyelash at the thought of picking up that phone and getting the president of Neiman-Marcus on the line."

"That's different."

"It doesn't have to be."

"It does. The president of Neiman-Marcus hasn't been batted around for years by Willow Enterprises."

"You didn't bat Patrick around. Peter did it."

"But I was married to Peter! And the world knows that."

Sally surged to her feet. "Screw the world, Jordanna Kirkland. You've never been one to make decisions based on what the world thought. You've made decisions based on what you thought was right. Call him. Pick up the phone and call him."

"No! I want him to call *me!*"

"Ahh. The ultimate fantasy." Sally's voice was gentle, as were the hands she placed on her friend's shoulders. "You, Jordanna Kirkland, are an old-fashioned girl at heart. I should have seen it sooner—the way you cry at weddings, the way you insist I take the day off when one of the kids has a birthday, the way you send champagne on anniversaries. You're a romantic. Even your marriage to Peter was that way at the start, wasn't it?"

"Yes."

"But you've grown cynical."

"Cautious."

"Whatever. And because the present fairy tale has a little glitch in it, you're willing to throw it away?"

"I never said that. All I said was that there were problems that I didn't know how to solve."

Sally shook her head, a sad smile on her face. "I wish I had the solutions, love, but I don't. You and Patrick are the only ones who can find them, but you've got to get together."

"I know," Jordanna whispered.

"He'll call."

"How can you be so sure? Maybe he's decided that fighting one Kirkland was enough."

"He's not going to fight you. He's going to fight for you."

"How can you be so sure?"

"Because I know you, Jordanna. I've seen the spell you cast over people. If Patrick Clayes spent that delicious weekend with you, he's hooked. And besides, I'm a romantic at heart myself. It'll work out. You'll see."

"I wish I could be as confident as you are." She pouted. "I'm not even sure that I *want* it to work out."

"You do. I can see it in your eyes. Don't forget, I've known you for nearly ten years now. I was with you in the aftermath of your divorce. I've been with you through years of occasional dates. And I've never seen you this way before. You do love him. And love is a stronger force than some stupid rivalry between little boys."

Jordanna laughed. Though Sally's conviction was subjective at best, she did feel better for the sharing of her woes. "Little boys. Stubborn little boys."

"Jealous little boys." Sally's eyes suddenly widened. "Hey, Craig doesn't know any of this, does he?"

"Lord, no! And I don't want him to know. Any of it. Got that, Sally?"

Sally turned an imaginary key at her lips. "Got it." Her eye skipped back to the ad mock-up on Jordanna's desk. "Now, about this campaign...."

THE AD CAMPAIGN was the last thing on Jordanna's mind when, two weeks later, she received a call from Alexander Shane. Drawn from her reverie concerning another call, one she had not received, she was slightly off balance.

"Alexander Shane?" she echoed when her secretary buzzed her to announce the call. "Of the Widener Corporation?"

"That's what he said."

Jordanna had heard of Alexander Shane *and* his Widener Corporation. In the past three years, the corporation had made headlines any number of times. She cringed at the reason.

"Put him on," she instructed, then straightened in her chair. A gravelly voice came on the line.

"Mrs. Kirkland?"

"Yes."

"This is Alexander Shane."

"Yes, Mr. Shane. How are you?" It was a formality. Her mind was already jumping ahead.

"Fine, thank you. I want to congratulate you. Willow Enterprises is doing quite well."

"Thank you. We believe it is."

"The Widener Corporation *knows* it is. Which is why I'm calling. We'd like to make you an offer."

Jordanna's heart began to thud. "An offer?"

"Yes. A merger. Willow Enterprises and the Widener Corporation."

Stunned, Jordanna cleared her throat. "I'm sorry, Mr. Shane, but we're not looking to merge with anyone, particularly a corporation that deals almost exclusively in electronics and defense gadgetry."

"Actually," came the other voice, undaunted, "we've expanded in recent months. You're aware of our takeover of Grossner Foods?"

Takeover. The word sent a frisson of fear through Jordanna. She gripped the phone more tightly. "Yes. I read about that. But what possible interest could you have in Willow Enterprises? We're still very young—"

"You've got six plants spread across the country. Your profit margin has steadily increased. And, as the deal with Grossner Foods shows, we've begun to diversify."

More like trying to soften the image, Jordanna mused angrily. "I'm sorry, Mr. Shane. We're simply not interested."

"Is that a definite no?"

"Very much so," she said. Her pulse raced. Her eyes were glued to her desk. She waited.

Then it came. "In that case, I'd like to inform you that tomorrow morning we'll be filing a statement of intent with the Securities and Exchange Commission. Ads will be run in the major papers. A direct-mail offer will be made to your stockholders."

Shocked, Jordanna couldn't seem to catch her breath. She looked frantically around her office as though somewhere the proper words to quash this demon lay hidden.

"Well?" Alexander Shane prodded. "No response, Mrs. Kirkland?"

His smugness was enough to snap her from verbal paralysis. "My response, Mr. Shane, remains the same." She swallowed hard. "Willow Enterprises will not become a subsidiary of your organization."

"You may not have much choice. We've already bought up a substantial amount of your stock, and our tender offer will be for forty-eight dollars a share. As you know, that's ten above the market—"

"I know what the market price is," Jordanna cut in, blood boiling, "and I believe we have little left to say to each other. If you wish a friendly takeover, I'm afraid you'll have to go elsewhere. I'll fight, Mr. Shane. I haven't spent the past ten years of my life working to build a business, only to have it taken over by a warmongering conglomerate!"

Her caller only laughed. "It's that very spirit of yours that has made Willow Enterprises so successful, Mrs. Kirkland. We're fighters. All of us. We'll look forward to a successful union."

Over my dead body, Jordanna fumed, hanging up the phone and gripping the edges of her desk for dear life. "This is incredible. Absolutely incredible." Her eyes were wide, panic-filled. "They can't do this!" she wailed to no one at all. "They can't just call up and steal my baby from under my nose! It's not fair! *It's not fair!*"

Bolting from her chair, she began to pace the room, only to return to her desk with a rush and lift the phone. "Leila, get Tom Cherwin on the line." Tom was vice-chairman of her board of directors and a practicing lawyer.

Unfortunately, he wasn't much help. "It's perfectly legal, Jordanna. You know that as well as I do. Widener has every right to attempt a takeover. At least we know they haven't got too much stock; we would have to have been notified otherwise. All we can do is work fast."

"A board meeting tomorrow?"

"If possible. I do know that Margery Dodd is out of town. Henry Walker may be too. If we have to let it go another day, we can. Try to reach everyone else."

Jordanna's mind was reeling. She was amazed she could sit still. But then there was this god-awful quaking of her knees.

"I will. Tom, what are our chances?"

"Of emerging with things exactly as they've been for the past few years? Next to nil." He paused, then spoke very quietly. "Damn it, I never dreamed this would happen. Fortunately, we have a clause in our corporate contract to the effect that any change in the status of the company has to be approved at a meeting of the stockholders. Arranging such a meeting will take time. If Widener has borrowed money to finance the acquisition, time for them may be at a premium."

"Their ads will be in the papers tomorrow. What if they manage to buy up enough of our stock to swing the vote?"

"We've got to prevent that. Get on the phone, Jordanna. You, personally. Call the largest of the block stockholders and explain what's happened."

"Damn it, Tom. Widener's offering forty-eight. It's an attractive deal. We can't match that."

"We'll have to. Somehow. I'd suggest a leveraged buy-out, borrowing money ourselves to buy back the stock and go private, but that'd put us on shaky ground financially." He paused. "There's always the chance of finding a friendly buyer."

"But I don't want to sell! Willow Enterprises is my life!"

"Which is why a friendly merger may be the only answer. If Widener takes us over, you and I and the board as we know it are bound to go, not to mention the greater part of your executive force. I don't care what Shane says on the phone about working together, I've seen how the man operates. He'll use us for his own ends. Don't tell me he's really interested in the welfare of the sportswoman. Hell, his fancy heat-seeking missiles could blow her away in a minute."

"You're supposed to be making me feel better, Tom," Jordanna scolded. "Let's not worry about heat-seeking missiles for the time being. Let's concentrate on keeping the guy's finger off our button, okay?"

"Sorry, Jordanna. Damn. We should have clauses to protect management."

"Why don't we?"

"Because we never thought in terms of being taken over before."

They were wasting valuable time. "Well, we are now. Listen, I'm going to start making some of those calls. I want to reach as many of the major stockholders as possible before Widener's ad hits the papers. What do I tell them?"

"Tell them to hold off while we look into counteroffers."

"Right." She was furiously scribbling notes. "And the board of directors—I'll call Marge and Henry first. If they can't make it until Thursday morning, we'll meet then."

"Fine. In the meantime, let me get an analyst on it. If we're going to need a white knight, we'd better get on the stick."

White knight. Jordanna pondered the term, a common one in takeover jargon. In her mind's eye she pictured Patrick, and a pang of need joined those ones of desperation that filled her. More than ever she wanted to talk with him. He'd understand, give her encouragement and strength. But he hadn't called...and there were others she had to talk with now.

As she'd done so often in the past four weeks, as she'd done so often in the past ten years, she put her personal needs on hold.

JORDANNA SPENT the entire day and much of the evening on the phone. She contacted each of the members of the board and set up a meeting for early Thursday morning. She called each of the major stockholders and made her plea for restraint. It was hard; without a concrete counteroffer, she was appealing to them on grounds of sheer loyalty. Fortunately, though money was the name of the game, those she spoke with appeared to be the loyal type.

She called each of the six plants across the country, explaining to her managers what had happened and enlisting their aid in convincing those of their employees who held stock not to sell. This task was somewhat easier. The employees of Willow Enterprises were treated well; a threat to the organization was a direct threat to their own well-being.

Between calls she met with her executive staff, all of whom were stockholders as well. It was from this group that she found the greatest support. Their fury at the takeover threat and determination that it wouldn't succeed was a source of encouragement.

Nonetheless, by the time she'd returned home and made calls to several stockholders she hadn't been able to reach earlier, she was totally drained. It was all she could do to stumble into bed, and then she tossed and turned fitfully until dawn, when she dressed and returned to the office to renew the campaign for survival.

By ten in the morning, she was exhausted and discouraged. When her secretary knocked on her door bearing a fresh cup of coffee, Jordanna slumped in her chair and gave a wan smile. "Thanks, Leila. I need this."

"How's it going?"

"Oh, who knows? You make the calls and put forth your case and then hope for the best." Setting the coffee to the side, she opened the *Wall Street Journal.* "Have you seen it?"

"Yes," Leila answered. "It's pretty awful, don't you think?"

"God," she said in a defeated tone, "I've seen so many ads like this, never imagining that one day Willow Enterprises would be the target. It seems so unreal." She slapped the page. "But there it is. In black and white. A tender offer that may be too sweet for some of our stockholders to resist.

They've probably all seen it by now. I can imagine what other papers it's in."

"They'll stick by you, Jordanna. I know they will. You've been good to them. They can't ignore that fact."

"I'm hoping that's so. They've got to know that if Widener takes us over things will change. And I doubt for the better—"

The ring of the phone from beyond the door broke into her words. With a quiet, "Excuse me," Leila ran back to her desk to answer it.

"Take a message!" Jordanna called after her. "Have them call back in ten minutes! I need a break!" She watched Leila slip into her chair and lift the receiver, then turned off thought of who it might be. Coffee cup in hand, she walked to the window.

She felt tired, so tired. And very, very empty. Things had happened so fast. It seemed hard to believe that a mere twenty-four hours before she'd been so innocent. Willow Enterprises had been hers then.

Tom had been right. With Alexander Shane's call, things had changed irrevocably. They would never quite return to the old status quo, Jordanna knew. And facing the loss of her company, she was suddenly less adverse to the thought of a compromise solution.

For an instant she imagined what would happen if she did lose. The business was her life. She had nothing else. Nothing . . . but dreams.

And he hadn't called.

Setting her coffee cup on the sill when her hand began to shake, she pressed her fingers to her mouth. Even before all this had happened, she'd felt empty. There was only one man who could fill that emptiness, and he was—

"Jordanna?"

Certain she'd only imagined his voice, she closed her eyes against the sting of tears.

"Jordanna?"

This time the voice was closer, very familiar, very dear. And real. Turning sharply, hand still pressed to her mouth, she focused through misty eyes on the man she'd missed so desperately for the past four weeks. She tried to say his name, but her lips only made the movements.

Patrick walked steadily forward, his heart pounding at the simple sight of her. He felt her anguish, had felt it the instant he'd opened the paper that morning. And suddenly who she was hadn't mattered, whose wife she'd been, who saw. He'd had to come. He needed to be there for her.

When he was a hand's width away, he stopped. He had his needs. But what about hers? What if she didn't want to see him, particularly at this time? He saw the pain in her eyes, the glimmer of tears. And he thought he'd die if he couldn't help her.

The tears welled higher, then began to trickle one by one down her cheeks. He was about to reach out and smooth them away when Jordanna swayed toward him. Then she was in his arms, clinging as tightly to him as he was to her. And the waiting was over.

"Ahh, angel," he crooned, hugging her as she wept softly. "Shh. It's all right. Everything's going to be all right now."

She didn't argue. She couldn't. Somehow, in Patrick's embrace, she believed it for the first time. The conviction was irrational. Emotional. She knew it, but that didn't matter. Things had indeed taken on a different perspective.

"Oh, Pat," she whispered, when at last she was able to speak. "I'm so glad you're here."

His arms trembled as he held her tighter. "I've been wanting to come. You have no idea how much. But I was afraid. Of so many things. Then, when I saw Widener's notice this morning, those other things didn't seem to matter anymore. I love you, Jordanna. I want to be there. I want to help. I know how much Willow Enterprises means to you."

But she was shaking her head against his cheek. "I love you too, Pat. I'm glad you're here. So glad you're here."

He held her face then, brushing at her tears with his thumbs. His gaze adored her, reacquainting itself with each of her features as though it had been years rather than weeks since he'd seen her last. When he kissed her, his lips spoke of the pent-up longing, the anguish that was hers, now theirs.

He smiled. "You've grown."

"I'm wearing heels."

"And a skirt and silk blouse and makeup."

Self-conscious, she ran a finger beneath her eye. "I must be a mess."

It was Patrick's turn to shake his head. "You look beautiful. Very chic and sophisticated. Of course, I still like the way you look totally bare."

She smiled for the first time in more than twenty-four hours, and rubbed her forehead against his chin. "You men are all the same. One-track minds, all of you."

"No, angel," he murmured gently. "I love you the way no man ever has or ever will. I've been a fool to wait this long to tell you. These past four weeks I've been surviving on memory alone. But I need more now. You're warm and wonderful. The thought of you gives me life. You have no idea how much I admire you."

His words brought reality back with a thud. "Oh, Pat," she whispered, eyes filling again, "what am I going to do?"

Taking her under his wing, he guided her to the sofa on one side of her office. "You're going to relax first of all. You look like you haven't slept in a week."

"It was really only a night. Funny how a takeover attempt can do that to a person."

They were sitting on the sofa, knees touching as they faced each other. Patrick took her hands in his.

"It's so awful, Pat. I mean, it never occurred to me that we'd run into trouble like this. Hostile offers are for other firms. Not Willow Enterprises. We were doing so well on our own. And I've poured so much of my life into this. If it's taken away, I don't know what I'll do!"

"It won't be taken away, angel. There are ways to fight."

"I know. But it's hard. And it costs." Pausing, she looked down. "Were you ever in a car accident, Pat?"

"A car accident?"

She raised her eyes. "I had one once. Not long after I got my license. There was a blind intersection. I never saw the car that hit me until well after I came to a stop crunched around a telephone pole." When Patrick winced, she was quick to assure him. "Oh, no one was hurt. But my car was totaled. There were police and insurance forms to fill out, the inconvenience of being without a car, not to mention the money to shell out for the new car that the insurance didn't quite cover. I kept thinking that none of it would have happened if I'd been ten seconds faster or slower. I kept wanting to turn back the clock, to replay the scene and have everything bad go away."

Her shoulders slumped and she focused on Patrick's hands, so strong in hers. "I feel that way now, only I don't know what I could have done differently. A day ago, none of this was happening. Now, suddenly, my business—my sweat and tears—is up for grabs. I want to turn back the clock, but I can't."

"No, you can't. Life isn't that way. But you're not unique in wishing it, angel. It's a normal feeling for someone in your position. I know. I've had any number of friends go through the same thing."

"How did they handle it?"

"The first thing they had to do was to accept the fact that they couldn't turn back the clock. That accomplished, they sought the best possible solution to the problem."

Jordanna took a deep breath and let it out slowly. "The best possible solution. Right now, *anything* looks pretty bad."

"That's because you're still at stage one. It takes time."

"Just what we haven't got."

"But you've got people working on alternatives to a Widener takeover?"

"Oh, yes. And I've contacted most of the major stockholders. We're sending wires to the rest. The board's meeting tomorrow morning." She smiled sadly. "But I'm discouraged." As she looked at him, she found the respite she needed. "God, you look good." Freeing a hand from his, she stroked the side of his head. His hair was thick and rich. She dropped her gaze. "Pin-striped suit, crisp white shirt, dashing rep tie and these sprinkles of silver in your hair."

"Those are from thinking about you all month. Wondering. Worrying."

"Don't give me that. I saw those strands of gray last month in New Hampshire."

"They came from needing you all my life and not knowing who you were."

"You've got an answer for everything, don't you?" Slipping her arms inside his jacket, she leaned against him. He felt so solid, so strong. When his arms went around her back, she felt very, very safe.

"I may."

At his cautious tone, she tipped her head back. "What does that mean?"

"It means," he went on, taking a breath, "that I'd like to help you."

"You are helping me. You're here."

"More than that. I'd like to help you fight Widener." At her puzzled expression, he continued. "The best way to fight a hostile tender offer is to counter with an offer from a friendly source. I may just be able to provide that source."

Jordanna inched back, a frown on her face. "The Houghton Group?"

"Uh-huh. I've got investors just waiting for a good cause. This might be it."

"But . . . but you work with new ventures or businesses that need rebuilding. I didn't think you were into acquisitions."

"There's not much difference in the mechanics of it all. Just because we haven't made a name for ourselves in the takeover field doesn't mean we haven't dabbled in it. Right off the bat I can think of four major investors who would be interested in forming a group to back Willow Enterprises."

"How can you say that? I mean, you didn't know about any of this until the ad appeared in the paper this morning. You can't know much about us."

Patrick snickered. "Evidently you don't know much about the way of boys. When they have their first big crush on a girl, they find out everything about her. Where she lives. What she likes to eat. What her favorite color is. What time she leaves for her piano lessons."

"I never took piano lessons," Jordanna whispered. "And this is a crush?"

"No, ma'am. No more than I'm still a boy. I'm a man. And in love. Which means that I haven't spent the past month just staring out a window." He smiled, a faint red tinge creeping above his collar. "Well, I guess I've done my share of that too. But I also did my homework. I read everything I could about Willow Enterprises. Between that and what you've told me yourself, I know that it'd be a sound investment, one I could recommend to any number of my clients."

She simply stared for a minute, then, dazed, shook her head. "Oh, Pat. I don't know...."

"Have you got another possible suitor?"

"No. Not yet."

"Then why not me...uh, my group?"

"Because I don't want to be bought, period!"

"You may not have much choice."

Stricken, she sat back. Alexander Shane had used identical words on the phone yesterday. Coming with such gentleness from Patrick, they had the ring of authenticity rather than spite. "No, I may not," she stated, sagging against the sofa.

"Would it be so terrible?"

"In that I'd lose control of my company, yes."

"But that wouldn't necessarily be the case. What if, between you and me personally, we held a majority of the shares?"

"I haven't got that kind of money!"

"But I do. Or at least I have access to it." He leaned toward her, propping an arm on the sofa back. "What if we included specific phrases in the contract that would assure your board control of the everyday workings of the company? What if we guaranteed that you would have sole authority over personnel? What if we took measures to assure that no other conglomerate such as Widener could possibly attempt a takeover?"

She thought about that for a minute. "Sounds idealistic."

"It's not. It can be done. Believe me, Jordanna. I know what I'm talking about."

That, too, she thought about. But it was all so sudden. Her mind seemed suddenly crammed to overflowing. "I don't know, Pat." She looked away. "There are promises . . . and there are promises. Fancy legal language can be as deceptive as anything else."

For the first time since he'd begun to set forth his proposal, Patrick hesitated. "Jordanna?" His fingers were firm as they turned her face toward him. "Do you trust me?"

"When you look at me that way, how can I help it?"

"But *do* you trust me? I mean, really trust *me*?"

"Yes."

"Why?"

"Because I love you."

"And because you know that I love you? That I would never do anything to hurt you?"

"Yes," she whispered. She found the urgency of his expression to be as mesmerizing as his words.

When he stood, reached out and drew her up into his arms, she went eagerly. "Then let me get to work on it. Let me discuss it with my partners and see what I can come up with."

"I have to talk with my people too."

"Of course you do. It'll take me a little time to put something together anyway. In the meantime you can tell them what I've told you." He smiled and crushed her against him. "If anyone gets the short end of the stick here, it's apt to be my investors. I think I'd give you the world if I could. Ahh, Jordanna." A low growl came from deep in his throat as he buried his face in her hair. "It's so good to hold you."

"And you," she whispered, wrapping her arms more tightly around his neck. Her lips were waiting when he sought them and opened hungrily for his kiss.

His hands released her only to slide along her blouse in search of her breasts. He found them full and warm, nipples responding instantly to his touch.

"Ahh. She wears a bra."

"I warned you."

"Mmm. I'm supposed to be thinking of putting together the deal of a lifetime and all I can think about is very slowly taking off every bit of this silky stuff from your body. You know what I'd do then?"

Suddenly and unbelievably high, she laughed. "What?"

He proceeded to whisper in her ear precisely what he'd do, and she went moist and quivery all over.

"When?" she countered with such urgent demand that it was Patrick's turn to laugh.

"How about tonight? Your place. Around nine?"

"Mmm. I'd like that. I live on—"

"I know where you live. A boy's crush, remember?" He pressed her to him a final time, leaving no doubt as to his very manhood, then, with reluctance, held her away. "Maybe I should pick you up here."

"No. I'll want to change and shower and . . . make myself presentable."

"Now that really *is* funny," he said, popping a kiss on the tip of her nose before heading for the door. Halfway there, he stopped, turned, then retraced his steps and swept her into his arms a final time. "I love you, angel. I love you."

His kiss echoed the words, to be echoed in turn by Jordanna's responding lips. It was with great effort that they separated. Pat shook his head as he crossed the room once more. "Lots to do. Lots to do." Then, without turning, he slammed a fist against a palm and threw his head back. "Wow, do I feel great!"

The only thing that was missing was a clicking of heels in the air. Jordanna watched him go, a look of loving indulgence on her face. When she was alone once more, she realized that, remarkably, she felt great too.

8

As THE DAY WORE ON, Jordanna's feeling of euphoria diminished only slightly. Buoyed by the knowledge that Patrick loved her even more than by the chance that he might have a solution for her woes, she felt in control of herself once again.

The influx of calls from worried brokers began. Though she'd known that the Widener ad would be read by many people, she had dared to hope that it wouldn't cause an immediate stir. For the most part, the calls she received were positive. There were those, however, that were tentative, others that were downright dubious.

Between calls she thought of Patrick, and her spirits inevitably rose.

When she called Tom Cherwin and told him of a potential suitor in the Houghton Group, he was more than pleased. The group was honest and well-respected, he told her quite unnecessarily. Though his analyst had already sniffed out several potential buyers, Tom promised to call immediately about the Houghton addition.

With what was left of the day, Jordanna put her thoughts together for the board meeting to be held early the next morning. Several well-placed phone calls gave her valuable information on the Widener Corporation, which she proceeded to organize for presentation at the meeting. Though she had every reason to believe that the board would vote down the merger, she wanted to take no chances. Along with her notes on Widener, she gathered the

atest figures on Willow Enterprises. After handing the lot
o Leila for typing, she returned to her desk to take care of
:he routine work she'd been neglecting for two days.

It was well after eight when she finally turned out the
ights and left the deserted office behind to begin the healthy
:wenty-minute walk home. Head high, she welcomed the
orisk December breeze. She felt tired but exhilarated, and
more excited with each step. It amazed her that Patrick's
reappearance in her life could make such a difference;
whether the Houghton Group could indeed come through
for her seemed secondary to the fact that, where emptiness
had existed before, now there was a rich bouquet of hope.
The knot that twisted in her stomach each time she thought
of Widener's bid seemed that much easier to bear.

Fifth Avenue was alive with lights, made all the more gay
by the approach of Christmas. Wrapping her cashmere scarf
more tightly around the collar of her coat, Jordanna turned
down Seventy-eighth Street with a smile. Regardless of
what tomorrow held, she was determined to enjoy tonight
to the fullest. *He loved her.* What a wonderful feeling!

Taking her front steps at a trot, she let herself into the
lobby of the narrow brownstone, snaked her mail from its
box, then took the elevator to the fourth floor. Moments
later, with steaks removed from the freezer and put in the
microwave to defrost, a head of Boston lettuce rinsed and
left to drain, and potatoes put on to boil in preparation for
an au gratin casserole, she dashed upstairs to quickly
shower.

With the freshest bit of makeup skillfully applied, she slid
into a pair of dark silk pants, a white silk blouse that bil-
lowed at the sleeves, and heels. A bright red scarf completed the outfit. After sending a brush through her
mercifully wash-and-wear hair and spraying her pulse
points with cologne compliments of Oscar de la Renta, she

raced back to the kitchen to drain the potatoes, slice them and layer them with onions and gruyere. Then she stuck the casserole in the oven while she went to work on the salad. She was in the process of fluting a cucumber when her buzzer rang.

Nine o'clock on the dot. He was prompt. But then, had she expected otherwise? Had she *wanted* otherwise? With a smug smile, she wiped her hands on a paper towel and headed for the intercom by the door.

"Hello?" She knew she was beaming, and she hoped she sounded less giddy then she felt. Given the threat to the business, it seemed indecent that she should feel so light-headed, but she couldn't help it.

"Room service," came the deep voice she'd recognize, fuzzy intercom or no.

"It took you long enough," she teased.

"I'm right on time!"

"Four weeks late. I just hope everything's still hot."

"Oh, it's hot, all right. And getting hotter." The voice lowered. "Damn it, Jordanna, buzz me in. One of your neighbors just walked by and gave me the strangest look."

Laughing, she pressed the button, waited until she was sure he'd have cleared the door before releasing it, then went into the hall to wait for the elevator to arrive.

The doors slid open with a soft hum. Arms laden with bundles, Patrick turned sideways to see her. She reached forward and drew him out, then scowled.

"That's quite a load. It's a miracle you haven't tripped and spilled the goodies. Then where would we be?"

"Depends on which goodies you're worried about," he drawled, taking a broad look around him as, led firmly by Jordanna, they entered her duplex. "Hey, this is nice!"

Not quite forward enough to start grabbing for the bundles he carried, one of which was very obviously from a florist, Jordanna clasped her hands before her and joined his inspection. "I like it. I've been here for five years now. The rooms are narrow, but that seems to be a regional hazard. The fellow who lived here before me took most of the walls down, so the place looks larger. And what with upstairs and down, it's plenty roomy."

"I can see."

What Patrick saw was a vision of impeccable style. Thick rugs carpeted the floors. Beautifully upholstered chairs and a love seat comfortably filled the living area, and an exquisite marble-topped dining table and four straight chairs drew the eye on. Sculpted pieces, each unique and of varied materials, rested upon coffee tables and a small oak buffet. Original oils hung on the walls. The overall color scheme was a blend of cream and powder blue.

"Classy. Like you," he said in soft appreciation, then turned to face her and raised his voice in imitation of a door-to-door salesman. "And for the classy lady, we have—" he juggled his bundles and began handing them to her one by one "—flowers...wine...ice cream...and—" he cleared his throat as he passed her the two largest packages "—a little something for later."

"For later?"

"Mmm. Not to be opened now." He shrugged out of his topcoat and tossed it onto the nearest chair, then retrieved the two large boxes from Jordanna, dropped them near his coat and went for the ice cream and wine. "These have to be stashed," he said, heading for the kitchen with such ease that Jordanna half suspected he'd researched the layout of her apartment as well. She followed, gently cradling the flowers, pleased that he should feel at home here.

"Pat?" Her voice held a touch of unsureness, hinting at the crisis that had brought him to her office that morning.

Having already deposited the ice cream in the freezer, he closed the refrigerator door on the wine, turned and put a finger against her lips. "Shh." Then he took her hand and began walking. "Put the flowers down. I want to see the rest of the place."

She barely had time to deposit the wrapped bunch on the table before she was swept back through the dining room and living room to the stairs. Her senses had already begun to quiver. All day she'd been excited about seeing Pat, yet the reality was so much better than the anticipation that it took every bit of her self-command to call his name again.

"Pat? What about—"

"The deal?" He was taking the carpeted steps two at a time. Jordanna had to trot to keep up. "It's looking good." He poked his head into the first room he reached. "A study. Nice. Do you do much work at home?" Already he was dragging her on.

"Yes. I try to bring papers—"

"Ah, angel. This is you." He was at the second room, clearly the one he sought. Tightly holding her hand, he took in every inch of the room, from the lacquered dresser and dressing table, both of which matched the carpet perfectly, to the single modern oil on the wall, to the pale-blue-covered bed. With the gentle pull of his hand, he brought her to him. His dark brown eyes suddenly saw nothing but her. "Have I told you tonight how much I love you?"

"You haven't told me much of anything," she complained, but it was in a whisper and there was the faintest smile on her face to say that those three little words were the only ones she really needed to hear at the moment.

"I love you," he murmured, taking her face in his hands. His lips brushed her eyes, closing them, then her nose and her cheeks before settling at last on her mouth in a kiss filled with need and purpose. "Mmm, do you taste good." He raised his head only to focus on the buttons of her blouse.

It didn't matter to Jordanna that she'd dressed mere moments before. She'd dressed for him. Perhaps simply to be undressed by him. Without hesitation, she slipped her hands beneath his jacket.

"You changed." In place of the gray pin-striped suit was a navy blazer and gray-flannel slacks.

He was down to the third button of her blouse and proceeding steadily. "I keep things at the office." He bent his head to lick her neck as she slid the blazer from his arms. "When I want to freshen up, it's easier than going home. And since I had to work late...."

She loosened his tie and worked at the knot. "No wonder you had to work late. You must have spent half the day shopping. Flowers. Wine. Ice cream. Ice cream?"

"Rum raisin." He untied her scarf. "I get this craving sometimes."

"What's in the boxes?" The knot at his neck came free. She tugged off his tie and tossed it aside, then began on his shirt buttons as he pulled her blouse from her pants.

"That's a surprise. I told you. For later." Pushing the blouse from her shoulders, he had her momentarily manacled. His mouth found the soft swell of her breast, just above the lace of her bra, and moistly kneaded the burning flesh.

"Pat!"

At her hoarse cry, he freed her arms of their silken bonds. The truth was that while he wanted to take things slowly, that was a pipe dream. He needed to feel her hands on him. Needed that desperately. He tugged his shirttails free while she worked feverishly at the last of his buttons. She smoothed the fabric to the side just as he unhooked her bra. Then they were kissing again, hands touching each other, and he was crushing her bare breasts against his chest, feeding on her excitement as she fed on his.

Suddenly time was of the essence. The only thing that seemed to matter was that they be naked, together, joined. Jordanna fumbled with his belt, then thrusting it aside, pulled at his zipper. Patrick nearly tore the button from her waistband in his effort to free her from her velvet pants. For several minutes, then, confusion reigned. It was a question of whose hands were supposed to be doing what where. Their pants, both pairs, hit the floor only after a bit of contorting. The scene was indeed comical. Between kisses they laughed, then renewed the farce.

But it wasn't a farce, because the outcome was breathtaking. There seemed no crisis more critical than the affirmation of their love on this most physical of planes. Swept into the immediacy of an overpowering need, Jordanna was aware of nothing but Patrick. Whereas moments before she'd had every intention of wheedling business news from him, now she could only think of her need to possess and be possessed by the magnificent man her frenzied hands had laid bare.

Both naked, they fell down to the bed. Lips met, tongues dueled. Made for each other, their bodies meshed so naturally that Patrick was inside her before she could begin to catch her breath.

There was no turning back from the fierce need that gripped them. It was as though, given the urgency of all else in their lives, they had to speak that much louder of their personal bond.

"I love you. I love you." Patrick murmured the words again and again. Jordanna simply arched higher to receive him, to give everything she had in return. Their shared adoration put their joining in that much more exalted a sphere, so that when the final moment of joy seized them, it was that much stronger, that much sweeter, that much more soul-reaching than it had ever been before.

"Angel...oh, God!" he gasped, collapsing on top of her. She could barely breathe, but just then she would have given her very life for him if he asked. "That was phenomenal!"

Eyes closed, she wrapped her arms as tightly as she could around his back. Her blissful smile spoke of her agreement as her vocal cords could not. When she remained silent, Patrick raised his head, looked down at her, then quickly slid to her side. She followed him over until they lay nose to nose.

"I love you," she whispered, combing her fingers through his hair. His brow was damp; she stroked it with her thumb.

"Do you? Do you really?" He'd had all day to assimilate the words, yet he couldn't hear them enough. Somehow he sensed it would always be that way.

"Uh-huh."

"When did you decide?"

"I'm not quite sure. I knew something was up when we left New Hampshire. The drive home was dismal. Then when I got back here, all I could do was picture you in this bed." She inhaled deeply, loving the scent that was uniquely his, and eyes moist, she shook her head in amazement. "I can't believe you're here. You came when I needed you most. Thank you."

"Don't thank me, angel. I needed you just as badly." It was his turn to look amazed. "It's odd how things happen."

"Does it bother you still . . . my having been married to Peter?"

"Not the way it did. Knowing that you need me helps. I don't think I'll ever be able to forgive him for trying to subjugate you in the way he did. You've got so much to offer.

A man would be totally selfish to try to curb that. Part of what I love about you is your commitment to Willow Enterprises."

For the first time since Patrick had arrived, Jordanna felt that now familiar knot form in her stomach. "You do think you can come up with something to save us?"

"I'm sure I can. Two of my partners are interested and among us we've got eight clients who are as enthusiastic. I'll make more calls tomorrow. In the meantime, our lawyers are working on preliminary contracts. What I need from you now are figures." He hesitated. "Do you think our man could take a look at your books?"

"Of course! That is, it's okay with me. I'll raise it with the board tomorrow. I'm sure they'll approve if you can guarantee us confidentiality."

"Done."

"Oh, Pat," she breathed, draping an arm around his neck. "Do you really think it would work? With the clauses you mentioned?"

"I don't see why not. You've got a solid organization. None of us wants to change that. The investors would be getting something good. How can they complain?"

"The price would have to be high, at least higher than Widener's offer."

"I know that, but we'll pay. It'll come back tenfold in time."

"What if Widener ups its bid?"

"We'll counter it. Trust me, angel. It'll work. You'll see. It'll work." He paused then, sniffing the air. "Is something burning?"

"Oh no! My casserole!" Within instants, Jordanna was out of bed and flying down the stairs, muttering frantic thoughts about scorched gruyere cheese. Wearing nothing but a pair of oven mitts, she removed the dish from the heat and set it atop the stove.

"Did it survive?" Patrick asked from behind staring over her shoulder at the crisp crust of what was supposed to have been a delicately browned accompaniment to the steaks, which lay on the counter, and the lettuce, now slightly wilted nearby.

"I don't believe this," she wailed. "I wanted to impress you with my culinary skills."

"It looks . . . good."

"If you're looking for something to gnaw on." She let out a long breath, then couldn't help but grin. "Well, at least you can't say I didn't try."

Patrick turned her around and clasped his hands at the small of her back. "I didn't expect you to be a cook. As a matter of fact, I had quite a different impression."

Her thoughts joined his in recollection of their first dinner on the trail in New Hampshire. "I never said I didn't cook. The guys suggested that. I mean, for myself I rarely do much of anything. But I *can* do it when the occasion demands."

"This occasion *doesn't* demand it. I just wanted to be with you tonight. I couldn't give a damn about food."

"That was obvious," she mused aloud, but blushed when she realized that there was good reason her casserole had burned. She hadn't been paying it much heed herself. When she was in Patrick's arms, not much else seemed to matter.

"I tell you what," he began, setting her back and heading for the living room. "I'll give you a hand with dinner."

"I thought you weren't hungry."

"The sight of that steak just changed my mind." But he wasn't focusing on the steak. He was snapping the cords from the two large boxes he'd brought with him. Jordanna watched, growing more curious by the minute. A bright smile broke out on her face when, boxes emptied, he returned to her with one white terry robe slung over his arm and the other held open for her.

"I don't believe it." She shook her head, then laughed. Turning, she slid her arms into the awaiting sleeves. "You came prepared."

"It's winter. I didn't want you catching cold."

"Pretty sure of yourself, weren't you?" When she would have tied the belt, Patrick's hands were reaching around her to do it.

His lips brushed her ear. "You weren't exactly discouraging this morning. I'd never force myself on an unwilling woman."

"Never?" Jordanna teased, closing her hands over his and leaning back against his strength.

"Well, not unless she wanted me to."

"But then she wouldn't be unwilling."

"Unless that was her particular fantasy."

Jordanna turned in his arms then and looked gently up. "You are into fulfilling fantasies, aren't you?"

"I try."

Standing on tiptoe, she kissed him softly. "You do well at it. I think it must be your forte. A professional white knight."

"They didn't call me Lance for nothing."

She recalled having said similar words to John, and smiled.

"What is it?" Patrick asked. He sensed her mind had wandered and was unwilling to let it go far.

Reaching for the robe on his elbow, she opened it and draped it around his shoulders. "I was just thinking of a discussion I had with John up in the woods. He's a nice guy. A philosopher, if mathematicians can be that. We were talking football."

"Oh?"

"Mmm. Funny, when I first saw you up there, I could only think of you as Lance. That changed pretty quick."

"Did it?" Patrick asked. His expression was suddenly serious. He'd wondered if it still bothered her that he had played football. She'd made it clear from the start that she had negative feelings about the game. And though she'd seemed to have come to accept that aspect of his past when they were in New Hampshire—hadn't she, herself, asked him all about it?—he'd had any number of fears that when they'd returned to New York those negative feelings might come to the fore. "How do you feel about it now?"

Jordanna knew precisely what he'd been thinking and, in hindsight, felt guilty for having made some of the statements she had. True, she was biased and true, with good cause. But she'd generalized. She saw that now.

"I think," she began slowly, "that you gave the game a very important part of your life. I can only respect you for that. I also think that there's far more to you than football. You've left it behind. You're a successful businessman now. And a very nice human being."

His mouth took hers in a slow, savoring kiss. "Mmm. I guess I can live with that." Unable to resist the appeal of the lips he'd left soft and moist, he kissed her again. But his body was quickly responding to other soft, moist sources of appeal, and lest he repudiate Jordanna's compliment and prove himself nothing more than a rutting beast, he set her back, secured his robe tightly and straightened his shoulders. "Now—" he cleared his throat "—about those steaks...."

Grilled medium rare on the broiling pan, the steaks were delicious, as was the salad and, miraculously, the potatoes once the top crust had been scraped away. With a dozen aromatic long-stemmed roses gracing the center of the mar-

ble table and Patrick scooping the last of his rum raisin ic
cream from its bowl, Jordanna sat back in amusement.

"You can lick it if you want."

His cheeks went red and he set his spoon down. "Sorry
I get carried away with this stuff."

She held up a hand. "Don't apologize. It's a deligh
watching a growing boy eat. As for me—" she patted he
stomach "—I don't think I've eaten as much in . . . in . . .
month."

"Let me see." His hand pushed hers away and caressed he
softness. "Mmm. You do feel stuffed. I think the best thing
for you to do is to stretch out somewhere comfortable." H
stood up.

"What did you have in mind? *Patrick . . . !*"

Lifting her in his arms, he started for the stairs. "The bed
Where else can one stretch out comfortably?"

JORDANNA AWOKE in the middle of the night in a cold sweat
Eyes wide in the darkness, she listened to those city sound:
that never seemed to end. They were as they'd always been
but there was a new sound joining them. Patrick's breath
ing. Slow. Even.

She'd dreamed she was alone, but he was right beside her
Turning to face him, she moved her arm until it touched his
The feel of his flesh was comforting, the memory of hi
lovemaking intoxicating. But still there was the matter o
her baby—Willow Enterprises—in danger. Unsettling, to
say the least.

Over and over she reviewed the situation. It occurred to
her that if the Widener Corporation had not attempted its
takeover, Patrick might not have come to her when he had
In time he would have. She was sure of that. If only it hadn't
taken this particular catalyst to bring them together!

Time and again she tried to imagine the future, but couldn't. Naive as she'd been, she'd never entertained thoughts of any kind of a takeover, let alone a hostile one. Despite what Patrick had said, she couldn't get past stage one; she simply couldn't seem to accept the fact that Willow Enterprises, against its will, was being forced to change its status. It was unfair and infuriating and not at all conducive to peace of mind.

Snuggling closer to Patrick's warmth, she closed her eyes and concentrated on how wonderful it was to be with him. But sleep was a long time in coming and she was up again at first light, unable to sleep a minute longer.

Stealing softly from the bed, she pulled on her running gear, left a note for Patrick and headed for the street. In her upset the morning before and her desire to get into the office as early as possible, she hadn't run and she'd felt it. Not that the exercise she'd gotten in Patrick's arms hadn't compensated to some extent. But today, given her wakefulness and the fact that she wanted her mind to be clear and alert for the meeting that morning, she set a rapid pace in the cold dawn air of Central Park.

Nearly forty-five minutes and five miles later, she returned to the brownstone half expecting to find Patrick still asleep. It was barely seven. She knew that he'd have to return to his own place before going into the office. What she didn't know was that he'd been awake for half an hour, sitting in the living room, staring at the floor.

Closing the front door very quietly, she turned, then jumped. "Pat! You're up!"

"Mmm." He raised a mug. "Made a pot of coffee. Hoped you wouldn't mind."

He sounded distracted. She assumed he was still half asleep. "Of course not." Crossing the carpet, she leaned forward to kiss his cheek. Her hand slid inside his robe to cover his heart. "You got my note, didn't you?"

"Mmm."

He sounded strange. She couldn't put her finger on it. "Everything okay?"

"Fine."

When she would have questioned him, something held her back. It was bound to be a tense day, what with the board meeting and her continuing campaign against the Widener Corporation. With a frown, she headed for the stairs. "I'll take a quick shower. Be right back."

He was in the same spot when she returned wearing the white robe he'd brought. Her hair was damp, her face still bare of makeup. She stopped before his chair.

"Pat?"

He looked up, jarred from deep thought. "Hmm?"

"Is something wrong?"

"Wrong? Uh, no." But his brow was creased even as he pushed himself from the chair. "I'll give you a hand with breakfast."

She stared after him for a minute before following him into the kitchen. In silence they made a breakfast of French toast. In silence they ate it. As the clock ticked on, Jordanna knew she should be rushing to get dressed and to the office, but somehow something was happening—or not happening—here that was more important. It was only when it occurred to her that Patrick might be having second thoughts about their relationship that she crushed her napkin and looked up.

"What's wrong, Pat? You haven't said two words to me since I got in. *Something*'s on your mind. If it's about us—"

Patrick's rising gaze stopped the words at her lips. His intensity pushed them back into her throat and she swallowed hard.

"It is about us. Very much so." At her apprehensive look he raced on. "I want you to marry me."

For more than a minute Jordanna was speechless. Of the things she'd feared he might say, this hadn't been one. "Marry you?" she murmured at last.

His smile had a daunted cast to it. "Is that so hard to believe?"

"Yes. Uh, no. It's . . . it's just so sudden."

"I know." The urgency was back in his expression. "I hadn't planned it either. I mean, I've known that I loved you for weeks now, but it wasn't until a little while ago that I realized how badly I want to marry you."

"A little while ago?"

"When I woke up it was barely light. It took me a minute to realize where I was. Then I reached for you and you were gone." He took her hand and held it tightly, as though the reminder of that other moment created a new need. "Sheer panic. That was what I felt. Sheer panic. Even after I saw your note, I couldn't stop shaking. I realized then that I have no ties with you. You could very easily get up and walk out of my life."

"But there *are* ties. I love you!"

"Then marry me! I want to know that you'll always be here, that you'll always be waiting for me."

"Pat," she whispered, slowly shaking her head, "that was what I escaped when I divorced Peter. I won't be the one to sit around and wait—"

His own headshake was vigorous. "Wrong words. Or rather, figuratively offered. It doesn't matter where you are, angel. You can be at the office working your tail off or out at the plant in Tucson. You can be doing whatever you want

for as long as is necessary. I wouldn't dream of holding yo
here. All I need to know is that you'll be thinking of me, tha
you'll come back to me. I guess after all these years I'm sti
insecure. I need to know that of all the people you'll run int
in a day or a week or a month, I'll come first." He lowere
his voice. "Is that selfish?"

"No. Oh, no. It's not selfish. I want it too!"

"Then marry me."

Tears formed in her eyes. Looking down, she clung to hi
fingers. "It's not selfish to want what you want, to wan
what *we* want." She raised her eyes. "But it's unfair to as
that of me now. In the past two days, my life has turned up
side down. Ten years, Pat. *Ten years.* That's how long I'v
been living and breathing Willow Enterprises. Suddenly I'r
gasping for breath, struggling for survival. I don't knov
what I would have done if you hadn't come to me yester
day. Even if you hadn't been able to do a thing to help th
company, you would have been the comfort I needed. I ge
strength from you. I never thought I'd say that to a mar
never thought I'd allow myself to say it. But it's true. Still
I can't rush into something. We met under unique circum
stances at Wild River. You said it yourself. And now here
the circumstances aren't much less bizarre. I can't thin
about the future yet. Don't you see? I just can't thin
straight!"

Wearing a look of defeat, Patrick launched his final plea
"If you love me enough—"

"I *do* love you! But I've been through one marriage an
was badly hurt. I want it to be right this time. For *both* ou
sakes."

Inhaling deeply, he eyed the ceiling, then let out his breat
and dropped her hand. "Well, I guess my timing's off." Wit
a look of disgust he stood. "They'd have put me on waiver
for this one." Then he started for the stairs.

"Pat?" Jordanna stood.

He didn't turn. "I'd better get dressed. It's late."

She knew how late it was, knew she should be getting dressed as well. Important business faced her at the office. Yet she couldn't follow him upstairs. Instead, she busied herself with cleaning the kitchen. She was standing quietly at the sink, head bowed, when he returned.

"I'm sorry, angel. I shouldn't have upset you. Not today. I know how important this meeting is for you."

He was leaning against the doorjamb. His shirt collar was undone. His tie hung limply in his hand. Looking at him, Jordanna felt her insides melt. Going to him, she wrapped her arms around his waist and pressed her face to his chest.

"Will I . . . will I see you later?"

"If you want."

She raised her eyes. "Yes, I want."

"Shall I pick you up at the office? Around seven? We could go out for something to eat."

"Seven is fine." She hesitated for just a minute. "Can I call you after the meeting?"

The tense set of his shoulders seemed to relax. "I'd like that. I want to hear how everything went."

She nodded. "Of course. You have an investment—"

"Damn right I do," he cut in, eyes flashing in denial of her preliminary assumption. "I want to make sure you're okay. You, Jordanna, first."

Before she could properly comprehend, he kissed her once, briefly but firmly on the mouth, then strode toward the door, scooping up his topcoat in passing, and left.

9

THE MEETING that morning went well. Despite Jordanna's inner turmoil, she looked and acted every bit the self-confident chairman of the board, presenting her case clearly and with conviction. By a unanimous vote, the directors rejected the Widener Corporation's offer, a decision that was promptly put into a letter to be mailed to each of Willow Enterprises' stockholders. Possible defenses against the hostile takeover were discussed, including the search for a friendly buyer. Feeling vaguely uncomfortable, Jordanna related Patrick's offer. The board members were more than open to consider any formal proposal he might submit and agreed to make themselves available for another meeting at short notice.

It was only after the meeting had adjourned, when Jordanna sat back in her office catching her breath, that she pondered her discomfort. Somehow she felt she hadn't told the board everything. But what should she have said? *The man I love is willing to bail us out? My lover wants to buy in? He's asked me to marry him; wouldn't that be nice—a double merger?*

Life was so complicated. With a touch of self-pity, she wondered why it had to be so.

But there were no answers, not at the moment. There were too many ifs—*if* Patrick could come through with his group, *if* the Widener Corporation gave up the fight, *if* she decided that marriage to Pat was what she truly wanted. She supposed it wouldn't be so bad, when a sufficient amount of time had elapsed, to announce to the board that she and Pat were getting married. Would they wonder, though, if she'd known all along, if she'd set the whole thing up with precisely this in mind? Was there a conflict of interest in her dealing with the Houghton Group?

She needed advice, and Tom Cherwin was the one to call. But such a call was still premature. She needed time. What she'd told Patrick that morning had been the truth. She'd been married once. If she was to marry again, she wanted to know beyond all doubt in the world that it was right and forever.

JORDANNA AND PATRICK had dinner at a quiet French restaurant on the Lower East side, then returned to her place for the night. He didn't mention marriage again, and for that she was grateful. They talked business some; he brought her abreast of his progress on putting together the investors' group and was as optimistic as ever that within several days he'd have a formal proposal to give her board of directors.

Sure enough, after a weekend of quiet intimacy at his town house overlooking the East River, Patrick called her on Monday afternoon to present a concrete offer. On one level, Jordanna was ecstatic; his offer was for five dollars a share above what Widener had bid, and the contract provisions were every bit as fair as he'd promised. On another level, though, she knew she had to move.

At her urgent summons, Tom Cherwin arrived in her office within an hour of Patrick's call.

"It sounds good, Jordanna," he admitted after she'd outlined Patrick's proposal. "If we have to merge with someone, we could have done a hell of a lot worse. According to what Clayes has suggested, the Houghton Group will guarantee us nearly complete autonomy." He paused to watch her rise from her desk and approach the window. "Is there a catch?"

"I don't know."

"You don't look as pleased as by rights you should be."

She turned quickly. "Oh, I am pleased. It's just... well...there's something more." She looked at the floor and frowned, searching for the right words, then realized that there weren't any right or wrong words, simply the truth. "Tom, I haven't been as forthright with you as I should have been. I met Patrick Clayes when I was away in New Hampshire last month. We, uh, we've been involved with each other since before this all came up."

"Involved?" Tom echoed, blankly at first. But if the sudden flush on her cheeks hadn't given her away, her evasive gaze would have. "Ahh. Involved." He smiled broadly. "That's wonderful, Jordanna. Is it serious?"

"Very." Bearing infinite worry, her eyes finally met his.

He understood. "You're concerned about a conflict of interest."

"Yes. He wants me to marry him."

"That's wonderful! Congratulations—"

She held up a hand. "Oh, nothing's happening yet. I haven't said yes. There's too much going on in my life right now to make a decision like that. But it may happen. Someday. And, even if it doesn't, the fact remains that I'm deeply involved with him. At some point, whether Patrick and I ever do marry, the board, the rest of the business world, is apt to find out about us. In the case of the board, they might suspect that I had personal motives for this merger. As far as the business world goes, can you imagine the hay they'd make of it?"

"I think you're worrying too much about what others will think."

"But that's only part of it. I'm worried about whether I can make an objective judgment where the Houghton Group is concerned."

"It wouldn't be your decision alone. Anything we decide to do will have to be by majority rule."

"I know. But still.... Tom, I think *you* should be the one to put the proposal before the board. I think *you* should handle this thing from here on."

"You want me to work with the Houghton Group."

"Yes."

"And we tell the board of directors why?"

"It seems the only honest thing to do. And it's an awful lot better than risking their finding out at some later point that Patrick and I are personally involved."

"You know, Jordanna," Tom said, eyeing her over the top of his glasses, "there's nothing wrong with your being personally involved with him. Do you have any idea how many mergers involve family members or friends?"

"I'm sure there are plenty. But at least in those cases the relationship is a known fact."

But Tom was shaking his head. "The only facts that really count in this kind of wheeling and dealing are those written in the contract. Those facts will have to stand by themselves, regardless of your relationship with Clayes."

"That's what I want you to make sure of, Tom. What I'm saying, among other things, is that I'm not sure I wholly trust myself when it comes to Patrick. I may be looking at this deal through rose-colored glasses. What I want is for you to be aware of the situation and to double-check everything. I mean, the Houghton proposal sounds wonderful. It could be precisely what we need. I just want to be sure that's the case." It was like marriage. She wanted it to work.

Tom was nodding. "Of course. I understand."

"I'll explain to the board simply that I'm a close friend of Patrick's and that, for the sake of impartiality, I'll defer to you."

"You're still the president and chairman of the board. They'll want your opinion, Jordanna."

"Oh, they'll have it," she replied with a half smile. "It may be slightly biased—"

"I doubt that," Tom replied, standing to take his leave. "Willow Enterprises means far too much to you to allow for any merger agreement but the best. No, you'd never compromise on the future of the business. I'll get our team to work with Houghton's. We'll have everything in writing before the board meeting."

"I'd like to call it for tomorrow afternoon. Think you can be ready by then?" When Tom raised his brows, she raced on. "With every day that passes Widener is buying more of our stock. According to the reports I'm getting, our major shareholders are standing firm. But there are those minor ones, and they can add up. The sooner we make a counteroffer, the better." She gave a begrudging, "Hmmph. Widener's in luck. If Patrick's offer of fifty-three stands and Shane decides to sell back his shares, Widener will make a bundle. It doesn't seem fair somehow."

"It's the way of Wall Street. We have to accept it."

Watching him leave, Jordanna felt somewhat better. She'd told him about her relationship with Patrick, and he hadn't been shocked or dismayed or incensed. Perhaps she *was* worrying too much.

Patrick said as much that night during dinner. "You didn't have to turn things over to Cherwin. You could've handled it."

"But I feel better this way. At least I'll have ensured myself against any possible future criticism by the board. Don't ou see? If I'd said nothing at this stage, I'd be in worse rouble when they found out."

"Are you nervous . . . about telling them?"

She heard the mild apprehension in Patrick's voice and hared it. "A little. I, uh, I wonder if any of them will comnent."

"My guys did."

"They did? You told them about us?"

"My partners. I felt they had a right to know."

"Like my board?"

He nodded. "They thought it was pretty funny that you'd een married to my rival and all."

Jordanna took in his sober expression. "Did it bother ou?"

He frowned and took her hand. "A little." He couldn't lie nd say he hadn't felt a twinge of anger. "But I got over it. nd they had to agree that the deal was sound regardless."

She was silent for a while, studying her hand in his. His ngers were strong, long and firm. No wonder he'd had uch control of the football. "I suppose it's something we'll ave to learn to live with," she said simply, but she had to vonder if what Patrick had come up against wasn't just the eginning.

LL THINGS CONSIDERED, the board of directors of Willow nterprises was remarkably indulgent. At its meeting uesday afternoon, Jordanna briefly explained her dimma before turning the gavel over to Tom. If there were mug remarks to be made, they were kept from her ears. The oard voted in overwhelming support of the Houghton roposal, and a messenger was immediately sent to convey he news to the group.

The following morning Patrick filed his statement of innt with the SEC. Ads appeared in the appropriate papers.

Jointly signed letters were mailed to the stockholders, accompanied by phone calls to the major ones.

Jordanna was busy. Between those calls conveying her personal endorsement of the agreement with the Houghton Group, and a refocus on the everyday workings of Willow Enterprises, her days were filled to brimming.

As for her nights, they were filled with Patrick. He didn't mention marriage again, but everything he did with, for and to her spoke of his love. Her own blossomed all the more fully, a warm lush feeling that brightened every aspect of her life, binding her to him more and more closely.

They spent every possible minute together, either at home or out. On occasion, in a restaurant, at a party or show, they bumped into people who knew of that earlier link between them. There were comments it was to be expected. For the most part they were positive, offered on a kidding note. Even the small newspaper mention they received simply stated the fact that Jordanna was the former wife of Peter Kirkland, Patrick Clayes longtime rival. It seemed harmless enough, Jordanna thought. Until she received a call from Peter himself.

"Well," he began in his own inimitably arrogant way, "you're making headlines this time, aren't you, babe?"

She was at the office, deeply involved in a meeting with her marketing vice-president, and was tempted to quickly put him off. But she sensed he had something to say. She knew she had things to say to him. And one phone call from Peter Kirkland was all she wanted to receive.

"Hold on a minute, Peter." She muffled the phone. "Fifteen minutes, Jill? This has to be taken care of now."

With a smile of understanding, the other woman left. Only when the door was firmly shut behind her did Jordanna remove her hand from the mouthpiece. "How are you, Peter?"

"Surprised, if you want to know the truth. I guess I underestimated you, Jordanna. I didn't think you had it in ou."

"What are you talking about?" She had an idea, and idn't like it. But she wanted him to say the words himself.

He proceeded to do just that. "Revenge." It wasn't quite vhat she'd expected. Eyes wide, she listened as Peter ranted n. "Patrick Clayes. You've really done it, haven't you? Not nly are you letting him buy out the company, but you're nvolved with him personally! I couldn't believe it when Mac called." Mac Heinsohn had been one of Peter's closest laying buddies. Evidently they were still close. "He hought it was pretty funny. I don't."

Jordanna had begun to simmer. "For your information, 'atrick is not buying me out. His company is buying *into* Willow Enterprises. There's a difference."

But Peter wasn't listening. "You wanted to get back at me, lidn't you? Well, you've done it. How long have you been olanning this little coup, Jordanna? Months? Years?"

"If you're as well informed as you claim to be, you'd know hat none of this would be happening if Widener hadn't attempted a hostile takeover. That was barely three weeks igo."

"But the two of you—Patrick and you—don't tell me you've only been with him since then."

"We're divorced, Peter. You and I. It seems to me that you shouldn't be concerning yourself with my private life."

"When it affects mine, I'll be as concerned as I want. Hell, ordanna, I look like a fool."

"Because you couldn't hold me? That's your problem. You were only concerned with yourself. Even now. Nothing's changed."

"What about you, sweetie? Has it ever occurred to you hat Clayes gets his revenge too?" Jordanna couldn't be-

lieve what he was saying. Her silence tipped Peter off. "God
you're as naive as ever. Well, let me tell you. Clayes wouldn't
be doing any of this if it weren't for me."

"That's not true," she argued, but her voice shook as did
her limbs.

"Come on," Peter spat. "It's too damn coincidental to be
anything else. I have to hand it to the guy. He's pretty clever.
Sat around all these years waiting for the right moment.
And it fell into his lap. He's a smooth one. You're probably
head over heels in love with him. I remember how it was
with us. You fell pretty quick then too."

Jordanna called on every bit of the self-control she possessed to keep her voice steady. "I think you've said enough,
Peter."

"I don't think so, babe. But then, you never were very
good about listening to advice."

"From *whom*? *You*?" She couldn't help herself. Her anger boiled over. "Let me tell *you* something, Peter Kirkland. You know *nothing* when it comes to human beings!
You couldn't see an honest emotion if it hit you in the face
because you're so damned convinced you have all the answers. Well, you were wrong about me ten years ago. My
divorcing you was the smartest thing I ever did. Willow Enterprises gave me back the self-esteem you denied me. If you
really want to think that I've built a relationship with Patrick out of revenge, go ahead. You always were self-centered
enough to believe that everyone and everything revolved
around you. And that goes for Patrick's motives too. If you
honestly want to believe he's been waiting around all these
years simply for a chance to get back at you, be my guest.
But you know *nothing*, Peter. Patrick is a *man*. Football is
behind him. He's built a very successful life for himself, one
that he wouldn't jeopardize for cheap revenge any more
than I would."

"So naive," came the caustic retort.

"Not naive," she countered firmly. "Realistic. And by way of realistic advice, let me suggest that you simply tell our adoring audience that what your *ex*-wife does is her business, and her business alone." She sat straighter. "I haven't got time to hold your hand if your ego happens to be bruised. I've got work to do. Now, if you'll excuse me—" Slamming down the phone, she severed the connection, then sat trembling in anger for the few minutes it took for her to regain her composure. When she lifted the receiver again, it was to buzz Leila.

"Leila, that was my ex-husband. If he calls again, I'm unavailable. Understood?"

THE DAMAGE had been done. Jordanna was as furious at Peter for having suggested what he had as she was at herself for having listened to him. For, much as she tried to categorically deny his allegations, she couldn't totally erase them from her mind.

That night, when she appeared somehow withdrawn, Patrick questioned her.

"What is it, angel? Something's bothering you."

She forced a smile. "Oh, nothing. Just tired, I guess. Things must be getting to me."

"But everything's going well. Widener's going to be selling back its stocks. You've nothing to fear from them anymore."

But from you? she wanted to ask, but didn't. She knew she should come right out and tell him about Peter's call. Somehow she couldn't. She was embarrassed. Patrick would think she didn't trust him at all. She was frightened. What if some of what Peter had said was true?

They didn't make love that night. Patrick simply held her in his arms until, at last, she fell asleep. Long after, he lay worrying, fearing that it was the intensity of their relationship that was getting to her. He thought about cooling it for a while, but he couldn't. He needed to see her, to speak with her, to be with her. As it was, he was exercising the greatest control in not pestering her about marriage. More than anything in the world, he wanted her to be his wife. With each day, the need grew. And it was never more dire than at times like this when he realized how unattached she truly was.

THEN CAME THE DAY, nearly a month after the agreement with the Houghton Group had been formalized, when Jordanna had to go to St. Louis. She'd put the trip off twice, just as Patrick had limited himself to day trips so that they might have the nights to themselves and each other. But she couldn't delay it longer. Her plant manager was resigning and his replacement had to be interviewed and approved. When hiring was done at such an important level, Jordanna had always reserved the final judgment for herself after her personnel department had narrowed the field to the three top contenders. This time, given the fact that she'd have to be away from Patrick for two nights, her heart wasn't in it. But her mind was. Particularly in light of the recent changes in the ownership of Willow Enterprises, she knew that this was no time to abdicate her responsibility. As a show of command, if nothing more, she had to go.

The parting was difficult for Jordanna, enlightening in its way. Patrick accompanied her to the airport for the early-morning flight.

"Are you sure you'll be okay?" he asked, hands firmly gripping the lapels of her coat as they stood by the boarding gate.

"I'll be fine. I've done this many times before."

"I know, but still . . ." He cast a worried glance through the sheets of glass. "It looks like it might snow. They're predicting it."

She laughed softly. "By the time it comes, I'll be up there above it all. You're the one who'll be stuck with it."

"I wish you'd let me come."

They'd discussed this before. "You've got your own work to do, Pat. And I've got to let our people down there know that I'm still firmly in control. No, it's better that I go alone." Her voice cracked. "Though I will miss you."

Enfolding her in his arms, Patrick held her tightly. "I'll miss you too, angel. You'll call when you're free?"

"Every night."

Boarding began. While the other passengers flowed by, he held her silently. When they could put if off no longer, he kissed her. "I love you, Jordanna."

She buried her face against his neck, breathing deeply of him for a final time. "I love you too."

"Will you . . . ?" His voice trailed off with indecision.

"Will I what?"

Unable to stop himself, he went ahead. "Will you think about us while you're there?" The slight emphasis he put on the *us* left no doubt in Jordanna's mind what he referred to.

"I will," she whispered.

"And you'll behave?"

"I will." Reaching up, she kissed him once more. Then, fearful she might lose her composure altogether, she quickly hoisted her shoulder bag and headed for the door.

Patrick watched, feeling helpless and empty as she walked away from him. Her departure was a harsh reminder precisely how much she meant to him. She was his light. Without her his world was dark and lonely.

As PROMISED, Jordanna called him that night. She told him about the flight, which had been smooth, and about the interviews she'd had with two of the three finalists that afternoon at the plant. These had been more perplexing. Something was missing in each of the two men she'd interviewed. She couldn't put her finger on it. Intuition, she told Pat. He simply chuckled when she tried to apologize and told her that her intuition was very definitely something to be trusted. Hadn't it gotten her this far in life? he asked. She wondered.

The third interview was scheduled for the following morning, after which she had meetings scheduled with various of the plant personnel and the decision on the manager to make. On the third morning, she would have a meeting with the chosen one. In her briefcase she carried detailed reports on each of the candidates; these she reviewed time and again.

From the moment she sat down with the third candidate, she knew what her decision would be. She also knew what had been missing in the other two men. A plant manager, *her* plant manager, had to be ultrasensitive to people. This third man had called half an hour before he was due to come, saying that there was an emergency at the plant he was presently managing and that he might be several minutes late. He wasn't. But he explained his call. One of his workers had collapsed on the job. He'd wanted to be sure that the woman was taken to the right hospital, that she was given immediate attention by the best doctor and that her family was gently notified and on their way.

Jordanna hired him on the spot. Intuition, she told herself, not to mention the fact that his qualifications had been impeccable, his references superb. Or was it simply that, with the decision made and the congratulatory meeting held there and then, she was free to fly back to New York that night?

She didn't stop to analyze her motives, but pushed herself headlong into the afternoon's meetings. She was tired but enthusiastic when she called Patrick to tell him of her change in plans. He was delighted. There was no way he could have fabricated his pleasure, she told herself, even if he *had* had reason to do so. If, as Peter had so callously suggested, he had sought her and her business out of revenge, by rights Patrick would have been looking forward to this break from her. But she believed him when he said he loved her, when he said he missed her, when he said he'd be there at the airport to meet her at whatever time the plane touched down.

In a state of immense satisfaction, she took a cab to the airport. Several of the plant personnel had offered to drive her, but she'd wanted the time alone. Nothing, no one, should intrude on her thoughts of Patrick, she decided. She was going home.

The plane was filled. She'd been fortunate to get a last-minute seat. Buckling herself in, she put her head back and took a deep breath, then awaited the takeoff. It went without a hitch, right on time, smooth and, for Jordanna, with promise.

St. Louis was no more than an hour behind when that promise was shattered by the quiet announcement from the captain.

"Ladies and gentlemen." He cleared his throat. "I'm afraid we'll be taking a slight detour. There's a gentleman here in the cockpit with us who insists on being taken elsewhere. He may be armed." There was a break before his voice returned more tensely. "He is armed but wants no harm to come to any of us. On his behalf, I ask you to remain calm.

I'll keep you informed of our flight plan once it is determined."

Jordanna sat in her seat as a wave of disbelief, then fear, swept the large cabin. *Hijack.* The word was a murmur, bouncing in a wave from one row of seats to another. Flight attendants moved deftly up and down the aisles, their pale faces in contrast to the smooth words of assurance they delivered on cue.

Hijack. It seemed unreal. But then, so had *takeover* been, and she'd seen the end results of that. A slow trembling started deep within Jordanna, seeping steadily through her limbs until she had to grasp the upholstered arms on either side for support.

Hijack? Was it possible? After everything she'd been through during the past few months, it couldn't be! She looked frantically from side to side but found nothing reassuring in the faces around her. Those too were pale and searching hers for the answers none of them had.

"This is too much," the man on her left muttered. "I've been flying for thirty years and nothing like this has ever happened. I mean, I've had engines go dead. I've had lightning all but strike the plane. But . . . a hijacking?"

"The worst that's ever happened to me," ventured the younger man on Jordanna's right, "was to lose my luggage. It went to Greece while I went to California. I had to go out and buy new clothes. My bags made it two days later."

Eyes straight ahead and dazed, Jordanna heard herself join the conversation. "I was supposed to fly home tomorrow. This was a last-minute change of plans. I wanted to be back. I thought—" She stopped talking when a lump formed in her throat. Sensing the state of her emotions, the man on her left patted her hand in a fatherly fashion. In other circumstances, she might have thought it condescending—the little lady needing comfort. But she did need comfort. And he appreciated the gesture.

"How can this kind of thing happen?" the man on her right demanded of no one in particular. "My God, with all the security precautions at airports you'd think they'd be able to prevent it. Everything goes through X-rays. How could some kook walk up there and say he's armed?"

"Maybe he's bluffing," the man on her left conjectured. "They're probably trying to find that out now."

"Either that, or they're trying to talk him out of it," Jordanna offered, trying to gather her wits and assess the situation in whatever small manner she could. It was hard. Her stomach was in knots and her thoughts kept wandering, mostly toward New York where Patrick would soon be waiting. Incredulous still, she shook her head. "Where do you think he wants to go?"

"Cuba?" suggested the man on her right. In vague maho fashion, he was wearing jeans and a Western-style shirt. Jordanna thought him to be in his mid-twenties and prayed that he—or any other of the passengers—wouldn't be so foolish as to try to storm the cockpit.

"Maybe the Middle East," suggested the man on her left. "If we land in a country we have no extradition treaty with, a hijacker would be safe."

Jordanna looked over at him. Perhaps in his early fifties, he wore a business suit and might have seemed perfectly calm except for the sweat that dotted his forehead. When he met her gaze, she gave him a worried smile and looked down. Again he patted her hand. Again she welcomed the kind gesture.

Very slowly, the shock aboard the craft gave way to a thick, quiet tension. What conversation there was was muted. All ears were attuned to the moment the captain's voice would return. The flight attendants came through bearing drinks, explaining that dinner would be served later. It went without saying that the food provisions might have to be stretched somewhat, depending on their final destination.

It seemed an eternity before the captain came back on the loudspeaker. His voice was low, obviously strained. A ripple of apprehension passed through the cabin. All other noise ceased.

"This is your captain speaking. I've just been given clearance to head for Philadelphia, where we'll be stopping briefly to refuel. If there are any medical conditions that need special attention, please notify one of the flight attendants now. Once we leave Philadelphia, we'll be heading for Benghazi."

With a curt click, the speaker went dead. In its wake, silence reigned, but only long enough for the passengers to absorb this new bit of information.

"Benghazi?" the man on Jordanna's right echoed. "Where in the hell is *that*?"

"Libya," returned the man on her left in a dull tone of voice. "It's on the other side of the world!"

"Should've been Cuba," the first growled. "Would've been faster, cleaner."

Wearily, Jordanna closed her eyes and withered into her seat. Libya. It *was* on the other side of the world. So far away from Patrick. So far away from everything she knew that was safe and predictable. God only knew what the Libyans would do with an American aircraft jammed with people! God only knew if they'd make it there in one piece!

Suddenly the world seemed a very bleak place with the only bright light shining from New York. Patrick would be there, waiting, worrying. But she'd be landing in Philadelphia, so close, so very close, then taking off again for Africa and a far and hostile land. What was in store for her—

or the entire planeload of people—was unknown and herefore terrifying. Most terrifying of all was the thought hat, should something go wrong, she might never see Patick again.

10

PATRICK STOOD at the arrival gate in a state of disbelief "What did you say?"

"We don't know when the flight will be in," the young airline official repeated softly, apologetically. "It's been hijacked."

"Hijacked. You've got to be kidding."

"I wish I were."

Patrick made a face. *"Hijacked?"*

"The plane should be landing in Philadelphia right now It'll refuel there."

"And then?"

The woman's voice lowered. "They'll go on to Libya."

"Libya! This has to be a joke."

The woman shook her head.

"You're serious?" When she nodded, his heart skipped beat. "Oh, my God!"

"I'm sorry, sir. We're doing everything we can to try t talk the man out of it."

Patrick's eyes flashed. "How could something like thi happen? I thought you people were so careful!"

"We are," she replied as calmly as she could. "The cap tain says the man's got an explosive hooked to his pace maker."

"Pacemaker!" Patrick cried, then dropped his voice a octave. "This is too much."

"We had no way of knowing. Since the man couldn't pas through the metal detectors, he was searched by hand. Th

cemaker was an external one, secured near his waist. No
e ever dreamed it wasn't legitimate."

"No one ever dreamed...." Patrick muttered. "Damn it,
y woman's on that plane!"

The official tossed a pained glance toward the other peo-
e somberly clustered at the arrival gate. "They've got
iends and relatives on it too. I'm sorry. I wish there were
ore I could say. There's no reason to believe that the plane
on't land in Benghazi, drop the hijacker and then quickly
turn here. If you'd like to wait, we'll fill you in on any news
we get it."

"Wait. Uh, yes, I'll wait." His brow furrowed, then
eared as he tried to sort out his whirling thoughts. "How
ng? How long will it take to get to Benghazi and back?"

When she grew flustered, a male official stepped in. "The
ying time one way is close to thirteen hours."

"Thirteen hours! And they'll have enough fuel?" He could
e the plane running out midway, and shuddered.

"It'll be close, but they should be okay. If necessary they
in land in Tripoli but the hijacker insists on going to
enghazi. If the Libyans allow them to land and take right
ff again—"

"*If,*" Patrick interrupted in anger. "But if the Libyan gov-
nment detains them...."

The official shook his head once. "We have no reason to
elieve that the Libyans would detain them for any reason.
lease, sir. There's no cause for immediate alarm."

"*No cause?* My God, man! This isn't exactly your aver-
ge flight!" He looked down, eyes terror filled. "Hijacked.
can't be. Jordanna's on that plane." Suddenly he looked
ack up. "Maybe she's not. She only got a seat at the last
inute. Maybe it was overbooked ... or she missed it...."

"Her name?" Already the official was studying the clip-
oard before him.

"Kirkland," Patrick stated, heart pounding. "Jordanna Kirkland."

One page of names was studied, then turned. Patrick's hopes rose. He didn't care if she hadn't called. Or maybe she had; he'd been out of the office since he received her first call and had wanted to get to the airport in plenty of time. He didn't care if she'd have to take tomorrow's flight after all. Just as long as she was safe.

But his hopes were shattered when the official pressed a finger midway down the second sheet of paper. "Jordanna Kirkland. Yes, I'm afraid she is on the flight."

Patrick squeezed his eyes shut. The young woman came from behind the counter to gently take his elbow. "Why don't you have a seat, sir? We'll have coffee brought out in a little while. As soon as we hear anything, we'll pass it on."

Dumbly he looked at her, then followed her glance toward the others waiting in small, quiet groups. "Uh, yes, I think . . . I think I'll just go stand by the window."

"If there's anything we can get you. . . ."

"Get me Jordanna," he ordered. "Just get her back here safely."

"We'll do our best," the woman offered softly, then left him to give her attention to another worried party that approached.

Patrick stared out the window for what seemed an eternity. Disbelief, shock, anger—each yielded in turn to the next. When at last he turned and took a seat, he was filled with an awful helplessness. And fear. So much could happen. A hijacker had to be crazy to begin with. What if he completely lost his mind midflight and detonated the explosive he carried? What if someone tried to tackle him and the explosive went off by accident? What if the Libyans detained both the plane and its crew. Torture? Mayhem? Or they refused to grant the hijacker asylum and he went berserk there and then?

Beads of sweat covered Patrick's brow. He mopped them with his forearm, then thrust his fingers through his hair. It was unreal! All of it! Jordanna was coming back to him, *rushing* back to him. She'd advanced her schedule, taken an earlier flight. For him. Guilt joined terror to consume him. If anything happened to her, he'd never forgive himself. Why couldn't it have been *he* on that plane? Why Jordanna? Why now, just when things were looking so good for them?

Hours passed. The terminal slowly filled with anxious friends and relatives, silent in their vigil. Representatives of the media quietly worked the crowd, interviewing those who would speak, deftly bypassing others. Standing once more at the window with his back to the rest, Patrick waited angrily, almost daring someone from the press to approach him. He'd tell them what he thought, crude bastards. To shove a microphone at a person who was obviously in pain was low and dirty and heartless.

"Got someone on it too?"

Snapping his head to the side, Patrick found himself staring at an elderly gentleman whose eyes were moist. Instantly contrite, he curbed his anger and nodded.

The man gripped the wood rail with gnarled hands that shook slightly. "My daughter's on it. Didn't even know it until my son-in-law had the good grace to call. We're not close." There was sadness in his broken voice and regret. "Heard about it on the eleven o'clock news. Never imagined she'd be aboard."

"Did the news have anything to add that we don't know?" Patrick asked as gently as he could, but there was an underlying urgency in his tone that he couldn't hide. Despite hourly updates by airport personnel, real news had been scarce. The plane was indeed en route to Libya. Beyond that nothing was known.

The old man shook his head. "Just mention of some of the passengers. A singer. Never heard of him. Couple of company presidents. Never heard of them either. Course, no one's heard of my Jane."

Patrick wondered if Jordanna's name had been mentioned, but he didn't ask. It didn't matter. The only thing that mattered was that the plane and its passengers should return intact. And soon.

In as blind a daze as Patrick felt himself, the old man wandered off. A long table had been set up at one end of the room with sandwiches and hot drinks. The thought of food made Patrick sick. He wondered if Jordanna had eaten, wondered whether there'd be enough food and drink to sustain the passengers through their ordeal. He tried to remember what he'd read about other hijackings, but drew a blank. Slamming his fist upon the rail, he gritted his teeth against the pain. But the worst of the pain was inside, and it only grew as the long night wore on.

By dawn, he felt desolate. Slumped in a chair, he watched the sky pale. Around him, others shifted and fidgeted. Those who'd fallen asleep awoke with urgently whispered inquiries about news. Those who'd gone home for the night slowly trickled back.

Helping himself to a cup of hot coffee, Patrick wandered aimlessly about the room. He felt, in turn, like a caged animal, then a grateful hostage. Rubbing a hand to his shadowed jaw, he wondered if he should go home to shave and shower. But he didn't want to go anywhere. Not while Jordanna was out there. Not while there might be news.

At nine in the morning, slouched once more in a seat, he was roused from his depression by a familiar voice.

"Pat, I just heard!" Andrew Harper, one of his partners
nd close friends, slipped breathlessly into the seat next to
m. "I got here as soon as I could."

"You heard?" Patrick echoed, numb.

"Read, actually. The newspaper." He held a copy folded
his lap, but Patrick was too weary to reach for it.

"They mentioned her?"

"Yes. She's one of several big names on the plane."

Patrick thought of the old man who'd talked with him
ours before. "They're all big names, Andy. Every one of
em—" he tossed his head toward the crowd behind him
—to these people here."

Andrew looked appropriately chastised. Then he eyed his
iend cautiously. "Is there any news? The paper simply said
e plane was on its way to Libya."

"It should be arriving within the hour." Word had come
rough a few minutes before. "That's all we know."

"Well, at least that's something. They're getting there."

Patrick shuddered and stared straight ahead. "Now we
ave to wonder what the Libyans will do with them. Once
ey land, they'll probably sit on a runway sweltering in the
eat. If the hijacker remains on board, they'll be in contin-
ing danger from him. If he gets off, they may be in danger
om the Libyans." Leaning forward, he knotted his hands
ogether. "All we can do is to pray that the plane will be al-
owed to take off with everyone but the hijacker aboard."

Andrew raised a hand to his friend's shoulder. "It'll get
ff okay. You'll see."

Patrick closed his eyes tightly. "I keep thinking of En-
ebbe. What those people went through—"

"That was a political thing, Pat. This is not. It's one crazy
an. The Libyans wouldn't do anything to risk this coun-
ry's retaliation."

Opening his eyes wide, Patrick sat back with a tired sigh. "I keep telling myself that but, damn it, it doesn't help. Jordanna's on that plane. If it weren't for me, she'd have flown in safely this morning. If anything happens to her, I don't think I'll ever forgive myself. Not to mention the idea of living without her—"

"Hell, Pat. Since when were you such a pessimist?"

Patrick looked at his friend then. "I'm talking reality."

"You're talking morbid. They'll all be okay. Sure, maybe hot. Maybe tired and hungry and thirsty. But they'll be okay. Got that?"

"I have your word?" Patrick asked, sarcasm in his arched brow.

Andrew simply sent him a chiding glance, then softened. "Is there anything I can do?" Pat shook his head. "I'll cover you at the office. Any important meetings that can't be postponed?"

Nothing was so important that it couldn't be postponed. Not when Jordanna was in danger. Again he shook his head.

"You really should go home and change. You look awful."

Patrick was still shaking his head. "I can't. Not yet, at least. Once we get word that the plane's on the way home I may leave for an hour." He glanced at his watch. He'd calculated and recalculated all night. "In the most optimistic circumstances, they could be back tonight. Until I know something, anything, I'm staying here."

"Want me to stop back later?"

Patrick's smile was sad but it held his appreciation. "No. Thanks anyway, Andy. I'll just...sit here. I'll be okay. Don't worry about me."

"You're sure?"

"Yup."

But he began to wonder as the day dragged on. There was
news, other than that the plane had indeed landed in
nghazi. No word of a takeoff. No word of a seizure.
thing. Patrick's frustration was shared by the others
nding watch. His worry was reflected on their faces, his
nse of helplessness in the way they seemed to wander in
mless circles, sitting, only to stand and walk again.

When, at midafternoon, a reporter approached him, he
as too tired to muster immediate fight.

"Excuse me," the young woman said, "but aren't you . . .
u look very much like. . . ."

"I am," he conceded, staring off toward the runways he'd
ready imprinted inch by inch on his mind.

"Do you have someone on this flight, Mr. Clayes?"

"Yes. My woman."

The reporter began to write.

"Must you do that?" Patrick snapped, tossing a glance
ver his shoulder. "Have you made notes on each of these
eople and the names of those they're waiting for?"

"Some," the reporter returned calmly.

"And you've asked how they feel, whether they're wor-
ed?"

"Logical questions, given the circumstances."

"Doesn't it occur to you that this is an invasion of pri-
acy? That they may not want someone poking her nose in
t such an awful time?"

"It's news, Mr. Clayes. You should know that."

"Oh, I know it, all right, which is why I always did avoid
e press." Standing, he thrust his fists into his pants pock-
s. "If you'll excuse me. . . ." Without another word, he
alked off.

It was shortly after five when a somber-faced airline rep-
sentative announced that the plane had not yet left Libya.
enewed expressions of anxiety rippled through the air.

Patrick stood stiffly while the representative explained th
both the airline and the government were doing everythir
they could. Turning, head bowed, Patrick walked to tł
window once more.

How was Jordanna? She had to be exhausted. An
frightened. If he thought the waiting hard, he could barel
begin to imagine what *she* had to be going through. Nearl
twenty-four hours—that was how long she'd been on tł
plane. *If* she was still on the plane. He shuddered when ł
thought of the alternatives, then tried to think more pos
tively. Most likely there was some simply explained dela
But what? Red tape? *Why hadn't the plane taken off?*

Dropping into a chair, Patrick realized that he was mor
bone tired than he'd ever been in his life. He felt as thoug
he'd played three football games back-to-back and then ł
had been forced to run around the entire field a dozen time
Moreover, those games had been Super Bowls and he'
blown each one.

Nothing, no, *nothing* could compare with the way he fel
Worried. Fearful. Empty. Alone. The others waiting s
tensely in the terminal might have been some comfor
sharing the ordeal, there was a gentle bond between then
But he couldn't share his thoughts with them, didn't war
to hear their tales of woe. Rather, he drew into himself an
centered his thoughts on willing Jordanna safe and well.

Six o'clock became seven. The winter's night had lon
since fallen. Seven became eight, then nine. The crow
thinned out again as some of its members went home for
few hours' rest. Patrick dozed once or twice in his seat, onl
to snap awake to a vision of an explosion or gunfire an
screams. Andrew stopped by again and tried to persuad
him to go home for a bit, but Patrick was adamant abou
not leaving until he heard something positive.

Finally, at three in the morning word came. With a ra-
n of fuel, the plane had taken off from Benghazi and, af-
a stop in Gibraltar for food, drink and sufficient extra
l to see it across the Atlantic, would be heading home.
e words were sweet, bringing tears of anguished relief to
eyes in the room, including Patrick's. Numb with fa-
ue, but elated by the promise of having Jordanna in his
ns that night, he finally left the airport and went home.
By the time he returned, with several hours' sleep, a
ave, shower and fresh clothes to his credit, he felt almost
man. Almost. The rest would come when Jordanna was
ck with him.

The atmosphere at the arrival gate was one of quiet ex-
ement. With word from Gibraltar not only that the plane
d left there on schedule but also that everyone aboard was
ll, if tired, the friends and relatives who waited in New
rk broke out in smiles from time to time. But an air of
ardedness remained; not until the plane actually touched
wn would anyone fully rejoice.

As afternoon became evening, the crowd swelled. Join-
g those who had so faithfully kept the long vigil were other
mily members and friends. Moving from group to group
scavenger fashion were representatives from both the
int and electronic media.

Patrick kept to himself for the most part, eyes glued to the
y. As the minutes passed, his excitement grew. The plane
as due in at six. With a mere fifteen minutes to go, and the
n a faint memory in the west, he turned from the window
get a drink of water, only to stop, dead still and stare
ead. There, looking fresh and alert, chatting amiably
th two reporters, was Peter Kirkland.

Patrick's first response was to haul back and punch the
an in the mouth. He'd come for the show, the bastard! He

intended to cash in on Jordanna's ordeal, to milk it f
whatever publicity he could get!

Then Peter met his gaze with a message that was hard a
direct. Patrick looked away, then back, then away agai
deep in thought. When he looked back a final time, it w
to calmly nod to Peter. Very deliberately he unclenched l
hand and tucked it comfortably into the pocket of his slack
Then, accepting the challenge Peter had issued, he went f
his drink of water.

As the landing time grew closer, a sense of anticipati
filled the arrival area. Ignoring Peter Kirkland's presen
and the press contingent he courted, Patrick stood at a f
side of the room, alternately watching the lighted runw
and the information monitor suspended from the ceilin
The minutes seemed endless. Somehow fatigue was forgc
ten, as was the anguish that had dominated the past tv
days. In their place was an excitement just waiting to bu
ble and overflow.

When the airline official announced that the plane h
touched down and would be approaching the terminal m
mentarily, a collective sigh of relief seemed to waft into tl
air, accompanied by random cheers and an exultant shou
The crowd inched forward, restrained in its joy only l
airline personnel who struggled to leave an open path f
the passengers.

Patrick remained at the side. Given his superior heigl
he could easily see the door through which the passenge
would pass. Likewise, he knew Jordanna would easily s
him.

Heart thudding, he caught sight of the aircraft's lights
it pulled up to the terminal. His throat felt suddenly tigh
he tried to swallow the lump there but couldn't. All he cou
do was to imagine the airplane's door being opened and i

ssengers, who'd traveled such a long way, streaming out,
the corridor, onto home soil at last.

It seemed an eternity before the first of the bedraggled
velers emerged to be crushed into familiar, welcoming
ns. Patrick's eyes filled with tears; he brushed them with
sleeve and focused again, waiting, watching, his life
spended until she came into view.

Inside the aircraft, Jordanna waited for those before her
begin to move. She wondered how something so simple
uld take so long, particularly after all they'd been
rough, then realized that, exhausted as she was, her pa-
nce was next to nil. Those around her were as quiet as she;
was as though every bit of the energy they possessed was
cused on terra firma and home. She shifted from her left
ot to her right, then hoisted the strap of her shoulder bag
ore comfortably when, at last, the line started forward.

She needed to see Patrick, needed to hold him. Had it not
en for thought of him, she might have gone mad during
e harrowing hours of flight, the more harrowing hours of
ent detainment on Libyan soil. If she'd needed something
help her sort things out regarding her life, this ordeal had
en it. Forty-eight hours of enforced inactivity, of near
nstant fear, could do that to a person. Oh, yes, she knew
hat she wanted. It was simply a matter of physically get-
ng there.

She thought she'd scream when the line slowed down
ain, but it moved on again quickly and, heart pounding,
e kept up. Weary as she was, both mentally and physi-
lly, she suddenly had all the energy in the world. It was
though her life passed through a funnel, narrowing in on
e one element that held meaning. Patrick.

The corridor leading from the plane into the terminal
emed endless. The clamor of joyous reunions reached her
oments before she stepped into the light. Blood thunder-

ing through her veins, she searched the throng of fac┊
Tears blurred her vision. Walking over forward, s┊
blinked.

"Jordanna! Over here!" She turned her head to see a lar┊
man approaching. But it wasn't Patrick. It was...Peter. T┊
nightmare continued!

Before she could move much farther, she was envelop┊
in a hug expansive enough to be captured by the camer┊
that rolled. "How are you, babe? I was so worried!"

Frantic now, she continued to search the crowd. Pe┊
kissed her soundly on her cheek, but she didn't notic┊
Could it be that Patrick hadn't come? Could it be that h┊
ordeal had been for nothing? Tears streaming down h┊
cheeks, she struggled to focus.

Then she saw him, as different from Peter as night fro┊
day. Where Peter looked fresh and well rested, Patrick w┊
the one who had obviously lived through the ordeal wi┊
her. Where Peter was surrounded by the press, Patrick stoo┊
alone, waiting in anguish.

"I've got to go," she heard herself murmur, and push┊
against Peter's arms. "Excuse me...I've got to...." Th┊
she was free, dodging her way through the crowds, until┊
last Patrick was holding her and she knew she was home┊

Heavy sobs came from deep within then, expressing bo┊
the heartache she'd endured and the joy of reunion. H┊
arms circled his neck, clinging with desperation and ne┊
and love. She couldn't talk through her tears, could on┊
hold him tighter, and tighter. He was as silent, and as firm┊
His strong arms surrounded her. His own tears fell freely┊

How long they stood like that, they neither knew n┊
cared. The only thing that mattered was that they were t┊
gether again. Gathering his composure mere momen┊
ahead of her, Patrick moved his lips by her ear. His voi┊

as hoarse, but she heard every word. "There's a diamond ng in my pocket. Want it?"

Face buried still against his neck, right arm remaining piled in tight possession, she lowered her left hand to his pocket. The small box was easily opened, her finger quickly id through the ring. Then, without so much as a look at ie exquisite gem, she resumed her hold of him.

"I love you, Pat. I love you so much!"

"Mrs. Kirkland. A moment, please?" The interruption ame from one of the several press people who'd gathered round. Jordanna pressed her head more tightly to Patck's neck. "How was it?" came the intrusive voice. "Did ie passengers ever panic?"

"Did the Libyans board the plane?" demanded a second.

"Did you talk with the hijacker at all?" shot a third.

Very slowly and with deliberation, Patrick eased Joranna to his side. Wiping the tears from her cheeks, he roke out into a broad smile. "I love you," he mouthed, rearded by her own smile. Then he turned to the microhones that seemed to have gathered in a swarm. "I believe iat Mrs. Kirkland is well, but tired. She's been through an rdeal. We've *all* been through an ordeal."

"She saw her husband—" a reporter began, only to be oundly interrupted by Patrick, whose gaze had returned Jordanna's and was not to be dislodged.

"Her *ex*-husband. She's engaged to me now."

"Engaged?" A second reporter frowned down at his otebook as though in search of information he'd someow missed.

"That's right," Patrick said with a grin.

Sniffing a new story in the works, an astute television orrespondent waved his microphone closer. "So the rialry goes on?"

Patrick's grin didn't fade, nor did he shift his eyes fro Jordanna's. "No. The rivalry's over. Now, if you'll excu us...." Turning, he began to lead Jordanna from the crow

A final question followed them. "When's the wedding

"Within the month," Patrick stated, his arm wrapp firmly about Jordanna's shoulders as he quickened his pac "Is that all right?" he murmured softly, when at last the porters had given up.

"Oh, yes," she breathed, her bright eyes beamin "Oh...yes."

"HI, SLEEPYHEAD," Patrick whispered, smiling broadl "How do you feel?"

Opening her other eye, Jordanna stretched, then reach forward and took his hands. "Better. I was exhausted."

"Good reason for that." His eyes lowered briefly befo returning to her face. "Maybe you should cut back yo hours."

She smiled at his concern. "I already have. And I'm oka Really. A nap before dinner always does the trick. Have y been sitting here long?"

"Long enough. I like watching you. My beautiful wife Leaning forward, he caught her lips in an exquisitely gen kiss.

"Mmm," Jordanna breathed. "I like that." In the eig teen months they'd been married, it had only gotten bett and better.

"Angel?"

She opened her eyes to find him looking at her in co cern.

"Are you sure this is what you want?"

Laughing, she pressed his hand to her swelling stomac "It's a little late to worry about that, isn't it?" She was s months pregnant and growing by the day.

"But I do worry. I know how much the business
eans—"

Leaving his hand on their child, she put her fingers to his
os. "Shh. I thought I'd made that clear. The business
...the business. You're my life. And now we'll have a child
love." She paused. "You're not sorry, are you?" She re-
lled her first marriage and the reluctance Peter had had
share any part of her. In her heart she knew Patrick was
fferent. Still, from time to time, she needed to hear the
ords. As had always been the case in the past, she wasn't
sappointed now.

"God, no! I've dreamed about having this baby. You
now that." Raising the edge of her loose blouse, he leaned
w to kiss her rounded belly. "I love you so much I think
l burst at times. It'll be a relief to have someone to absorb
e overflow."

For Jordanna, it was the same. Threading her fingers into
s hair, she held his head as he brushed his lips back and
rth over her flesh. When he gently gripped the elastic band
f her pants and eased it down, she closed her eyes against
e heady pleasure.

"Oh, Pat, I love you," she whispered, then caught her
reath when his lips moved lower. And lower. Suddenly her
ulse was racing at the excitement of his touch. "Pat,
t's—"

"Shh. Let me."

And he did. Using his lips and tongue and those phe-
omenally agile fingers of his, he brought her to the fur-
est reaches of desire and back, before at last sliding up her
embling body.

"You're wonderful," he murmured, careful not to hurt her
s he moved his large body over hers.

It took her a moment to catch her breath. But it was hard given the sensual rock of his body. "Patrick," she chided "you're fully dressed."

"Not for long." Grinning, he reached for the buckle of hi belt. "Not for long."

When he took her then, it was with precious care an tenderness. She enveloped him, gave him every bit as muc of herself back, and then some. He was first in her life. had been that way since the moment they'd set eyes on eac other in the woods of New Hampshire. If it was reassur ance he sought, Jordanna intended to spend a lifetime an beyond giving him precisely that. For in the giving she re ceived. It was what their love was all about.

Back by Popular Demand

Janet Dailey
Americana

A romantic tour of America through fifty favorite Harlequin Presents, each set in a different state researched by Janet and her husband, Bill. A journey of a lifetime in one cherished collection.

In November, don't miss the exciting states featured in:

Title #19 MAINE
        Summer Mahogany

#20 MARYLAND
        Best of Grass

Available wherever
Harlequin books are sold.

JD-N

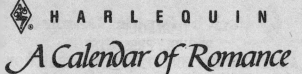

HARLEQUIN
PROUDLY PRESENTS
A DAZZLING NEW CONCEPT IN ROMANCE FICTION

One small town—twelve terrific love stories

Welcome to Tyler, Wisconsin—a town full of people
you'll enjoy getting to know, memorable friends and
unforgettable lovers, and a long-buried secret that
lurks beneath its serene surface....

JOIN US FOR A YEAR IN THE LIFE OF TYLER

Each book set in Tyler is a self-contained love story;
together, the twelve novels stitch the fabric of a
community.

LOSE YOUR HEART TO TYLER!

The excitement begins in March 1992, with
WHIRLWIND, by Nancy Martin. When lively, brash
Liza Baron arrives home unexpectedly, she moves
into the old family lodge, where the silent and
mysterious Cliff Forrester has been living in seclusion
for years....

WATCH FOR ALL TWELVE BOOKS
OF THE TYLER SERIES
Available wherever Harlequin books are sold